RISE of the FLAME

K.N. LEE

INTERNATIONAL BESTSELLING AUTHOR
BOOK ONE OF THE EURA CHRONICLES

www.knlee.com

Rise of the Flame/ K.N. Lee.—2nd Edition

ACKNOWLEDGEMENTS

Rise of the Flame is the first book I've ever written. It started as a short story that I typed on my mother's typewriter when I was eleven years old.

How it has grown!

Throughout the years, my dreams have shaped Lilae and Liam's world, and unique creatures and powers began to seep into this world. With each passing year that I added more and more chapters, Lilae began to be shaped by my experiences, insecurities, and dreams.

While Lilae is a powerful being who is faced with saving the world, I believe that she is the most like me in many ways. From a girl in my dreams and daydreams to a character put before the world, Lilae is a cherished being whom I have long loved and looked to for solace. Writing her story has helped me through the toughest times.

When my home was broken into and my laptop was stolen with the only file that I had of Lilae's story, I almost lost the desire to write. I lost years of work and entered a six-month depression that made it impossible to even pick up a pen and paper or open a file on my computer. It was Lilae's incessant reoccurrence in my dreams that gave me the courage to get over the pain of having lost her and to start the entire book from scratch. I must say that starting over was the best thing I've ever done. I may have lost thousands of written words, but Lilae's story was engrained in my mind. And so, the story morphed into the epic trilogy that I present to you today.

Throughout the years, many people have encouraged me and given me the strength to pursue my dream of becoming an author.

I must thank my family for always supporting my writing. My mother always encouraged me, and my grandmother introduced me to the incredible world of fantasy, and my younger brother was always there to let me read my stories to him.

Thank you to my beta readers, Melinda Metz, Carrie Enders, Jacqueline Pfhal, Julia Fe Chala, Zachary Katz-Stein, Erica Li, Caridad Ortiz, and Kenichi Kamihara.

Thank you to my editor, Ann Wicker. Special thanks to my amazing artist, Jennifer Munswami of JM Rising Horse Creations, and to my fairy godmother, Colleen M. Albert, The Grammar Babe.

It is with the help of these incredible individuals that I present to you *Rise of the Flame*.

Dedicated to Ava and Beckham

BARRIER
BARRIER
BARRIER
SILVER RIVER
FROZEN PLAINS
CHIMERIA
CAIR OCEAN
MERMAID TERRITORY
GARDENS OF FLORN
TOLRIN
RAFDEN
OXEN
TERRINTON
JORDAN
INDU
GOLLUSH
GOBLIN CITY
AUROBIA

Table of Contents

Ellowen World Info

Realm: Eura

Human, mermaid, and Mithrani territory

Human Traits

Focus—prominent trait; increased focus

Evasion—the ability to confuse an opponent by making one's image flicker and shift to another spot

Split—the ability to split into two identical beings Reach

Accuracy—increased precision when using a weapon

Mermaid Traits

Breath—prominent trait; the ability to breathe under water and bestow the power to do so to others temporarily

Hypnosis—the ability to hypnotize others with their eyes

Mithrani Traits

Mock—the ability to manipulate the prominent trait of every race

Realm: Kyril

Tryan, fairy, and mermaid territory

Tryan Traits

Enchant—prominent trait; the ability to make weapons or items stronger and more powerful

Creation—the ability to create objects from ordinary materials or invent new ones

Blessed shield—a shield of energy that protects its user
Vex—the ability to confuse an opponent temporarily
Mind Telling—the ability to read the thoughts of others

Fairy Traits

Heal—prominent trait; the ability to heal wounds with energy power

Enchant—the ability to make weapons or items stronger and more powerful

Flight—the ability to fly
Soothe—the ability to calm others, including animals

REALM: ALFHEIM

Silver Elf and mermaid territory

Silver Elves

Agility—prominent trait; the ability to climb and increased balance

Focus—increased focus
Accuracy—increased precision when using a weapon
Stealth—the ability to go invisible
Shift—the ability to change into an animal

REALM: NOSTFAR

Shadow Elf and mermaid territory

Shadow Elf

Dart—prominent trait; lightning-fast speed
Rage—the ability to become more powerful when angry
Camoflage—the ability to blend into their surroundings

PROLOGUE

EVEN IN THE LOWEST LEVELS of the Aurorian palace, where the servants slept, the castle staff sat up and listened to the queen's cries of pain. No one wanted her to die. She was only the fourth queen of the Black Throne, and yet she was the most loved.

King Torek paced the dim, narrow corridor; the only light came from the brass torches placed against the stone walls. His brow furrowed as he waited for his summons.

He wondered if it had been wise of them to try for a second child. He was growing older and weaker. But one son wasn't enough of a legacy for an Aurorian king. Torek had grown up with four brothers and seven sisters.

The time for doubts had passed. They were twenty hours into labor, and either the child would finally come or both the baby and the mother would die.

King Torek sat down on the carpeted corridor's floor in exhaustion. His legs were tired from standing. Sweat ran down his balding scalp.

"Do you need anything, sire?"

King Torek waved the young guard away as one last scream, more agonizing than the rest, broke him from his thoughts. Torek drew a fearful breath and waited.

After a few moments of complete silence, the short midwife opened the doors to Queen Sysil's quarters and ushered him inside.

The air inside the room was thick and steamy, the candlelight dim; it bathed the room in a faint orange glow. The smell of blood and sweat invaded his nostrils, so he covered his nose with his long velvet sleeve.

King Torek noticed his young wife sprawled motionless on the bed. "Is she all right?" A look of worry creased his aging face.

Queen Sysil's eyes seemed sealed shut from tears of pain. Her scarlet hair was in disarray and sweat beaded her pale face. Her chest rose slightly and fell, and he sighed in relief.

The midwife nodded. "She's only resting." Her aged eyes seemed to hold something more.

"Where's the child?" His dark eyes roamed the room. There were no screams or cries from the baby.

The midwife pointed a chubby finger to the small bassinet at the queen's bedside. The midwife's aide stepped aside timidly, careful to avoid eye contact as the king towered over them on his path to the baby.

An attendant wiped the sweat from the queen's face with a cool rag. Sysil's lips trembled. "I am sorry that it is a girl. We can try again, if it is your desire."

If only they had time to try again. Sysil was only twenty-two, but Torek was nearly seventy, and his body reminded him of his mortality every day. Two children would have to do.

"A baby girl?" To everyone's surprise, Torek smiled.

He looked in at the daughter who seemed so calm and peaceful. He picked her up, and his thoughts of having another boy vanished as he stared at her appealing yet eerie beauty.

The girl was tiny with a head full of short, curly hair. He'd never seen anyone with hair that shade of red before. It was so bright that it seemed to have traces of gold throughout.

The king's body tensed as though under a spell when his daughter looked up into his eyes. Under long, thick golden lashes she had eyes of a rich, bluish green. He gasped, almost dropping her, when a faint flicker of light moved deeply within them. The child yawned innocently, her little mouth opening in a perfect circle, before she closed her eyes to sleep.

"Do not look too deeply into the child's eyes."

"She's bewitched," one of the attendants whispered.

Torek turned and looked at the midwife; one of his bushy white eyebrows rose in search of answers. The queen's attendants avoided his eyes as they busied themselves with cleaning the room of the blood-soaked rags.

The babe did indeed resemble the queen as far as her hair color; however, her blue-green eyes were rare and unsettling. Though many humans of the North had special traits, there was something more to this girl.

Torek already felt a deep love for the child, his baby girl. He gently hugged her close to him.

"Let me hold her, your grace." The midwife held her arms out, her small eyes never leaving the baby.

"My king, what is wrong?" Sysil weakly tried to sit up in the bed. Her face paled even more when she saw Torek's smile fade.

The child's eyes… did that *thing* again, flickering with light. Torek swallowed hard, fearing that something was wrong. He watched as the midwife examined the baby, the room full of tension.

Heavy boots trampling down the corridor broke the silence. The door burst open, and the captain of the palace guards, Pirin, charged into the room.

"What is going on?"

Pirin pointed to the midwife. "Get the child from that woman! She is a witch." Pirin looked to the king and spoke quickly. "We found the *real* midwife's body in the stables." He glared at the woman who stood there with the princess in her arms.

There was a collective gasp from the aides.

"I've been called many things over the centuries, but never a witch."

Torek's heart raced as he watched the midwife transform to a woman of a younger age. He stepped back, startled. His jaw hung open as his eyes searched her face. Torek balled up his fists as rage filled his veins.

She *did* look evil with her black hair and pale skin. Her blue eyes looked at him without fear and that made his anger intensify. She stood there holding his beloved daughter.

"I assure you," she said, "I am Delia, Elder and gatekeeper of the Underworld. Not even a witch is safe from my power. Now, lower your weapons and listen to me."

"Sorcery! Seize her!"

Delia shook her head, gripping the baby close to her chest. "I have not come to harm the child." She raised a hand as if to calm them, meeting all of their eyes.

"Seize her!" The soldiers charged for her.

The calamity and uproar upset the wee princess, who wailed into the air.

"Silence!" With a flick of her small hand, Delia seemed to rip their voices right from their throats. It was so sudden and immobilizing that no one could even scream. The room was flooded by light, and all sound was sucked away. When she lowered her hand, everyone was frozen in place like a statue.

Delia slumped onto a chair, exhausted from her sudden burst of energy. She looked down at the child whose cry was the only sound heard in the room. She sighed and gently rubbed the girl's tiny hand, as if to soothe her.

"I warned you," Delia said, shaking her head. "I have come a long, *long* way to help you humans."

Torek watched as Delia gazed into his daughter's eyes. He saw the woman's body shiver and knew that she, too, saw the light flicker there.

"The Ancients have asked me to protect this child, and, as an Elder, I am more qualified than any of you to help her fulfill her destiny."

The veins in Torek's neck strained as he watched the woman cradling his daughter. Elder or not, he wanted to break free from the hold she had on all of them and wring her neck.

She reached inside her leather side-purse for a clear vial of blue liquid. When she opened the cask, a slight cloud of frost escaped. Torek watched as Delia drank a tiny sip; she squeezed her eyes shut and breathed deeply, as if waiting for something to happen. Finally, she stood.

"Listen, Torek. You should be glad that I arrived first." She wrapped the baby in a blanket and secured her to a sling upon her chest. "I don't have the time to explain everything, but you have to know that others will come, if the child stays here. You have to trust me."

Delia knew that she was asking the impossible of Torek and Sysil.

"Our world is about to change," Delia said. "There are beings who would seek to kill the princess and destroy your kingdom. Understand that I will protect her, train her, and prepare her for the time when she will be called upon to save our world."

Delia looked toward the captain of the guards; he was tall like most Aurorians and very well built. "Pirin, is it?" His eyes widened. "I shall take you with me. Lilae will need training, and—" She looked him over. "—you will do."

Delia released Pirin from his frozen state, and he fell to the floor. His hair was so blond that it was nearly white, and it fell into his eyes as he looked up at her. He winced as he began to move his limbs, as if shaking out pins and needles. He stretched his arms and picked up his sword.

"What do you mean, 'will do'?" Pirin frowned at her, furrowing his thin eyebrows. "I haven't agreed to anything."

"Do you understand that you have been chosen to join the child and me?"

Torek looked around at the others, whose eyes were now glazed over; he sensed that they were no longer aware of what was occurring.

"Why?" Pirin asked. "You're still an enemy as far as I'm concerned. I know you have power. I've seen that. But try to harm the king and queen, and I will find a way to kill you."

Delia blinked at him and sighed. "I know you have no reason to trust me, but in time the Ancients will reveal to you what I have seen."

Pirin stood there and glanced at the king.

"The Ancients created the races who populate the world, and they have put their trust in this me. Can you understand this?"

"You're obviously not from Auroria," Pirin reasoned, his eyes grazing over her dark hair. "You don't have our pure blood, nor fair hair and light eyes." Though Delia's eyes were blue, they were dark, like the ocean at night. "But you haven't come all of this way just to kill the child, either. That is what I understand."

"I have not, Pirin. But there are those who would come from afar to do just that. I wish to protect the child from those with power, who would use it to kill her. She is a weapon that, if in the wrong hands, could cause great harm to this world."

"You are really an Elder?" Pirin remained calm, looking at the woman who claimed to have once ruled the Underworld.

"I am."

Pirin frowned. "You don't look like an Elder."

"Have you ever seen an Elder?"

He shook his head.

"Good. And you don't want to see me in my *true* form." She watched his face. "Pirin, look at me."

He glanced up at her.

"I will tell you everything you need to know after we are far from danger."

"What danger?"

"I don't think you are quite ready to know such things," she said. "But in time, I will tell you."

Though Pirin's stance looked imposing, his eyes filled with worry. "I need more than that, Elder. I have a wife and two little girls.

What will become of them? Who will protect them if I come with you and the princess?"

"Bring them," Delia said without hesitation. "We will give this child a family and protect her until her time has come."

"Do I have a choice?"

"You do. But wouldn't you still be serving your king and queen by protecting their daughter?"

Pirin looked up. "Yes, but I'd be putting my twin daughters in harm's way."

Delia lifted her shoulders. "Are there any other soldiers who could do as good of a job protecting and training the princess as you?"

He shook his head.

"And wouldn't it be wise to keep your family close, to protect and train them as you would the princess?"

Pirin looked back at his men. They were still frozen.

"I know *your* secret, Pirin…"

His face lost what little color it had when his eyes lifted to hers. "What?"

"You heard me."

He shifted from one foot to another. "What do you think you know?"

"I know everything." There was a tense silence between them, as she watched him with a straight face. "So, are you coming or not?"

"I'll do it."

Delia nodded, a small smile forming at the corners of her lips. "Are you doing it because I know all of your secrets, or because you want to?"

"Everyone has secrets. I care about the child. You have given me a chance to protect her, and I accept."

"Well said. I see much good in you, Pirin. You will go down in history for your part in this."

Pirin put his sword away and looked at the queen, whose tears were trailing down her face. "I don't care about history. I only care about this child and my own. If what you say is true about danger heading this way, then we'd better get going."

Pirin crossed the room and wiped the queen's face. He leaned down and whispered something to her. Pirin unhooked Sysil's silver necklace and balled it into his fist.

Delia narrowed her eyes and asked, "What exactly are you doing?"

Pirin turned, his hazel eyes wet. "For the princess. She will need a token from her mother. It's the least we can do, isn't it?"

Delia nodded, staring at the necklace for a moment before putting her hand across the baby's face. Instantaneously, the little girl fell asleep.

"One more question, Elder?"

"Call me Delia, please," she replied to Pirin.

He nodded, dropping the necklace into his pocket. "Fine… Delia." He lifted his shoulders in a shrug and asked, "Why me?"

Delia pulled on her cloak and covered the girl's head, holding her snuggly against her chest. She walked toward the door but glanced back at Pirin, an eerie smile on her pale face.

"It was always you, Pirin. Coincidences don't just happen. We have all been chosen, so long ago that the world has forgotten. We cannot escape our fate; not when the entire world is at stake."

CHAPTER 1

LILAE FLOATED BARE-SKINNED beneath the bright crescent moon, her arms outstretched on the lake's calm surface. Winter never seemed to end in northern Eura, but she braved the frigid water for the solitude offered by an evening swim.

Alone, she thought, *just how I like it.*

Just as she began to relax, Lilae felt the presence of her Elder in the black shadows of the forest.

This is not good. She peeked over and saw Delia in the human form she'd stolen when she was forced to leave the Underworld, her pale face illuminated from beneath the hood of her wool cloak. She held her wooden staff in one hand and Lilae's discarded cloak in the other.

"Lilae!"

Lilae swallowed and then flipped over to swim back toward the shore, closing the gap between them. She quickly got out of the water and dressed, taking the heavy cloak from Delia's grasp and flinging it over her shoulders to ward off the chill in the air.

"What is it? What's happened?" Her breath escaped her lips like a puff of smoke in the darkness.

Delia looked over Lilae with dull blue eyes. "I don't like how close they are getting. We need to leave before dawn."

Lilae tucked her boyish pants into her boots. Only a few years ago, she would have refused; she would have run away to stay with another family in their village. Now, at almost eighteen, Lilae resigned herself to their nomadic lifestyle.

That's because she had finally learned why they moved so much: Lilae was being hunted.

Lilae followed Delia through the forest to their little cottage on the edge of town. It was a small structure, built into the side of a hill. Though it was once a cave, Pirin had made it into a real home. A squat chimney protruded from beneath the soil, a trail of smoke wafting from its mouth into the gray sky.

Lilae ducked as she stepped inside. Pirin, Lhana, and the twins, Risa and Jaiza, were already awake. Her surrogate family. They glanced at her and, without a word, returned to their preparations. They all moved slowly as the cold air in the room bit at them.

Pirin put his arm around Lhana. She stopped packing and buried her tears in his shoulder, sighing. "Just tell me why? Every time we finally get comfortable and make friends, you make us leave."

He smoothed her blonde hair and kissed her cheek. "And every time you ask me this same question. The answer will not change. They are coming. We don't have time to waste."

"Let us stay behind. It's not the girls and me that he wants."

Pirin grabbed Lhana by the elbow. The room fell silent, and Lilae tensed, her eyes darting from Lhana's stunned face to Pirin's stern expression.

Pirin lowered his voice, but Lilae heard every word. "We stay together. She is my responsibility."

Lhana swallowed and arched a brow, her jaw clenched. Her eyes may have glared in defiance, but her voice wavered. "I thought she was the Elder's responsibility. You trained her. Your duty is done."

Pirin pulled Lhana closer. "I will not hear another word about it." The discussion was over. Pirin's word was law. Everyone went back to packing.

Lilae glanced at Lhana and wondered if the Ancients knew how much Lhana hated her. Lhana met Lilae's eyes with what was clearly resentment. It was a look that hurt Lilae more than anything;

there was almost nothing she wanted more than to finally feel that woman's love.

Despite the tension, they all enjoyed a hasty breakfast of buttered toast, eggs, and fried potatoes, aware that this might be the last they would have for quite some time. They all ate silently and packed their leftovers in sacks. Lhana also packed dried toast and fruit for the journey. They would have to buy more supplies as they went on or rely on Pirin to hunt while in the wilderness.

While the others gathered their belongings, Lilae sharpened her dagger. For her, packing was always quick. She had nothing of value. She wore her only trinket of worth around her neck. It was a simple silver necklace with shiny stones around a ruby. Besides that, a sack of clothing and an extra pair of boots was all Lilae needed.

Jaiza's grunt sounded like exasperation as she stuffed her favorite dress into her travel bag. She reached for her bow and arrows and headed toward the door, not even looking at Lilae as she passed by.

Once everyone was ready, Lilae hooded herself and followed the procession into the woods. Soon, the sun would rise, and farmers would tend to their cattle and crops.

Delia led the way as they quietly crossed the village to the path leading east. Always east. She cut through the darkness, taking them from gentle paths directly into the thickness of the woods, where the grass was knee high and the hungry bugs were ready to feast on any exposed skin they could find. They were all used to it by now. It would be just another long, hard journey to a foreign land.

Whenever she saw Delia look into the sky, eyes glowing and staff raised, she imagined that she could actually see the Ancients peering down at them from their homes in the Overworld. When Lilae glanced upward, she saw only stars.

"I am glad we have a moment to speak, Lilae. I've been wondering how you feel, now that you're approaching your eighteenth birthday."

"I feel fine." She stuffed her gloved hands into her pockets to warm them. "I am ready for a new journey. I feel more at peace in the wilderness. No one can be mean to me out here, and no one can hurt me." She shrugged it off and forced a smile Delia's way. She didn't want to complain.

"No one can hurt you, Lilae," Delia said, "unless you let them. Have The Winds spoken to you lately?"

"No, they have been quiet."

"Well. Perhaps it is a good thing. They warn you of danger that even I cannot see."

Lilae nodded. "Yes. I don't need The Winds to tell to look out for boys. I'm glad to be free of Jameson's taunting."

"Tell me about this boy."

"He smells like the pigs and always tries to wrestle me in the pits." Lilae scrunched up her nose. "I won't wrestle him, even if I want to twist his arm off."

Delia chuckled softly as she glanced at her. "I'm glad to hear it. I hope you know he wants more than to wrestle, Lilae. I'm sure he fancied you."

"Gross."

"Risa and Jaiza enjoy the company of boys. I'm sure they are ready for marriage, but you know you're different, right?"

"I know. I guess I don't care about the same things that they do. I do not care about friends or boys or starting a family of my own."

A small smile formed on Delia's lips. "Of course not…" She winked at Lilae. "—you're too young to think of such things."

"Am I?" She couldn't see a boy falling in love with her or raising children of her own. But that didn't mean she wouldn't like an adoring, handsome boy professing his love to her; she just didn't think that it was possible. She looked odd. She acted differently. It was better not to dream about such things.

"Don't most girls get married at my age?" She stepped over a fallen tree and waited for the others to do the same.

The grass grew taller, nearing their necks. It was covered in ice, making it so sharp that they had to walk through it with caution. So many years of walking, of moving. When would they stop?

"Sure, some do. There are scores of young girls who, at the first sign of womanhood, begin bearing children, too. And they will do so continuously until the seed no longer catches. But that's not the life for you. *You* have a future, Lilae. There's a bigger, more important task for you than just producing babies. You are different."

"How? Why? Because there's something wrong with me?"

"No!" Delia waved a flippant hand and peered at Lilae. "Nonsense. There's nothing wrong with you. You're special. You have a very important destiny."

"But *why,* Delia?" For as long as she could remember, she just went with whatever Delia or Pirin said was best. "How am I special? *Why* am I being hunted? I've never hurt anyone innocent. I have killed, but I follow the judgment of The Winds."

Delia was silent for a moment. "Soon," she said and patted Lilae on the shoulder.

"*She is ready,*" Lilae heard Delia whisper to herself, as if praying to the Ancients above.

CHAPTER 2

WEEKS HAD PASSED SINCE Lilae and the others had seen another village. They kept off the worn paths and stayed as close to The Barrier as possible. The massive stone structure stood as a constant reminder that they were far from civilization. No one ventured near The Barrier; it was feared.

As they climbed over foothills and through mountain passes, Lilae glanced at the top of The Barrier, where a green haze rippled from the top of the stone to the clouds. She hoped that she'd catch a glimpse of a Silver Elf. Silver Elves shared a wall with the humans, and, in her mind, they were the friendliest of the six remaining races.

The terrain changed from treacherous mountains and valleys, where the snow and wind whipped past their nearly frozen faces, to smooth plains and dense forests. It was like a dream to see the different landforms of Eura.

They crossed over a bridge that connected two massive mountains. When they reached the top, it felt as if they were in the clouds. Whenever Lilae had the nerve to look down, all she saw was a white mist that resembled smoke. Though she couldn't see it, she knew that a river rushed through the valley below. Its waters crashed along the rocks, causing a deafening roar to fill the valley.

Too high, Lilae thought. The wind whipped around her, making her red hair fly into her eyes.

Lilae gulped and tried to catch her breath. Her hands started to shake as she imagined herself plummeting to her death. She hoped the bridge was sturdy enough to support them. Her hands gripped the rough ropes that served as railings so tightly that they cut into the palms of her hands.

Lilae was usually at the head of the pack, but now, she was the last to gather the nerve to cross. She willed herself to move her feet, forcing her mind to stop feeding her images of falling and hitting her head on every rock that lay below.

Her breath sped up. The slats of the bridge were cracking; some were already missing. She looked to Pirin with terrified eyes.

He seemed too far away. Lilae saw him motion for her to cross.

"You can do it, Lilae," Pirin yelled above the roar of the river below.

Lilae looked down again, the mist curling up around her ankles.

"Just take your time."

His patience with her gave her courage. She nodded, more to convince herself that she was ready than anything else.

Lilae took a deep breath and headed toward Pirin. She would hate for him to think of her as a coward. She walked carefully across, praying the entire time. She drew a breath of relief when she safely reached the other side and joined the others.

They began down a steep trail that led back into the wilderness. They were all tired. Everyone was moody. Risa and Jaiza stayed close to each other, as always, and looked simply miserable.

Lilae walked ahead of them all, trapped in her thoughts, clinging to her more pleasant dreams to keep her going. Hunger nagged at her stomach. Her feet were callused and sore from hundreds of miles of walking. Still, she refused to complain.

Pirin once told her that complaints and excuses were signs of weakness. From as early as she could remember, his words were like law, and she lived by his and Delia's teachings.

"Please, Pirin." Lhana stopped abruptly. She breathed heavily, coughing from the cold in the air. She dropped her bags onto the ground with a thud and folded her arms across her chest. "We have been walking since dawn and without a decent break. I am *exhausted*." Her shoulders slumped. "Please, darling, can we rest now?"

Pirin gave her one look. She was pale, her cheeks red from the wind. There was a small clearing at the mouth of a cavern. He looked to Delia.

The Elder placed her staff in the ground, looked around, and nodded her approval.

That's how it always was: Pirin checking to make sure Delia was in agreement. He shrugged his heavy pack off of his back and held it with one hand.

He nodded toward the cave. Lilae looked at it. It was a small opening in the side of the gray mountain, and all she could see was black inside. She was glad that she wasn't as afraid of the dark as she was of heights.

"This way," Pirin said, leading them to the clearing. They climbed the rocks and heaved their sacks inside the shelter. "This will suffice for the night."

There was a collective sigh of relief and everyone busied themselves with setting up camp inside the hollow mouth of the cave. They would make it as comfortable as possible.

"Looks like rain anyway," Pirin said and peered into the night sky. He sniffed the air. "I'm sure of it. Build a fire inside the cave and we'll sleep there."

"How long can we stay?" Lhana wrapped her arms around his waist.

Pirin looked at Risa. "Until morning."

Jaiza's gaze went to the dark woods on the other side of the cave. "But what about wolves? I saw at least three carcasses on the way up here."

"We'll make a fire. Don't worry," Pirin assured her. "Lilae, go out and place the rabbit traps."

Lilae nodded, uncaring about the cold; it never affected her as it did the others. She wanted to talk further with Delia. Their nights beside the fire, learning and hearing stories, were what Lilae looked forward to each day.

"Who will keep watch?" Jaiza eyed the dark cave and then the forest again. If there was one thing that Jaiza was afraid of, it was wolves.

Pirin had already started to gather wood from fallen branches around the camp. "I'll watch for half of the night, and then you girls can take turns. We'll get horses from the next village and I promise we can stay at an inn."

The twins smiled. Lilae watched their faces light up, and it brought a small smile to her lips. The thought of sleeping in an inn excited them all. There, they could drink ale and meet new people. The food was always hearty, even if the beds were sometimes infested with bed bugs.

Lilae lingered near the slope into the woods while the others set up. She heard something. Her head tilted as she listened to The Winds.

Delia looked back at her, concern spreading across her face. "What is it, Lilae?"

Lilae held a gloved hand up and continued to listen. The Winds spoke to her. They were always there like an old friend. The voices that floated along the breeze or rushing winds always warned her when something was amiss. She had relied on them since she was a child, and they never lied.

Now, they issued a warning.

"Bandits," Lilae said, standing tall. Her eyes searched for movement in the bushes.

"Oh, great. She's talking to herself again," Risa whispered.

"*Shush*, Risa." Jaiza nudged her sister's arm. "She may talk to herself, but has she ever been wrong?"

Risa didn't reply. They both watched as Lilae stood near the edge of the woods.

"*Murderers*." The Winds were sure to tell Lilae that, and she gave the twins a look that they understood.

"They followed our tracks, and they wish to rob and kill us." Lilae said it as if she was discussing the weather.

"*Humph*. I wish they'd try," Jaiza said with a glower in the same direction as Lilae's gaze.

Delia drew in a deep breath. "Holy Elahe. We can never travel in peace?" She stabbed her staff into the ground. "Those bandits are damned fools to be this close to The Barrier."

"I don't like this." Lhana's eyes darted toward the forest as she withdrew to hide near the cave. "Why does this always happen? One day they'll sneak up on us, I just know it!"

"I won't let that happen," Lilae said, glancing back at her.

"You will be the death of me," Lhana said as she turned her back on Lilae.

Pirin gave her a sidelong glance. "Perhaps you'd let me train you sometime, Lhana. You are not as defenseless as you pretend to be. Your trait is quite rare—it could be of use to us."

Lhana glared at him. "I don't want to hear it. You seem to forget that I am a proper *lady*. Only warriors use their traits."

Pirin shrugged. "Suit yourself. I don't understand why you'd rather waste something you've inherited."

Lhana shook her head. "Never. So stop asking me." She raised a finger. "The first queen of the black throne gave my family my dowry. Who else can make such a claim?"

Risa sighed and gave Jaiza a look. They both set their things down without a word. They'd trained with Lilae for times such as this since they were all children; and this wouldn't be the first group of bandits to threaten them.

Jaiza grabbed her bow, securing her quiver of arrows onto her back.

Risa drew her sword quietly and put the scabbard down. She rolled her shoulders, as if loosening her muscles.

Lilae grinned, her teeth shining in the moonlight. She loved when the twins were like this.

Jaiza stepped beside Lilae, who was younger yet taller. Her keen eyes looked into the growing darkness. "I'll go ahead and see how many there are." She twisted her blonde hair into a knot at the top of her head to keep it from getting in the way.

"There are eight."

"You know everything, don't you?" Jaiza rolled her eyes. "Fine. *I* can take them out."

Lilae's grin widened. The thrill of a fight excited her. "*I'll* be right behind you."

Pirin continued to unpack their supplies, shaking out their wool blankets. "This will be good practice for you girls. It's been awhile since you've had a real fight. Maybe you can practice working as a *team* this time…"

Risa lowered her sword. "Eight? What a waste of energy."

Pirin gave her a stern look.

"What? I was hoping for at least ten," she said as though it was a sport. "*That* would have been good practice. I can handle eight on my own." She put her sword away and started to help Lhana prepare the salted pork and beans.

"Risa…"

"Father…" Risa said as she squatted down and pulled out an iron pot. "Lilae and Jaiza can take this one."

"Don't be so cocky. You're not the best fighter in the realm by any stretch of the imagination, so stop acting like you know everything. Even your Evasion can be countered if someone has the right skill. Trust me, killing people isn't a game and should not be taken lightly."

Risa raised a brow. "I know it isn't. But Lilae and Jaiza can handle it. We've done this how many times now? At least seven."

"Never underestimate your enemy, Risa. You never know if those men are as trained as you or better."

"You can't be serious." Risa huffed. "I doubt it. We both know that most bandits are nothing more than boys who can barely hold the weight of their own cheap sword."

"You're not listening, are you?"

"Yes, Father. I get what you're saying. I will try not to be so cocky about it. That better?"

Pirin sighed. "You girls are impossible," he said, though a small smile played across his lips.

"You didn't train us to be warriors for nothing," Risa said, as Jaiza slunk into the forest.

Without a sound, Jaiza climbed into a tall tree and disappeared into the branches and leaves.

Lilae stepped out of her cloak with her dagger sharpened and ready in one hand. It was warm on her palm and pulsed for action. She listened to The Winds as they led her to the men who approached her family's camp, careful not to crunch any of the fallen branches beneath her feet.

As the sun's last light faded, she peered silently at the bandits from her place behind a tall oak tree. Energy flowed within her body, and there was an anxiousness filling her throat, and a fire within her veins.

The Winds warned her that the men were merciless. They preyed on innocent travelers, robbing and killing even defenseless women. In return, Lilae and Jaiza would show no mercy.

There was a sudden whistling sound as Jaiza's arrow cut through the dark forest and slammed into the chest of the leader. He gasped loudly, clutching his chest as he was thrown back onto the ground with a solid thud. The arrow was made of the strongest wood and impaled him to the dirt so that he couldn't lift himself.

Lilae noted the look of shock and pain on his face as he strained against the arrow. That look always interested her. It was the look of one surprised by death's touch.

Shouts and frantic orders ensued from the other bandits as they drew their weapons and searched for the source of the arrow. They held their weapons but ducked and cowered toward the safety of the dense, dark forest.

Lilae watched them in silence. She could feel their fear, knowing their hearts were thumping with terror of the unknown. She wanted them to feel that fear. It was the same fear countless others had felt when those men harmed them. Risa was right about one thing: their weapons were cheap. But these were not boys; they were men who had done this countless times, with success. This would be their last.

"Who's there?" someone shouted in a high-pitched voice that cracked with his words.

"Demons!" another wailed.

"Shut up, Gred. There ain't no stupid demons in this forest!" Lilae heard someone reply, yet she could hear the fear in his voice as if he were uncertain about his own reassurances.

"I told you we shouldn't tempt the Ancients! We're too close to The Barrier!"

Lilae worked quickly, hoping to get some action before Jaiza killed them all with her skilled archery. She took a deep breath, and her vision changed. She could see their moves before they even did them. Everything stilled for her; all sounds muted, and Lilae activated her Focus.

Silence welcome Lilae as she raced into the battle, calculating their every action.

She darted into the mob with her dagger in her fist. She sliced Gred down before he even saw her coming. Lilae didn't waste time making sure he was dead. Her dagger had cut his throat with such precision that there were no doubts.

She slammed into a tall, burly man who seemed more like a solid tree. His body was made of pure muscle, hard as stone. Lilae climbed his body and stabbed him in the neck. Blood spurted into the air.

As he fell backward, his hands racing to cover his wound, she hopped from his body and went on to the next. She didn't need to look back; Lilae always struck true. She could hear him gasping for breath.

Someone grabbed Lilae by her hair from behind. She used her Evasion. Her image flickered before his eyes, and, in an instant, she yanked herself free from his grasp. She kicked him in the back with such force that she heard his spine crack.

His scream resonated throughout the woods, and Lilae put him out of his misery, pouncing onto his back. Her hands were secure against his thick, coarse beard as she snapped his neck.

She stood and turned around. The remaining men were lying on the ground, covered in blood and dirt. Jaiza's arrows protruded from their bodies. Lilae calmed her breathing.

She stood at the center of the massacre. Her eyes closed as she listened to the last groans of pain and gurgles of blood coming from the bandits' mouths. Her Focus subsided, and her vision of the world returned to normal.

Lilae waited until their sounds of dying ceased before making her way back to the camp. She emerged from the forest, her hands and clothes covered in blood splatters. She wiped her face free of a few speckles with a rag that Risa handed her.

Everyone stared at Lilae across the dancing flames as she warmed her bloodstained hands over the burning logs. Her pale face was streaked with blood, and her eyes watched the fire without a trace of emotion.

CHAPTER 3

THE RAIN POURED OUTSIDE the mouth of the cave. Its song was soothing, dripping steadily onto the stones. Lilae enjoyed such private moments with Delia. While the twins had their mother, Lilae had Delia. She still wondered why Lhana had shed that tear earlier. She sensed a deep sadness hidden within that woman.

Lilae sighed, snuggling closer to Delia with her wool blanket. Lilae rested her head on Delia's soft shoulder. She always smelled like mint from the oils she used.

Lilae broke the silence. "Why *exactly* am I different, Delia?" She had been waiting to ask that question for years now. It was always in her mind. From kingdom to kingdom, she never fit in. "Or *special,* as you say. Even more importantly, Delia, why is someone hunting me? Why would anyone want me dead?"

For as long as she could remember, Delia and Pirin had only told her the same thing: *Someone very bad is after you and will stop at nothing to accomplish his task.*

Delia looked down at Lilae, as if considering what to tell her first. "They don't necessarily want you dead, Lilae. They want something from you." She sighed at the perplexed look that Lilae knew crossed her face. "I suppose you're ready."

Delia rose to her feet and held a hand out for Lilae. Lilae accepted the help and stood beside her. Delia was a small woman but that never made Lilae respect her any less. She looked on curiously as Delia held her willow staff out toward the mouth of the cave. A ripple of air floated from the staff and spread. A pale blue light connected to the ripples of air. It covered the entire opening of the cave like a sheer film.

The cave grew warm as if the film stood as a door that closed them inside. Lilae shrugged off her blanket and perked to attention.

"Let's go." She headed toward the ripples of air and stepped through.

Lilae hesitated for a moment, and Delia waved her forward. "Come," she whispered.

She could see Delia through the film. She reached a hand out first, and her body turned frigid. It felt as if a million thorns prickled her flesh, and she winced. She saw Delia standing on the other side, waiting patiently.

"Don't be afraid. It only stings for a second. The shield will not harm any of us. It is laced to shock anyone or anything that I have not named to protect. Do not worry."

She took Lilae's hand and pulled the rest of her body through. Delia walked into the darkness of the forest, expecting Lilae to follow. She held her staff before her, leading the way. Lilae was surprised that they walked deeper and deeper into the forest.

The rain stopped but the ground was muddy and squishy beneath their boots. She could barely see ahead of her. She was afraid that they were being watched, yet The Winds were silent.

Lilae held on to Delia's small waist to keep from falling over. They walked for what felt like hours, and Lilae fought to keep her questions to herself. She could feel that it was time. Finally, she would know who she was, and what her future held. They stopped by a body of water.

Lilae stared at the lake, feeling the cold air drift closer to her. The soft patter of drizzle sprinkled onto its surface, bathed in moonlight. Lilae held her hand out, catching a cool droplet of water in her palm. Rain was one of her favorite things in the world. It was cooling and calming.

Delia walked to the edge of the water and waved her closer. "Kneel."

Lilae took off her boots and stepped closer. She loved the feel of the mud on her feet and stepped close enough for the water to lap over her toes. She knelt down beside the lake and looked up at Delia.

"Good. Now bow your head and close your eyes."

Lilae breathed deeply and looked out over the water. She bowed her head, and her eyes fluttered closed. Lilae nearly choked as she was grabbed violently and dragged into the water.

Lilae's eyes popped open as the water slapped her face. All she saw was darkness. Her mouth filled with water; she quickly tried to push the liquid out and close her mouth.

She could hold her breath for only so long, and her entire body froze with fear as something held her hand and pulled her deeper and deeper into the water. Lilae fought the urge to scream. Whatever held on to her was rough and unyielding. She could feel the hate and evil radiating from it. She fought to see ahead of her. She wanted to see what had hold of her, but all she saw before her were the inky depths of the lake.

Her ears filled with fluid, and her eyes began to burn. Two yellow eyes glowed back at her, and Lilae felt her body shake.

She screamed. "*Delia*!"

Water flooded every orifice, and she panicked. She tried to regain her composure, but those eyes bore into hers. A hand went over her mouth and pressed her face deeper into the water until her head scraped the bottom of the lake.

Lilae flailed and fought. She needed air. Her mind became a torrent of screams and pleas. Her lungs burned. Her nose burned. Her heart thumped so fast that she was sure it would explode. And then, she saw a face. Bronze skin, yellow eyes that glowed beneath the water, and high cheekbones. Terror filled her very bones, creeping into her soul.

"Join me, *Lilae*. Or die," the creature said in a voice that was unlike anything Lilae had ever heard. It wasn't human; it had to be some sort of a demon from the Underworld.

Lilae shook her head. She felt lightheaded, as if she was dying. Still, she refused.

"No!" She swallowed more water. She reached past the face and toward the surface. She could see light. She craved that light.

"Join me and I will ease your pain."

"No!"

Pain jolted through her body like a flood of hot acid.

"Then, your fate it sealed. You will be mine whether you choose to or not."

Like a slap to the face, Lilae was jolted back to the surface. Delia had her by her shirt's collar. She leaned over Lilae, closely watching for her reaction. Lilae coughed and choked as air flooded into her lungs. Cool, delicious air. She breathed it in greedily. She saw Delia nod with approval and sit back on her heels. She wrapped Lilae in her cloak, giving her a moment to calm down.

"What was that?" Lilae shrieked.

Delia put her hand out. "Quiet your voice."

Lilae shot to her feet, flinging off the cloak. She looked over at the lake. It was still now, peaceful. She would never look at water the same way.

Lilae's face heated, and tears stung her eyes. She had thought that she was going to die under the lake's surface; she never wanted to feel that way again. Lilae looked at Delia as tears slipped down her cheeks. She wiped furiously at them.

"What was that, Delia?"

Delia picked up the cloak off the ground and draped it over Lilae's shoulders. "First, tell me your choice. Did you choose to side with him?

"Who was that?"

"Answer the question, Lilae. It's important!"

Confused, Lilae tried to gather her thoughts. Wiping her face she shook her head. "I told him no."

Delia closed her eyes and let out a breath of relief. "Good girl. There is still hope then." She opened her eyes and pulled Lilae in for a hug.

Lilae buried her face in the warmth of Delia's chest. The comfort of her embrace still didn't banish the fear that threatened to make her cry out in hysterics.

"That was an apparition of the Ancient, Wexcyn. He has returned from his imprisonment in the abyss. He has come to claim his throne. And now, he knows that you cannot be swayed to fight on his side. You have denied him."

Lilae pulled away from Delia. That name did not sound familiar. She shook her head. "I don't understand." Cold water dripped from her clothes. She pulled the cloak closer to warm herself. She shivered and slumped to the ground, resting her back on a smooth cluster of rocks.

Her gaze went back to the water, and her eyes glazed over as she recalled the terror she had just experienced. There was a time when Lilae thought that she feared nothing.

Delia made a fire with the tip of her staff onto a rock. Lilae glanced over her shoulder. Such a fire was not possible, but Delia had a talent for the impossible.

Sitting beside Lilae, Delia put a hand on her shoulder and stroked it tenderly. "I'm sorry, Lilae, but I had to show you. Showing you what evil we are up against is better than just telling you. I find it much more effective."

Lilae scoffed. "It was quite effective, Delia. And it was uncalled for."

"I don't think so, Lilae. Wexcyn is a threat to everything you know and love."

"Was that real?"

"It was." Delia looked up at the stars. "It was real in your mind. I could see nothing of the encounter, but that doesn't mean that it didn't happen. Wexcyn invaded your thoughts. We are lucky that he is not strong enough to actually harm you from a distance. But soon, anything will be possible."

"Who is Wexcyn?"

Delia pulled her journal from her bag. It was a small book made of supple leather and filled with parchment.

It was the book Delia used to teach Lilae ever since Lilae was a child. There were ancient maps, history lessons, illustrations, and prophecies. Delia licked her thumb and flipped through a couple of weathered pages; she held open a page with a map on it. The map was drawn with such precision that Lilae wondered if Delia was an artist and had done it herself.

"You know about the four realms, Lilae, right?"

Lilae nodded. As a child, she had loved to learn and recite what she memorized. It was rare for anyone other than royalty and nobility to even be able to read. "Yes, of course. There's Eura, the human realm. Alfheim, the Silver Elf realm. Kyril, the Tryan realm. And Nostfar, the Shadow Elf realm."

Delia smiled. She smoothed a wild ringlet of Lilae's hair behind her ear. "Good girl. And who created the races?"

"Delia, we have traveled for as long as I can remember, and I've never heard anyone even mention the other races. Why is that?"

"Because it has been so long since anyone has seen someone from another race that it simply isn't thought about anymore. Can you tell me who created the remaining races?"

"Pyrii created the Tryans, Inora created the Shadow Elves, Ulsia the Silver Elves, and Telryd created the humans." Then, Lilae lifted an eyebrow. "You said… the *remaining* races. There were others?"

"Yes. Lord Elahe, the creator of the entire universe, created many Ancients to start new worlds… But we'll get to that another day. I am afraid I don't have time to explain the origins of the universe quite yet."

"But the others?" Lilae persisted. "What happened to them?"

Delia pointed to the lines that separated each realm from one another.

"The Barriers," she explained, "were created by the Ancients to keep us from warring with each other. When they created the different races, it was glorious. First, there was peace, and they were pleased. However, everything changed… when death was discovered. With the first death, the perfect world they had created and loved started to crumble. Quests for power and greed took over. Evil was born, and it infected some of the Ancients as well. Things were so bad when all of the races lived together that they almost destroyed our world." Delia turned the page to a picture of the Ancients.

"The Ancients created The Barriers to keep us safe from one another's powers, to return the world to balance."

Lilae examined the drawing of the Ancients.

Delia pointed to a picture of what resembled a man, except he seemed to be made of some type of metal.

He sat on a dark throne with a long spear in his hand and an intense look on his bronze face. Even as a picture, he seemed to stare back at Lilae, looking into her soul. She shivered and turned her eyes to the fire, scooting closer to Delia for warmth and protection. Before that night, Lilae thought that she feared nothing; she now feared Wexcyn with every fiber of her being.

"Wexcyn was the first Ancient created by Elahe. He was so powerful that his creations were able to manipulate any power that the other races could. He was almost too powerful, and he knew it. He wanted to rule his brothers and sisters. He wanted to *be* God."

"What Ancient was he, Delia? Who were his people?"

"They were called Mithrani. They were a beautiful race."

"And now they are all gone?"

"After the war, they hid. They are out there… Somewhere. And he was imprisoned in the abyss for his crimes. Wexcyn started an alliance with a few of the other Ancients. What they did in the Great

War changed everything. They discovered something that threatened the entire world."

Lilae sat up straighter. She could picture everything Delia spoke of. The races, the gods, the war. "What happened? What did they change?"

"They discovered that each death of an individual makes their Ancient weaker."

Lilae nodded. "It makes sense," she said and ran a finger across her bottom lip as she thought. "Delia… the Great War wasn't about us, was it? It was really a fight between the Ancients?"

"Indeed."

Lilae stared at the picture again. Those eyes would haunt her until the day she died. He had once been the most powerful Ancient in existence. What would he do to her if he was close enough? He resembled a human, yet he seemed to be a supernaturally enhanced version. Seeing him hold that golden spear worried her. She could picture that spear impaling her.

Lilae furrowed her eyebrows as she looked at his picture. "Is that what is coming, Delia? Another war?"

"They have already taken sides, my dear. This war has been brewing for ages. I am afraid we can no longer avoid it. The Ancients knew that Wexcyn couldn't stay imprisoned forever. He has too many supporters who have been trying to free him for centuries."

Lilae looked at the sky, imagining as she always did that she could see the Ancients up there in the Overworld. "And who is on our side, Delia?"

"The odds are in our favor… for now. Telryd, Ulsia, and Pyrii fight for life, for the preservation of this world."

"So that leaves Inora, the Shadow Elves' Ancient. She betrayed us, then."

"I wish it were that easy, Lilae. I really do. I fear the other Ancients have returned, as well. There are races that you've never even heard of, hiding out there… ready for revenge."

"Bellens, you mean?"

"Where did you hear that word?"

"I overhead a woman in Sabron say something about them to a little girl. She told the girl that if she didn't do her chores, a Bellen would come and eat her."

Delia signed. "Damned idiot, whoever that woman was."

Lilae folded her arms across her chest and held her blanket tightly. She had waited so long to hear this story, and yet, something told her that she was already a part of it all. "That's what you meant though, right?"

"Yes. As we speak, they prepare for war in my home. They have made the Underworld into something it was never meant to be. The Underworld was supposed to be a place for the dead to reconnect with their lost loved ones, and go to their last home." Delia looked off then, and Lilae felt badly. She couldn't help but forget that Delia was not of this world. Her home had already been taken, and now she hoped to help Lilae keep hers. "I escaped when Wexcyn killed my brothers and sisters. I was aided by the Ancients, so that I could take you before someone else did."

Lilae rested her head against Delia's shoulder again. She scratched at a mosquito bite. "Tell me, Delia. Where do I fit into all of this? Why did you take me?"

Delia stroked Lilae's hair. "Lilae, you are a remarkable young woman. Do you know that?"

Lilae half smiled as she watched the fire. She didn't want Delia to keep anything from her anymore, so she tried to look as if she were brave. "No more stalling, Delia. Go on—tell me. Am I an Ancient or something?" she joked.

Delia didn't say anything. Instead, she pulled back and stared at Lilae. "What did you say?"

Lilae sat up straight. "What? I was joking."

Delia's face was paler than Lilae had ever seen it. She narrowed her eyes at Lilae so that only a small glow replaced her irises. Lilae shuddered. "What is it?"

Delia shook her head. "Lilae, I don't know what possessed you to say that. You are too smart for your own good."

"You're not saying…"

Delia shook her head and waved her hands. "No. No, you're not an Ancient."

Lilae sighed in relief. "That's a relief." Her shoulders slumped. "What then?"

"You were close though, my dear. You are of the Chosen class. With the end of the Great War, the losing Ancients fled, and Wexcyn, the leader, was imprisoned. As a truce, The Barriers were created. However, the truce said that one day another war would be fought… This time for total domination. But here is the thing, Lilae. It was agreed that each race would produce an heir of the Ancients. You are Telryd's heir."

"How is such a thing possible?"

Delia sat up and leaned a little closer to Lilae, her tone rushing with excitement. "The truce states that the fate of the world would be put in the hands of the people. The Ancients are letting their creations decide who will lead in the Overworld, and there will be no further disputes. They all agreed. It is set in stone. *You* are the one they call the Flame. You were chosen to lead the humans in this war."

Lilae folded her legs and looked over her shoulder again, feeling as though someone watched her from the dark forest. "You're saying that I will fight Shadow Elves, all to keep Telryd's place secure in the Overworld? Why can't he fight for himself?"

"Lilae, if an Ancient stepped into this world, the balance of power would shift, and the world would not be the same. There's no telling what damage would be done. It must be done by the races."

Lilae squeezed her eyes shut and touched her temples with her fingertips. Her head throbbed. There was just too much to process. "What do I have to do?"

"You will lead the humans against Wexcyn and the forgotten races, and we will hope for the best. For, if you fail, there will be new leadership in the Overworld. Do you understand what that would mean?"

"There would be no more humans."

"Exactly. There would be no more humans, Silver Elves, or Tryans. Shadow Elves will thrive, and Wexcyn will re-create his fallen race." Delia sat back and pulled her cloak tighter. The air grew colder, and the wind picked up speed. "Those of the Chosen class are all named. You are the Flame, there is also the Storm, the Inquisitor, the Seer, the Steel, and the last is the Cursed. *He* will be Wexcyn's greatest weapon."

Lilae sighed. "Delia, this is too much." She was having a hard time keeping up a brave front.

"I know that this is a tough fate to accept." Delia leaned back. "I really thought you were ready. I have no choice but to tell you all that I can. Soon, we might not have an opportunity to talk about these things. We must prepare. The Storm is already heading this way. You have to be ready for his arrival. He will be the closet to you, for Pyrii and Telryd are like brothers. Tryans have always been great friends to the humans. As for the other Chosen, they have been ready for years now. We all have been waiting for you."

Lilae stared at the fire. The flames were dying down. She had an odd urge to touch them. Somehow, she knew she could do it. She almost reached out but resisted. She sighed and gazed sidelong at Delia.

"But…" She cleared her throat and tried to straighten her back. "What if I don't want to? Will they replace me? If I am too afraid… can I choose my own path?" Delia shot her a look that made her face pale. She immediately felt embarrassed by her question and looked away.

Delia folded her hands on her lap. "Lilae, dear, I know this must be very hard for you. I've studied human emotion for centuries, and while I do not have such feelings, I *am* empathetic. But my duty is to see the bigger picture. This entire thing is about more than just you. However, you are the one who must do it. We have waited for someone to be born with all of the necessary power. That someone is you. There will be no replacements."

Lilae looked down at her hands. Delia couldn't understand how she was feeling. She wasn't human and never would be. She was a supernatural being in human flesh. Could Delia even love her? It hurt to think that she was just business to Delia.

Delia noticed the look in Lilae's eyes. She put a hand on Lilae's. "You are strong, Lilae. You *can* do this."

So, there are five others out there just like me. I wonder if they are as miserable with this burning power as I am. Somehow, she couldn't tell Delia that she had been feeling stranger than normal lately, that she could feel the power that Delia was telling her about. It kept her awake at night, begging to be released.

"I'm afraid, Delia." She avoided eye contact with the Elder. She said it calmly, but she could feel the fear rising in her throat, making her almost giddy. "Is that normal?"

"It's the most normal emotion of them all, my dear."

Lilae pulled her blankets closer. "At least that part of me is human enough." She stared up at the stars, listening to the fire crackle.

"Good girl." Delia smiled and kissed her forehead. "You are the best choice the Ancients could have made, and one day, you'll understand why."

Lilae smiled. She felt comforted by Delia's kiss. Such affection was so rare from her.

Delia stood. "Let's return to camp before the others wake up."

Lilae nodded and followed her back through the forest. When they returned, everyone was still asleep. Delia kept the shield up and put her bedroll beside the fire. She leaned her staff against the wall and watched Lilae as she stood staring past the shield into the darkness.

"Get some rest, Lilae. We will be reaching new territory soon enough." Delia moved away from the fire and pulled her blanket over her. "Soon," Delia said, and smiled at her warmly, "you'll see a real spring."

Lilae nodded absently and grabbed her pack.

"Good night, Delia." She sat down and looked into the fire. She had so much information to process. Lilae always knew she was different, but now that she finally started to realize what was brewing inside, it frightened her.

She looked over her shoulder and into the woods. The quiet all around her made the hairs on her arm stand on end just thinking that Wexcyn was there, watching her. She lay on her bedroll and folded her arms across her chest as her mind drifted, wondering if the other chosen ones were as afraid as she was.

CHAPTER 4

"I KNOW WHAT YOU'RE AFRAID OF, my love," Sona whispered into Liam's ear.

Liam grinned and closed his eyes. She was the only one welcome to disturb his solitude. Sona kissed the back of his neck and ran her fingers through his hair. She smelled of lavender and honey. He caught her in his arms. She was light in his grasp and smiled up at him.

"And what is that?" Liam leaned in to kiss her on the lips. They were as soft as rose petals and similarly colored.

"Our wedding night." Sona giggled, and he showered her with passionate kisses all over her white throat. "You're afraid you won't know what to do with me." She wrapped her arms around his neck as he grabbed her skirts into a bunch, pressing her against the mantle of the fireplace.

He lifted her by the thighs. She wrapped them around his waist and let his hands slide up her stockings. "I'm sure I'll figure it out," he whispered, as his hand caressed her smooth legs.

"Prince Liam!" a shrill voice called.

Liam sighed, resting his forehead against Sona's. She looked up at him with the most unsettling blue eyes he'd ever seen.

"That woman," Sona growled under her breath. "Does she follow you everywhere?"

Liam agreed with the sentiment; he never got a moment's peace. There was always something to do, somewhere to be, for as long as he could remember.

"What?" Liam couldn't mask the irritation in his voice. He rolled his eyes as he heard the high-heeled footsteps enter the room. He knew those clicks along the floor all too well.

Lady Cardelia stepped into the quiet room. Liam quickly put Sona back onto the floor and straightened his clothing. His tutor frowned as she looked at the both of them. Her glare lingered on Sona in particular.

Lady Cardelia's serious blue eyes lifted to Liam's face. Her spectacles made her eyes look even bigger as she regarded him. He remembered when he used to draw caricatures of her during their lessons. He also remembered being struck across his hands with a stick whenever she caught him.

"Queen Aria asked me to find you. It is your birthday ball, after all." Lady Cardelia spoke slowly, precisely, always proper and composed. "You have guests, Prince Liam. You shouldn't spend the entire night hiding."

Liam gave a nod, even though he cared nothing about being paraded for guests he didn't know. "I'm coming."

"And you, Lady Sonalese Rochfort—" She shot a raptor-like glare at Sona. "What would Lord Rochfort think if he knew you were back here without a chaperone, with your dress gathered up around your waist? That is *not* ladylike at all."

Sona looked back at her. Her blue eyes held an icy glare. "I dare you to speak one word to my father."

Liam watched as Sona walked directly up to Lady Cardelia. He once thought that Lady Cardelia was one of the most intimidating women he had ever seen; that was, until he met Sona. The young woman fluffed out her petticoats and indigo skirts and retied her white bow around her tiny waist.

Sona was a noblewoman. Her father, Lord Rochfort, owned all of Klimmerick's Row, the wealthiest street of row houses and shops in Oren. He was a prominent political figure, and yet Sona didn't care about the constraints her title should have put on her. Sona did what she wanted. Liam envied her. Perhaps that was why he had proposed to her.

"But, haven't you heard that I am going to be your queen one day... Lady Longneck?" Sona grinned evilly at the look of shock on Lady Cardelia's face. "That *is* what everyone calls you."

Liam dared to look at Lady Cardelia. The tension in the room was stifling. Sona never censored her speech; she said whatever was on her mind. Lady Cardelia's face turned red.

Sona began to leave the room. She glanced back at the wiry older woman whose ruffled collar was buttoned all the way up to beneath her chin. Liam's brows lifted. Lady Cardelia almost seemed to shrink under Sona's glare.

Impressive, Liam thought. *No one can make that woman as much as flinch.*

"I don't care what you tell him. He'd probably have you killed anyway," she said with a flippant shrug of her shoulders, "for spreading such *vicious* lies." She grabbed her silk shawl from the back of a mahogany chair then flashed a smile at Liam. "I'll see you later, darling." She waved graciously and disappeared into the crowd outside the door as if nothing had happened.

Liam stood there silently as Lady Cardelia waited. He almost rolled his eyes when she lifted a long thin finger to wiggle at him. He knew the scolding was about to begin.

"Liam." Lady Cardelia looked to him.

Liam raised an eyebrow. "Prince Liam to you," he said.

She put her hands on her hips and gave him her best scowl. "Oh, don't try that with me, Liam. I've been your tutor since you were a little *wild* toddler wetting your pants. Don't give me any sass. That girl you're marrying may have a filthy tongue, but you know better."

Liam sighed. *No point arguing.*

She shook her head, her face softening. "Why are you hiding in here, Liam?" Her voice came out much gentler that time.

Liam shrugged, glancing at the doorway. *Too many people.* Outside those doors were thousands of people waiting to see him.

They were crowded in all of the public rooms of the Orenian castle. So many people made him nervous.

She offered a small smile. "You're twenty-five years old today, Liam. You cannot hide anymore. All of those people out there are expecting you to protect the kingdom. No masks or disguises can hide you now. Your time has come."

Liam put his hands in his pockets. He swallowed. She was right. It was time. This would be the last night that he would be in the castle. For years, he'd thought he wanted nothing more than to escape his studies and see what the real world had to offer; and now, the time had come, and only he knew just what that meant. Being a scholar brought more than knowledge.

He'd studied the prophecies. He knew what was coming.

"I know, Lady Cardelia. We've prepared for years now. I am ready," he said, standing just a little taller. He tried to give a reassuring smile.

Liam knew she already doubted him in her head. Many of his subjects looked at him with skepticism. *This was supposed to be our savior?* He could read that very question in their eyes. He wasn't a big man or remarkably tall. He was too skinny compared to his warrior friends. Liam feared that he was too… *ordinary* to be someone special.

He started toward the door and she caught him by the wrist. "Prince Liam, listen for a moment."

He lifted a brow. Her face looked troubled.

"I know you're leaving tomorrow and everything, but promise me something."

Liam nodded. "What is it?" He wanted to make his way to his private quarters. He wanted to get a good night's rest before he left with the Order of Oren. His friends would be ready and waiting for him in the morning.

Lady Cardelia's eyes were wet with tears. It made Liam uncomfortable. She had always been the strictest of tutors. He didn't like seeing her façade fade.

"Don't let anything you see out there in the wild lands change you. Don't let anyone taint your good heart, especially that foul woman who dares to call herself a lady."

"Watch yourself. Lady Rochfort is my fiancée."

She shook her head. "I'm sorry, but I don't know how you chose her out of every lovely young woman at court. She isn't good enough for you."

He turned away from her. *Why wasn't she being fair about Sona? Sona never did anything to hurt anyone.*

"She loves me," Liam replied. "And who says I'm good enough for any of those women outside those doors?"

"You speak as if you are incapable of being loved. We all love you, Liam. There is no need to settle. Most of those people out there have no idea what you really are, but *I* know. You fight for our entire race. Stay focused, and don't let us down."

She had never spoken this way. Her words worried him. "I promise." He left her in the empty cloakroom and entered the busy hallway. It was after midnight, and the ball was still in full swing.

He walked with his hands in his pockets, and then remembered Lord Eisenmoore's gentleman's training and quickly took them out. While Lady Cardelia had spent years training him to be a scholar, Lord Eisenmoore had tried his best to train Liam to be the perfect gentleman, the future king. Still, he forgot some things at times.

"Prince Liam," the guests said whenever he passed. They bowed and glanced at him in awe. Sixteen years secluded in the vaults, and nine more spent in the walls of the military stronghold in the north, and none of his civilian subjects had ever seen his face, until tonight.

Liam nodded to each of those who addressed him. Though he walked with his back straight and his face calm, inside he was a ball of nerves and nausea for being stared at so. His black hair had been brushed and styled differently than any man who attended the ball.

"A future king must set the trends," Lord Eisenmoore said, *"not follow them."* Tomorrow, most of the men in court would try to sport the same hairstyle.

Liam wore a rich red-and-white tailored suit and walked with his jewel-encrusted sword at his hip. There was a time when a weapon felt foreign to him, but after being locked away with the other soldiers of the elite Order of Oren, he was never without his sword again. It was an extension of him now, and he wielded it with an expertise that couldn't be explained in someone so young.

Faces: smiling faces, judging faces, envious faces, adoring faces. So many faces, and he didn't recognize any of them. He wished his best friend, Rowe, were a nobleman. He wished the captain had been allowed to come. Instead, he was forced to mingle with complete strangers, people who probably secretly wanted him to fail.

Liam was the only heir, and there were those who wanted him dead. There were fools who coveted the throne. They still went about their political intrigues and scheming as if everything was the same. They had no idea what was coming to their realm.

Liam avoided the stares and looked up at his mother. Queen Aria seemed to glow a little brighter than the other Tryans around her.

This was Kyril, realm of the Tryans and the fairies. Every Tryan had a glow that reached from the inside out, and yet she stood out as if a light shone only for her. He felt a lump in his throat. Her piercing gaze rested on him, and she smiled. This might be his last night seeing her beautiful face, and in an instant, he could see that same thought reflected in her eyes.

Oh, mother, he thought. *Stop reading my mind!*

She grinned. It was a secret smile, and only Liam knew its meaning. *Forgive me, it is a terrible habit,* she said silently back to him.

Liam walked up the short staircase to the row of thrones. There were only two, when there had once been three. His father had been dead for twenty years now, and he still remembered where he used to sit up there.

"Liam, my boy," Queen Aria said and hugged him.

Liam stood beside her, and there was a loud cheer from the crowd. She raised his hand up with hers and smiled down at the large ballroom packed with Tryans dressed in their absolute best finery.

"Tonight," she called, "my son salutes you all, for he is the chosen one who will deliver us from the hands of evil. These are indeed dark times. He will rid our realm of the murderous Shadow Elf clans that invade our territory. He *will* protect us."

The crowd cheered even louder. Liam almost wanted to shout at them. They knew nothing. Shadow Elves weren't nearly as bad as what they really should fear. As Queen Aria smiled at the crowd, she locked arms with Liam.

Liam, I love you, she said silently to him. Even while she smiled at her people, Liam could feel the tension. *I've tried to protect you for as long as I could, but I fear The Barriers are being opened. We both know there are more sinister things in the works. We both know that Wexcyn wants you dead.* She looked at him, worry lines tainting her forehead. She gave his hand a squeeze. *Please, don't get yourself killed out there. Get the talisman from the Alden clan in Raeden and wait for my word. I fear the time to meet the others is upon us.*

Liam nodded. *Do not worry mother,* Liam thought. His mother could read most anyone's mind; his was not immune. *The Alden clan will willingly give us the talisman for safekeeping. And as far as the Shadow Elves are concerned… They don't know the havoc I will unleash upon them.*

He could feel his adrenaline start to rush. The time for reading books and scrolls was over. The time for training and preparing had come to an end. He thumbed his hilt. Tomorrow, his sword would taste blood, and there would be no turning back.

CHAPTER 5

LIAM TILTED HIS HEAD and listened to The Winds as they whispered to him.

They're coming for you, they warned.

"What?" Without a reply, they faded with the crisp breeze.

Liam looked to the dull, gray sky. Dew clung to the thin overhanging branches and the mountain air smelled sweet. It was just before dusk—when the Shadow Elves would awaken for their nocturnal activities—and Liam was ready for battle. He sat tall above his black horse, waiting for the right moment to attack the Shadow Elves below.

Liam patted Midnight, his battle horse, and smoothed his hind leg. He leaned forward and spoke in a hushed tone to the horse. "Are you ready?"

Midnight neighed in reply and kicked his legs.

Liam waved a hand and motioned for the troupe of soldiers behind him to move closer. There were about a hundred Tryan soldiers waiting for his command. They looked around at the empty space before them and the long drop beneath them. Still, Liam had their complete trust.

Liam held the reigns tight in his grip and took a deep breath. The cool air entered his lungs, and he closed his eyes. He focused on his power, the energy that flowed within his veins. The clouds began to move closer together, creating a tight knit form in the sky that completely blocked the sun. When Liam opened his eyes, they were no longer blue. They were as black as night.

The Tryans behind him were unafraid. They were the elite warriors of the Order of Oren. Liam had been locked away with these men and women for nearly ten years. He had trained with them and lived with them as an equal.

Commoners like Rowe and nobles like Sona, none of that mattered in the Order. This group was like family, and they would follow him into the Underworld, if necessary. They waited for Liam to signal them. One hand clutched the reins of their horses, the other on the hilts of their swords.

Liam raised his large jewel-encrusted sword into the air with a loud cry and urged Midnight on. Midnight jumped, and over the cliff they went. Liam held tight. His eyes narrowed fiercely, and his sword began to glow white in the darkness. The horse's hooves searched for footing and found none.

Thunder cracked loudly above them, as if the sky was about to break open and fall upon them with rage. Liam sucked in a breath of the cool air and lightning shot across the sky. Liam caught the light in his sword and directed it beneath them, making a pathway of blinding light so that his men could file steadily behind him.

The horses' hooves sparked along the road of lightning, a shrill sound deafening the soldiers as they slid toward the ground. The valley led them directly to the camp of Shadow Elves.

The effect was perfect, so perfect that Liam couldn't help but crack a smile. Liam wanted it to look as though he and his men were coming straight from the sky. The Shadow Elves woke with a start at the noise as an army of horses jumped from the path of lightning and trampled into the rocky valley. The vibrations shook the terrain, and their enemy was frozen with obvious terror. In an instant, the battle began.

A swarm of Shadow Elves scrambled from their tents. They moved with such speed that their figures were barely traceable. However, Tryan eyes were equipped to spot them. Even though they darted in and out of the shadows, they couldn't hide.

The Shadow Elves hissed like snakes when they saw the royal colors of the Oren palace. There was blue and red on their breastplates and armor. With Liam leading them, it made them all the more fearsome.

The Shadow Elves had heard about the prince. Liam was the first male heir in centuries, and his reputation in the field was notorious amongst the invading elves. Ten years in training and smaller battles with rival clans and wildlings had made Liam a force to be reckoned with. His grim expression was illuminated by another flash of lightning. He swung his enchanted sword, and lightning whipped out like a terrifying rope of electric currents. It cut through groups of elves like butter, slaying them by the dozens. The remaining elves began to flee from its path.

Yes, just run away. Liam grinned in triumph as they retreated back to their own barrier. *This can end quickly if you just run*. And many did run, back to the cruel, dark realm of Nostfar.

The Shadow Elves who remained were quick and agile, with fighting styles that the Orens had never seen. They were like predators, calculating and precise. One leapt from the ground and reached for Liam's sword.

Liam saw him coming and sliced the elf's outstretched hand off. The glow of his sword made the wound sizzle as though it had been stuck with a hot poker. The smell of burning flesh struck Liam's nostrils as the Shadow Elf shrieked in pain and tumbled to the ground.

Before Liam could turn, another was on his back, a blue crystal dagger clutched in its grasp. It never ceased to amaze him how lightning-fast they were; like cats, they pounced and darted. His eyes widened as the blade came toward his face.

He turned his head and grabbed the Shadow Elf by its long black hair, slinging it to the ground with such force that it flew into a nearby tree. Liam's eyes tracked the body, and, with a point of his sword, he sent a flash of light that knocked the Shadow Elf from the branches and onto the hard ground. *One more down.* Liam grinned as he turned Midnight around and charged headfirst into an oncoming flurry of Shadow Elves with the power of the Ancient Pyrii flowing through his veins.

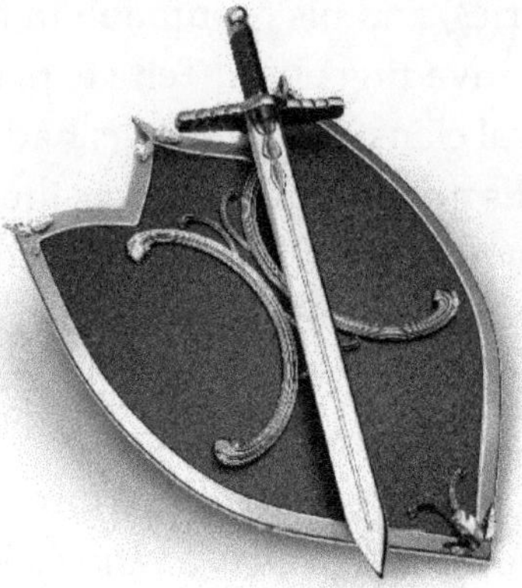

ROWE CHARGED THROUGH THE MASSES with untamed vigor. His ax hung low at the side of his horse. His pulse quickened as he gripped the heavy ax in his large fist, the bands on the hilt pressing hard into his roughened palm.

Rowe lifted it slightly and, with a grunt, he leaned forward, swinging the ax powerfully into the heads of the surrounding Shadow Elves. A spray of blood filled the air like a fog.

Skin split open and bone crushed beneath his ax. It glowed blue, and he knew that it stung their flesh as it cut through. The yells and noise were deafening, and so was the blood that rushed as his heart pumped with adrenaline.

Rowe's horse wouldn't slow. Like every other horse riden by a Tryan on the battlefield, his was connected with its rider. Each horse could feel the same, sense their thoughts, and anticipate what the rider wanted. Rowe's veered right and into another group of Shadow Elves that tried to slice the horse's belly or legs, trying anything to get the Tryan soldier to the ground.

Rowe kicked one with his heavy-booted foot and thrust the ax into the neck of another. The glowing blade sliced straight through the soft flesh of its neck and barely paused to cut through the bone. Other elves looked in horror as the head rolled off of its body to the muddy ground.

Rowe sat up and swung the blood from his blade, not stopping as he continued on to the next unfortunate being in his eyesight.

"SONA!" THE TRYAN WOMAN on the white horse heard someone shout her name from beyond the dense cluster of elves she was attacking.

Her head snapped up toward the voice, her hands tight on her horse's reins. Rowe pointed to a tent on the far side of the field.

"There!"

Sona nodded, and her horse instantly understood the orders. They galloped through the crowd as the Shadow Elves continued to fight with the Tryan soldiers on the ground. Sona grinned despite the calamity all around her.

The Shadow Elves reached for her as she passed by, but her horse was too fast for them. She ran them over with such a force that many lay crushed behind.

Once they reached the tent, she hopped from the horse's back. Sona reached both hands over her head and grabbed her dual swords from behind her. The swords glowed blue with her touch, and, with a face of determination, she charged through the tents flaps. Inside, three Shadow Elves crouched over a circular table.

Her large blue eyes widened. The surface of the table was black like smoke, and images of other Shadow Elves flickered along the smoke. The smoke disappeared, and the Shadow Elf captains lunged at her.

"Kill the Tryan!"

With a curved sword in each hand, she crisscrossed them and sliced the first elf straight through his abdomen. With a pull of the swords, she cut him in half. Blood splattered onto the tent's walls as she flung one sword at the elf to her right.

He fell backward with the force of her throw, as the sword lodged into his spine. The screams filled her ears, but she was in a trance. With only one sword, she saw the other elf dart to her like lightning.

Sona grunted as he elbowed her in the face before she could catch him with her sword. She tasted the saltiness of her own blood, and it enraged her. Her eyes narrowed. He may have caught her off guard with his Shadow Walk, but he would only get one hit. She would not make that mistake twice.

Her sword caught the handle of his dagger and tossed it into the air. He growled and ducked as she tried to cut off his head. The glowing sword missed, but she anticipated his move and kicked him in the chin, knocking him backward. She lunged on top of him, her sword's blade pressed against his neck.

"Who sent you?" Sona clenched her teeth as he tried to push her off.

His thin eyes were completely white and matched his tattoos almost perfectly. A smile spread across his face. "Is that a trick question?" he asked with a raised brow and a grin that was meant to taunt Sona.

Sona's gaze bore into his, watching the light fade from his eyes as she pressed the blade into his neck. He wrapped his thin hands around her throat in a desperate attempt to stop her. She closed her eyes and finished the job. His hands fell back to the ground, limp and lifeless.

Sona stood and closed her eyes. Heart thumping, she wiped a streak of the Shadow Elf's blood on both cheeks, readied her swords, and stepped from the tent into the blackness of night that only her fiancé could have arranged on a spring morning.

She saw him on his black horse, regal and full of a confidence he didn't normally display. She watched him as she let the light from her glowing body seep into her swords. A tiny bit of light made them blue. A tiny bit more made them yellow. She shook a bit as she poured nearly all of her light into the swords, and made them red with power.

CHAPTER 6

IN THE DISTANCE, LIAM WATCHED Sona run through the surrounding masses with her swords overenchanted so much that the red glow caused a cloud of smoke to encircle her.

Seeing her in action was like witnessing a tale from the storybooks he'd been read as a child. He was proud of her.

He never doubted any of them, but he could see that some of the men were fighting only to be surprised by the elves' speed. This made them focus even harder and fight with more intensity. Once you had an elf in your sight, you'd better kill them quick, lest they slip through your fingers and stab you in the back.

Liam breathed hard, the adrenaline surging through him. He saw Sona climb onto her horse again, bloodstained but as beautiful as a goddess.

The Tryans had so much to prove to the other races, and Liam was confident that his Order was made up of the perfect warriors for the task.

The fairies were busy keeping track of anyone wounded, ready to heal anyone in need. His reflexes were sharp. He heard the wind swish as a Shadow Elf raced through the crowd and onto the back of Liam's horse. He felt the cold hands reach around his neck, a small blade at his throat. Liam clenched his jaw.

"You sure you want to try that?" He looked down at the Shadow Elf's ash-colored arm, the white tattoos standing out against his skin.

"Shut up," the Shadow Elf spat. "You better end this now, or I will slit your throat. We'll see who wins this battle when your precious royal blood spills onto the ground."

Liam felt the blade dig into his flesh, and he elbowed the Shadow Elf in his stomach. There was a grunt of pain, but the blade barely moved. Liam clenched his fist around his sword's hilt, and the lightning radiated through his body and into the Shadow Elf.

The blade at Liam's throat dropped. The Shadow Elf convulsed with a cry as the lightning circulated throughout him. His organs burned and then his muscles, until the currents ate away at his bone and skin.

The remaining Shadow Elves saw this, and Liam could tell that their resolve wavered; they slowed to a stop and backed away. They raised their weapons above their heads in surrender. The Tryans watched Liam to see what he would do, if he would show mercy to the stragglers.

When the Shadow Elves saw that Liam merely glared at them, they lowered their hands, their shadowed faces draining of their will to fight. Only a couple dozen were left alive and they reluctantly backed away, making sure that Liam or the others weren't going to come after them.

When the elves saw that he stood his ground, they turned and joined the others in fleeing. They ran as fast as the wind, looking like nothing more than haunted shadows as they disappeared into the forest. The army camp was overthrown within minutes, and every Shadow Elf had either fled back toward Nostfar or lay dead on the grassy field.

"WE LOST THREE," Rowe reported to Liam. He stopped a few feet from Midnight and looked up at the prince. Liam kept his face absent of emotion. He was captain of the Order. The title had been passed to him, and, at merely thirty-two, he was the youngest to ever earn such a title.

Liam lowered his sword, his eyes returning to a most crystalline blue that mocked the purest sea. The clouds began to part, and the sun shone its light onto the carnage that tainted the valley. Liam hopped from Midnight's back and bent down to a corpse.

Three losses out of a hundred weren't bad, but Liam felt partly responsible for those deaths. He was supposed to protect them. He sighed and nodded. All of those men were like brothers to him. He hated to imagine which ones had died.

"Offer them to the Silver River. May they have better luck in the Underworld." The men would be laid upon rafts and set ablaze before being sent down the river. It was a proper soldier's funeral. "May Lord Elahe bless them."

Rowe nodded and gave orders to Tuvin to take care of the task. The soldier gave a quick nod and hurried off. Rowe watched Liam for a moment as he knelt over a dead Shadow Elf, staring at it.

Liam rubbed the blackish blood between his fingers. He was in deep thought. He remembered the first time he'd seen a horde of

Shadow Elves. It had been his fifth year in the Order, and they were attacked in the early dawn.

The Elves were like demons that stalked the night at speeds that left Liam and the other men on edge. Liam had almost been slit by a glowing dagger before his eyes could even adjust to their speed. The elf's maniacal sharp-toothed grin still lingered in his mind. He was thankful that Rowe had been by his side. It wasn't the first time that Rowe had saved his life…

"Liam?"

Liam looked up at his best friend and raised an eyebrow. "What?"

"Are you all right?"

Liam nodded and came to his feet. "I'm fine. Tired is all. I may have overdone it on the lightning." The other ninety-seven soldiers were gathered around him.

Rowe reached into his side pocket and tossed him a vial. Liam thanked him and popped the cork. A cloud of fog escaped, and he drank the liquid gingerly. He savored its replenishing waters.

Rowe waited for him to return the vial. He handed it to a passing fairy to refill it. The waters of the Silver River ran through Kyril and Alfheim, but only a fairy could bless it and encourage its rejuvenating properties.

"They managed to get a lot closer this time."

"Yes. I know. I can't understand how, though." Liam hated lying to his friends. He knew why, and the explanation was an impossible one.

The Guardians were awakened. They were the only ones who could open the doors to The Barriers. They had guarded and protected the doors for centuries, keeping the races safe from each other, keeping dark things from polluting the realms.

He wiped his hands clean on his pants. Liam stood tall amongst his kinsmen and cracked his knuckles. He spoke to them in a solemn tone.

"Gather all of the enemy bodies and burn them." His jaw clenched. This wasn't what he'd expected to see so soon. There had to be a couple hundred in this small force, but it was more elves than they'd ever seen.

"I don't want their stinking blood tainting our soil." The soldiers voiced their agreement; some spat on the bodies and went to follow their orders.

Liam looked up at the mountain that they had jumped from; it was massive, reaching toward the clouds. Its rocky terrain led down the valley and through the rushing Silver River. He had dreamed of such mountains when he was a child.

There was a time when he had been confined to the palace, when his mother, Queen Aria, had been too overprotective to let him leave the courtyard. She had held his hand when they visited other kingdoms, and his eyes had widened with wonder at the different landscapes of Kyril. He was grateful for her love and protection, but the day he had first picked up a sword had changed his life.

Rowe's approach broke him from his thoughts. The tall, brawny man came closer and spoke quietly. "What do you think this all means?"

Liam glanced at him and up at the sky. All of the storm clouds had vanished. "It means the Realm Wars have begun."

Rowe shook his head. "This is getting out of control. I don't even know if we're really helping. The Shadow Elves outnumber us at least ten to one."

"No matter. Like today, we will cut their numbers the best we can."

"Someone's a bit ambitious today," Rowe grumbled. "How long do you think we'll be out here? You know Cammie is going to give birth in three months."

Liam met Rowe's blue eyes and forced a smile. "I'll try to get you home in time to meet your new son."

Rowe returned the grin. "We can only hope it's a boy, but I'll be okay with a girl just as well."

"Maybe you'll have twins," Liam suggested, and Rowe gave Liam's shoulder a shake as he chuckled.

It was odd, hearing laughter when they were surrounded by dead bodies. He almost felt guilty for thinking of joyful moments right after a bloody massacre; as if he hadn't just revealed that, soon, they'd be fighting in a war that could go on for centuries.

Rowe's laughter died down, and there was a tense silence. Liam knew that distant look in Rowe's eyes. Neither of them wanted to say the obvious: Rowe might never return home to see his wife or unborn child.

Liam watched the fairies congregate toward the trees. He could see that they were saddened.

They had let three men die. A healer's job was never easy. They had to be entirely focused and ready, watching every man to make sure he didn't suffer from a blow that could prove fatal. Liam knew what pressure was put upon them. He shared that burden with them. They would beat themselves up over it for days.

Liam looked down at the grass. The battlefield was no longer green. The grass was brown now. Its life and energy had been sucked up and used by the fairies to heal the wounded soldiers.

Liam clicked his tongue and Midnight trotted closer. He smoothed the horse's flanks and laid his face close to his. "Good riding today, boy."

Midnight neighed in reply, stomping his hind legs.

Midnight was a stallion, both quick and aggressive. In battle, Midnight was agile, aiding Liam in his quick attacks as they weaved in and out of the masses. He was the most loyal and intelligent horse Liam had ever encountered, and he had trained him from a foal. Their bond was strong and pure.

Liam pulled a flask of water from Midnight's saddlebag. He drank the warm water deeply and handed it to Rowe. Rowe took a swig and sealed the top.

"We stick to the plan. It's off to Raeden we go."

Rowe nodded. "I still can't believe the elves are actually here."

Liam shrugged. "You'll see much more than just that if you stick with me."

"That better be a promise." Rowe clamped a hand on Liam's shoulder. "I'll get the men to hurry with the funeral pyres and the burning of the elves."

Liam gave a nod of approval. He wanted to tell Rowe what he knew, but he was too afraid of his own knowledge to put that burden on his friend. The world was about to change, and he was partly responsible for making sure it didn't plunge into total darkness.

He had immense power, but he sometimes wondered if it was enough. Despite his doubts, Liam refused to let his people down. He was driven by duty. It was his destiny, and he was a slave to it.

"Why the long face, pretty boy?" Nani teased as she hovered before him. Her glittering fairy wings caught the sun's rays so that he had to shield his eyes as he looked directly at her.

She smiled and landed onto the soft ground. He knew she was faking the smile. She was as heartbroken by the loss of the three soldiers as her team of healers.

Nani was a prodigy. No fairy village had known a healer as powerful as she, and she chose to follow Liam. She believed in him even if none of the other kingdoms and villages did.

Nani batted her eyelashes at Liam, bright green eyes full of affection for him. "You did well today. You showed the enemy a taste of what they're up against. A little flashy, but you know how I like theatrics, my dear prince."

Barely taller than four feet, Nani walked over to him, her deep purple pigtails bouncing with each step she took in her supple thigh-high brown leather boots. Nani ignored the stares of some of the men as she walked by. Her eyes were set on Liam.

Liam chose not to mention the dead soldiers. "Are you sure you're up for staying with this army? Things are only going to get worse. We are heading deeper and deeper into the wild lands to eliminate these Shadow Elves. It's going to be dangerous for you girls."

Nani scoffed. "I have the most powerful man in the world on my side. I think we'll be all right." She winked at him.

Liam grinned. "Not the most powerful," he corrected. "There are the 'others.'"

Nani turned up her nose. "I won't believe it until I see it."

"Talking about the Chosen class again?" Rowe stood with his legs spread apart. He folded his arms across his large muscle-bound chest. "I don't know why the Ancients won't just come down here themselves and set things straight. Save us all a load of trouble."

"There's a lot that you don't know, Rowe." Nani smirked. "Why don't you stick to your brutish ways and let Prince Liam do all of the thinking."

Rowe shrugged. "Works for me."

Nani laughed. "That's why I like you, Rowe. I think the safest place to be right now is by your and Liam's side."

What were the other Chosen ones were up to? *Together* they were supposed to unite the entire world and end all evil.

Maybe they could unite the races, but there would always be a new evil to conquer.

Sona stepped through the crowd. "Heal me," she demanded.

Nani flew toward Sona with a grin. "Say *please*." She flew away before Sona could push her. Nani laughed softly, nearly a child by comparison to the Tryan woman before her.

Nani flew closer and brought her face close to Sona's. This time, she mocked a serious expression.

"Getting a little sloppy." A twinkle filled Nani's green eyes. "I am *not* impressed."

Here we go, Liam thought.

"Just fix it, you little twit!"

Nani raised an eyebrow and spoke to Liam. "Whoa, lady!" She mocked a gasp of shock. "The manners on this one! Where'd you find her, anyway? A slum?"

Sona ignored her. She looked over at Liam as Nani's healing hands mended her swollen jaw. A yellow glow covered Sona's face, sealing the wound and decreasing the swelling.

"Done." Nani stepped onto the ground and curtsied. "*My lady*."

"Thank you," Sona said, though she sneered and turned on her heels to walk away. She wrapped her arms around Liam's neck.

Liam tensed, seeing the others eying them. "Not now, Sona," he said quietly into her ear.

She kissed his cheek and nodded. "Of course, darling." She glanced back at Nani. "Wouldn't want the fairy to get jealous."

Nani tossed her head back and laughed. She looked back at Sona. "Jealous? Of what? You can't even fly!"

Sona gave Liam another kiss, on his lips. "Good job today. You handled the battle well."

Liam watched Sona as she headed toward the other soldiers. She only let her hardened persona relax around him.

Liam sauntered toward the Silver River. It was the only body of water that stretched from Kyril to Alfheim, where the Silver Elves lived.

He listened to The Winds. They were unusually quiet lately. He missed their voices.

It was nice to know when danger was around, before it reached him. There was rarely anything exciting in the palace; however, when he had finally been sent away for his soldier's training, The Winds had revealed themselves with vigor each time he was in a battle.

Liam ran a hand through his hair and knelt down to the riverbank. He absently picked up a few pebbles and tossed them into the water as he listened. It was as if the air grew dense, and every other noise was muted.

He looked back into the direction of the camp. He wondered how many more he would lose before he was able to return home. What his mother had led the people of Oren to believe was a simple mission to rid the lands of a few rogue elves was something much more serious.

Liam felt something dark and evil approaching. *The Ancients are warring, what does that mean to their creations?* He shuddered. What would they do if their creators abandoned them? What would be the point of fighting if that happened?

Stop it, Liam, he sighed. *You really do worry too much.*

He turned to head back toward Midnight when he heard yells from the forest.

"Wait! Prince Liam!" Jonev, one of the sentries, shouted.

Liam felt his skin crawl with dread when the ground began to shake as something ran toward them. Liam's jaw tensed. Something was approaching. Something… big.

Jonev ran behind Liam, his eyes wide as he pointed toward the forest. "The elves, they set them loose!"

Liam swallowed. He had already used too much energy with his lightning skills. He took a long deep breath and rested his hand on the hilt of his sword. They were all watching him. The Order depended on him to lead. Liam refused to let those men and women down. They were his only friends.

Liam glanced over at Nani, whose smile completely faded. Her olive skin paled as she stared past him with wide eyes.

"Nani," he called. He drew his sword. "Get ready to work."

CHAPTER 7

OUT OF THE TREES emerged a pack of wild wolves.

No, Liam realized with horror. *These aren't wolves.* They were nearly twice the size and had matted ash-black fur that stuck to them like tar. These were creatures born of evil. They were actually *people* whom the Shadow Elves had transformed into horrible beasts specifically to hunt down other men. *Riestlings.*

Liam swallowed the hard knot in his throat. The wars before The Barriers had produced countless monstrosities, and it seemed as though no one was safe from those they thought they'd never see again.

The Tryan army drew their swords and slowly backed away. They had seen many horrors in the Order, but most members had never seen a Shadow Elf, let alone their minions.

There were nearly thirty riestlings trampling through the forest like horses. It was obvious to Liam that the Shadow Elves were quick in their revenge. They weren't going to be so easy to crush as he had hoped.

Behind the riestlings, however, was the reason the ground shook as though an earthquake ripped through the land. Liam sucked in a breath as a massive Nostfar giant came running through the woods.

Like pounding on a drum, his footsteps could be heard for miles all around.

His head was covered in a metal helmet so that only his eyes were visible. They were large and completely black. The giant's large chest was exposed. He had spiked, metal shackles on his wrists and feet and ran full speed toward the Tryans, who looked like children in comparison.

Nani waited above them. Liam watched as she cracked her knuckles and readied herself.

The other fairies were positioned above the Tryan army.

"Holy Elahe. You better do something, Liam," Rowe warned as he looked up at the giant.

Liam rarely ever saw Rowe looking afraid. However, he could see shock line his face as he beheld something he'd only heard tales about while growing up.

"You never said there'd be blasted giants."

"What can I say, Rowe? I promised you a battle that you'd never forget." Liam worked quickly. Once he enchanted his sword until it glowed, red beams pumped from the steel, and the spark of power brought all eyes to him. Even though he began to sweat with exertion, he held it ready and unwavering. The power crackled and warmed the air around him.

The riestlings' eyes went from Liam to the others, as though choosing whom to attack first.

Liam could feel himself growing weaker. He glanced at Rowe. "Can I count on you, Rowe, if this kills me? Will you break your vow and use your power?"

"You're not dying today, my friend. My vow is safe."

Liam reached his other hand out and blew it. A cloud of black smoke flew from his palm, encircling the pack of wild beasts. Their nostrils sniffed the air, and they were immediately drawn to Liam, angry and with purpose.

The giant growled. His blunt teeth curled into a snarl as the smoke lured him in, as well. He raised his ax high into the air and swung it at Liam.

Liam grinned despite himself. He was amazed that his Vex worked. He had never tried it before, and now he had all of their attention. The beasts would focus only on him, leaving his men free to strike without opposition.

Liam took in a quick breath as the beasts began to close in. They were coming fast. Their clawed feet kicked up dirt as they ran. He ducked the giant's ax as it scooped up some of his men, tossing them into the air.

Liam cursed under his breath, seeing them fall to the ground with a crash. He rolled his wrists, the sword immediately creating a shield-like bubble around him, as the riestlings descended upon him. When he sank his blade into the ground, the shield was complete.

A glow stretched from Liam's body, feeding the shield as the creatures began nipping and clawing at it. The Vex had put them under a spell of blind hatred, and they desperately wanted nothing else but to rip Liam apart.

The giant beat on the shield that encircled Liam as though he were possessed. It was the perfect opportunity for the other Tryans to attack while the beasts were all focused on Liam.

"What are you fools waiting for? Kill them!" Sona shouted as she ran to tear the beasts apart with her dual swords.

Liam squeezed his eyes shut to stay focused. He felt no pain and would absorb all of the damage for the others. They had to kill the beast because the Nostfar giant would devastate the surrounding villages. Liam was still surprised that he had created such a shield but knew that he couldn't keep it up for much longer. Nani must have sensed this, too, as she was at his side in a flash.

Her wings flapped in a frenzy, like those of a hummingbird. Nani's eyes narrowed as she fed energy to Liam; he didn't need healing, but her powers would rejuvenate him. Shards of thin, golden light traveled from her fingertips to his body but bounced off of the shield. She tried harder, only to realize that it was impenetrable.

Liam watched as Nani changed her target to Rowe, making him stronger and faster so that he could quickly kill the beasts and get them off of Liam.

Nani's energy filled Rowe, and he chopped away at the riestlings until all sounds of their growls and squeals of pain had ceased.

Sona was already climbing the giant, who paid her no mind. His was intent only on Liam. He slammed his ax onto the shield, causing it to spark from the impact.

Liam could feel only the pressure from the ax as the giant struck again and again. It vibrated the shield, making Liam's bones and teeth chatter. He dug his feet into the dirt to keep his balance. Liam squeezed his eyes closed, and sweat dripped from his head and down his chest. He was weakening with each blow.

Sona was fast. Once her mind was set on something, she would never stop. She was upon the giant's shoulder in no time. The other Tryans below stabbed at the giant, with little reaction from him. They barely weakened him, but Sona seemed to know exactly where to strike. She was at his neck with her glowing swords.

She clenched her teeth and used all of her strength to slam her sword his flesh.

"Die, you stupid creature," she panted with each saw of her blade across his neck.

Each second that passed made him weaker.

Finally, the other soldiers made way, as the giant wobbled and fell to the ground.

The entire valley shook as he collapsed with a loud thud. Sona hopped off and rolled away just in time; the giant's head crashed into the ground, tossing a heap of dirt and rocks into the air at the impact. She sprang to her feet and checked to confirm that the giant was dead. She nodded to Liam, her blue eyes meeting his.

Liam pulled his sword from the soil and slumped to the ground.

"Liam!" Rowe called, pushing through to get to him.

Liam held a hand out to keep Rowe away. Liam could barely see anything and felt nauseous. His body tingled all over as if tiny bees had stung at him until he was nearly numb. When he opened his eyes, he saw only colors and then darkness.

"I'm fine," Liam said. His voice was raspy as he slowly succumbed to the darkness. His body felt heavy, his mind smothered by an intense weight. He didn't realize that he was crashing to the ground. "Don't worry about…" His voice trailed off as his eyes fluttered closed.

CHAPTER 8

THE SUN BEAMED DOWN on Liam's face, warming his skin. He opened his eyes and squinted, shielding the red sun's rays.

Red sun? Liam thought as his head lolled to the side.

He groaned. He wanted to go back to sleep. A blue and orange butterfly flew right onto his nose. Its wings seemed to make the air glitter around it. The moment it landed on Liam's nose, memories of what had happened came back to him in a torrent of images and sounds. He sat up and winced at the throbbing in his head.

His head whipped to the side as he took in his surroundings. Rowe, Nani, Sona, and the others were nowhere to be seen. Panic filled him as he came to his feet and realized that he was no longer in the valley with his friends.

Where is everyone? Liam tried to stay calm as his eyes scanned his surroundings. He stood in the middle of a meadow, a soft breeze rustling through so that the tall deep-green grass swayed gently.

Liam examined the scenery. This place was like nothing he'd ever seen. He looked out toward white snow-capped mountains, the icicles reflecting the sun's rays so that it appeared as though the mountain was covered in jewels.

Looking down at his body, Liam realized that he wore a white tunic and white linen pants that swayed in the breeze. A simple gold band was wrapped around his waist, and he felt the soft, cool grass beneath the soles of his bare feet.

His feeling of worry deepened. His stomach twisted into knots as he feared the worst.

Am I dead? Liam turned around, looking for clues as to where he was and what had happened. He had to get out of there—wherever he was—and get home. His people needed him.

Liam stopped abruptly. He could feel eyes on him. He turned and saw someone standing across from him in the distance.

It was a girl.

His worry and fear dissipated as he looked at her. She calmed him somehow. Liam felt self-conscious as her eyes examined him. He straightened his tunic. He felt naked without his sword, but he didn't sense danger as she approached him.

She wore a white gown that billowed around her thin frame. A similar gold band tied her dress at her waist. She was tall, nearly as tall as a Tryan woman, but clearly not of his race. Her skin didn't glow like a Tryan woman's, but she was no less enchanting.

He gasped when she stepped closer, the light of the sun illuminating her fire-red hair. It was odd. Her hair was scarlet, but gold strands stood out as the wind tossed it around her delicate face.

Liam's throat suddenly went dry. Though he was from a land where most of the women were natural born beauties, there was something special that drew him to this woman.

"Who are you?" He pursed his lips, surprised to find that he couldn't hear his own voice, and neither could she. He noticed that she desperately tried to have her own voice heard.

After a few attempts, it seemed as though they both gave up on being heard and focused on each other. Liam felt compelled to walk toward her, and she did the same. As he got a little closer, he noticed that she was as confused as he was and as cautious. Still, nothing stopped them until they were merely a few feet apart, facing each other.

He was oddly glad that they couldn't speak to each other. For once, Liam didn't know what he would say to her. If only Rowe could see this! This was the first woman to leave him awestruck.

Her jade-green eyes were flecked with hazel and drew him in like a spell. Liam felt an intense desire to touch her. He took a deep breath and reached out.

She looked up into his eyes, a little unsure but equally curious. She reached out, and the instant their fingertips grew close enough to touch, a blast of light struck them, separating them…

Liam woke as though he'd been drowning. He gasped for air as his eyes opened to see Nani's face leaning over his. Her eyes were closed as she focused her energy on healing whatever damage he had received. The instant her lids fluttered open and she saw that he was alive, she tackled him, straddling his body and squeezing him in a firm embrace.

He realized that he was back where he had fallen, the other men standing around him. Everyone spoke at once, asking what happened and if he was all right. He simply wrapped his arms around Nani's small body.

Liam closed his eyes, overwhelmed with joy at being alive. He buried his face in her hair and sighed with relief. The scent of pine filled his nostrils. He thanked the Ancients for bringing him back to his friends.

Still, the girl's face haunted his memory, and he sensed that he *would* see her again.

CHAPTER 9

A MONTH PASSED, and finally they found a suitable village. Lilae and the others passed by many small towns along their journey that the girls all thought would be perfect: quaint little farming villages or large cities filled with friendly people. Each time, Delia took one look and shook her head no.

They were all weary of sleeping in the forest. The hard forest floor and the threat of wild animals while they slept had everyone on edge and irritable. Their arms were covered in mosquito bites and Lhana's special ointment barely eased the itching.

The dense evergreen forest opened up to bright sunlight and a wide-open dirt road. It seemed heavily traveled because of the deeply embedded wagon and foot tracks. Fluffy white pollen spores fell from the trees like snow.

They had never seen a spring like that. Living in the north was always cold. There was so much green and orange around them that they felt out of place. The purple and yellow flowers bloomed and the birds flew ahead in packs by the hundreds.

Lilae looked in awe around her. She sighed in content. The sun's soft rays on her cheeks felt good.

Golden wheat reached for the sky on both sides of the road, and tall trees bowing low from the weight of their apples. Risa and Jaiza wasted no time in picking the apples and bit greedily into the crisp flesh.

Lilae cautiously followed them. Her stomach growled loudly in her ears as she looked up at the trees that were heavy with ripe fruit. The apples were plump and red and smelled delightful. The first bite was the best. The taste of something sweet, and fresh reminded her of better times. She didn't care that the juice dribbled down her chin.

"Lowen's Edge," Delia read from the sign posted on a stake in the center of the road.

"Partha," Pirin said as he walked beside her. "It's a commercial village, they forge weapons and sell goods, but Partha has a strong military."

Delia nodded. "Fine, we can stay here, for a while."

"It seems nice here," Lhana remarked.

"I'm just glad it's not so cold!" Risa added. "I am sick of snow."

Jaiza nodded. "Me too. I just hope the boys are cute and the girls are plain and frumpy." She and Risa snickered.

Lilae smiled to herself. She wasn't jealous. She wanted them to be happy. The twins would have no trouble finding doting boys.

Pirin shook his head at Jaiza's comment, but Lhana smiled. She reached to hold his hand.

They walked alongside a log fence that contained a large bull and a herd of cows. The farmers noticed them and slowly came to their feet. They stood with their wooden pitchforks and watched with curious eyes as the family passed by.

"Hmm, the cattle look healthy here," Lhana mentioned, pausing to view the herd. She sounded happy. "Though a lady, I used to run down to my father's land worked by the farmers. I always loved animals and would help out sometimes." She looked off as she reminisced. "The farmers would let me help milk the cows and feed the chickens." She smiled to the twins. "I used to name them, sometimes."

"I bet they were delicious," Risa joked.

Lhana ignored her. "The land must be fertile. Fertile land means healthy animals, which in turn means healthy people."

Lilae looked back at the women who whispered to one another as they looked on. They wore scarves covering their hair and aprons over their simple brown gowns. They carried baskets of bread and jam and jugs of water to the farmers.

They mocked her for the way she dressed. They wondered if she was a boy, but clearly, she was not because of her hair and delicate features. Lilae self-consciously tightened her hood and walked on. She tried to keep from staring back, but found herself glancing at the villagers.

They made their way down the heavily traveled path and toward the gated village. Lilae turned around curiously to the sound of heavy footsteps. She turned to see men on horseback riding toward them. *Four,* she counted to herself. *Swords, armor, blood on their boots.* She noted everything about them before they even approached.

Jaiza perked up. "Look, Risa! Boys!" She grinned. She turned to her sister and grabbed her by her shoulders. "How do I look?" The men were getting closer.

"Dirty," Risa replied, and smirked.

Jaiza's smile dropped and she punched Risa in the arm.

"So do you!"

Risa laughed and shoved her back.

"Hush girls," Lhana said softly. "We'll all be clean again soon enough." She straightened her own clothing.

"Halt!"

Lilae felt her jaw tense at the lead horseman's demanding tone, and she reached for the dagger in her boot. It was purely instinct. Pirin placed a hand over hers, stopping her. She stood slowly and looked at the men closely. They were dressed in uniformed hides that were dyed green.

For village folk, they appeared quite impressive. Each wore leather gaiters that looked of good quality and matching brass breastplates. They wore supple leather gloves and boots and each donned a sword and plate shield. Not cheap.

A brawny man with a thick, closely cut beard stepped forward. Even upon his horse, Lilae could tell that he was much shorter, and wider, than Pirin.

"I am Lukas, High Regent of Lowen's Edge. Better you deal with me than the Parthan soldiers," he said, and nodded to the armored men standing at the entrance to the gates. "Their interrogations are much more severe." He looked them over. "We are on the lookout for Imperial spies. But, I can tell just by looking at you that you're definitely not Avia'Torenian. Which clan do you hail from?" he spoke to Pirin directly.

"We do not belong to a clan anymore. We do not owe allegiance to any king. We travel alone," Pirin said. He stretched his arm around Lhana's shoulders and nodded to the girls. "My family and I just want to work for a while and we will move on. We do not look for trouble and we have no plans to stay for longer than a year."

Lukas nodded, as he looked them over. His eyes passed by Lilae and went to Jaiza and Risa as he stroked his graying beard. Lilae noticed that the other men all stared at the twins as well. They looked much younger than their leader without a lot less hair on their faces.

"Too bad," Lukas said finally while shaking his head. "Perhaps if you were allies with Partha we could negotiate a temporary citizenship." He hopped down from his horse and approached them with an easy gait to his stride.

He stretched his fingers from holding on to the reins of his horse for so long and stood before Pirin. "Trust me. I want to help you all, but you make it hard when you do not belong to a clan."

Pirin looked to Delia who nodded. "We are from the North."

Lukas nodded. "This is good news. It could help your case."

"We will stay no longer than a year. We are all good workers. My wife bakes the best pies and bread you've ever tasted, and my daughters all know how to help with the harvest, or anything in the fields or barns."

Lukas stroked his beard. After a moment of thought, he cracked his knuckles. "Why are you traveling?"

"We are taking a pilgrimage to the South. I want my children to see the Holy Temples of Shi'Yen."

Lilae almost laughed but restrained herself. Pirin cared nothing for the Holy Temples. He felt it was unnecessary, a way for the monks and priests to control those who were uneducated.

"What an ambitious journey," Lukas remarked. "But you'll want to stay clear of the eastern territories."

Pirin raised an eyebrow. "Why is that?"

Lukas lowered his voice. "Avia'Torena controls the entire East, the Guardians have unlocked the doors, and now all sorts of creatures are spilling through."

"What?" Risa and Jaiza said in unison. Lhana's face paled as white as ever.

Lukas nodded and sighed. "I'm afraid they have, girls. Soon, we'll be in the midst of all sorts of evil. I tell you these things the same way I tell the other foreigners who come through here seeking refuge, but I feel especially inclined to warn you. Such lovely young daughters should be kept away from unsavory beings. There are rumors that Swartelves are already getting free from The Barrier, through those doors."

Lilae's interest grew, as did Delia's. Swartelves was just another name for the Shadow Elves who lived in the Nostfar realm. For centuries, they were confined to their own realm, keeping humans safe from their terrible power and ambitions.

"The Guardian's unlocked the doors?" Lilae whispered to Delia. "Is that possible?"

Delia held a hand up. "Shh, Lilae. Not now."

Lilae bit the inside of her lip. She was really worried. She knew more history than most people did. She knew all about the Great War. These people had no idea what was coming.

The other men joined Lukas and dismounted their horses. A young boy ran from the gated village and gathered the reins, leading them toward the stables. He snuck a peek at the twins and grinned as he walked past. When Risa glanced back at him, he turned beet red and ran along. Like most boys, he fell in love instantly.

One of the men stepped forward. He resembled Lukas but his hair was cut very short.

"I heard that they fly around on wyverns." He spoke directly to Jaiza and Risa who nodded aptly, excitement in their eyes.

Lukas nodded. "Yes. This is Bryson, one of my sons." He looked back at the girls.

"What's a *wyvern?*" Risa asked. Her nose scrunched up as she spoke the foreign word.

Bryson stepped in closer to her. "They're creatures that resemble dragons. But these are much smaller and trainable, like horses; they have saddles and everything."

"And they're fast!" one of the others added.

"These are just rumors?" Everyone's eyes moved to Delia. "Or is there any proof of such things?"

Lukas gave a slight bow to her. "Yes, ma'am, there is proof. We've seen hordes of folk fleeing those areas, and all have spoken of the sightings. All of Eura is now at war with the Empire. And we hear that the emperor may be a sorcerer of some sort."

Pirin sighed. "Let's go."

Risa and Jaiza grumbled and didn't move.

Pirin waved for them. "I said let's go," he said sternly.

Lilae heard whispering as they turned to leave. She noticed that their eyes looked up at Jaiza and Risa occasionally and Pirin noticed as well.

"Wait!" Lukas called out to them.

"Yes?"

Lukas approached Pirin and they began speaking in hushed tones.

"I have an idea to get you temporary citizenship, if not permanent," Lukas said. He looked them all over. "You're Northerners, you say?"

Pirin nodded.

Lukas smiled wide. "Perfect." He clasped his hands together. "Well, the North is allied with Partha," he added. "I can't just let you and these young ladies wander such territories with the kind of terror we've been seeing out there." He nudged Pirin's shoulder. "Can you believe it, after centuries, we're going to have to deal with the other races again?"

Pirin shook his head, eyeing Lukas's hand on his shoulder. "We will manage." He shrugged free from Lukas's grasp. "Tell me; how can you help us?"

Lukas cleared his throat. "Your daughters…I assume they don't have suitors? Are they betrothed, perhaps?"

Lilae gasped. She looked from Lukas to Pirin in shock.

Pirin's eyes widened. He glanced back at Jaiza and Risa, then to Lilae, his eyes resting on her. While Jaiza and Risa stepped forward, Lilae withdrew closer to Delia, locking arms with the woman.

"I see what you're getting at, and you can stop right there," Pirin said motioning for the girls to start walking away.

Lukas held his hands up. "No, no, don't get me wrong. I have sons. They are good men, with titles. As High Regent, my sons are subsequently barons. They would like to *court* your daughters." He motioned toward two young men who stood beside Bryson. "Bryson, Andrew, and Jarred."

They were already making eyes with the twins, and Jaiza and Risa seemed to enjoy the attention. They gave the young men secret smiles.

"With a union of our families, you all would be considered Parthans. You could freely live wherever you choose in this territory." Lukas looked pointedly at Pirin. "More importantly, you'll be under the protection of the crown. King Morr takes care of his people. There are soldiers in every city, town, and village."

His expression suddenly darkened. "There aren't many eligible young women in Partha anymore. The Sisters come by and claim at least thirty percent of them every season. You are lucky you still have your daughters. Those Sisters are said to have a divine right to claim the girls that Elahe calls. Not even King Morr can stop them."

Pirin didn't care. He began to shake his head, but then noticed Risa and Jaiza smiling at the young men.

"Pa, please," Jaiza whispered. The twins looked at their father with eyes that seemed to beg their father to say yes.

"Come now, my love," Lhana whispered close to his ear. "We are tired, worn out from travel, and the girls need this. You'll have them waste their youth wandering around like this. At least give them a chance. Or a choice."

Pirin's shoulders slumped as he turned away from his daughters' anxious faces. "I don't like this," Pirin whispered to Lhana who nudged him to be quiet. "This is far too quick."

"This is good, Pirin. Don't ruin it." She spoke quietly as she straightened his collar. "We can have a home, and the girls would be cared for. Think of it, honey. *Baronesses*."

"We don't even know these people. You want to pawn our daughters off to strangers?"

She arched a brow and whispered, "And they don't know us, either. They want to court the girls, not drag them off unwillingly. Let the girls have a chance. You owe me at least that much."

Lilae saw the dilemma Pirin faced. They had to stay together, but he couldn't deny them the chance to find love and start families of their own. Maybe it would be best to let the twins stay in one place. Then he would only have to worry about himself and Lilae.

"What about that one?" Lukas added, breaking Pirin from his thoughts. His dark eyes had finally caught sight of Lilae's face, and Pirin could tell that her eyes intrigued him. "How old is she?"

Lilae had tried to keep covered by her hood, shielding her eyes, but it was too late. He stared at her so intently that Pirin put his arm across her, as though shielding her. Pirin pushed her behind him. She was glad for the cover. She looked nervously at Delia.

"No." Pirin clenched his jaw. "Only the two are up for consideration." Pirin's voice was firm. "Your sons can speak to me about courting my daughters, Risa and Jaiza, and *I* will decide if it's appropriate."

Lukas nodded in agreement. His eyes lingered on Lilae's face and she lowered her head again. "Fine. Follow me," Lukas replied turning toward the tall wooden fence that was still being built. "There is an empty flat near the blacksmith."

"That was fast," Lilae said to Delia. She couldn't believe that they hadn't even gotten inside the gates of the village yet and Risa and Jaiza already had suitors.

"It was bound to happen," Delia muttered.

"How much?" Pirin followed behind Lukas into the town square.

Lukas glanced back. "Sixty quinne." He raised a questioning eyebrow. "Reasonable enough?"

"We are all hard workers. We will all take jobs in the morning. I can hunt, and the girls can do a number of things: sew, plant, harvest, domestic work. My wife can bake and cook as well as any palace chef, and my sister here," Pirin said and nodded to Delia, "she is an herbalist. Your village would be very fortunate to have her. The sum shouldn't be a problem."

Lukas smiled. "Good man. We're happy to have you all."

They walked through a gate guarded by Parthan soldiers who nodded to Lukas as he passed. No one stopped to question them; Lukas's word was enough in this case. They entered the bustling market square. Lilae was intrigued by the expanse of it.

People sold their dried meats which hung from hooks. There was fresh fish, colorful produce, and expensive spices. Being so close to the kingdom gave the people of Lowen's Edge such delicacies and luxuries. Lilae looked curiously at the assortment of selling carts. The town was so lively, she already felt optimistic.

"Why are you building such a tall fence?" Jaiza asked, as she looked up at the men who worked above.

The men were shirtless, sweating profusely as they lugged heavy logs and rope. The fence was comprised of dark logs that stretched at least twelve feet tall and encircled the entire village.

Lukas glanced over his shoulder at her. "To keep out the beasts."

Risa was skeptical. "What beasts are that tall? Don't tell me you have giants here?"

"No, dear girl," Lukas said. "Worse. Ever hear of a basilisk?"

Delia stopped walking. Lilae noticed and stayed back with her.

"No," Risa and Jaiza said in unison, shaking their heads.

"Well, I hope you'll never have to see one."

"What are basilisks doing in Eura?" Pirin asked.

Lukas turned to face them, and his sons stopped behind him. "The Swartelves are not the only danger coming from Nostfar." He sighed. "Every now and again, I gather a few strong fighters and we go out and hunt these creatures. It's a dangerous task though, and we have lost more than I wish to count."

Lukas frowned as he looked out into the distance, as though he still grieved for his lost men. "You girls," he said, narrowing his eyes at Jaiza to Risa, "stay out of the forests after dark."

Risa and Jaiza nodded and quickly followed behind him.

Lilae trailed behind with Delia, who was as stiff as a statue. "What is it, Delia?"

Delia hushed her. Her eyes were fixed on the forest, yet Lilae could tell that she was listening to something. Lilae listened herself, to the quiet winds, and heard nothing out of the ordinary. She watched as Delia closed her eyes and tightened her grasp on her staff.

When Delia opened her eyes, they went directly to Lilae's. Lilae swallowed. There was something different in Delia's eyes that frightened her. Usually, Delia looked so confident. For the first time, Lilae thought she actually saw fear on the Elder's face.

"What is it?"

Delia held Lilae's by her shoulders. "Listen closely, Lilae," she began, and Lilae nodded fervently. "We must be *very* careful here. We are getting closer to The Barrier. You must control the urge to use your power. Do you understand?"

"What power?"

Delia squinted and pointed at Lilae's forehead. Her soft fingertips pressed into the space between Lilae's eyes. "For years you've been aware of your mental powers, Lilae. The Winds speak to you, and your fighting skills are heightened because of your power." She moved her finger down to Lilae's heart. "But, as you approach your eighteenth year of life, you've noticed something more, haven't you?"

Lilae looked away. She thought that it was her secret. She could feel that something was changing inside of her. "Yes," she admitted in a hushed tone. "I do feel something."

"You see." Delia stood up straight. "This power, the power of the Ancients, given by Elahe himself"—she poked at Lilae's heart "is the one you must control, for it can destroy, and it is so strong that our enemies will sense its presence. Wexcyn's disciples are looking for you. They will rip this realm apart to have your power."

Lilae frowned. "Why have we traveled so close to the Nostfar barrier then?"

Delia looked behind Lilae, far past her. "Your calling has arrived, my dear. Soon, you'll need to start the most important task of your life."

Lilae was about to ask more questions when Pirin came back for them.

"Come, we must settle into our new home." He motioned for them to follow.

Delia pushed Lilae toward the village. "Go, child. We will talk soon."

Lilae wanted to stay back and ask more. She sighed in exasperation but didn't have a choice but to obey. She followed behind Pirin and contemplated what Delia had said. It vexed her. Lilae had been trying to keep that burning power a secret for a while now. It was as though she knew the damage it could do, yet, something urged her to test it. It fought to be free.

They were led to a wide roadway near the town square. The buildings were made of log and brick and reached at least two stories. The stone road was shaped like a tree, with wider roads resembling branches that held clusters of homes and shops. Lilae was intrigued by the style of dress of these Parthans. The women all wore colorful bonnets on their heads even if their dresses were plain and almost uniform. It seemed as if their accessories were their only ways of expressing themselves.

Hyper children ran past them, playing and giggling. They rolled colorful balls down the street, kicking them to each other with such energy that Lilae couldn't help but smile. The cottages were set in attached rows. The architecture was impressive in comparison to the other villages they'd lived in. Most of the homes were on the second level, whereas the bottom floors were shops. Across from the blacksmith's shop was where Lukas opened a heavy door. It creaked on rusty hinges.

"The old apothecary used to live here." Lukas walked inside the dark room and started opening windows. Light spilled into the room. "She died about a month ago, so you can help yourself to whatever you find in here. Oh, and there's quite an herb garden in the back," he said. "If you don't mind, perhaps that sister of yours can fill a few orders for remedies during the week. Those fees alone should pay half of the rental fee."

Pirin nodded. "Of course."

"But don't worry," Lukas said. "If things go well with our children, you'll have to move to the Garden District with us. It would only be proper. Trust me, I know it sounds pretentious. I was only a councilman before the king gave my family titles. This whole nobleman system is still new to me."

Lilae covered her nose with her sleeve as she stepped into the dust-filled room. She waved the thick motes from before her eyes. It smelled old and full of mildew. Lhana lit a candle in a wall sconce and more light revealed scant furniture and shelves full of bottles, jugs, and stacked clay bowls.

There was a large living space right inside the door. The outside was deceptive. Lilae was surprised that there was so much room. She followed the twins as they ran through the cottage with excitement. Besides the large living space with a dining table, large fireplace for cooking, cabinets, and a washbasin, there were two rooms for sleeping.

"This small one will be for Pirin and me," Lhana said as she stepped into the bare room. She glanced back at Lilae. "You know, when Pirin and I were first wed, we had a master suite, as big as this entire cottage. It was a beautiful manor, with staff and horses."

"It sounds lovely," Lilae said. She offered a smile.

Without returning the gesture, Lhana quickly hurried into the small hallway to the other, slightly larger room. There was a loft space above a small bed. "Lovely," she said. "You girls can sleep in the loft and this bed will be perfect for Delia." She beamed. Lilae couldn't help but smile as well.

Lhana spun around. "A real home again!" She hugged the twins. Her eyes lifted to Lilae's. She tilted her gaze to the space beneath the window. "We can put some blankets down there for you, Lilae. It'll suit you well."

Lilae stepped back into the front room, bowing her head. Her smile faded. When would someone hug her like that? She didn't mind sleeping on the floor. It was the small spark of hate in Lhana's eyes that made her stomach twist with dread. She sighed and stood by the front door, her back leaning against the cold stone wall. She suddenly felt like sneaking out.

Risa and Jaiza grinned. They'd already rolled up their sleeves and started to rearrange the furniture. Lhana searched for a rag to clean out the large pot that hung from the hearth in the corner of the room.

"You girls get settled in." Pirin nodded to Lukas. "Let's talk outside." They left the cottage and Lilae walked out quietly behind them.

Lilae waited for them to head down the road, and turned to go the other way when they did. She paused when she saw a young man walking from the blacksmith's shop. She stepped away, her back pressed against the wall as he walked past her without a glance.

She watched as he carried a large crate of scrap metal. Chestnut hair cascaded over his eyes, and he tossed it out of his vision. His arms strained to carry the heavy load and she saw sweat dripping down his body. The smell of coal was thick in the air and she felt the heat radiating from the shop across the road.

He barely noticed her, but she noted every detail of his face. Something about him caught her interest. She darted down the road behind him and turned the corner to the marketplace. It was crowded and loud with merchants shouting about what they sold. He was lost and Lilae was caught in the mass. She stood on her tiptoes to try to spot him again, but he had vanished into the energetic crowd.

She pushed her way to the entrance of the forest. Once she was free from the crowd, she sighed with relief. She already felt smothered by the swarm of people; she'd never seen such a vibrant marketplace.

"Where are you going?" Pirin tapped her on the shoulder.

Caught off guard, Lilae faced him. "I thought you were speaking with Lukas," she blurted.

Pirin narrowed his eyes. "That's not what I asked you, Lilae. You heard the man tell you girls to stay out of the forest. You can't just go running off all the time like you did in Sabron, or Halwan before that. It is time to get serious about things. We are closer to enemy lines than we've ever been and you can get hurt."

Lilae nodded, looking off into the thickness of trees. "But I feel more at home…out there." She marveled at how the forest extended farther than her eyes could see. It was so green, not full of the browns of withered trees or the white of snow that she had lived in for most of her life.

Nature called to her. It was clean and fresh, and full of solitude. She yearned to be free from this life. No one had ever asked her if she wanted to be the Chosen one.

Lilae's shoulders slumped. She was trapped by this fate. *How many people will I have to kill in order to be free?*

"You've never been one to enjoy enclosed spaces, like the little wolf you are," he said, and smiled. "Wild and brave, my little Lilae."

She spoke softly as she looked up at the sun. "I like that, little wolf. It does fit me doesn't it?" Her smile faded. "Pirin, do you ever wish that you could stay in one place? That you didn't have to follow Delia and me around all of the time. I know I am being hunted." She loved Pirin deeply. He was the only father she had ever known, and he's always treated her like his real daughter. She would always remember and appreciate that. "Please, tell me the truth. I won't be upset."

Pirin raised an eyebrow and stared down at her. She saw that he was contemplating her words. She knew he wasn't her real father, but she would never say it to him. She loved Pirin and, in her eyes, he was her true father.

Lilae examined his face. He was growing old and deep worry lines now marred his forehead. Still, while he worried so much about the family, he also had laugh lines at the corners of his mouth. His eyes were bright and full of love; yet when he was angry, they became too unsettling to look into.

"Listen to me, Lilae." Pirin put a hand on her shoulder. "The day Delia came for you, I took one look at you, and I fell in love. You are my daughter in my heart as much as the twins are. It's funny. You're more like me than either of them. You're quiet and reserved, yet calculating."

Lilae felt her eyes sting with tears at hearing those words. They were all she'd ever wanted to hear. She drew in a jagged breath.

"And wouldn't a father do all that he could to protect his children, and prepare them for the dangers of this world?"

Lilae smiled up at him and he surprised her then. He pulled her into his chest for a hug. Lilae's eyes widened as they embraced. He held her tightly, as if he feared that she would be taken away from him. She inhaled his scent, relishing in the rare show of affection; but it was short lived.

Pirin smiled down at her and gently pinched her right cheek. "Come on, let's hunt for dinner. I bet when we return, Lhana and the twins will have the place as clean as a castle."

Her smile grew. She was excited to have Pirin all to herself for a while. It was like a game to Jaiza and Risa. *Let's see who Pirin loves best,* Risa would say. Lilae skipped a little as she followed him into the forest.

He had a crossbow with him and spear which he handed to Lilae. They quietly trudged through the thick underbrush, delving deeper and deeper. In the quiet, away from people and their judging eyes, was where Lilae felt most at peace.

They traveled to a clearing where a small brook ran behind it. Pirin settled behind a cluster of bushes. Lilae's eyes went right to the wild hog that drank from the trickling waters. It stood on the stones and never noticed their presence. Lilae imagined the bacon and chops they could have for a week.

She watched Pirin. His eyes narrowed and she could tell that he was using his Focus. The air around him grew tighter in its devotion to aid him. He let out a soft breath and shot his crossbow.

The hog barely had a chance to squeal before the arrow impaled its brain. It was a single, fatal shot that caused it to double over. Lilae grinned at Pirin and then at the dead animal. He nodded and she rushed over with her dagger.

Pirin put his bow onto his back and sat on the slick rocks. "Go on. You can gut it. We can use the skin for lard."

Lilae nodded and slit the hog along its underbelly. The cut was smooth and easy, and she pulled the intestines and liver out. Pirin held a sack out and she dropped the pig's innards into it. They would waste nothing.

Lilae heard rustling in the bushes behind them. She turned and saw Pirin shoot another wild hog. Lilae smiled.

"Another? That was a fat one!"

Pirin nodded, but his face looked troubled.

"What luck!"

"A little odd," Pirin mused aloud. He frowned at the second animal. "Cut the innards out before it poisons the meat. We can sell that one at the market."

Lilae climbed to her feet and began to run over to the fallen hog when something large catapulted out of the forest and pounced onto the carcass. Lilae gasped and froze as she stared up at the large beast. She barely got a good look before it grabbed the carcass in its mouth and ran away.

She stood anchored to her spot, trying to put together what she just saw. It was a large, hairy beast with a head the size of a barrel and sharp teeth. She'd never seen an animal with stripes before, but that beast had black and green stripes on its brown body.

She jumped when Pirin tapped her shoulder. His face showed the slightest trace of fear as he pulled her away. He held the hog she had gutted.

"That was a poulos. From Nostfar. Let's get out of here before its mate arrives. Pouloses always hunt in pairs."

Lilae voiced no objections. She grabbed her dagger and followed behind Pirin as they ran back toward town. Toward their new home.

CHAPTER 10

ONE THOUSAND SOLDIERS, led by one woman, a Sister from the Sisterhood of the Fallen, walked at a steady pace through the fields of Sabron. Black smoke filled the air; the sound of distant wails and cries followed them.

They were not in uniform, but it was no secret that these men were Avia'Torenan soldiers. And the woman wore a long black gown that was fitting for the amount of death that they were responsible for.

From the sky, Dragnor watched the gloomy procession. If it were up to him, they would have killed all of the girls instead of marching them along and slowing him down.

The girls who followed behind were bound by the wrists and connected to one another by chains clamped to golden collars around their necks.

They shivered violently. They hadn't had a chance to dress for the cold morning when the soldiers had ransacked their homes. There were tears dried and crusted on their cheeks, intermingled with blood and dirt. They all looked down at their feet, too afraid to meet the eyes of the soldiers who had massacred their village.

Other than the young women, the soldiers had taken only the men who had agreed to join the Imperial Army. That was all that they wanted: fresh recruits. The fate of the young women was uncertain, and that was what frightened the girls more than anything.

In the past, the Sisterhood of the Fallen had upheld their treaty with the nine kingdoms of Eura and collected only a small percentage of the young women every other year. Eventually that turned into each year and, subsequently, into each season. Now, they took every girl they could find. And still, no one knew what had happened to all of those girls who had been taken in the past.

They had simply never returned.

"Where are you taking us?" Dragnor heard from one of the girls who was brave enough to ask. Even from high above them, his ears picked up on her small voice.

The Sister turned back to look at the girl. She smiled way too big, considering that there was nothing to be happy about.

She floated toward the young girls. Her clogged feet weren't touching the ground. They all saw it. Even though black robes were meant to hide such a thing, it was unmistakable. That woman's feet were not touching the ground.

Everyone stopped. The soldiers, the girls, the horses… stopped. They all stared at her. So far, all of the girls had been too afraid to speak.

"Name."

The girl gulped. Her dirty face was streaked with tears. She stuttered, "Willa… Sister."

The Sister's smile widened. "Willa. Lovely name." She ran her finger along the clamp on the girl's neck. "How old are you?"

Willa straightened her shoulders, trying to look brave. "Fourteen."

The Sister laughed lightly. Then she tapped the chain, and, suddenly, Willa and every girl attached to it gasped and froze. All life was sucked out of their faces as their bodies turned gray, like stone. She gave Willa a tiny push. With a crash, all of the girls fell to the ground and broke into pieces. Their auras floated in the air like colors on the wind. The Sister reached out a hand and claimed them. Her green eyes looked up at the other lines of girls.

"Does anyone else wish to question me?"

They shook their heads. No one spoke. They held one another in fear, but no one made a sound.

The Sister smiled again. "Good." She looked up into the sky. "Hurry it up, Dragnor," she shouted and made her way back to the front of the procession. She frowned as she looked ahead. "I want her found before winter."

Dragnor nodded, even though it was that blasted army that slowed him down in the first place. He flew ahead of the men on his black wyvern. Its black wings were outstretched as it glided across the brightening sky. His keen eyes searched the grounds for any signs of life. He knew the Flame was fleeing, always one step ahead of him. Dragnor felt as though he might finally catch this elusive being. He would never tire of searching.

Dragnor saw a flicker of light below and, in an instant, the wyvern tracked it. They flew down with the wind until they reached the ground. He hopped from the wyvern's back before it even landed and darted to the light. The forest floor was covered in a blanket of leaves and fallen branches. He crunched on the dead leaves as he sauntered over to where he saw the glow.

His grin widened as he stooped down to pick up the golden strand of hair. To anyone else's eyes, the single hair that glittered between his fingertips would never have been seen. It belonged to the Flame, and he was certain of it. His eyes narrowed as he stretched the strand. Through the glow that only he saw, it was a scarlet red.

"What's this?" he asked under his breath. His thin eyes narrowed as he examined it. He looked back at the wyvern. It blended with the forest floor like a chameleon. "Take a look at this, Tari."

The wyvern lifted his head up from the brush of fallen leaves. He was cautious, his eyes darting from tree to tree. Tari's neck was long, connecting a small head to his sleek, leathery body. His eyes glowed for a moment as he looked at the red hair and then ducked again, blending with the underbrush.

"Iridescent. It's changing colors, even after being detached from the scalp. She *is* getting stronger," Tari said.

Dragnor raised an eyebrow then glanced back at the strand of hair. "You're certain?"

"Certain." Tari's voice rumbled low and steady as he rested.

"Fascinating," Dragnor replied, as the strand went from red to gold in his hand.

"The Ancients never cease to amaze me. They truly made a masterpiece of this one. I honestly cannot wait to meet her."

"The fire is only weeks old. She has a lead," Tari noted, as he took a long whiff of the ground.

Dragnor nodded and sniffed the air. He could smell the ghost of her long-gone presence.

"She always does."

"But not much," Tari added. "You may catch her this time, if you hurry."

Dragnor put the strand of hair in his cloak pocket. He observed the traces of an abandoned camp. A fire had been buried, and he could smell her presence.

For years, he had had only the Flame's scent to track. Now, he was able to see physical traces of her. He knew he was getting closer. Soon, he would have her in his grasp. The thought of draining the life out of her excited him. Seventeen years of hunting, and now he was closer than ever.

"I told you that they would do this. You're up against more than a couple of children, Dragnor."

Dragnor smirked, turning to face in the direction the Avia'Torenan soldiers were taking their new female slaves. "And they're up against much more than just a Shadow Elf," he replied, his eyes glowing as he traced the direction of her scent.

CHAPTER 11

LILAE FOUND IT ASTOUNDING how quickly the twins had fallen for Lukas's sons. Lilae thought them to be plain-looking men who acted too silly when they drank ale. Still, it wasn't Lilae whom they had to impress, and Risa and Jaiza were completely enamored.

They would be gone soon, moving into their new homes in the fancy Garden District, since Risa and Jaiza would become ladies.

Lhana had steadily grown more content with their life. It was a delight not to have to do the dirtier chores of the house all of the time or endure the constant pointing out of Lilae's flaws when the others weren't around. She had already developed friendships with Lukas's wife and the other women of the village.

Pirin hunted daily with a few of the townsmen, and, each night, he went out with Lukas to aid in the killing of wild beasts. The soldiers from the kingdom's capital had arrived nearly a week ago and filled the streets. They were to protect Lowen's Edge and monitor the forests and roads for bandits and Shadow Elves. They were civil, at least, and only rarely pestered Lilae as she passed them on the streets.

Lilae sat by the brook, listening to the water as it rushed across the shiny rocks. She let the water soothe her toes as she gently splashed. It had taken her a long time to feel comfortable even approaching water again.

She sighed, lying back onto the plush grass of the forest. She looked up past the canopy of trees at the blue sky and felt completely at ease. Her muscles were still sore from her morning sparring match with Pirin.

She was grateful for a little time to herself. She still enjoyed Pirin's daily sword and fighting lessons. Since Lilae had been seven years old, she had looked forward to it each morning. It was the only opportunity she had to exhaust her pent up energy and anger. Risa and Jaiza, however, were growing weary of sparring with her, losing more and more consistently, even when they fought her at the same time.

Lowen's Edge was more vibrant than the other villages that Lilae and the others had traveled to. Lilae found herself secretly hoping that this place might be their final move. It was beautiful and large enough to get lost in the crowd.

Merchants and performers passed through regularly, and royal soldiers patrolled the roads. Still, as much as she liked the more exciting scenery, no one bothered to talk to her. She harbored a secret that no one could know about. It was something that only Delia knew of, and, lately, she had been trying to teach Lilae about this secret.

Her keen ears now heard horses trampling through the forest from far away, and she felt the ground vibrate beneath her head. Lilae sat up and gathered her things. She put her brown leather boots back on, tucking her pants into them, and tied her cloak's dark brown hood beneath her chin.

She looked toward the noise in consternation. It was still early in the day. She wondered why the hunters were out this early. Poulos and the basilisk supposedly waited for the late afternoons and evenings to hunt their meals. She had kept her promise to Pirin about not staying out too late. Lilae grabbed her sack of berries and stood.

A group of horsemen emerged from the forest into the clearing and spotted her. She quickly turned away from them and headed toward the path to the village.

Lilae heard their boisterous chattering, their voices filling the forest.

"Hey!"

She ignored the call and quickened her pace.

"Who is that?" they questioned each other.

"Stop! I said stop!"

Lilae felt her heart beating faster and began to run. She didn't know what they wanted from her and didn't want to stick around to find out. Both Pirin and Delia would be livid if she hurt one of the villagers.

She was shocked at how quickly they got to her. When someone grabbed her cloak, she shrieked and grabbed his leg. She yanked as hard as she could and quickly pulled him to the ground. Out of her cloak spilled her fiery red hair, the sun reflecting off the golden strands that were intertwined throughout.

The boy found himself face down on the forest floor, pebbles embedded into his cheek.

Lilae planted her booted foot on his back and pressed him down when he tried to stand.

The others stopped and stared at her, their mouths hanging open.

She heard them whispering to each other.

"It's *that* girl."

"What girl?"

"The girls call her a hag, because she walks around cloaked all of the time like a boy."

"For a boy, her bosom's full enough!" joked Jacodi, the tailor's son. She recognized his wild brown hair and thick eyebrows.

Hearing those words, Lilae shot them an icy look.

"Hey, don't hurt him. We were just playing around with you," Jacodi said as he rested his hand across the pommel of his horse's saddle. He smirked. "Honest, we thought you were a boy." The others snickered.

Lilae glared at him, her chest rising and falling with her quick breaths. She knew she had to calm herself. She sometimes feared what would happen if she lost control.

"Be careful who you decide to play with." Lilae grabbed her dagger from her belt. She tossed it into the air and snatched it by the handle, pointing the blade's tip at him. She met Jacodi's eyes and his grin faded. "I don't play so nice."

"Anic, get up," Jacobi called.

Lilae continued to glare at him.

"Come on! Let's go!"

Lilae removed her foot and let Anic up from the ground. She recognized his face. He was the son of the blacksmith. She had watched him lug sacks of coal to his father's workroom on occasion and hoped that his eyes would meet hers. For the first time, his almond-shaped brown eyes finally looked up at her.

"It's you," Anic said when he recognized her as well. "I didn't know."

Her eyebrows drew in. Lilae was surprised that he knew who she was. "Go!" She threw her arm out and pointed for him to follow the others.

Anic stood and dusted himself off, but he didn't follow the others as they rode away. He raked his hand through his rust-colored hair, chopped sloppily by his mother, and cleared his throat. He was just as tall as Lilae, with full lips and a slant to his eyes that made him look forever sad.

She didn't shy away when he drew closer. Her fingers tightened around her dagger.

"*Um,*" he began, seeing the sharp blade. "I apologize. The others were just looking for some fun. We go out on the hunt tomorrow, and I'm new to the gang."

Lilae was silent as he spoke, watching his every move. She trusted no one.

"Really?" She rolled her eyes. "What a terrible excuse for trying to terrorize someone."

"Like I said," Anic reiterated, motioning for her to calm down, "I apologize."

Lilae examined his freckled face and then slowly nodded. She put her dagger into her belt. There was something in his soft brown eyes that told her he was telling the truth. She stepped away and pulled her cloak over her head once more, tucking her long tresses into the hood.

"No harm done." When Lilae began to walk away, she realized that he was following her. Anic held the horse's reins and walked alongside her.

"You're called Lilae, right?"

She nodded, unsure why he walked with her. Pirin would not approve of such a thing.

"That's a nice name."

Lilae pursed her lips. *What is he doing?* She continued on without a word.

"Can I ask you a question?"

"What?"

"Why do you always hide your hair like that?" Anic pointed at her hood as he tried to keep up with her. Seeing him so interested and staring at her made Lilae uneasy.

Lilae scrunched her nose. "Why do you care?"

Anic shrugged. "I just always wondered."

Lilae rolled her eyes. "So, you just sit around wondering about me?"

"Maybe."

Lilae glanced at him, unable to think of a clever retort.

"Forgive me for being forward, but you're *so* beautiful, Lilae. I don't understand why you would want to hide such a gift."

She stopped abruptly and turned around to face him. The color drained from her face, and her eyebrows furrowed. "What?"

"Why do you look so terrified? I said you're beautiful. Perhaps I am too blunt?" He shook his head with a smile. "My mother always tells me to keep my opinions to myself… but, I couldn't resist."

Lilae pursed her lips; no one had ever told her such a thing. Boys were incessantly telling Risa and Jaiza that they were beauties. However, Lilae had grown used to being so different from everyone else, never seeing anyone who even mildly resembled her.

"Thanks," Lilae replied, fidgeting with the string of her cloak. An awkward silence filled the space between them. "Now go away."

Anic's smile faded, the corners of his lips rounding down. He nodded and mounted his horse, ready to turn away; then he pushed on, pressing his luck.

"Can I see you again, Lilae?"

She looked down at her boots, seeing the mud caked along the soles. Lilae never imagined someone would show an interest in her; even in her dreams, she was alone. She examined his face and finally shook her head.

"No."

"Well, you can't keep me from 'seeing' you. I can do whatever I want with my eyes," he joked. "But can I call on you? You know, come by and take you out or something? I promise I won't try to kiss you, at least until the second date."

Lilae felt her cheeks redden and quickly turned away from him. She couldn't believe his bluntness. She wasn't sure if he was still joking.

"No!" She was flustered, embarrassed by the thought of kissing him.

Lilae ran along, leaving Anic behind with little hopes of speaking to her again. What he didn't see was that a small smile started to appear on her face as she ran through the forest. She tried to repress it. She couldn't let anyone catch that secret smile.

She darted through the trees and jumped over fallen logs and branches. She wasn't entirely sure how she felt about what Anic had said to her. One word of adoration had ignited a small ray of hope within her that she might one day find love. Still, Lilae wasn't certain that she wanted such a thing. She shook her head to clear it of the thought.

She crashed into the cottage to see Lhana and Delia talking on the wool rug by the fire. They were discussing Risa's and Jaiza's weddings, she presumed. Her chest heaved from the exertion of running, and she couldn't control the beaming smile on her face.

"Lilae?" Lhana called, frowning at her from her place on the floor. She removed her knitting from her lap and motioned for Lilae to sit down. "Come, you little heathen. Let me fix your hair."

Delia examined Lilae's face. Her brows furrowed as she looked into her eyes. "What happened to you?"

Lilae slumped onto the floor at Lhana's knees. She looked into the crackling fire, her head swimming with thoughts of Anic. "Could you braid it tighter this time?" she asked. She hid her smile when she noticed Delia staring at her.

Lhana nodded.

"I asked you a question, Lilae," Delia said firmly.

She tilted her head as she looked at Delia. A mischievous smile came to her lips. "Nothing. I just had some fun with the local boys."

Delia raised an eyebrow but didn't pry. She shook her head and continued writing in her little brown leather journal.

"Tell me again—why can't I just cut it all off?" Even though Anic had told her that she was beautiful, she couldn't help imagining what she would look like if she had straight blond hair like Risa and Jaiza. He would like her even more then, and the girls might want to talk to her, instead of treating her like a troll.

"Nonsense," Delia interjected. "You should be proud of your hair."

"Why? I hate it. Everyone stares at me as if I am a strange creature invading their land. It gets annoying."

Delia poked the fire and stood to stir the stew in the large cauldron that hung from the hearth. "It's different. Beautiful, even. Only royalty can grow hair as long in some regions. One day you'll appreciate it."

"Oh, hush about your stupid hair, Lilae," Risa snapped, entering the front room from the sleeping quarters. She and Jaiza shared a loft bed that sat above the space where everyone else slept. She stretched and filled a mug with water from a clay jug. "I think you go on and on about it to tease us."

"*Tease* you?" Lilae asked, her nose scrunched in genuine confusion. "What are you talking about?"

"Seriously, Lilae? Only you can pretend to be oblivious about such things. Sometimes I wonder if it's all an act with you. Look at it. It shines like there's magic in it or something!"

Lilae grabbed her hair, angrily. Her face heated. She couldn't understand why they were talking this way. "I don't know what you mean."

"You know exactly—" Risa started.

"Girls, quiet," Lhana interrupted in a hushed tone. "Your father is sleeping."

"What are you complaining about," Lilae whispered, leaning forward as Lhana grabbed a few strands of her hair to braid. "You'll be fat with children soon enough. You won't be bothered with me anymore," she said with tears burning her eyes. "You'll never have to see me or my stupid hair again."

Risa folded her arms under her bosom and glared at Lilae. "That's right. You'll be off to another village, far away."

"Where we won't have to hear your pestering," Jaiza added.

"I can't wait for the day we are rid of you," Risa quipped over her shoulder, and they both left the house.

Lilae stared at the door as they left. She didn't want anyone to see that their words had stung her heart. She looked at the fire silently. She missed when they were younger and settled into a small village in Halwan. Those were the times when they could actually make friends and the family was full of love and contentment. Risa and Jaiza actually treated her like a loving little sister back then.

"They didn't mean it, Lilae," Delia said softly.

"Lies," Lilae replied, but without her usual venom; her voice was hollow. "They hate me. I know it." She didn't let her voice waver, she was careful of that. She refused to let anyone know the girls had hurt her. "They hate me because I keep them from living happy lives. I'm the reason they've gone so long without a real home. I don't blame them. Not at all. I'd hate myself, too." Her heart thumped with both anger and sorrow.

Lhana was silent as she braided, yet she seemed to tug at Lilae's hair a little tighter that night.

"Foolishness, child! I think they would have followed you forever, if you'd have given them a chance."

"Humph."

Delia pursed her lips. "I've never seen a more stubborn person in my life."

"Or one so selfish," Lhana mumbled under her breath.

Lilae shrugged, feigning indifference. She had to use all of her strength to avoid lashing out at Lhana. She bit her lip to keep her sharp retort at bay.

"You don't even see that it is you who pushes people away."

Lilae didn't respond. She watched the flames dance and smother the logs in the hearth and bottled those feelings of hurt deep, deep inside.

CHAPTER 12

WITH A MIGHTY SHOVE, Risa blocked Jaiza's sword and knocked her off of her feet.

Jaiza fell hard onto the ground with a grunt. She glared up at her sister, ignoring the scrapes on her hands.

"Jaiza," Risa jeered with a grin. She held her sword down at her side. She was barely breathing hard. "You fight like a girl." With a laugh, she twirled her sword masterfully, just for show.

"Come on, Jaiza," Pirin coached. He leaned against a tree and motioned for her to get up. "You can do better than that."

Jaiza's face turned red, and she pushed herself up. She clutched her sword and stood before her sister. She focused on catching her breath, as Risa ran a finger along her wooden training sword.

Pirin sighed. "You can't always rely on your bow, Jaiza. Arrows run out too quickly, and a bow is almost useless in close combat. You all need to master more than just one weapon."

"Well, why don't we practice with bows then?" Jaiza demanded.

"Very well," Pirin nodded. "Tomorrow, we'll pull out the bows."

Jaiza grinned and went in to try another attack.

Lilae sat on the grass and watched their every move as they practiced. Each move of offense and defense became engrained in her mind. She held her training sword's hilt tight and waited for her turn.

Pirin glanced at her. "Jaiza," he called. She looked back. "Switch out."

Risa's grin turned into a scowl.

Lilae came to her feet and turned on her Focus and Evasion.

Risa was tricky, and Lilae never underestimated her. She had truly mastered Evasion more than Lilae could ever dream of doing. It was difficult to master one trait when you had them all.

Risa didn't waste any time letting Lilae prep for her attack. She charged at Lilae without a shred of amusement on her face. Her eyes were set with a cold determination.

Lilae drew in a breath and planted her feet, waiting. Her eyes watched in anticipation as Risa's image started to flicker. With a grunt, Lilae dove to her right. Risa's sword crashed down on her own, sending shards of wood into the air between them. Lilae rolled out of the way of Risa's aggressive attack. She had to get back on her feet before Risa took advantage.

Risa appeared above her, and Lilae used her free arm to forcefully push her off by slamming her head to the ground.

"Ouch!" Risa cried. Her cheeks reddened.

Lilae gulped. Her cheeks flushed. She had angered Risa. She backed away slowly, keeping her eyes locked on Risa. She quickly wiped her sweaty palm on her pants and held her sword's hilt tighter.

Risa grabbed her sword with both hands, bared her teeth like a wild animal, and swung it with all of her might at Lilae's side. Lilae flicked a wrist, countered the strike of Risa's sword, and stopped Risa by swirling out of her path, around her body, and back in front of her.

She pointed her wooden sword directly at Risa's neck.

"You're dead," Lilae said as Risa eyed the sword. She growled and pushed Lilae's sword away.

"Whatever. Cheap tricks," Risa said, catching her breath. "You're only good for a workout, Lilae. Anything more simply doesn't count. You're some kind of creature in a human guise. Like Delia."

Lilae smiled. "Thank you." She winked at her. "Glad to know I can give you a good workout. I learned that move from you, Risa."

Risa scoffed and stalked back to Pirin and Jaiza.

"That was quick," Jaiza remarked, as her sister drank from her flask.

Risa drank greedily and poured the rest on her head. "I barely had a chance to rest my legs."

Lilae hid her grin as she returned. Pirin nodded his approval. He wouldn't gloat over her while the twins were around, but Lilae could see the pride on his face from the way his eyes crinkled at the corners and the small smile on his lips.

He stopped before them and folded his arms.

"Right." He pointed to Risa. "Try not to get so wild with your attacks. Anger should be contained. If you lash out like that, you can expose your weaknesses. Anger makes you sloppy. Anger kills you," Pirin explained.

"Yes. Certainly, father. I'm too cocky and quick-tempered." She shot a glance at Lilae. "But what about *Lilae's* critique?"

Pirin shrugged and took a bite from an apple. "Don't hold back, Lilae. You should be cautious, but don't hold back to spare anyone's feelings."

Lilae blushed, and Risa's jaw dropped.

"Well, that was a joke," Risa exclaimed.

"That *was* pretty funny," Jaiza laughed. "Not so cocky now, *huh*?" She gave Risa a nudge in the ribs.

Pirin grabbed his sack. He grabbed Risa's head and gave her a quick kiss on the side of her forehead. "You did well. We can always improve, though. Don't forget that."

Risa looked up at Pirin. "Thank you."

Pirin clasped his hands. "All right, girls. You'd better run along before you're late for work."

"Right… work. I can't wait." Risa rolled her eyes.

Jaiza smirked. "Oh, you don't really mind. All of the boys enjoy our company."

Risa shrugged. "Well, we shouldn't be focused on that anymore now, should we?" She glanced at Lilae as she wiped her face of sweat and water. "We'll be fat with children soon enough. Isn't that right, Lilae?"

Lilae twirled a lock of her hair and looked down at her weathered boots. "I'm sorry about that. I didn't mean it."

"It's okay. We're sorry, too. Right, Risa?"

Risa nodded. She grinned and put an arm around Lilae's shoulders. "You know how I get when I wake up, Lilae."

"Cranky?" Lilae laughed.

Risa nodded. "Exactly. Don't take what I say too seriously."

"It's probably true though, the whole fat with children bit." Jaiza smiled at Lilae. She grabbed her sack. "I've always wanted children. Three, maybe. *I* took it as a compliment."

"Speak for yourself." Risa folded her arms across her chest. "I'm not too keen on sharing any of the attention. I want Jared all to myself. I don't want any crying babies to care for."

"I don't know if that's possible, Risa," Lilae said softly. She blushed as she spoke, whispering so that Pirin wouldn't hear. "I mean, once you lie with him, you're bound to be with child. Right?"

Risa and Jaiza both burst into laughter. "Innocent little Lilae. I'm surprised you know even that much about what happens between a man and a woman." Risa pinched her cheek.

"One day you'll find out," Jaiza said with a smirk.

Lilae's blush reddened.

"Well, let's go." Risa led the way back to the path.

Lilae followed them from their secret spot at the edge of the meadow on the outskirts of the village and along the dirt road. Lilae didn't run along, as the twins did. She wasn't particularly looking forward to her duties.

Risa and Jaiza were lucky. They helped bake pies and cakes at the bakery that Lukas's wife owned. For them, they had a chance to bond with their future mother-in-law.

Lilae, on the other hand, worked the fields. She entered the village and went to join the other girls in filling buckets of water from the well.

Well, Lilae thought as her eyes met with some of the village girls who waited in line to fill their buckets. They already shot her glares and her shoulders slumped. *Here goes.*

CHAPTER 13

AT THE STRIKE OF THE VILLAGE BELL, everyone was allowed to quit work for the day. Lilae was glad to meet up with Pirin so that he could walk with her back to the village.

Lilae walked a little behind, dabbing her shirt against her skin to soak up some of the sweat.

Her eyes nervously looked from side to side, and Pirin had an idea why. Lilae knew that he noticed everything, but she particularly wished that he hadn't noticed what had been going on lately.

Every morning since that day in the woods, Anic had left a handful of wildflowers at the cottage door with a message written on tiny pieces of parchment. It wasn't unknown for a blacksmith's son to know how to read and write. There were always written orders from the nobles to read, but she found his handwriting refined, and his words poetic.

Good morning, Lilae. Let the sun rise so that all can witness your enchanting beauty.

I dream of you each night and awaken early to see you before you vanish into the crowd.

Your smile fills my heart with joy, if only you smiled more.

Why do you torture me with you silence? I yearn to hear your sweet voice again.

Each day, Lilae scattered the flowers into the dirt but secretly kept the notes in her sack of belongings that was always packed and ready for the next move. She read them to herself at night and stared at the ceiling with a smile on her face and a flutter in her heart.

Soon enough, she found herself searching the crowd in the marketplace just for him and smiling when he waved at her.

On this evening, Lilae knew that things were about to change from friendly smiles and notes to something more. His last message both brought her joy, and fear.

After the work of the day is done, I will come to you, because I cannot wait any longer to hear your voice.

As promised, Anic walked over from the blacksmith's shop to Lilae's cottage with a hopeful smile on his face.

Pirin ignored him. He walked into the cottage and closed the door behind him. Lilae knew that she only had a moment before Pirin left that very door with his hunting gear. Lukas and his men were calling for volunteers to hunt wild beasts in the woods.

"Come on, men. We shouldn't have to ask for volunteers," Lukas's voice boomed down the streets as he walked with his sons behind him. "Grab your spears, and you can come home to dinner after. We are all responsible for protecting our children and families."

Alone, Anic stood on the other side of the street and grinned at Lilae. "Evening, my lady," he shouted with a mock bow.

Fearful that Pirin would come back out at any moment, Lilae scratched her forehead. "Keep your voice down," she whispered with raised eyebrows. "You're mad. Go back into your home before my father sees you."

Lilae held her breath as the door opened, and Pirin stepped out. His things had been waiting for him at the inside of the door against the wall.

Pirin looked back at Lilae, not even glancing at Anic. He stood with his back to Anic and spoke to Lilae as if he weren't even there. "Don't stay out late. You must get your rest for tomorrow. It's an important day, Lilae."

Lilae's face tingled with embarrassment at being stared at by both her father and the young man. She swallowed and nodded. "Yes. Of course."

Pirin gave her shoulder a squeeze and walked toward the gathering huntsmen. Many of the men already looked weary as they left their houses. They had had a full day of work already, but Lukas had a way of convincing people to come out, despite their fatigue and fears. He may have been playing on their feelings of guilt, but it certainly worked.

Lilae saw Anic still waiting there, propped against the window sill of his cottage and straightened her clothing. She held her necklace in her fist for strength. She contemplated what she would say to him. She couldn't let this go on. She enjoyed the attention, but he couldn't be led to believe that there was a future with her.

She crossed the heavily trafficked paths toward her house as the villagers retreated to their own homes for supper. The smell of roasted hens and spiced breads wafted through the warm evening air. Lilae wanted to be mean to him, to scare him off from his conquest, but when she saw the friendly smile on his face, she found herself unable to think of anything.

Lilae released her necklace and put her hands on her hips. "What do you want?"

Anic grinned. He reached out and presented a handful of sarie flowers.

She stared at the red flowers in awe. The red petals were beautiful and full, with smaller yellow flowers inside, held together by a white ribbon. "How did you get those?"

Anic shrugged. "I picked them."

Lilae accepted the bundle of flowers, and he put his hands in his pocket, a self-satisfied smile on his face.

"Saries don't grow here, Anic."

Anic's grin widened. "I searched, and I found some." He paused, lengthening her apprehension. "Near the Utinia Lake."

Lilae pulled back, stunned. The Utinia Lake was a long walk from the village, far from the protection of the clan. She had found that the villagers were too afraid to venture near it. It was said to be the lake that the beasts tended to drink from. There had been large tracks sighted near it, and it had been ordered that everyone was to stay away. She couldn't believe that he had done such a dangerous thing for her.

She held the saries down at her sides and stared down at them "That was foolish, Anic."

He shrugged with that same smile on his face. "You see, I'd do anything for the prettiest girl in all of Lowen's Edge."

"How did you know I liked saries anyway?"

"Jaiza told me. Your sisters have told me quite a bit about you," he admitted with a grin.

Lilae wondered what exactly they had talked about. She wanted to grab him by his shoulders and shake him and find out what he knew about her. She squeezed the stems of the flowers as she thought about the possibilities.

"You're not quite the menacing person you try to make yourself out to be."

Lilae reached out to hand him the flowers and sighed. "Anic, you have to stop this."

Anic raised an eyebrow, folding his hands behind his back. "Why?"

It was such a simple question that should have been easily answered, yet she had no idea how to explain anything to him.

"Just because."

Anic smirked. "That's not an answer!"

"Well, you're just going to have to accept it."

He nudged her forearm, and she scowled at him, folding her arms.

"Loosen up, Lilae," Anic urged. He gently unfolded her crossed arms. Lilae tensed at his hands on her skin. "You can let your guard down… just for a second. Okay?"

Lilae turned to walk away from him and go into the cottage when he grabbed her wrist.

"Come on," he pleaded. "Don't be so cold to me!" His eyebrows were wrinkled in frustration. His sweet smile faded.

She looked at him with curious eyes. Anic seemed to be genuinely enamored with her, and she couldn't pretend that she wasn't flattered. Still, Lilae was hesitant.

"Tomorrow."

Anic perked up, and his face brightened. He gently took her hand into his. She stared at his hand then looked at his face. She had never held a boy's hand before.

She felt her heart flutter at his touch. It was gentle and warm.

"No." He urged her closer.

She pressed her lips together, unsure of how to react when he pulled her into him. Lilae sucked in a breath, expecting him to kiss her, when he simply leaned into her ear. His warm breath on her ear made her close her eyes and swallow.

"How about I show you some fun for a change?" Anic whispered, and before she could protest, he whisked her away down the alley. "It is your birthday tomorrow, after all!"

Lilae was shocked that he knew. She felt exhilarated as she followed behind Anic, racing through the crowds. Just like that, her guard was down, and she did something she did not expect. She giggled and drew in a refreshing breath.

Maybe it will be okay, she thought to herself. *Maybe this is a good thing.*

The sun was setting on Lowen's Edge, and the streets were now filled with musicians and people looking for entertainment.

Lilae held on to Anic's hand, afraid that, if she let go, she'd fall. She enjoyed the rugged warmness of his palm against hers. She felt safe somehow.

It was as if her eyes were finally opened to the town, like she was really seeing it for the first time. Now that the work was done, the people of Lowen's Edge were out to enjoy the city's nightlife.

When they stopped before the double doors of a tavern, Lilae looked to Anic questioningly. She read the engraved markings on the dark birch oak doors.

"The Blind Cow." Lilae laughed at the name.

She paused when a group of royal soldiers walked in. She'd never felt comfortable around soldiers, even if they were from Partha's military. The people of Lowen's Edge seemed to appreciate their presence, though. Lilae supposed it was kind of the king to try to protect his people. It was more than she could say about some of the other kingdoms she'd lived in.

"Why are we here?" Lilae looked around cautiously. She tried to ignore the fact that the eyes of some of the villagers were on her. She looked back at them and felt oddly at ease. The villagers weren't glaring at her or judging her. If anything, they seemed to look at her with curiosity.

Anic pushed the doors open to the dimly lit room, welcoming her with his smile. "For some fun, of course," he declared. "We're young. We work every day. We should enjoy our free time. Now come on, my lady." He motioned for her to enter and held the heavy door open for her.

Lilae stepped inside the tavern. "I wish you wouldn't call me that," Lilae said under her breath.

So many knew sights and smells affronted her. She'd never been to such a place. The smell of apple cider and rum overwhelmed her nostrils. It wasn't an offensive smell, but rather festive.

Royal soldiers from the capital sat in big groups, chanting and singing with their mugs raised and their dirty boots stomping to the beat of the songs. The villagers also drank from mugs of ale and wine at the bar.

There was a group of young women sitting by the fire at the corner of the tavern, giggling loudly with mugs of their own. Lilae was captivated by how some of the girls danced to a lute player's music. She'd rarely seen dancing. The girls looked happy and free, their movements flowing and full of feeling.

She stood there for a moment, unsure of what to do, when Anic took the lead toward the bar. Lilae followed closely behind. The room quieted noticeably as people stared at them. She felt the eyes on her and wanted to turn and run away, but Anic took her hand and gave it a squeeze.

Lilae looked in wonder as he gave her a sidelong gaze, smiling at her. He was attractive but not like the boys from the north. His brown eyes were large and so innocent that she felt like she could maybe trust him. She could tell that he was trying hard to impress her. It still felt odd to her. No boy ever showed her any attention the way Anic did.

He gave a wink, and she looked away. She couldn't let him see her vulnerability. She had to always appear confident and strong. But what would Pirin or Delia say if they found out she was out with a boy after dark, without a chaperone? At least she was in public, she kept reminding herself. Her reputation would be protected.

Lilae shook her head, thinking to herself how much she really didn't care about reputation. They would likely move away in a year, and she would never see these people again.

"Good evening, Reeka! Two pints of your finest ale!" Anic called to the bar maid. He put two bronze quinne onto the bar, and the round, chubby young woman quickly swiped them into her apron pocket. With overly-rouged red lips, stark against her white face, Reeka smiled. She slammed onto the bar two large, heavy looking mugs that frothed at the top.

Lilae looked at it curiously, watching the amber liquid spill over the side of the mug. Anic slid a mug over to her and picked up his own.

He turned to face her. "All right, Miss Serious, I dare you to be so cold to me after you finish this ale," he said, grinning.

Lilae took the mug, held it high, and nodded. "We'll see," she said.

He took a large gulp and chuckled. She followed suit and drank down as much as she could fit into her mouth. She swallowed hard and coughed.

"What is this? Poison?" Lilae eyed the contents of the cup.

Anic laughed loudly and pulled out a chair for her at a nearby table. Lilae sat down and sipped the ale this time. The cool liquid slowly filled her mouth. It didn't taste much better, but at least she didn't gag. She looked to Anic and couldn't help smiling.

Anic returned the smile. "Thank you," he said.

"For what?"

"For that smile. I was beginning to think you were simply incapable of smiling."

Lilae shrugged. "What is there to smile about when war is at our heels?"

Anic shook his head, frowning. "No war talk, please. Tell me something about you."

Lilae was silent. She stared into her mug.

"Come on, tell me something interesting."

Lilae drank again. "You first."

He nodded. "Fair enough." He looked up and thought. "I want to see what Alfheim is like, when the Realm Wars are over, of course."

Lilae raised an eyebrow. "Why?"

"Don't you? It's supposed to be the most beautiful place in the entire world. With silver palaces built into the side of mountains. Snow covered castles and creatures we've never even dreamt of."

"Well, the Silver Elves don't like us, so you might want to think of another dream."

Anic grew serious. "Who says that they don't like us? Have you ever met a Silver Elf?"

Lilae thought a moment. She was speaking solely on rumor and folklore. "I guess you're right. Good luck with that dream of yours."

"Sarcasm." Anic grinned. "I like that in a girl."

Lilae shrugged but smiled behind her frothing cup. She looked around at the people enjoying themselves. They all seemed so normal. So carefree.

"Anic, I've been wondering," Lilae began. "Do you know of anyone in Lowen's Edge who was born with a special trait?"

Anic nodded. "Sure. Jacodi has Accuracy. Mela, the girl who knits bonnets for her mother's shop, she can change colors of anything with a touch. Not sure what you'd call that."

Lilae made a face. "Sounds pretty useless. Changing colors? Really?"

Anic chuckled at the look on her face. "Yeah, I guess it does. There aren't many people around who can do anything special anymore. Except the old apothecary who used to live in your cottage. She was interesting. She could call on birds, even get them to deliver messages for her or guard her house. But she was a little paranoid and would have an entire flock of birds watching her house when she went out for supplies."

Lilae felt her shoulders slump. All of those traits seemed unimpressive. "So, nothing extraordinary? Not even a shifter?" She sighed.

"Sorry that we're too ordinary for you, Lilae," Anic said while shaking his head. "Come one, tell me. You can do something different, can't you?"

Lilae tensed at the question. "No," she answered quickly.

A group of girls walked past, and one of them bumped into Lilae. Lilae was pushed so hard that she knocked over her mug. Ice-cold ale spilled all over her clothes. The girls giggled to each other as they watched the embarrassment on Lilae's face.

Lilae flung ale off of her hands and pulled at the soaked front of her shirt. It clung to her, and she felt sticky and cold. Her cheeks flushed as she watched Anic's eyes rest on her shirt, which revealed an outline of her bosom.

"Oops," blurted Yonna, one of the girls who worked with Lilae in the fields. She smiled, but her dark eyes narrowed in malice. Lilae knew that look quite well.

Lhana cast it on her every day.

"Why are you here with that hag?" Kelsi asked Anic, as if Lilae weren't standing right there. Kelsi put her hands on her hips as she regarded him with disapproval.

"Shut up, Kelsi." Anic stood to put his arm around Lilae's shoulders. "I know you did that on purpose. You need to apologize to Lilae."

Kelsi looked Lilae up and down. "You can't be serious. Please tell me you're with this freakish outsider out of pity."

Lilae watched the shock on Anic's face at hearing Kelsi speak like that. He clenched his jaw. "Get out of here, you stupid girl," he replied, and Kelsi's grin vanished. "Go home before you become a drunk like your father, or I'll have *my* father stop giving you charity."

Lilae looked at the girls in surprise. She couldn't believe that Anic had stood up for her. The look on Kelsi's face pleased her. Apparently, Anic had cut her deeply with his words.

"Let's go," Kelsi ordered the other girls, seeing that everyone was staring at her. Kelsi's cold glare met Lilae's. "You better watch out, you filthy fire freak," she said, her voice lower and more dangerous than Lilae had thought possible.

They shuffled from the tavern, throwing icy glares at Lilae as they left.

Lilae sighed deeply as she looked down at her soaked shirt and pants. "I don't know what I did to them," she said, still embarrassed that one could almost see straight through her shirt.

She looked up to see Reeka holding a dry rag for her. Lilae gave a half-smile as she accepted the towel.

"Thank you." She began soaking up the ale on her clothing.

"Yes, thanks Reeka."

"No problem, sweethearts. Those girls are a pain in my side," Reeka replied as she wiped the bar clean. "Always so haughty, like they are princesses or something. Princesses of the bloody stables, if you ask me."

Lilae and Anic shared a look and snickered.

Reeka smiled. "And what do you do, lass?"

"I gather water for the fields. It isn't the best job in town, but at least it isn't the worst."

Reeka made a face by twisting her mouth. "Really?" She shook her head. "If you're keen, I could use an extra hand here. A pretty face like yours will surely bring in more customers." She winked at Anic. "Probably keep them here drinking ale a lot longer, too."

Lilae's face lit up. "Yes!" she blurted. She withdrew and lowered her voice. "I mean… if you really need some help… I could do that for you."

Reeka beamed and slapped her hand across the table top. "It's settled, then! You start in the morning. Who do you report to?"

"Mrs. Denny."

She turned around and filled up two mugs at the cask. "I'll handle Mrs. Denny. Now, here's another ale. On the house!" She winked as she slid Lilae another mug.

"Thank you, Reeka. I promise I'll be a good worker."

Reeka laughed. "I don't need you to work, child. I just need you to put on a bar maiden's clothes and look pretty." Her laugh carried as she went to the back of the room toward the bar kitchen.

Anic stood from his seat. "Remarkable. We come in here for a drink, and you get a job. Come on, drink up."

Lilae stood with him. "All of it?" She looked at the mug reluctantly. If nothing else, it was cold, and she was thirsty from a long day of work in the fields.

He grinned and raised his mug. "Of course. Don't waste a drop of that free ale."

Lilae put the mug to her lips and waited for Anic to begin. She was surprised at how fast he drank and hurried to catch up. She held her breath as she drank every drop of the cold ale. When she was done, she burped. She laughed and covered her mouth. "Pardon me."

Anic laughed with her and took her hand. "Come on."

Lilae followed Anic, her mind starting to become hazy. She couldn't stop smiling. She was happy, and… having fun. Not only that, but she was sure she was drunk. And it felt good. Her body felt light and warm. Her mind was clear. She didn't have to think about wars and powers and people hunting her. She just wanted to enjoy her time with Anic. It was dark outside and quiet, except for a few men coming back from the hunt.

Lilae gasped and grabbed Anic by the arm. She quickly pulled him into an alleyway, hoping that Pirin wouldn't see them. She pulled him close, her eyes wide with fright. Pirin would be furious if he caught her out drunk. She held her breath as the men passed by without pausing to even notice them. She sighed in relief and looked up at Anic, whose body was pressed to hers.

Lilae noticed that his hands were on her hips and that he looked deep into her eyes . His finger ran along the outline of her pelvic bone through her tucked shirt and onto her waist. She gulped, looking down to avoid his gaze. He was warm beneath her hands. She felt his muscles through his shirt and dropped her hands to her sides. She looked away again.

When he lifted her chin so that she looked up at him, she drew in a breath. Her heart pumped. Her ears grew hot. Her mind raced. Anic leaned close to her, and she felt his lips brush hers. She pulled away from his embrace and ran into the street.

Lilae stopped and stood there awkwardly for a moment, her eyes darting from left to right to make sure no one saw… what had almost happened.

“Thanks for tonight,” she said, avoiding his surprised stare. “I'll see you tomorrow!”

Lilae ran home in a daze, happy but afraid of what she was beginning to feel. Something nudged at her stomach, like a faint warning.

CHAPTER 14

"I COULD USE A COLD MUG OF MEAD," Rowe said as he drank water from a flask.

Liam tied his supplies to Midnight's back and grinned. "I don't care much for the stuff. Too bitter."

Rowe made a face. "I'm sorry, Liam, but sometimes I wonder about you. What kind of man doesn't like a mug of mead or ale?" He took another swig of his water and gave it a distasteful look.

Liam looked at him and pulled himself up into his saddle. "Alcohol dulls the senses," he said, tapping his temples. "I want to be alert at all times."

He nuzzled Midnight, and the horse neighed in bliss.

"I think I actually fight better after a mug or two. Drink some ale… inhibitions fade… nothing holds you back from completely destroying an opponent."

Liam laughed. "How can you think clearly when you're drunk?"

"Like I said… what kind of man are you?" Rowe laughed. "Drinking takes practice."

"I've more important things to worry about."

Rowe raised an eyebrow. "Yes, of course. Like your first woman, no doubt."

Liam's face nearly reddened.

"What are you two laughing about over here?" Nani buzzed over. She landed beside Rowe, who towered over her like a giant. "No one invited me? A girl can only take so much chatter from Clerics. They can be *so* drab. Recharge this. Recharge that."

"But *you're* a Cleric, Nani."

Her purple pigtails swung as she shook her head. "I'm not. I tell you I'm different. You can't tell me that I'm as boring as those other girls."

Rowe rolled his eyes. "Yes. Yes, we've heard all about it. You're *different*. You just happen to heal… like a *Cleric*."

Nani smiled. "It's okay, don't believe me. I'll show you one day, funny man."

"We are what we are, Nani. I'm a brute who happens to be extremely good at killing creatures, and you're a Cleric." He grinned. "It's best that we accept these things."

"Liam," Sona called softly.

Everyone grew silent. No one had seen her approach.

Liam turned to her. She looked as if she'd seen something horrifying. "Is something wrong?"

"Can you come with me please? Just for a moment?"

He nodded. Something told him that something was amiss. Sona motioned for him to follow her.

The others watched as the couple walked into the forest. She took his hand and led the way.

Liam gave her hand a squeeze and looked at her curiously. "What is it?" They stood in a shallow part of the woods where the sun's light was given just enough space to shine dimly.

"Do you remember when I met you?"

He looked down, noticing that she was nervously wringing her hands. Her face looked troubled.

Liam nodded. "Of course I do. It was my first day on the training grounds. We were sixteen, and you were the most beautiful girl I'd ever laid eyes upon. Every man around stared at you in adoration as you walked through the gates." He smiled warmly and fingered her long black braid. "Your hair wasn't as long as it is now. It brushed the shoulders of your recruiting uniform, but it blew in the breeze right when our eyes met."

Sona frowned. She folded her arms across her chest and looked down at her leather boots. "It's nice that your memory of that moment is so vivid, but that's not when we first met."

Liam's smile faded. He was embarrassed. *What is she talking about?* he wondered. *I would never forget the day we met.* He reached for her, and she pulled away.

She stared at his face a moment. "We were nine when we first met."

Liam put his hands in his pocket. At nine, he had still been confined to the palace walls. No one had seen him but palace staff.

He shook his head. "What are you talking about?" His brows furrowed. "Are you feeling well, my love?"

Sona sighed. "Of course you don't remember, Liam. I wasn't beautiful then. You wouldn't have noticed me. But I noticed you." She looked off into the trees. Two birds noisily flew out of a thick oak, as if chasing each other. Then it was quiet again in the lush forest.

"No one even knew who you were that day when you ran away from the castle. You wore a cloak and tried to hide your face, but you could have walked through the streets of Klimmericks Row shouting, 'I'm the prince of Oren,' and no one would have believed you. And you… were the most beautiful boy I'd ever seen." She smiled at the memory.

Liam's brows furrowed. "What?"

"You were trying to hide in the crowd that day, and even then, I knew you were someone special. I saw you give your *entire* money bag away to beggars that day. Beggars who were too lazy to work or too drunk to do anything to help themselves. You wasted all the money you had to run away with on *them,* and I knew there was something good about you."

Realization finally flooded Liam's mind. His eyes widened. He remembered what she was referring to. "Wait a moment. You were the girl?" His face blanched. "*That* girl?"

Sona nodded. "When those beggars beat you in that alley to see if you had more money on you, I ran over to you. It was foolish, I know. I hit them and screamed for help." She grinned bitterly. "I got this scar on my neck because I was trying to help you." She pointed at the almost-faded scar that stretched across her neck. He'd always wondered where the scar had come from, and she had always refused to talk about it.

Liam reached for her, stunned. He wanted to make her forget such a horrible memory. He had tried to forget it himself. It was a reminder of how foolish he had been, and how he should have listened to his mother.

"Sona, why did you never tell me? This brings us even closer together." He held her face in his hands, and she looked away, gently removing his hands.

"It wasn't important until now. That day, we both almost died. If my coachman hadn't come to check on me and called for help, they would have killed us."

"Sona." Liam took her hand. He pulled her close. Finally, she gave up resistance and let him hold her.

"You held me while I lay there bleeding. Your innocent face was so bloodied and bruised, and yet, I looked up at you, and I loved you that very day, Liam." Her eyes welled. "And I never stopped. I don't think I ever *could* stop loving you."

"I love you too, Sona," he said as he embraced her. He was overwhelmed with emotion. Liam had tried to forget that memory. At the time, he had thought he wanted more than being stuck in the vaults with his teachers and his studies, and he had nearly gotten himself and a little girl killed. Sona was that little girl.

She looked up at him tearfully. It was the first time he had ever seen her show such emotion. Oddly, it seemed like the first real moment they had shared. She was vulnerable, not the woman of stone she tried to portray. She was genuine.

"When you fell and blacked out that day with the Nostfar giant, I thought I was going to lose you."

Liam swallowed. He had been obsessing over that day every passing moment. He felt guilty for thinking of that dream girl with red hair when he had Sona right there with him.

He cupped her head and kissed her. Her lips tasted salty from her tears, but he didn't stop. The girl with the red hair started to fade from his memory the longer he kissed her.

Sona closed her eyes and held him tight.

"You're not going to lose me, Sona," he replied. "I will always be here for you. Nothing can break us apart."

Sona shook her head. "You can't make such a promise," she told him. "Betrayal is in a man's nature. My father taught me that."

Liam pulled away. He frowned. "What do you mean?"

Sona sighed. "It means that, if you die, I won't have a reason to live anymore. All that's good in me… will die with you." Her lips trembled, and she turned away.

"But, Sona, I'm not going to die." Liam felt helpless as she sobbed. Her words disturbed him. He turned back to the direction the Order waited. They were about to make the trek to Raeden. "I need you to trust me. I have so much power within me that you cannot even imagine. I will never let anything happen to you. I swear that I will never leave you. In this life or the next."

"We shall see," he heard her whisper, and his blood went cold.

"What was that?"

"Nothing, Liam. I'm sorry. I'm being emotional." She forced a smile. "You know how women can be sometimes. I just wanted to get that off of my conscience. Go on, Liam. I'll catch up." Sona wiped her face. "I need to compose myself." She cracked a smile, but not one of joy; of pain. "I can't let that damned fairy see me with tears in my eyes."

Liam forced a smile, but her words repeated in his head as he walked. He put his hands in his pocket. His mind wandered to the image of her face covered in her own blood that horrible day. She had saved his life and nearly given hers. This revelation made him love her even more… But still, the girl with the red hair haunted him.

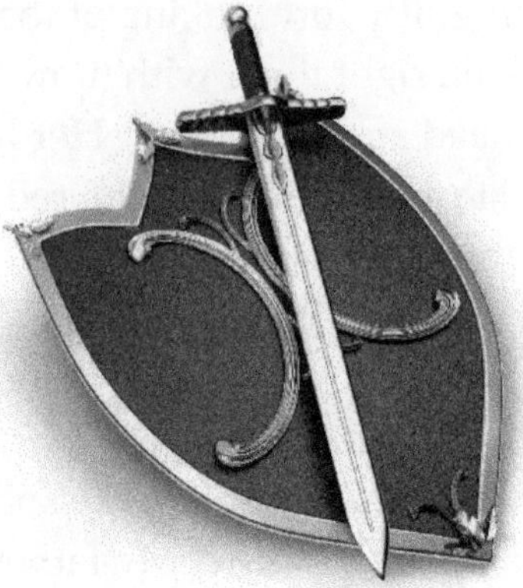

"PERFECT." Rowe's blue eyes brightened as they approached Raeden's shiny silver gates. "We've arrived just in time for the festival of lights."

It had been a little more than a week since they had encountered the Shadow Elf camp and fought the riestlings and the Nostfar giant.

They were all weary and looking forward to finally reaching civilization again. Raeden was a grand Tryan kingdom, ruled by the Alden clan. Like his mother's family, they were an ancient clan who ruled their respective kingdom. Also, they were Oren's greatest ally.

Seven days of feasts, games, and celebrations were what everyone in each Tryan kingdom looked forward to each harvest season. It was a welcome distraction from their conquest to keep their lands free.

Liam was trapped in his thoughts when Nani buzzed over to him with a grin on her face.

"Liam?" She flew beside him, her legs outstretched behind her. "Are you all right?"

"Of course," he replied shortly.

"Are you sure? You seem distracted." Nani waited for a reply, watching his brows start to furrow. "What happened that day when you passed out? What did Sona say to you? You two haven't been as mushy since that day."

Nani was right. Sona had kept her distance from Liam, and he had done the same. He wasn't sure what had happened, himself.

"Nothing, Nani. I'm sorry, but there's a lot on my mind is all."

"Never mind that. Tell me. We've been friends for long enough now that I can tell that something is bothering you. Go on, fess up."

"Nothing I said. Don't bring it up again," he snapped. Liam didn't want her pointing out his weaknesses in front of the other soldiers.

Nani stared at him. Her small face morphed into one of sorrow. She pursed her lips and flew ahead without another word. She met with the troupe of fairies and flew in line with them above the Order.

Liam sighed with regret. He reached out to her.

"Nani!"

She flew too fast to even hear his apology. The moment those words had escaped his lips, he wished he could take them back.

"Liam," Rowe spoke up, taken aback by their exchange. His gaze followed Nani then back to Liam. "I hate to press the matter, but…." He paused. "You *have* been acting very strange since that day. You've always been the quiet sort, but even I can tell that you are not yourself."

Liam glanced at his friend. "I don't know. I just feel…" his voice trailed as he tried to come up with the perfect words. He shrugged. "I just feel different."

He met Rowe's eyes. "Something happened that I can't explain."

Rowe raised an eyebrow, riding closer to Liam. "What was it? What did Sona say to you?"

Liam shook his head. "It's not Sona. Well… maybe she has something to do with it." He frowned. It was rare that he couldn't eloquently express himself. "I don't know." He cleared his throat and shifted uneasily in Midnight's saddle. Liam gave Rowe a sidelong glance. "Remember that year in the Order, when we were out training and faced that horde of elven raiders?"

Rowe slowly nodded. He kept his eyes forward. Liam noted how Rowe tightened his jaw. Rowe knew where the conversation was going.

"We were heavily outnumbered, and I was poisoned by that arrow. I saw what you did to them. It was appalling."

"What are you getting at?" Rowe shifted in his saddle. His eyebrows were bunched in annoyance.

Liam shrugged. "I just want you to know that I can keep a secret. I'd never tell anyone about that vow you made. The one you broke once for me. I hope you never have to break it again. But I just hope you can keep my secret, as well."

Rowe met his eyes. They were serious. He gave a single nod. "Of course. We are brothers. Forever."

Liam smiled. He was the one person whom he could count on. He took a deep breath and went on. "Good. Well, let's just say, this all revolves around a girl."

There was silence and Liam waited for Rowe's reaction, already wincing at what he would say.

To his surprise, Rowe cracked a smile. It was a skeptical smile, but he didn't look at Liam as though he had lost his mind. Liam prayed that he hadn't.

"Did I hear you right?" Rowe snickered. He seemed torn between humor and worry that maybe something really worrisome had happened to Liam when he passed out. "Did you just say *a girl*?"

Liam nodded, unable to look Rowe in the face any longer. Embarrassment had already washed over him.

Rowe burst out with laughter, his chuckles growing louder and more boisterous until Liam couldn't hold back a low chuckle of his own.

"Really, Liam? A girl? That's what's making you all solemn and brooding?" Rowe mocked a low serious tone. "You're unbelievable. I thought you would tell me something horrible. But really, a girl? You sneaky little bastard."

Liam sighed deeply. He already felt better for telling Rowe. He looked at the road as they crossed from a worn dirt path to one paved of stone. It led right to the gates of the city, which was encased in a stronghold of silver and steel.

Liam could see the palace of Raeden in the distance. It floated above the city, hovering like a shining cloud. Below the grand structure that had been built by both the Tryans and the fairies were dozens of courtyards and gardens. Behind it, facing south, was a blue-green sea that stretched outwards all the way to the Nostfar realm. Liam felt sadness within him as he looked at the palace. It was much like his own.

"So, tell me, Liam," Rowe pursued. "Who is this *mysterious* girl? Is it one of the soldiers? Myra, perhaps?"

Liam rolled his eyes. Rowe was going to drag this whole thing out. He would never hear the end of it.

"She's pretty enough I guess. But those lips… Imagine what she can do with those." He chuckled, giving Liam a sidelong glance. "Or is it Jedra? I wouldn't mess with that one." He laughed at Liam's expression.

"Rowe," Liam glowered.

"You know I'm just joking. Everyone knows Liam only wants the very best. But you already have the best girl in Oren…" Rowe glanced back at Sona and then to Liam. He lowered his voice. "So, who is it?"

Liam thought a moment. Rowe had witnessed Liam's darkest moments. There were countless nights of loneliness and regret. Days filled with constant training and drudgery. He had been tested both physically and mentally, and Rowe had been there every step of the way. Years in the Order could break anyone down. Fortunately, Rowe had taught him how to build himself back up. Liam was confident that he could trust him.

"That day, when I blacked out, I met her. It was like a dream, but something tells me that it wasn't." His eyes narrowed. "It was real. I just know it. Everything was real, until… we tried to touch." Liam held his hand before him, just like the moment he and the girl had tried to touch. His hand dropped. "It was like we were meant to touch, but something broke us apart, a light, and I woke up." He looked at Rowe.

Rowe scrunched his face up as he tried to make sense of what Liam was saying. "What?"

Liam nodded, looking off into the distance, remembering her beautiful face. He shook his head, wiping her face from his mind. He felt guilty thinking of her, yearning for her. "Yes, in a dream. I saw her, and she was as real as you sitting on that horse beside me."

Rowe stared at Liam for what felt like an eternity. Liam found himself wishing that he could read the thoughts of others, like his mother.

Then, Rowe shrugged. "Wow, she must have been something, to have you still thinking about her. I don't know of any girl that's kept your attention, not until Sona."

Liam smiled. "She was like nothing I've ever seen. The most beautiful face. Fire red hair. Green eyes."

"Oh," Rowe said with realization. He nodded. "I see. This dream girl of yours is completely different from Tryan woman with their black hair and blue eyes. Tryan women are all the same, never a variation. You want something different, that's all. Maybe… you made her up. She's as far from a Tryan woman as you can get. To think, *red* hair? Sounds like a fairy."

Liam shook her head. "I don't think that's it. I can't explain how it happened, but I feel that I must see her again." He sighed. "It kills me to admit it, when I have a great girl like Sona at my side. A girl who really loves me and to whom I've committed myself."

Rowe nodded and watched Liam's face.

"If it's meant to be, you will see her again."

Liam hoped so. He lowered his head. He looked back at Sona as she rode behind. She met his eyes, and it was almost as if she knew. It was as if she could see into his very soul. He swallowed hard. Liam felt horrible. *What is happening*?

Liam looked back at Sona now, as she rode in front of the other men. He noticed her gaze leave him. She looked past him.

"Liam!" Rowe shouted, breaking him from his thoughts.

Liam turned around, and his face blanched. He felt a knot in his throat as they grew closer to the gates.

Raeden lay in ruins.

CHAPTER 15

THE CHILD SHIVERED AND SHOOK. Her knees were drawn into her chest as she held them close.

Her eyes were red and vacant. There was a long gash across her cheek, as though someone had meticulously sliced her little face. She sat beside the corpse of a small boy. Pieces of his brain spilled out onto the cobblestone.

Liam cautiously reached out to her, and she flinched. He withdrew his hand, and she scrambled to her feet. She gathered her tattered skirts and ran down the dark alley between the tall stone buildings.

He looked to Rowe and Sona. Their eyes followed the girl until she disappeared around a corner between the stone edifices. Ashes and embers fell from the sky, landing on their heads and shoulders like snow.

"What happened here?" Nani flew to them. She landed beside him, standing nearly as tall as his waist.

Sona cracked her knuckles and looked to Liam. "This is quite a welcome. What now?"

Liam swallowed hard as he turned to look around him. Everyone watched him, waiting for direction, waiting for orders. The smell of burnt flesh and hair filled the air. Blood pooled in the streets, coursing through the grooves of the cobblestone that paved the roads and alleys.

He had seen too much death in his young life, but he had never seen so many of his own people so brutally killed. Liam couldn't fathom how the Shadow Elves could have destroyed Raeden like this. That nagging feeling flooded over him again.

The sky was darkened by storm clouds, and Liam closed his eyes. A cool wind softly wrapped around him as he called the rain.

Light rain began to fall, extinguishing the wild flames that ate away at the ancient structures. Steam began to rise from the paved roadways in the center of the intersection of houses and shops. Bodies that had been ripped apart littered the streets, and the rain cleansed them of blood and ash.

Nani took his hand gently. She wrapped her small hands around his.

"You know," she began quietly. Nani looked up at his face as he concentrated on the rain. She could see the tension in his face. "It's not your fault."

Liam opened his eyes and looked down at her. He didn't know what to say. He was supposed to protect his people. This was what he had been chosen to do.

"Well, Liam." Sona swung herself onto her horse. "You'd better get what we came for."

Liam looked up at her and nodded. "The Talisman of Alden." This wasn't how it was supposed to happen. He was to meet with the Alden clan and be their guest. They were supposed to give him the Talisman and teach him how to use it. Now, he feared that they were dead along with their people.

"What's that, Liam?" Nani looked to Liam.

"Our realm's divine weapon. It had once been the only thing that could protect the Tryans and fairies, if there was a threat. It was used in the Realm Wars. The Alden family of Raeden has kept it safe and hidden all of this time." It was a secret that only the ruling classes of Kyril knew about.

He ran to Midnight, mounted the horse, and began to ride toward the palace.

He needed something to take his mind off of the destruction all around them. Midnight maneuvered over rubble and jumped over fallen carts. Liam looked over his shoulder and shouted orders to those who rode closely behind them.

"Look for any survivors. Gather them and meet me by the south gate entrance."

Rowe and the soldiers nodded and split into four directions at the intersection. As Liam rode Midnight through the wide streets, jumping over bodies, he prayed that the Shadow Elves didn't know Tryan lore. He couldn't imagine what the Shadow Elves would do if they had that talisman.

Wexcyn already had enough of an advantage. He was an Ancient. Liam still couldn't figure out how they would ever defeat him, let alone Inora and their armies.

The rain continued to fall as he rode through the city. It pained him to see the bodies of children strewn about in the streets, hanging lifeless out of doorways and crumpled on the stairs.

The brass gates of the palace were bent and torn down. Tryan soldiers were impaled on the sharp ends of the main gate. He slowed Midnight down as they passed through the broken gates and into the courtyard.

At the center of the courtyard stood the bottom of the staircase that led up to the floating palace. It was all that grounded the palace to Raeden's soil. Even in the midst of destruction and death, the palace was radiant.

The silence was unnerving. He had been to this palace many times throughout his life, and it had always been bustling and full of life and joy. As a child he had looked forward to seeing the large water fountain in the palace courtyard.

In the center of the fountain, mermaid statues crisscrossed, sprouting green water. They were enchanted statues that moved across one another, as if in an entrancing dance. Those waters ran red now with the blood of bodies that were impaled and drowned in it.

Raeden was now a ghost town.

He climbed off of Midnight and patted him on the head. The horse bowed, and Liam hugged him. "I'll be right back."

Midnight nodded, nuzzling Liam. Liam held his neck for a long while, fearing what he would see inside that palace.

Liam sucked in a deep breath and drew his sword. He ran up the stairs two at a time for what seemed to take hours. He avoided fallen bodies and abandoned weapons as he neared the top. The wind grew colder as he ascended, and, when he looked down, Midnight seemed much smaller.

The doors were smashed in and lay in splinters. It had been barricaded, but now that barricade was crushed. Liam wondered how the Shadow Elves had managed such a thing. The hairs on his flesh began to rise as he feared that maybe Wexcyn himself had done this. Just the thought that Wexcyn was inside made Liam take pause.

At that moment, he imagined ending the war right then; finding him inside and killing him. He pictured Wexcyn sitting on the throne, tall as a giant and bronze like a statue, just waiting for Liam to walk in. They would fight, and Liam would call the lightning to strike him down.

Liam entered the palace. His eyes darted to each direction, and yet there was nothing waiting for him but silence. He saw the piles of dead soldiers. They were fresh. Dread washed over him, and he stepped into the shadows.

How could an army destroy an entire kingdom and escape so quickly without a trace?

He heard nothing, not even a tiny breath. *Wyverns*, he figured. He had studied the creatures. An army could do just that in a matter of hours.

The fallen soldiers' weapons were scattered across the polished floor. The tapestries and statues were overturned. Broken pieces of glass littered every inch of the foyer.

Liam slowly walked through the grand entrance that led to the double stairwell. He ran toward the lower staircase. He looked down the deep descent. He heard nothing but a low hum coming from below. Liam wasn't sure where the talisman would be hidden.

Where would I hide such a thing? The vaults?

The Alden family had one of the most extensive libraries in their vaults, where the history of the races was stored. It had to be down there. At the bottom of the stairs, Liam slid on some water. He fell hard onto the ground.

Not water. Liam could tell by the smell. It was blood. He glanced at a servant whose eyes looked up at him blankly. With the life drained from him, his skin had become a pale blue. His Tryan glow had faded.

Liam climbed to his feet and used the glow of his sword to lead the way. There were few sconces still lit inside the dark corridor, and he used caution to step over the dead servant. Liam's attention snapped to the far end of the long corridor when he heard a vase crash. He stood completely still, listening and seeking the source of the noise.

His ears perked when he heard shallow breathing. Liam let the glow of his sword fade and slowly crept to the intersecting hall. The breathing he heard grew closer.

Liam turned the corner and nearly sliced a young servant boy in the face. The boy's large blue eyes looked up at Liam in utter horror. His pale face flushed. His palace uniform was stained with blood, and he had a gushing wound on the side of his head. His hair was matted to his head with the blood.

Liam lowered his sword and caught the boy as he began to fall.

"It's okay. It's okay," Liam said. "I'm not here to harm you!"

He held the boy, who couldn't have been more than ten years old. He untucked his shirt and ripped the cloth. He tied the scrap around the boy's head to stop the bleeding.

"Who are you? Is anyone else alive?"

The boy was weak, yet stared at Liam with suspicion.

"I don't know you."

Liam rolled up his sleeve and pulled his shirt back to show his royal mark. The crescent moon glowed against his skin. He looked back at the boy.

"I am prince Liam of Oren."

The boy's eyes widened as he looked at the symbol. He sighed with relief. "I'm the prince's valet, Jorge. I was checking to see if the Shadow Elves had gone. There were thousands, Prince Liam. *Thousands."*

Liam shook his head. It was what he had expected. There was an even larger army in Kyril, and they were a step ahead of him. "Where is the prince?"

Liam slowly stood to his full height. He couldn't imagine so many running through the kingdom. The Shadow Elves must have filled the streets. No wonder the Tryans were massacred; they had been outnumbered. He wondered what unfortunate kingdom was next.

"*I* protected the prince. He is alive."

"Show me where the prince is." He helped the boy to his feet. He gave Jorge an arm for balance as they walked as quickly as the boy could manage.

Jorge grabbed a torch from its place on the wall and walked ahead. Liam knew that they were getting further and further to the bottom of the palace, where the floor looked down onto the sea. When they reached the glass-plated foundation, it was beautiful. The sea was calm and clear, but Jorge walked past without looking.

"What of the rest of the royal family?"

"All dead," Jorge said, lowering his eyes. He coughed into his shoulder. "They tried to fight, but there were too many Shadow Elves. They swarmed the castle like flies." He glanced back at Liam. Jorge's face was troubled as he thought about everything he had seen that day. "*I* saved the prince. He is my friend."

"Thank you for saving the prince." Liam smiled down at him.

Two survivors of the palace, and they were young boys. The other two princes of Raeden had been Liam's age. They must have tried their best to protect their people.

He knew they were excellent warriors and felt such dread that they had been so unfairly matched. Nonetheless, they had died fighting, with their honor intact, and that was something the Tryan's valued.

"You were brave to save the prince."

Jorge shrugged. "He would have done the same for me." They entered the musty cellar, and he handed Liam the torch.

There were hundreds of barrels of wine and ale. The floor was stone, unlike the rest of the palace bottom. The entire room was made of stone and felt damp. It smelled just like the sea inside. Jorge went to the back wall, which looked like any other wall. He pushed it with all of his strength, revealing a secret door.

"Is that you, Jorge?" a little voice whispered.

Once the door slid open Liam saw the young prince. He was still in his silk pajamas. His shoulder-length hair was wild and tousled all around his head. He shivered when his eyes met Liam's. His hand reached for a small sword that glowed green with his touch.

The young prince crawled to his feet, standing about five feet tall. He pulled Jorge into the room, pushing him behind so that he could stand ahead with the sword. He shook as he held the sword out toward Liam. "Don't come near us, or I will kill you." His eyes looked worried. "Please, don't make me kill you."

Even though Wilem put on a brave face, Liam could tell that he was still shaken up from all that he had witnessed that day. "I'm here to help you, Prince Wilem."

Wilem didn't lower his sword. His eyes narrowed. "Lies."

"I'm Prince Liam of Oren. I am your ally."

"He's telling the truth, Wilem," Jorge whispered into the boy's ear.

Wilem nodded but didn't take his eyes from Liam. "Show me the mark."

"Don't be afraid," Liam said, revealing the royal mark once again. "I will lead you both to safety."

Wilem reached out a cautious hand to touch it. "A crescent moon with two swords," Wilem said. He showed his. "Mine's a dragon with black wings."

Liam smiled. "Good to see you are who you say, as well."

Wilem straightened his shoulders, tilting his head up. "I am not afraid."

Liam nodded with a smile. "I know. You're a brave boy," he said softly. "Now, let's get out of here."

"Wait," Wilem said. He lowered his sword and stepped out of the secret room. "The talisman. I can't leave it here."

"You know about it? So it is actually in the castle?"

Wilem nodded. "Of course I know about it. I may be third in line for the throne, but I am as important as the rest."

"Show me," Liam said, moving aside. Wilem eyed Liam as he walked around him.

Wilem and Jorge ran off, and Liam followed closely behind. Out of the darkness of the lower halls and to the brightness of the grand staircase they ran.

Sunlight spilled from the large skylight as they crossed from one side of the palace to the west. Inside the grand dining hall, there was nothing.

Everything was calm.

There were no dead bodies; everything looked to be intact, and it was silent.

Liam raised a perplexed brow when he watched Wilem crawl beneath the table.

"Help me with this!" Wilem started tugging on the heavy wool carpet. Liam hurried over and helped him pull it from underneath the massive, stone table. They folded the carpet over, and Wilem knocked on the floor. There was a clicking sound.

Wilem smiled with relief. "It's still here!" He reached for a silver spoon from the table's place setting and bent it. His thumb rubbed the metal until it began to glow. His eyes began to glow, as well, as he shaped the spoon into a key.

"You're good at that," Liam said. "Creation is a rare skill. You are lucky to have it."

Wilem looked up at him, his eyes returning to blue. Even for a child, Liam could tell that he was wise beyond his years. Those small eyes were serious.

"Father taught me. I was the only one born with Creation. My brothers both had Stealth." Wilem paused. His eyes clouded with tears, and he fell onto his bottom, dropping the key he had just made. He began to sob, his shoulders shaking, and he covered his face with his hands.

Liam knelt down to hug him only to be pushed away.

"I'm fine," Wilem said. Wilem sniffled and wiped his eyes. He rubbed his wet nose with his silk sleeve and grabbed the key from the floor. Still, his breathing was uneven as he fought to hold back his tears.

Liam watched him with sadness. His eyes snapped to the lock when it clicked once and spat out the key. Wilem touched the door, and it creaked open.

Inside the hidden compartment in the floor was a box. It had brass claws molded into its lid as though they held it closed. Wilem pulled the small box out and suddenly, with a swishing sound, a knife was thrown into the side of it. Attached to the knife was a glowing strand.

Wilem gasped and scrambled beneath the table.

Liam stood with his sword glowing and ready. A Shadow Elf pulled on the glowing strand, and the box was ripped from Wilem's grasp. Liam hopped over the table, sliding to the other side. He slammed his sword down onto the strand as the Shadow Elf tried to pull it toward him. It split in two, and Liam caught the box from the air.

His eyes widened when the Shadow Elf crouched down onto all fours. His thin eyes glared up at Liam as he slammed his fist to the ground. There was a loud ringing sound that made Liam, Wilem, and Jorge flinch and cover their ears.

The room vibrated, and they had to steady themselves. Liam looked around and gasped.

Out of the shadows appeared elves. The once quiet room was suddenly filled with the snarls and voices of the Shadow Elves who had slaughtered the Alden family.

"Thank you," one of them said, "for leading us to the talisman."

Liam backed away closer to the boys, as the elves began to close in. He pulled the talisman from inside, and it was warm to the touch.

"Oh my god," Wilem gasped. "What's happening?"

"Use it, Wilem!" Liam said quickly. The elves were getting closer. Liam caught an elf with his sword, slicing its jugular. The elves all gasped and charged. They outnumbered and were nearly smothering him. Liam began to sweat and panic. He slashed through the closest ones with his sword. They reached for him and clung to his arms in an attempt to try and hold him down.

Liam's gaze darted to Wilem. He couldn't call his lightning, not inside, not where he could hurt the children. "Do it! *Now*!"

Wilem fumbled as he took the talisman from Liam's hand. "I've never done this!" he admitted and raised the talisman toward the Shadow Elves, who reached for it in awe. "I call the power of Alden!"

"Who calls?" a voice boomed, filling the room.

Liam stepped back in disbelief. He could feel a low rumble on the floor. The talisman glowed yellow. There were circles of light crisscrossing and radiating from it. Everyone quieted.

Wilem swallowed, afraid of what would happen next. "Wilem Alden," he spoke and fell to his knees as the talisman burned into his palm. He cried out, holding the talisman outstretched before him.

Liam gasped and stepped away as the glow nearly blinded them all. Out of the tiny trinket emerged a glowing shadow. The Shadow Elves ducked as the light blinded them. They all shielded their eyes, and out of the talisman stepped a massive dragon. It grew and grew until it filled the room with its body and looked down at Wilem, sniffing him.

With shining gold scales and black wings it towered over them all. It roared. The sound resonated throughout the room.. The Shadow Elves trembled with fright. Their bones shook. Their teeth chattered Hundreds of them became clumsy as they stared at the dragon and tried to flee at the same time.

As they stumbled and ran, the dragon blew fire onto them all.

Liam pulled Wilem and Jorge close and surrounded them with his shield of auras. They watched from safety as the fire singed and burned every other living creature in that room.

CHAPTER 16

WILEM HELD ONTO LIAM as the fires began to die down. The dragon sat before them and bowed its head. Liam was unsure if he should let the shield down yet. They stared at the dragon, watching to see if it would rekindle its anger and turn the flames on them.

"You can come out now," the dragon said in a female voice that sent chills through them.

Liam looked at the two little boys and saw the fear in their eyes.

"I don't know," Wilem said. They could smell the burnt flesh in the air. It was pungent and overwhelming.

"I'm scared," Jorge whispered, hoping the dragon wouldn't hear him.

"I know, Jorge, but the dragon is part of the Alden family," Liam reasoned. "I don't think it can hurt us." At least he hoped not. Dragons were virtually impossible to kill.

"Well, *I'm* not part of the Alden family, and neither are you! Only Wilem is safe!" Jorge exclaimed in a high pitched voice.

Liam sighed and looked into the dragon's amber eyes.

"I will not harm any of you. You are safe."

Liam nodded and, hesitantly, let the shield dissolve. He put his sword into its scabbard, and they stood exposed before the dragon. Jorge still clung to Liam, his grip tightening, but Wilem stepped forward.

"Who are you?" Wilem asked.

The dragon bowed its head to Wilem, its nose at Wilem's feet. "I am Vleta. I am yours."

"Mine?" Wilem repeated in awe. "Remarkable!"

Liam put a hand on Wilem's shoulder. "You will protect the boy? And do his bidding?"

Vleta nodded. Her golden eyes examined Liam. "And you, Storm. I will protect you, as well, as you fight for what is good."

Liam raised an eyebrow. "Of course I'll always fight for what is good."

"You can always be led astray," Vleta said. "As all men are inclined to do at times."

Wilem huffed. "Hey! I thought you were mine!"

"I am here to protect the Tryan race. Each realm has a secret weapon. I am yours."

Liam nodded. "We see."

Wilem folded his arms across his chest. "I don't," he mumbled.

Liam ruffled his hair. "Why don't you ride Vleta down to the south entrance of the kingdom? Just you and Jorge. How does that sound?"

Wilem's eyes brightened, and he nodded excitedly. Jorge looked at the dragon cautiously.

"Yes! Yes!" Wilem grabbed Jorge's hand. "Let's go!"

Liam was pleased that he could cheer up the young prince. He knew the boy didn't want to share his new prize. He imagined that at ten years old, he himself probably would have reacted the same way. He helped Wilem and Jorge onto Vleta's back. Wilem's smile was radiant, and Jorge held on tight to his young master.

Vleta craned her neck and lowered her nose toward Liam. She smelled him and returned to her statuesque position. "You smell tainted."

Liam scrunched up his nose. "What does that mean?" *Tainted*?

Vleta didn't respond for a moment. "I will tell you when I find out who tainted you."

Her words vexed him, but then he reminded himself that he was talking to a dragon. Her senses must have been enhanced; who knows what she had picked up on? He nodded cautiously and looked to the boys.

Wilem was still smiling. He was happy to see that the dragon had turned into the perfect diversion from reminding Wilem of what had occurred that day.

"All right, Wilem. I'll see you all very shortly," Liam called up to the boys.

Vleta nodded to the ceiling.

"Oh yes." Liam looked up, as well. He crashed the glass and slowed its descent to the floor, so that he wouldn't harm the boys. Like rain, crystalline glass particles floated all around them. Wilem and Jorge squeezed their eyes shut and held their heads down until all of the glass was out of the air.

With a puff, Vleta outstretched her shiny black wings. They were so large and long that they filled the entire room. She took off into the air and out of the palace with the new king of Raeden and his only subject.

"LIAM," ROWE CALLED. "

The little boys sat by the fire in the center of the camp. They had set up their camp west of the city after hours of searching for survivors.

"That boy is a Legacy. We couldn't find any survivors of his line. Whoever was behind the attack on Raeden will be looking for him."

Liam knew the implications of rescuing a Legacy. Legacies were sole heirs to a line of powers and traits. Whenever an entire clan died with one survivor, all of their powers were passed down to that individual. It was done to keep the traits alive, to be distributed in whatever offspring the Legacy bore.

"Well, what would you have me do? We couldn't just leave them in the city. That young prince is important to the preservation of our people."

Rowe stared at Wilem and Jorge. "I know. But they will need to be hidden."

"Of course. We'll take them to the fairy colony. They'll be safer there than anywhere."

"Indeed," Nani said. "My people would be glad to take in the boys. Tolrin is well hidden, where no one will find them."

Liam clasped his hands. "It's settled then. We'll head for Tolrin first thing in the morning."

Rowe nodded and they all returned to camp.

"All right, let's pour ourselves a drink."

"I'll have some," Wilem chimed. His licked his lips as he looked at the bottle of ale.

Liam shook his head as he sat beside Wilem and crossed his legs. "No, thanks. None for me."

Wilem held out his cup further. "I'll take his, too."

"Sure, little man. Chug away." Rowe hid a grin as he filled Wilem's cup with the dark liquid.

Wilem licked his lips and held the cup with both hands. He smiled and took a mighty gulp. Immediately, the ale spurted out of his mouth and into the air.

Everyone laughed at Wilem's look of disgust, while the liquid fell off his chin.

The boy looked around, embarrassed. When even Jorge joined in, Wilem couldn't help but chuckle along. He fell onto the ground and laughed hysterically. It was the most endearing thing Liam had ever seen.

Liam sat back and watched them. He smiled at how easily Wilem fit in with battle-worn soldiers. More responsibility had been tossed onto his already leaden shoulders, yet this time, he welcomed the task. He knew it was his duty to get that child to safety.

CHAPTER 17

THE NIGHT AT THE BLIND COW began a whirlwind of excitement and fun for Lilae. She found herself looking forward to the evenings, when all of the work and chores was complete. At sunset, she would slip out into the warm air and find Anic waiting for her with a hand outreached.

She smiled and took his hand then followed him as he led her to a variety of places.

"Where are we going tonight?" She looked ahead with a smile on her face. She even let her hair fall free from her cloak now, no longer caring as much about what others thought. Anic liked it, and that was enough for her.

Anic glanced back at her with a grin. "It's a surprise."

Many of the villagers were heading the same way that she and Anic were walking. In the center of the market square was a stage. It was a festival of some sort. It seemed as though everyone from the village was in the square that day. Even the soldiers were gathered around the festivities. They were in uniform, as always, and drinking frothy mugs of ale.

Lilae saw Kelsi, Yonna, and a few other girls chatting with the younger soldiers. They fingered the soldier's sword hilts and batted their eyelashes.

Lilae stopped beside Anic and looked around at the different forms of entertainment.

"What is this?"

Anic gave her hand a squeeze and ran his thumb softly over the back of it. "Partha's traveling festival. It comes through here at the beginning of each summer. You see?" He pointed to a box-like shape on their right. "There are puppet shows, plays, and even dances."

"Dances?" Her face paled. Lilae took her hand away and put it in her pocket. "I can't dance."

Anic laughed. "You don't have to know how. I can teach you. There are only a couple of moves. We aren't dancing at a royal ball or anything."

She forced a half-smile. She pictured herself tripping over her own feet and embarrassing herself. She didn't think she could handle having Anic laugh at her. "No, thank you."

Anic shrugged. "Fine. We don't have to dance." He waved for her. "Come on, the play's about to begin."

Lilae followed him through the thickness of the crowd and toward the front of the stage. She shielded her face when she saw Risa and Jaiza standing with their future husbands.

Lilae took a step away from Anic as they hurried over with amused smiles on their faces.

"Well," Risa said as she stood before Lilae. She gazed at Anic with a big grin on her face then pushed Lilae's shoulder. "What is going on here?"

"Looks like Lilae has a boy." Jaiza wrapped an arm around Anic's shoulders and leaned her head close to his face. "Meet Mr. Anic Treu. The son of the town blacksmith. I hear your father makes quite a few *gold* quinne a week." She winked at Lilae.

"Really, Lilae, you've managed to snag a man of trade. Impressive." Risa nodded in approval. "I didn't know you had it in you. I didn't even know you were interested in boys, Lilae. Have you really grown up while we weren't looking?"

"Looks like Lilae might not be a pauper all of her life," Jaiza added. "I mean, Risa and I will be married to barons, but Anic here makes armor and weapons for the king… Perhaps he could buy you two titles someday."

Anic cleared his throat and shrugged Jaiza's arm from his shoulders. He sidestepped her toward Lilae. "Jaiza, that's enough."

Jaiza raised an eyebrow. "What is it, Anic?"

He shook his head.

"I think he's being modest." Risa nudged him. She looked up at the sky. "But I can hear the gold quinne falling from the sky already."

"I just think it's improper to talk about money. Especially with women."

Risa's smile faded into skepticism. "Who said we were proper? Did you know that our little Lilae here is quite an animal? I'm surprised you've managed to tame her."

"What next… dresses?" Jaiza grinned. "Rouge? High-heeled slippers?"

Risa laughed. "You have your hands full, Anic. You don't know Lilae like we do. But if you're good, we'll tell you all of her childhood stories."

Anic was the one to grin now. "Childhood stories?" He pulled Lilae close to him. "I think I'd like to hear those."

Risa folded her arms. "Oh yes. You'll love it. Remember Mordrow?"

Jaiza's eyes widened with the memory.

Lilae cringed. *Oh no*, she thought. *Not this story.*

Jaiza chuckled. "How could I forget? You see, Anic, Mordrow was a little fishing village where we used to live. One time, our little Lilae decided she wanted to take a bath in the lake. Of course, she was only five, but it didn't make it any less hilarious!"

Lilae's cheeks reddened. She glanced at Anic to see that he was avidly listening. She felt her fists ball up.

"Honestly," Risa added, "she has an odd obsession with water. Hang out by the lake in the morning, and you might get a free show."

Lilae pushed Risa. "Shut up! All of you." She shot a stern look at Risa and Jaiza. "What do you think you're doing? I don't need your opinion on *everything*." Then she glared at Anic. "Don't encourage them, Anic. You think I need you judging me, too?"

Lilae stormed off, her face reddening from embarrassment and anger. She fought her way through the crowd, wanting to get as far away from the three of them as possible. She knew the whole thing with Anic was going too far. She liked him, but she feared he expected so much more from her. She only wanted to have fun, for once in her life.

Who knows how long before we have to pack and leave again?

She had almost made her way to the newly finished village gates. She stood facing the gates to the roads when she overheard the soldiers standing patrol.

"Are you sure, Jessup? I think you like to spread rumors. Like the one about the dragon you supposedly saw when you were a boy."

"Listen, I'm quite sure of it. I'm not fooling. The general really sent us here because the villages further north are being ransacked by Imperial forces. They are heading toward Partha."

The men grumbled. "Right, Jessup."

"I'd be on my guard if I were you."

"You sure you're not just trying to scare young Roddie here? The Avia'Torenians are coming from the west, not the north."

"I wouldn't have believed it, either. But my sister is the chambermaid of the general's wife, and she heard him talking about it. There is a force of two thousand men scouring the entire realm. They never lose even one soldier, and they double every year. That force isn't even a sliver of what Avia'Torena really has. I hear there are millions of soldiers waiting."

"I don't like this. Why in the name of Holy Elahe would they send us here? What can we do against these monsters?"

Lilae hid in the darkness, listening, when someone pushed her into the wall. Lilae gasped as her face was pressed roughly into the cold stone of the back of the building. Her arms were pinned to her sides. She tensed, ready to strike out.

"I told you," she heard Kelsi whisper in her ear.

Lilae froze. Her fear fleeted. She could tell that the other three girls were with her. They held her arms. She clenched her fists and tried to remain calm. She breathed carefully, but her blood began to boil.

This girl just won't let it be, Lilae thought.

Kelsi pulled Lilae's hair, yanking her head back in an awkward position. She held a hand out to Yonna. "Scissors."

Lilae waited. She looked sidelong at Yonna as she pulled a pair of rusty shears from her pocket. Yonna saw her looking and gave her a wicked smile. Lilae smiled back and used her Evasion to wrench free from their frail grasp, her body flickering before their eyes, and snatch the scissors from Yonna's startled hands.

Lilae held the pair of scissors like a weapon and grabbed Kelsi by the front of her blue dress. The girl's brown eyes looked up at her fearfully. She started sniveling before Lilae even had a chance to say anything to her. Yonna and the other girls shuffled uncomfortably, their eyes looking for an escape.

Lilae was nearly a foot taller than the girl and slowly lifted Kelsi from the ground as if it were effortless. Her toes searched for the ground but felt nothing, and Lilae smiled a wicked smile but there was no trace of humor in her cold, green eyes.

Kelsi saw the light flicker in Lilae's eyes and shuffled. Lilae's smile faded when she glanced down and saw urine trailing from Kelsi's dress and into the dirt. Lilae rolled her eyes and put the girl down.

Lilae's shoulders slumped, and she pushed Kelsi with a disinterested arm.

"Get away from me." She held the scissors up like a pointing finger. She glared at their terrified faces. "All of you!"

They scrambled and ran from the alley. Lilae watched them run away and sighed. She had almost hurt Kelsi. She had wanted nothing more than to hurt that girl. Kelsi had had three girls with her, but she would have been defenseless. Shame slowly crept onto Lilae as she stared at the puddle of Kelsi's urine. She kicked dirt over it.

"Lilae," Anic said softly as he approached her. His face was troubled. "I'm sorry."

Lilae avoided his eyes, still ashamed at her outburst. He came over to her and took her hands in his.

"It's okay, Anic. I overreacted. I know you didn't mean anything by what you said."

He shook his head. "Of course not. I really like you… but you already knew that." He tried to smile for her.

Lilae stared at his face. Her eyebrows scrunched together. "Why?" she asked suddenly. She wondered why anyone would like her.

"Because you're different. You didn't know my father had money or of my inheritance. You like me for me." He held her face in his hands and leaned in to kiss her.

Lilae pulled her head back. "I'm not in the mood to kiss you, Anic. Not now."

His head hung as she pulled her hands from his. "I understand."

Lilae tilted his chin and feigned a smile. "It's nothing you did. You have no idea all that's happening. I fear for all of these good people in Lowen's Edge. Reeka, you, your family, my family. I fear for myself."

"I know what you mean. My father's workload has increased. I think something's going to happen. King Moor refuses to submit to the Empire."

Lilae nodded. "Exactly. This emperor is supposed to be ruthless, and he is allied with Shadow Elves, Anic. You think those royal soldiers can protect us against them?"

Anic looked reflective. "My god, Lilae, you sure have been thinking about this a lot. I never really thought about it. No one has ever seen a Shadow Elf. No one around here, that is. How do we know they mean us harm?"

Lilae made a face. She wondered if any of the people swarming the square knew what the other races were like. "Trust me. They won't come through The Barrier to make friends."

Anic grumbled. "You are in a gloomy mood today." His eyes brightened. "Want to get a drink? I could use one. There's no work today or tomorrow. Might as well, right? It will cheer you up. We can go to The Bling Cow and then the grotto, to watch the sunset."

Lilae shook her head slowly. She tried to ignore that warning feeling in her stomach. It was annoying her not knowing what it was. Anic didn't seem to feel the coming danger. The people of Lowen's Edge, except for the royal soldiers, were oblivious to what was happening beyond their borders.

She sighed. There was no use talking to him about such things. "Can we just get away from all of these people?"

Anic nodded, growing excited at the notion of having Lilae to himself. "Sure. Whatever you want. Come on. We can go to the Garden District."

Lilae's face brightened. She nodded with growing excitement. "I would love to see a garden, actually."

"I can't figure you out, Lilae," Anic said. "You act all hard, but I think you're actually a sweet girl. Why do you try so hard to pretend you're not?"

Lilae shrugged as they walked along the outer road that led to the Noble Square. She hadn't been to the area where Risa and Jaiza would soon move with their husbands.

"It's easier to be short with people or blend in the shadows."

"Blend? You're crazy. You could never blend in. You're too beautiful." He grinned as he looked her up and down. "And tall."

She gave a small smile. "It's just that when you move as much as I do, there's really no point in making friends. Is there?"

"Of course there's a point," Anic said. "I get what you mean, but it sounds like a boring life. Aren't you glad we met? We have fun together, don't we?"

"Yes, we do."

He put an arm around her shoulder. She tensed when he kissed her cheek. "I'm glad I met you, Lilae. Even if it does make those other girls jealous… Not to mention Jacodi."

"What?"

Anic chuckled, leading her to the paved roads of the Garden District. "Kelsi always assumed we'd get together. I guess it made sense. Our fathers are really close friends, but she's not like you. She can be such a brat."

"Oh." Lilae nodded. "That explains why she and the other girls hate me. But what did you mean about Jacodi? He never even speaks to me. He just waves and runs away. It's weird."

Anic gave her a sidelong glance. "He's practically obsessed. He won't even speak to me anymore."

"Weird."

Anic shrugged. They arrived at the brass gates, and Lilae's eyes widened. Something warned her to not enter those gates, and then she saw why. Women in robes were walking through the square, going from house to house. Lilae took a step back.

Anic frowned. "What are they doing here?"

"Perhaps it's not a good time. I'll see you at sunset." Lilae looked at the sky.

Anic nodded. "You're right. Best to stay away from them." He smirked. "I can't have them take my Lilae off to a monastery. I'd never see you again."

She took her hand from his and started away when one of the Sisters' eyes met hers. An unexpected memory came to her then. She'd seen that woman before.

Lilae frowned. It couldn't be the same woman. Her eyes, though, were familiar.

Was it Sabron? Halwan? Perhaps Mordrow? All Lilae knew was that each time they'd seen those women in robes, the same thing had happened. She knew then that their time there would soon come to an end.

"Meet me at our spot tonight." She sighed. "There's something I need to tell you."

CHAPTER 18

"CLEAR YOUR MIND, LILAE. FEEL YOUR POWER, LILAE," Delia said.

She stood a few feet away from Lilae, her voice calm and low. Lilae could hear her soft footsteps behind her.

"When I was created at the beginning of this world, I saw what power looked like. I am created from Ancient power. My entire body." Delia tilted her head. "Well, my *true* body is composed of it. But what people don't know is that power is like a separate being. Like a mist or a current, it soars through your body, seeking out uses for itself. I believe you use it more than you know. Once you clear your mind, though, you can tap into more energy. Your power is in your core, but you have to learn to tap into it and use it without wasting so much energy. This is something different than your Focus or Evasion, Lilae."

Delia waved a hand, and red light hovering before her. Lilae stood completely still as she watched the red light spin in circles before her. She flinched when it flew out to her and vanished.

"It's more animalistic. The Ancients made it so that you could use it instinctually, if necessary, but, in order to fully use it, you need to understand everything about it. Like the miles you run with Pirin and the girls each morning, the exercises and mock sword fights, you need to practice. You train so that you'll know what to do when you really need to fight. Embed the power and forces within your muscles so that they will come naturally."

Lilae could feel Delia's presence, even if she couldn't see her. She knew exactly where she stood and couldn't help feeling that what they were doing was silly. She could feel it inside of her, but, like a stubborn child, her power refused to come when called. She reached and willed it to sprout forth, but that warm evening, her mind was elsewhere.

Lilae couldn't focus. She had promised Anic that she would meet him at sunset. She imagined him waiting there for her, thinking that she had stood him up. She held her dagger and stood in the center of Delia's cottage.

It was completely dark in the room, and she couldn't concentrate on her task. For weeks, she and Anic had been together every day. Between the taverns and the shows he had taken her to around the village, she had been exposed to fun that she had never known. She finally felt as though she were making up for lost time, for the lost childhood she had never experienced.

"Are you focusing, Lilae? You should be able to do *something* by now."

Lilae could hear Delia growing irritable by her lack of results and tried harder. Still, she was unable to do anything. She felt cold to the power. Other feelings and emotions were taking its place. She thought of Anic and how his lips had come so close to her own. She knew that tonight she would maybe be brave enough to experience that first kiss.

"Lilae!" Delia called, breaking Lilae from her thoughts. "By Elahe's grace! This is important!"

Lilae's shoulders slumped, and she lowered her dagger. She looked over her shoulder at Delia sheepishly. "I can't do it." Her face flushed with embarrassment. She couldn't believe that she had let her mind wander like that. She knew she was losing grip on what was important.

With a flick of her hand, Delia lit the assortment of candles all around the room. She ripped the dagger from Lilae's hand. She looked into Lilae's face with eyes of ice. Lilae stepped away from that scowl.

"What's wrong with you lately?" Delia was visibly frustrated. Her cheeks reddened with anger.

Lilae shrugged. She looked down at the stone floor. She couldn't stand to have Delia give her that look. "I'm sorry."

"You come home drunk almost every night." She wriggled her finger in Lilae's face. "I need you to take this seriously. You cannot do this, Lilae. Do not let a *boy* lead you astray."

Lilae stood there awkwardly. She didn't know that Delia was aware of her nightly excursions. She looked down. A spider walked across the floor between them. She watched it, with its long skinny legs, hoping for a diversion from Delia's heated scolding.

Delia's voice softened but only slightly; the edge was still present. "You don't understand how important it is for you to learn this skill, Lilae. You can do things that people couldn't even dream of, and we're losing time every day you slack on your studies. You are the only human who can attempt this."

"I said that I was sorry. What do you expect me to do?"

Delia threw her hands open. "There is so much dependent on you. You have no idea how long we've waited for you."

Lilae lifted an eyebrow and looked at Delia skeptically. "Why, Delia? Why now? You are hiding something. I know it." She pointed a finger at Delia. "Why are you so anxious to teach me about my power now? How can I do anything when *you* are keeping secrets?"

Delia pursed her lips. She began ridding the cottage of clutter, silently fuming.

"Exactly," Lilae said, exasperated. She motioned toward her dagger in Delia's hand. "Maybe if I knew what we are actually doing, it would be easier to focus! I wake up before anyone else, to train. I work all day! And then, you expect me to come here each night to summon some power that obviously doesn't want to be summoned. When do I get to have a life of my own?" Her face saddened and her chest heaved as she felt herself growing agitated. "When do I get a break from all of these demands? Is this what I am, Delia? Is this all there is for me?"

"We're done for tonight." Delia shook her head and started toward her room in the back of the cottage. "I don't know when you started to lose focus. But," she sighed, her hands dropping to her sides, "you disappoint me."

Lilae sucked in a breath. Those words infuriated her more than anything. Her pulse raced as her cheeks grew hot. She was tired of the secrets. "I'm sorry I disappoint you so much!"

The candle flames blazed wildly, and Delia paused at the door. She sucked in a breath and looked over her shoulder at Lilae, whose hands were balled into fists.

"Lilae?" Delia called softly.

Lilae didn't respond. She didn't move. Delia motioned for her to calm down, slowly approaching her. She took a chance and placed a gentle hand on Lilae's shoulder. She caressed her softly.

"Don't touch me!" Lilae growled, her voice booming in the small room.

Delia stepped away, and Lilae stormed from the room before she could stop her.

Lilae ran from the cottage and into the dark forest. She knew she had to control her emotions. She couldn't help wanting to please everyone; it was what she had strived to achieve all of her life. Not a day went by when Lilae didn't crave affection and approval. To hear Delia say that she was disappointed hurt her deeply.

She could hear Lhana laughing at her already. Anytime Lilae failed at something, Lhana had a snide remark; the failures were a reminder that Lilae wasn't the prodigy Pirin and Delia thought she was. Lilae fumed. She didn't want to go home. She wanted to run far, far away. And so she did. She ran.

Lilae's anger rose, and the power boiled within her. She barely felt the ground beneath her feet as she raced through the woods. She ran deeper and deeper until she became tired. She paused and caught her breath. Through her rage, she didn't even know which direction was home anymore. All she saw was black darkness all around her.

It was abnormally quiet. She turned around, but it was too dark to see where she was. The trees were clustered closely together, blocking out any light from the moon. Something ran across her feet, and she jumped with a squeal.

Must have been a mouse or something, Lilae thought to herself. Her eyes tried to see what it was. Normally she wouldn't have worried, but with the strange beasts of Nostfar running wild, she was on edge. She wished she had paid attention to where she was going. She scolded herself for letting her anger get the best of her.

She felt uneasy. Something watched her. Lilae turned to her left, and her heart nearly stopped when she saw something large staring at her with glowing eyes from between the thickness of the trees. Lilae gasped and stumbled backwards. She fell hard into the dirt, the color draining from her face. The darkness was smothering. She felt her skin crawl with fear.

Her eyes widened as she met the large orange-and-black eyes of a basilisk. The eyes, shaped like crescent moons, were nearly as large as her head. Its body was covered in shiny black scales, and it drew up its barbed tail like a scorpion, pointing the sharp edge toward Lilae.

The basilisk's massive body towered over her. It blocked the light of the moon, and she gazed up at it in horror.

Lilae stiffened and held her breath. It sniffed the air as it walked. She gulped as large, blunt teeth flashed through its snarl. She shivered as she realized that the basilisk had two sets of teeth, the pointier set crisscrossing through its snarl. Her anger at Delia dissipated and was replaced with terror.

It seemed as though they were in a staring match; nothing but tension and silence passed between them. Her mind raced as she tried to decide what to do. Lilae was afraid that, if she breathed too loudly, the beast would strike. She didn't want to die.

She risked crawling an inch backwards, and their eyes locked. The basilisk growled deep within its throat and charged toward her. With a shriek, Lilae sprang into action, scrambling to her feet. The basilisk stomped closer to her, the ground shaking beneath its clawed feet.

Her breaths were erratic. She ran blind. For once, she wasn't fast enough. The barbed tail swung and landed square across her stomach. Lilae grunted at the sudden pain. The wind was knocked out of her. The barbs penetrated her flesh. Her hair whipped around her face as she flew through the night and into a tree.

Lilae's head barely missed slamming into the trunk, and she was grateful. She slid to the ground with a cry and gasped for breath, as the sharp pain overwhelmed her. She held her wounded stomach. The blood soaked through her thin tunic and onto her fingers. She hadn't the time to nurse her wounds or focus on the excruciating pain, for the basilisk was quickly after her again.

Lilae barely had a chance to scramble to her feet as it galloped after her.

She had never felt so helpless in her entire life. She was weaponless and weak against the beast that chased her. While holding her wounded stomach, she ran deeper into the woods. The basilisk relentlessly tracked her. She imagined it had an endless supply of energy that would outlast her own and that it would not stop until she was a meal.

Her breaths came out ragged and labored. Everything seemed to burn. Lilae's eyes searched wildly for an escape. The Winds whispered incoherently, and Lilae's mind filled with too many thoughts so she couldn't understand what they were saying to her. Lilae glanced over her shoulder to see the large body quake the earth as it followed. The night air fogged out of its nostrils, and it grunted like a bull.

Lilae shrieked when it abruptly stopped and swung its barbed tail at her again. The creature slammed her into the ground with one large paw, pinning her thin body to the forest's floor. Lilae squirmed and screamed at the top of her lungs. Her stomach and legs felt as though they were being crushed. She hoped that someone would hear her.

"Help me! Help me! Please!"

She beat at the beast's face and kicked with all of her strength as its fangs drew close to her face. Thick, acidic saliva dripped onto her face as the tip of the basilisk's tooth began to pierce her throat. A spark ignited inside of Lilae. Energy soared through every vein, heating her to her core. She gasped as a bright light began to crackle between her palms.

For the first time, she had enough light to see the nightmarish face of her assailant. The sparks grew until it became a blast of fire. She reached out toward the basilisk, her eyes wild and her hands covered in flames. The fierce flames lit the entire forest clearing with a brightness that made her squint.

Dumbfounded, Lilae stared at her hands as fire sprouted from her palms. The flames licked and flickered wildly, traveling to her elbows. She let out one last scream, fearful that soon she would be burnt to ash.

Lilae grabbed the creature's face. A loud, shrill sound of pain came from the basilisk as flames consumed its body. Lilae took the chance to crawl from beneath the beast on her elbows. She stared in awe and confusion.

The basilisk writhed and squealed as the fire ate away at its scales, gnawing into the creature's flesh. Lilae's mouth was still wide and her throat dry when the basilisk turned to a mere pile of bone, scales, and ash. Her chest heaved.

Lilae held up her pale hands and stared at them. The flames were nowhere to be seen, and her hands seemed unharmed. She fell back onto the ground and tried to control her breaths.

She felt the darkness start to smother her as her blood spilled onto the forest floor. She grew cold and barely heard someone call to her. She looked up at a face, unclear in the darkness.

"Lilae!"

The world grew dark as her eyes fluttered closed. She fought the black void fiercely, but it grabbed her and dragged her down. Her breath grew shallow to a near hum as she was pulled deeper into the darkness.

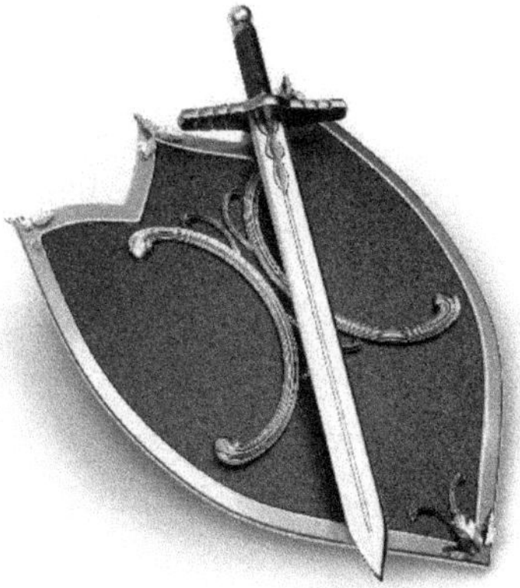

LILAE'S CHEEKS FELT WARMED. She groggily sat up and shielded her eyes. The sun was red. The sky was the bluest of blues. Lilae stared up at it in astonishment. She suddenly remembered her wound and looked down at her stomach. She gasped. She wore all white, and both the blood and pain were gone.

She pushed herself up to her feet clumsily. Her billowy white dress blew in the breeze as she looked around. Frantic thoughts filled her mind.

"Where am I?" Lilae was mesmerized. The place was oddly… familiar to her. She had been there before.

Lilae was in the middle of a field of tall grass that reached to her knees. Large blue and orange butterflies fluttered all around her. She stood completely still and watched as a few landed on her shoulders. She let out a slow breath, and they floated in the air again. Lilae turned in a circle, taking it all in.

There were gray mountains in the far distance and a nearby waterfall. She looked at the crystalline waters as they rushed down stones into a shallow body of water. She cautiously knelt down and dipped her hand into the water. It was cool. It was real.

She sprang up and gasped. Lilae put her hands over her mouth and let out a long, slow breath. She sighed and dropped her hands. She hoped that it was a dream and not death. The Underworld was not such a beautiful place. At least, this wasn't how Lilae imagined it.

"Am I dead?"

She felt eyes on her. Her cheeks paled. There was someone standing across from her. She shrieked and took a step backwards in surprise. Her eyes grew large as she stared at the tall young man a few feet before her. He looked at her in the same way.

She remembered him. He had been in her dream weeks ago. She would never forget that face. Lilae wanted to hide from his gaze. He was the most attractive man she had ever seen. He had wild black hair and the brightest blue eyes that seemed to have a glow. He wore white as well. A tunic and pants with a gold band at his waist.

The muscles in her face relaxed; somehow she wasn't afraid of him. He calmed her.

"Who are you?" Lilae realized that she couldn't hear her own voice. It was the same as before. She couldn't talk.

Lilae felt her heart beat faster and her face flush when he was near her. She looked up and found herself entranced by his eyes. He was one of the first men who actually stood a good deal taller than her. She wanted to touch his face. It was perfect. His skin was untainted and pale, much like her complexion, but there was an odd glow that radiated from his skin.

He brushed a lock of black hair from out of his eyes, and it sprung back into place. He looked into her eyes searchingly, and she felt her pulse quicken. It was loud, filling her ears. Her cheeks flushed when he looked at her like that.

In unison they both felt compelled to touch the other. The instant their fingertips touched, a light separated them, and Lilae was catapulted back to reality.

She shrieked, *"No..!"*

With a gasp, her eyes popped open, and she found herself lying on her blankets on the floor of their cottage.

Risa and Jaiza sat beside her, watching her with widened eyes red and swollen from tears.

"Lilae!" they said in unison. Their voices were filled with excitement.

Lilae's eyes darted around the room. She recognized it. She was back in their sleeping quarters. The small room was the same, with log walls and dark wood floors. There was an open window at her right, letting the breeze into the room. Lilae could hear chatter from the street. She could smell coal from Anic's father's shop across from their home.

She sat up and winced with pain. She saw that her stomach was tightly wrapped in bandages. She looked completely bewildered when Risa grabbed her in an embrace. Jaiza wrapped her arms around them both. They wept with joy, and Lilae was speechless.

"You are not leaving our sight ever again!" Jaiza scolded, but Lilae could tell that it was full of love.

Risa nodded quickly, tears falling down her face. She sniffled. "Never ever!"

Delia sat in the corner and covered her mouth in relief. She looked at the three girls in utter happiness. She smiled at Lilae. "I knew you'd come back to us," she said.

Lilae was disoriented and confused but clung to them, holding her hand up to caress Risa's hair. She closed her eyes and breathed a breath of relief. She was alive. She never wanted to linger that closely to death again.

Pirin peeked in after hearing the girls' cries. He wiped his forehead and smiled down at her. The twins moved aside as Pirin knelt down beside Lilae. He pulled her into his chest and smoothed her hair more tenderly than she'd ever known him to do. He clutched her as if he were afraid to let go.

He let out a long sigh of relief. "My Lilae," he said softly. "We all missed you."

CHAPTER 19

QUEEN ARIA SQUIRMED in her bed. She knew she was dreaming. She was held frozen and powerless as the eerie sensations continued. A force tugged at her mind, pulling her subconscious into a room where a man and a woman stood waiting for her.

The room was small, but it looked out into entire lands and peeked into other worlds. It was composed of a floor made of clouds and walls that depicted scenes of events that were occurring at that moment. The current scene was of a girl with hair as red as a rose lying in bed with bandages covering her abdomen.

Aria wore a turquoise sleeping gown, in stark contrast to the pure white room and white Ancients' garments. The Ancients stood around her as the vision continued. Aria reached out, the walls' message wavering as her hand tried to touch the girl.

"She is stronger than we thought."

"Is that the one?" Aria slowly walked toward them.

Telryd nodded. He was the creator of the humans. He resembled his complex creations. They were by far the most diverse of the races. His hair was a bright red and his eyes were a striking green. He towered over her as he stood with his back to the flickering screens.

"Yes. She is the Flame that we have been waiting for. There might be hope after all." He was in a white robe with a gold and purple tasseled belt wrapped around his waist. Telryd stroked his red beard as he looked over at the screen again.

"The Elder is taking her closer to The Barrier. She knows the strength of the Flame. We are in agreement that she is ready." Ulsia moved closer to the image.

As Ancient of the Silver Elves, Ulsia resembled her creation as well. Her long silver hair reached the small of her back, and she wore a silver circlet. Aria couldn't bring herself to look directly into her silver eyes. They were so unsettling.

"What would you have me do? I have done everything I could. I made him study and train. I showed him both love and suffering so that he would grow into a well-rounded man. I have done my best."

Aria was never truly comfortable with being in the presence of the Ancients. She had been the first Tryan born with the ability to Seek. It was historically a human trait. She was a just and mighty ruler because she could read the minds of others. Because of her ability, her mind was open to the Ancients, where they could draw her mind to their meeting place and converse with her as if she was in the Overworld.

Telryd nodded. "You have done well. We were wise to let him stay with you instead of Elder Drefen. The Storm is more than we could have hoped for."

"Agreed." Ulsia nodded. "He is the perfect specimen. But…," she sighed.

Aria was observant. The Ancients were getting more and more restless. Such an observation made her worry.

"He does have his weaknesses," Ulsia continued, still watching the images with curiosity. The Ancients had all put a part of themselves into that girl and Aria's son.

"As all mortals do, sister," Telryd said. Aria found it odd that they referred to each other in familial terms.

"You've sent him on a crusade to fend off the Shadow Elf invaders?" Ulsia asked with a raised eyebrow. "After we purposefully told you to send him to The Barriers?"

Telryd looked to Aria.

Aria purposefully avoided his stare. She glanced at Ulsia. "I did. They have been pillaging and killing villagers in our wild lands."

"But we gave you orders, Aria. An Elder wouldn't have questioned our orders or followed their own will. You promised us that you would be just as subjective. You cannot let your own emotions get in the way. Wexcyn will use your misjudgment in his favor," Ulsia said.

Telryd nodded. "She is right. Wexcyn has already sent out his disciples, and they are unlike anything we could have imagined. Wexcyn's disciples are loose on the entire world, and *they* follow orders. Do you understand?"

Aria nodded, feeling her ears heat at being scolded. She was afraid of them. It bothered her that they were starting to doubt her.

"Good," Telryd said. "We see everything, Aria."

Ulsia stepped beside him. "But soon, we will no longer be able to communicate with you. The Overworld will soon close its gates, to keep Wexcyn out. That means you will be on your own."

Aria looked afraid. "What do you mean? How will we know what to do?"

Telryd looked at her with compassion in his face. It was comforting to know that the Ancients knew how they were feeling. They were chosen to create because of their understanding of life.

"We can only lead you to the door, Aria. You have to go through it. You have to decide how you want this war to go. Tryans, humans, and Silver Elves are united… for now. It is up to you if it will remain that way."

Ulsia's eyes glowed. The silver was too bright for Aria, but she couldn't help but look into them. "The Mithrani numbers are growing. Wexcyn has beaten us. He has brought them into the world, and they have been thriving in the shadows. Inora's Shadow Elves are allied with them. Do you know what that means? Two of the most powerful races, with equal hate for the rest of you… I almost worry if we have done enough to prepare you all for what is coming."

"What about the others?" Aria folded her hands before her. "Ulsia, tell me, who is the Steel? Who is the Inquisitor?"

Ulsia looked to Telryd. "They have to present themselves to you."

Aria raised an eyebrow. "What? We don't have time to waste. You said so yourself."

"We cannot force them to come out. It is up to them to make themselves known."

Aria sighed in frustration.

"Send Liam a message. He must go to The Barrier. Do it quickly, before it's too late."

Aria nodded. She knew this moment was coming. It was foolish of her to once again try and stall. He was twenty-five now. Liam was no longer her little boy.

"This is proof that their link is very, very, strong. They are already drawn to each other." Telryd produced a golden throne. It materialized out of the air. He sat and draped his arms along the armrests.

Ulsia did the same. The image faded, and the walls became that of a shimmering plethora of colors that rippled all around them. Telryd and Ulsia's eyes met, and it was as if they spoke without words.

"They have healed together in their dreams… here, in the Overworld. *There* is the proof."

Aria's lips parted. "Healed? Is he all right?"

"Of course he all right, child. What a silly question." Ulsia waved a dismissive hand.

"Enough questions," a voice boomed, as Pyrii entered the room. He materialized right in the center of them, sitting in his own throne.

Aria stumbled back in shock. Pyrii was the creator of the Tryans. His long black hair hung long and loose over his shoulders. His glow was like nothing she had ever seen. It was so iridescent that the light seemed to circulate around him like golden discs.

Aria trembled, avoiding his gaze. *How long had he been listening*?

"This meeting is over. You do not ask questions. Who are you to question your creators? There will be no more stalling. You have your orders. Now leave."

With a jolt, they sent her back to her bed, and she woke. She opened her eyes and lay there for a moment. Tears soaked her cheeks as she tried to calm herself. Her stomach was burning with the pain of such stress. The Overworld would be closed. They would no longer lead her. She'd never felt so lost.

Aria slowly sat up and looked around her empty chambers. She was hot and sweaty. Her white covers were sprawled across the massive bed. She pulled a string at the head of her bed, and, within seconds, a young girl scurried into the room. She kept her head bowed low as she entered the room.

"Your highness?"

Aria lay against her cushioned headboard. "Mindy, darling. Water. Please." Her voice came out raspy. She tried to clear her throat and felt a new pain.

Mindy gave a quick nod and hurried away.

Aria sighed. *She is fast. When will she learn that I won't strike her if she doesn't show up in less than a minute?*

She stepped onto the plush carpeted floor and stretched. Before she could finish a yawn, Mindy had returned with a tray arrayed with a pitcher of water, a teapot, sugar, honey, lemon, and two small cups.

"Thank you, Mindy. This is perfect." She poured herself a cup of tea and drizzled some honey into it.

She thought she caught a small smile on the girl's face as she left the room. Aria walked out to the balcony with her cup of tea. She sipped as she walked. The air was warm and sweet with the smell of the honeysuckle bushes just outside the door. Her long, black hair hung loose, swaying in the gentle ocean breeze.

She walked through her exotic flower garden to look over the white stone balcony at the ocean. She rested a hand on the cold stone and sighed as she looked at the still waters. Her palace hovered above the water as if by invisible columns and beams. It was connected to the land by only a steep white staircase.

Most ancient Tryan castles had been built that way. In the beginning, Tryans rode dragons, and the height was practical. Now, the single staircase was quite a nuisance. Dragons hadn't been seen since the Great War.

Aria stared out at the moon. It seemed to settle right above the water, causing the gently rolling waves to sparkle under its light. She looked up as a large black and white eagle soared through the sky and landed next to her.

"What is it, Aria?" Yoska's voice was anxious with worry. "Has something happened?"

Aria looked down at him. His tiny eyes were black as coals. He was her oldest friend. Yoska was always there when she needed him, and only he knew all of her secrets. He knew her fears, every mistake she had made, and every love she had lost.

"Yoska," she said to him, smoothing the feathers on his back, "the war has started. Wexcyn has an army. His disciples are already here. And now Liam must be sent to The Barriers."

There was a brief moment of silence.

"The Ancients say that the Flame is strong, that she is ready, and that the prince must journey to her right away."

"They are right, Aria. Liam is more qualified than anyone in our world and would die before letting his people down." Yoska moved closer to her, his clawed feet near her pale hands.

That's what I'm afraid of, Aria thought. *Liam could actually die on this journey*. Aria didn't know if she was strong enough. Liam had spent his entire life training. She had made sure that he was strong and skilled in everything. Aria sighed and sat on the ground. She drew her knees into her chest. She felt defeated. He was all she had left.

Yoska saw the look on her face. "Poor choice of words, my queen. Liam is strong and powerful. He will be fine."

"Why do I have to be responsible for all of this?" She sighed. *Why complain*? At least they had let her keep her child. Otherwise, it would have been a strange Elder, and she might never have seen him again.

Yoska hopped from the balcony and stood beside her.

"I know it's hard," he said. "But you know better than anyone that doing what's right is rarely easy."

"I know." Aria nodded. "Time just went by so fast, Yoska."

"It has. I remember when you were just a child. Those innocent years, when you had nothing to worry about except what doll you would play with next."

Aria looked at him with a half-smile. She wished she could go back to such innocence. "Seems like ages ago."

"Yes, but we must all grow up, Aria. There is much responsibility that comes with age."

She forced a smile. "Very wise, Yoska. How old are you, anyway?"

"Old enough."

"You always say that, you know?" Aria grabbed the balcony and pulled herself up. "How long do you think it will take for you to send a message to Liam?"

Yoska flew up to her. "He cannot be more than a few days outside of Oren territory. I can be there and back in a week."

This is really happening. How long before things start to fall apart? Nothing ever went according to plan. Never. "Hurry back, Yoska." Her eyes turned glossy. "Tell him that I love him."

Yoska nodded and took off into the moonlight. She watched as his wings spread, and he soared over the moonlit ocean.

CHAPTER 20

LIAM THOUGHT OF HOW MUCH he was going to miss this Kyril, the Kyril before Wexcyn's destruction. Still, he knew it was coming. He sat with Sona outside their circle of tents. The others were sleeping, and he couldn't even imagine falling asleep with all of the worrisome thoughts in his head. His only comfort was having Sona by his side.

"Liam, tell me what you know about Eura," Sona asked as she picked up her water flask and drank. "Tell me something interesting. I've always wondered what it was like. I never thought we'd actually have a chance to see it."

"Besides being full of humans…," Liam thought a moment. "They have four seasons. I find that quite amazing."

She lifted a brow. "Seasons?"

Liam smiled. He loved to teach. If he hadn't been born a prince, he would have been a wonderful teacher. "They are changes in weather patterns. The humans have an autumn, a winter, spring, and summer."

Sona looked confused. "I don't understand. What are those?"

"Well, if we were in Eura, we would be living in the summer season. It is characterized by warm, temperate climates. Kyril's weather never changes. It rains and the sun shines, that's it. In Eura, they have snow."

She nodded. "That is interesting. Like the Silver Elves, then?"

"Yes, but the Silver Elves only live in winter… like the Shadow Elves only live in autumn."

Sona leaned back on her elbows and looked up at the stars. "I'm really not going to miss Oren. I think Eura will be nice."

Liam didn't show his surprise. He smiled and reached over to pull her closer. She welcomed his embrace. Her hands went through his hair, and she sighed. "It's just, my father. You know how he is."

Liam nodded. "Yes, I know. Lord Rochfort is pretty frightening. I honestly don't like being in the same room as him, but he is your father. I am sure he is worried about you being out here with me."

"If you say so."

Liam came to his feet and held a hand out to her. "Come on. Let's get back to the others."

They walked together as the sun began to set. He held her hand and felt at peace with her by his side. He tensed when he heard a whistling sound approaching them. He and Sona both paused and turned to see something fly at them from the trees.

"Yoska?" Liam stepped forward to get a closer look as the eagle landed on a tree branch before them. His face brightened when he recognized that it was indeed Yoska.

Liam smiled. It felt like so long since he'd seen his mother's companion. It was a blessing to see something familiar. Yoska reminded him of home.

"It is I," Yoska said. "I come with news from the Ancients."

Sona frowned as she looked at him. "The Ancients?" She shot a surprised look at Liam. "The Ancients speak to you?"

Liam put a hand on her shoulder. "Go back to camp. I'll catch up with you." He kissed her cheek and went over to speak with Yoska.

Sona lingered for a moment before hesitantly following orders. She paused and stood before him.

"But— "

Liam cut her off with a rare authoritative look. She pursed her lips and frowned but turned and stalked off.

Once she was gone, Liam stood before Yoska. His thoughts immediately went to his mother's welfare. "What is it? What do the Ancients say?"

"You are to go to The Barrier."

"Already? There was much danger on the road to The Barrier, let alone the Shadow Elves that were blocking the doors."

Yoska nodded. "Yes. It will take you some time. The Flame is finally ready. If things go well, she should be able to meet with you in time."

"She? Who are you talking about?"

Yoska looked at him with his expressionless eagle face. "The Flame. Didn't you hear me?"

Liam shook his head. "Wait. Wait a minute… the Flame is a girl?"

Yoska nodded. "Yes. Is there some sort of problem I am unaware of?"

Liam couldn't help but smile. At first his smile was wary, but as he started to put the pieces together, it grew. "The girl from my dreams?"

"Yes. The girl you have been dreaming about is the Flame, and the time has come when you must unite."

CHAPTER 21

"DELIA?" LILAE GROGGILY SAT UP sat up and peered into the darkness of the chilly room.

Delia's shape stood in the doorway. Lilae rubbed her eyes. Delia looked frightening, standing like that in the dark.

"What are you doing?"

Delia knelt down and kissed Lilae's forehead. "Get some rest, darling. I need you to get better soon. Dream for me."

"What did you just say?" *Does she know about the dreams*? Lilae wondered. She hadn't stopped thinking about that magical place.

"I have something important that I need to do."

Lilae clutched Delia's arm. "What? You can't leave me! I've never been without you."

"I know." She put a hand over Lilae's and gently removed it from her arm. "You must trust me. I will be back. I promise."

Lilae shook her head. "I don't understand. Where are you going?" She looked at the loft bed that the twins shared. One of them stirred, and she lowered her voice to barely above a whisper. "Tell me. Please," she pleaded. "Can't I go with you?"

Delia sighed and came to her feet. "I don't have time to explain everything to you, dear. You forget that I am an Elder. I have other tasks that I need to complete. It won't take me long. Please, get some rest." She put her hand across Lilae's face then, and Lilae no longer had the energy to ask any more questions.

Her eyes fluttered closed, and she fell back onto her pillow. She didn't mind, she went back… to her dreams.

AFTER A WEEK OF RECOVERY, everyone was amazed by her quick healing ability, including Lilae. She secretly believed that that magical place in her imagination had helped her heal. It should have taken twice as long for her wounds to close and scab over. Now, the skin was already smooth with only a faint scar left to remind her of her most terrifying moment.

Deep down, Lilae knew that her dream land was an important place, and she spent her time obsessing about the man she had met. She looked forward to sleep, with hopes that she would see him again.

She waited for Delia's return. She vaguely remembered Delia's departure. The Elder had been very secretive about the whereabouts but assured Lilae that she would return. Lilae missed her terribly. Lilae had never been away from her for more than a couple of hours. She didn't know what could have been so important, but the look on Delia's face convinced her that it must have been serious.

Lilae was grateful that Anic had been there to carry her back to town that night she was nearly killed, and their bond had strengthened. Whenever he was done working, they spent time together in the groves and by the river, talking and sharing secrets. He almost made her feel like a normal person. Anic was a best friend to her now, and she finally let him see her softer side.

"What do they say about me, Anic?" Lilae drew in the dirt with a short stick.

"Who?"

Lilae shrugged. "I don't know, the other girls in town, the other boys…" Her voice trailed off. "What do they say about me when I am not around?"

"Oh." Anic paused, thinking. He tossed a pebble into the calm lake. "They just think that you are different." He shrugged.

Lilae glanced up, her face serious. "I am."

Anic smiled. "I know," he said, moving a long strand of hair from her face. "That's what I like about you."

Lilae tried to suppress her own smile, but it was useless. She beamed and leaned back onto her elbows. He scooted closer and did the same, as they stared at the lake where they had first met. It had become their sanctuary.

"So, you never told me where you and your family are from."

She thought a moment. There were so many places. One for each year of her life. How could she choose? "I guess you could say Sabron was my favorite home of them all."

Anic nudged her with his shoulder. "Until now, I hope."

She laughed and grabbed a red berry from her basket. "Yes, until now." She popped the berry into her mouth and looked out to the lake. She watched as a duck glided along the surface of the water, her ducklings trailing behind.

"How many children do you want?" Anic gazed at the ducklings as well.

Lilae sat up, wrapping her arms around her knees. He came up with her.

"Did I say something wrong?"

Lilae was silent, frozen as she stared at the ducks. She didn't like where the conversation was going. She knew Anic was falling in love with her. He reached for her hand, and she sprang to her feet. She gathered her skirts, still surprised that Risa and Jaiza had convinced her to wear a dress. She only wore it to make them happy.

She relished the attention they had finally given her since she had almost died.

"I think it's time to go back Anic." She avoided his concerned eyes as he looked up at her.

She grew tense as The Winds swept through, drowning out his voice. They enveloped her, shouting, warning. She tilted her head.

What is it?

"I'll see you later," Lilae blurted. The Winds drowned out the sound of her own voice.

"Now wait one second Lilae! You can't keep running away from me. Talk to me!" He was firm, holding her still by her forearm.

Lilae shook her head. Something terrible clung to her mind. She couldn't make out what the images meant.

So much screaming. So much blood.

"I have to go!"

He let her arm go and took a step away from her. Hurt, he said in a voice laden with with sadness, "Why do you have to leave?"

So much that it made her stomach turn with dread. She tried to soften her voice. Her eyes darted around. "Trust me, Anic, I don't want to leave."

Anic looked perplexed then alarmed. "What do you mean? *Where* are you going?"

Lilae shook her head; she didn't have time to explain. "Don't waste your affections on me." There was a scowl on her face. She couldn't hear her own voice over The Winds. "I'm sorry."

"But you still haven't told me why!" His face was twisted in confusion, his cheeks reddening.

Lilae was moved by his outburst. She stared silently at him, examining his face. She wanted to tell him everything.

"You won't understand."

Lilae grew apprehensive when he grabbed her wrist, holding her hand to his heart. "I'm twenty. I can take care of you." He spoke quickly, full of passion. "I can build us a house of our own, if you'd let me!" Anic closed his eyes and kissed the back of her hand. "I will take over my father's blacksmith shop, you could raise our children. We would have a good life." He was breathless, desperate. "Please give me a chance. I pledge before Elahe, I love you."

She couldn't help but smile at his quick-paced speech and all of the wonderful things he promised. Still, the fear nagged at her insides. It warned her, it ate at her. She couldn't take it.

Anic could sense that he was losing her, that she was ready to bolt at any second. He didn't let her go; his grip tightened around her hand. "Stay with me, Lilae. *Please.*"

The tears stung her eyes. Crying was for the weak. Pirin had told her so years ago, and she would never forget it. She pulled her hand away from his and turned to leave. She began to run but stopped after a couple of feet. She turned back to him.

"Some nice girl will be lucky to have you. And most girls here don't even deserve you."

Lilae didn't give him a chance to respond. She darted through the forest without stopping. She felt the vibrations all around her, and it was maddening. The Winds pushed Lilae along. They screamed that something was wrong. All it told her was that she must flee. Fast.

She began to feel ill. Lilae grew weaker. The air felt thicker, seeming to deplete her of her energy. Her insides raged. The pain grew worse, and she collapsed when she reached the cottage.

Lhana stood at the hearth over a pot of stew that hung over the blazing fire. She usually loved the smell of lamb and turnips, but tonight it made Lilae's stomach churn.

"Supper is almost ready." Lhana turned, setting the ladle in the pot. She wiped her hands on a rag that hung from her waist. A worried expression settled on her face when she saw Lilae.

"Lilae?"

Lilae wanted to speak, but the room became a blur. She coughed. She groaned in pain. Her head spun, and she started to twitch.

"Help me." She panicked. This had never happened before. "Help me!" She fell to the floor, shivering.

Lhana knelt down to her and touched her sweaty forehead. She snatched her hand away as if she had touched the flames in the fire.

Lilae couldn't open her eyes. They were sealed shut. She feared what she would see when they did open.

CHAPTER 22

"WAKE UP, LILAE."

Something nudged at Lilae, urging her to awaken.

"Wake up."

She heard footsteps from afar. Then, she heard the screams.

"Wake up!"

Within her feverish slumber, Lilae wasn't sure if she was dreaming.

"WAKE UP!" The Winds screamed at Lilae, lifting her from her bed.

She fell to her bed and instantly sat up so fast that it made her dizzy. She squeezed her eyes shut and waited for the room to stop spinning. Lilae fell backwards into the wall. Her head pounded. She was soaked with sweat. Her clothing clung to her chest and back. Her body felt weak and ached all over.

As her head spun, her heart raced at the loud screams of terror she heard coming from outside. She climbed up from her place on the floor. The old wooden floorboards creaked.

Darkness filled the house. She rushed to the small opening that served as their tiny room's window and saw that it was early dawn. Then she saw the chaos and destruction in what had once been a peaceful village.

What she witnessed made the blood drain from her face. There was smoke and fire everywhere. Dozens of muscle-bound men were scattered about. Their attire was unlike any she had ever seen. Most had long black hair in ponytails that were held by gold bands at their nape. Some had bald heads with bright tattoos drawn on their flesh.

Gold rings pierced their ears and hung from their lips or the corners of their eyebrows. They sat above large horses, trampling along the dirt paths, and they were merciless in their killing of the men. She noticed that they were gathering the girls and young women.

She almost called out to Jacodi for answers as he ran past her house. He ran with such purpose that she felt his tension and fear. Lilae sucked in a breath.

"No. No," she whispered. Then she saw Jacodi slashed with a sword across the back by a man on a horse. The other villagers wailed and ran in every direction as they tried to avoid a similar fate. Lilae gasped when Jacodi's body was trampled to a bloody mess by the soldier's decorated battlehorse.

Her stomach lurched. Her hands went to her head as she tried to make the vision go away. She couldn't take her eyes away. Her stomach churned into acidic knots. She would never be able to forget the frantic look in Jacodi's eyes or his body splattered all over the street. She squeezed her eyes shut and let out a long groan of pain.

When Lilae opened her eyes she looked across the road to see the soldier throw a torch into the blacksmith's shop across the road. The flames grew larger and larger, consuming the lower floor, and Lilae called out when she saw Anic look out a window on the second floor.

"Anic!"

Not only Anic heard her scream; a group of soldiers glanced up at her and headed toward her house. Lilae felt her heart beat faster, her hands tingle. She had to rescue Anic.

Lilae squeezed her eyes shut, wiping the tears away from her face.

Through her fever, she didn't waste time in grabbing her dagger and making her way to the door. Just as she did so, the front door was kicked in. It was knocked from its hinges and crashed to the floor.

Lilae grunted as she dove out of the way. Two large soldiers entered the house. Lilae stabbed one in the chest. She saw the shock in his eyes as he fell into the wall, crashing into a shelf of clay bowls.

She spun around just as the other swung at her with his sword. She ducked as she tightened her grasp around the hilt of her dagger and stabbed his booted foot. His yell was deafening. Lilae grunted as she withdrew the blade from the thick leather to pierce the bearded flesh beneath his chin, the warm blood dripping onto her knuckles.

As she tried to pull her dagger from his wound someone grabbed her by the neck. His hand was large, crushing her throat.

Lilae frantically tried to fill her lungs with air the instant his grip released her neck. He slammed her onto the table. She banged her head on the wood and squeezed her eyes shut to block out the pain.

"Little savage," he growled.

Tears stung her eyes, and she screamed when he reached underneath her sleeping gown. She heard her undergarments rip. His fingers pressed deep into her skin as he roughly pulled her closer to him by her thighs.

Lilae punched and kicked, eying her dagger on the ground. She clawed at his face and tried to wriggle free. He slapped her hard across the face, and she gasped at the pain. Lilae grunted when he pressed her face into the table so that her cheek became embedded into the rough crevices of the wood.

Lilae felt her eyes stinging as tears clouded her eyes. She saw a knife near the edge of the table above her head and tried to reach it. It was too far, and she began to feel her resolve waver. He barely made notice of her struggles as he unbuckled his pants, his eyes glazed as he looked at her exposed body.

He held her still as he stared down at her. "Such a waste." He shook his head. "Let's say we enjoy this moment, before the Sisterhood claims you."

Lilae focused on the knife.

"Better yet, maybe I'll buy you for myself."

Lilae's entire body tensed when his hands went between her legs. Her face grew hot. Such an unwanted touch both angered and terrified her.

"Get off of me!"

Her anxiety rose as his pants were now around his ankles.

This cannot be happening, Lilae thought with terror. Sweat dripped from his forehead and onto her face as he leaned in to kiss her.

She felt a force deep in the pit of her stomach, rising within her chest, and the tips of her fingers began to tingle. Lilae reached for the knife on the table above her head once more. The tingling sensation increased.

It slid into her hand. Her fingers curled around the wooden handle.

Without a second thought, she stabbed him in the head with all of her strength.

Lilae let out a guttural scream with the impact of the blade into his brain. She then stared in silence, breathing heavily. Her icy glare met the shock in his eyes. His body began to jerk, and his eyes rolled into the back of his head. Thick, dark blood trailed down his forehead from the stab wound. Knife sticking out of his head, his large body fell backwards onto the floor with a loud thump.

Lilae stood and tried to fix herself. Her clothes were ripped, most of her flesh exposed. She wiped tears from her face, remembering Anic. She had to save him.

Lilae jumped over one of the dead bodies and pulled her dagger from his chin, his blood dripping from the blade onto her white knuckles. She wiped it quickly on his shirt to keep it from slipping from her grasp. She wouldn't be caught off guard again.

Lilae ran from her house and instantly stepped back as a horseman swept past her. She sucked in a breath at seeing his large sword raised high, the rising sun reflecting off of its metal blade. Lilae watched the direction that he was galloping in. The ground trembled beneath the horse's hooves, a cloud of dust trailing him.

She looked up to see that Anic wasn't waiting at the window as he had before. The flames had destroyed everything, and her heart sank into her stomach.

Lilae darted across the dusty road and turned the knob to Anic's door. She was cautious as she reached for the knob. The knob was hot from the flames. When it didn't burn her hands, she ran into the shop.

Everything was ablaze. The floorboards were being eaten away. The smoke was thick and stifling. She ran for the stone stairs and gasped when the flames seemed to chase her.

Lilae shrieked as the flames migrated toward her and attacked her. She flailed and stomped the fire frantically, but it swarmed her. She paused. She sucked in a breath when she realized that she was fine. The flames didn't harm her. Somehow, she was immune.

Lilae was covered in fire when she made her way to Anic's room. His eyes grew wide as he stared at her. His jaw dropped, and he rushed to help her.

"My god." His face turned ashen. "Lilae! What is happening to you?"

The flames captured her in a red aura that protected her from being burnt. She looked frightening to him, smothered in flames like a creature from his childhood nightmares. Her hair danced lightly with the flames and he gulped.

"Are you all right?" she asked awkwardly, trying not to focus on the flames that engulfed her. She was the Flame. Her secret was out.

Anic nodded hesitantly, his eyes staring in horror at the flames that covered her.

"What's going on, Lilae?" Anic coughed raggedly into his hands and looked around. Lilae saw a black cloud above their heads and realized that the smoke was thickening,. She wondered how she would get him out of the house.

"Why are you asking me? I don't know!"

"What do we do? I tried to leave through the front door, but the fire is too intense down there. God only knows how you managed to get up here." They both looked around for an exit as the flames began to enter his small room. They heard the crackling sound grow louder as the floor began to sink into the fire.

The ceiling began to collapse onto them. She took Anic's hand, and he shouted when the fire burned him.

"Sorry about this, Anic!" She pulled him behind her and out the window. She only hoped she was right about her abilities as they fell to the ground. Delia had warned her. She was the Flame.

Anic held his breath as they glided down to the road. The flames reached out and pulled Lilae and Anic to the ground, slowing their descent so that they lightly stepped onto the dirt.

Lilae quickly withdrew her grasp, and Anic shook the flames from his hand. He winced and grunted with pain as he smothered it in his shirt. A hole was burnt into it. When the flames were extinguished, he stood silently, staring at her, bewildered.

Lilae closed her eyes, and the flames were absorbed into her skin. It was as if the flames had never been there. Steam, however, radiated from her body.

"I knew I wasn't imagining it," he said, mesmerized. "It *was* you that started that fire in the forest that night!"

Lilae started to speak when she saw Lhana motion to her from a cottage. She looked from side to side and saw that it was clear of soldiers.

"Come on." She ran over to the neighboring cottage, and Anic followed. They quickly ducked inside before the soldiers saw them.

Inside were the dressmaker and her little girl. They clutched each other in the corner. Lilae caught her breath as Lhana shut the door behind them.

"What's happening out there?" Maude asked. She held her daughter, Stella, in her arms. The toddler had no idea that something was wrong. She shook her rag doll at Lilae and smiled.

Lilae stared at the girl, unable to come up with the words to respond to her mother.

"Foreign soldiers are here," Anic said. "They are killing everyone."

Lhana shook her head. "No. Not everyone. They're taking the girls." She looked to Lilae. "Have you seen Risa and Jaiza?"

Lilae shook her head. "Hopefully they are with Pirin."

Anic put a hand on Lilae's shoulder. "We can't hide out in here. We need to make it to the forest. I know a secret way."

"He's right," Lilae said to everyone. "Is there a back door? The streets are filled with soldiers."

Maude nodded. "Yes. But, my husband—"

Lilae shook her head. "No time to wait for him. Let's go."

Lhana nodded. Her calmness was unnerving. Anic went to the back door and peeked out the small window above the door. He froze.

"What is it?" Lilae whispered. Everyone in the room fell silent.

Anic slowly turned to them. "They're coming around the front."

Lilae felt her heart race. She looked out the front window. There were soldiers coming to the door.

"We have to go now," Anic urged, reaching for her hand.

Maude let out a muffled yelp and hugged Stella close. "They're here!"

Lilae motioned for them to follow Anic. She drew her dagger. There were four men at the door. She would have to kill them all. She breathed in deep. Her face was set as she glared toward the door. "Lhana, go."

"Lilae," Lhana called. Lilae felt her heart pause at the look on Lhana's face. Her eyes were wet. She smoothed Lilae's hair and tilted her head down to kiss her forehead.

Lilae froze as she looked into Lhana's eyes. Lhana had never, ever kissed her.

Lhana hugged her. "I'm sorry. For everything. I'm sorry you had to suffer. I'm sorry I made your life harder than it already was. I've watched you for eighteen years, and I know, deep down in my heart, that you are special. You are going to save this world." She smiled a tortured smile as she stroked Lilae's cheek. "Kiss my girls for me, and tell Pirin that I love and forgive him."

Lilae caught her arm. "What are you doing? What are you saying?"

Lhana blinked away tears. "I'm saying… you need to live. Run, Lilae. Save our world." She pulled her arm from Lilae's grasp and took off her shawl. Her face settled into a focused look. They heard yells outside as a woman ran into the soldiers. Her screams trailed as some of the soldiers pulled her into an adjacent cottage.

"The people of the North are greatly feared. I never noticed until we began our travels. Seeing the separation always made me a little self-conscious about my inherited skill. You see, to my family, skills were for warriors. I always wanted to be a lady." Lhana rolled up her sleeves. Her eyes dilated, and she reached out a hand.

She met Lilae's eyes. "But there is no denying that we can do things that many humans cannot. This makes them fear us, even when we are the same race."

Lhana held out her hand to her, and her body did something she had never seen but only heard of.

Lhana Split. An inaudible puff of light made her into two of the same person. Both women let their arms down in unison, like twins but connected by the same mind. One pushed Lilae forcefully. The other ran toward the door.

Before Lilae could speak, Lhana's double ran through the front door and into the street. She pressed the door closed with her back.

Lilae gasped and reached for her. Anic grabbed her and dragged her away. "Lhana," she said in a strangled whisper. While her double was outside, Lhana watched Lilae with tears streaming down her face.

She felt her heart sink when she saw the soldiers grab Lhana's double through the small window above the door. She covered her mouth in disbelief and went limp in Anic's arms when Lhana's double was lifted into the air by her shoulders and run through with a sword. Lhana clutched her stomach and fell, just as her double did outside the wooden door.

She never even screamed.

CHAPTER 23

ONCE OUT INTO THE BACK ALLEY, Lilae fell to her knees.

For a moment, she was transfixed. The world around her stood still, and she heard nothing. Her voice was caught in her throat, and she felt such grief that she was unable to move. Despite never accepting Lilae as her own, Lhana was the only mother she had ever known. All of those years, Lilae had thought she was an ordinary human woman, when she hid a trait that was more rare than even the twins.

Lilae felt like she would vomit. Lhana's last words haunted her. Anic yanked her to her feet, and everything started to move fast again, the mixture of noises loud in her ears once more.

"Let's go, Lilae. Come on!"

Lilae shook herself awake, grabbed Anic's healthy hand, and dashed through the crowd of running people.

Maude ran into the crowd with Stella. Madness and chaos surrounded them. Lilae knew how they were feeling.

She had to shrug off the numbness she felt as she and Anic hopped over lifeless bodies of men and the elderly. Their blood was splattered everywhere on the dirt road. The soldiers rode through the village and killed as if it were for sport. Homes that she had seen built from scratch were now burning to the ground.

Lilae would not let them get away with it. Her hand tightened on the hilt of her dagger.

She wished Delia had waited to take her impromptu journey.

She knew they were after her. Delia's tales of evil beings who sought to kill her as they ran from village to village along with the years of training to fight filled Lilae's head. She was confused. She was frightened. These weren't bandits. These men were trained soldiers.

"Lilae! Anic!" Risa shouted from behind a mud-formed structure that stored food underground.

Lilae glanced at her. She was silent. Her cheeks were red and stinging as fury built within her. A horse stomped by, and she stabbed her dagger in the leg of the horseman. With a mighty yank of the dagger's handle, she brought him down to the ground. She was on his back so quick that he hadn't a chance to catch his breath. She grabbed his head and lifted it from the dirt. She slit his throat.

Lilae eyed his sword and then to her dagger. Her dagger was her weapon of choice, but she could do so much more damage with a sword. She tucked her dagger into her boot and drew the sword from its scabbard. It was heavy in her grasp and cool to the touch. The ring of steel was like music to her ears.

She ran a finger along the blade and closed her eyes. The cold steel was somehow soothing to the heat she felt within her. Lilae sliced through the air and got used to the feel of its hilt. The sword became one with her. She rested the blade against her shoulder and stood tall.

She glared at the soldiers around her. Lilae was ready to rip those men to shreds. She saw that few of the royal soldiers were still alive; most of their bodies littered the dirt road. She shook her head. *Amateurs*, she thought. They were trying their hardest to fight the foreigners off. They were doing a horrible job.

"Anic, take my sisters and hide." She couldn't risk him getting hurt.

"My sword hand is injured, but I will protect you with all of my strength."

"My sisters, Anic! Protect *them*." With a nod, he ran toward the twins. Then he paused.

"What about you, Lilae? What are you doing?"

Lilae ignored him. She walked right into the chaos.

Focus activated.

Evasion ready.

Her Accuracy changed her vision. The power within her begged to be released. Dust encircled her as she entered the battle. Her eyes squinted to keep out the dirt. It was a hot day, and she was ready to stop hiding.

Lilae was ready to make a scene.

She glanced back at Risa and Jaiza once more and tightened her grip on the sword's hilt. When she turned back toward the fight, men were already reaching for her, ready to simply collect her like the other girls.

Lilae shocked them all when she ducked beneath their hands, knelt onto the ground, and started taking them down, one by one. Her muscles were ingrained with moves that she had practiced for years. She shrugged one off to clash steel with another soldier. Her long legs kicked a soldier in the chest, and she crushed his throat with her boot while swinging an arm to make a fatal gash in another's head.

She didn't care. Villagers watched in horror and shock. She wanted them dead. She wanted their blood. Every spray fueled her.

Risa and Jaiza saw her in action and felt the blood drain from their faces. *This* is what it was all for. This is why they trained *every day*. They looked to each other and spoke a multitude with just one look. They ignored Anic's calls to them to run.

Jaiza stood first, and Risa followed. Jaiza weaved through the crowd, and Risa did the same. Risa and Jaiza had to obtain their weapons from fallen soldiers and entered the crowd with such vigor that more of the villagers began to slow down their running to watch in awe as the girls made a stand. Risa was a marvel. She was quick. Her face was one of stone as she made a path for her sister.

The three girls were fighting side by side to eliminate the threat. The remaining Parthan soldiers finally saw their chance to make a dent in the swarms of intruders.

Lilae barely noticed that they had joined her. She fought as though in a daze. The blood stained her face like never before. It calmed her. It quenched the blood lust that had been building for as long as she could remember. Her ears were hot. Her face was hot. Every part of her body throbbed as she killed.

She sliced through soldiers two at a time, so quick that they were stunned by her skill. She sidestepped the charging of one soldier. As he ran past her, she sunk the blade into his wrist, slicing his hand off. He screamed and wept as he held his bleeding arm to his chest. His eyes regarded her in bewilderment.

The soldiers never expected such a resistance. The scene urged the other village folk to try and defend themselves, as well.

Lukas and his fighters arrived and tried their best to help. They had only been in Lowen's Edge for a few months, and Pirin had already taught them valuable moves that helped refine their fighting styles.

Lilae could have gone for hours with her eyes closed but then she heard Risa scream out in pain. She broke free from her trance and saw that Risa had suffered a stab wound to her belly. A soldier stood over her, his body… flickering.

Evasion.

These were not normal soldiers.

Lilae's eyes widened, and she kicked the man whom she had been fighting in the jaw as forcefully as her body would allow. Blood spurted into the air as his head was knocked back. He fell to the ground, and she rushed to her sister.

Jaiza was surrounded. She couldn't keep the men from closing in on her.

"Risa! Jaiza!" Lilae heard Pirin call to them. He shot an arrow at the soldier above Risa.

Yes, Lilae smiled. Lilae was relieved that he was finally there.

Pirin never could have guessed that his venture to hunt would return to a massacre of their quiet village. He had his bow and arrows ready and began to take down anyone who was in his path.

He made eye contact with Lilae. "Lilae! Get them out of here. Go!"

Seven men fell to his arrows before he was out, and he then took to the dirt path with his waist knife and pure, brute strength. Pirin plowed through the crowd with the grimmest look Lilae had ever seen on his face. His chest heaved as he breathed in the thick hot air and put his mind in focus. It was the very day that he had been preparing for. When his entire family would have to finally face real danger and fight back. There was no more running.

As Pirin killed one with his knife, he grabbed the fallen man's sword in one fluid motion. The soldiers toppled over as he went through, punching their jaws and cutting their limbs off. He was a machine of strength and would never grow weary.

Pirin was a master at battle, and they recognized that immediately. It was quite a scene watching him effortlessly make his way through the fight to his daughters. The soldiers ran at him, and he cut them down as if they were children running at him with wooden swords. They didn't have a chance against the former captain of the Aurorian palace guard.

By then, the men had summoned their forces, and the four of them and royal soldiers became outnumbered by the dozens. Lilae saw another group of soldiers enter the town square. One was cloaked and didn't run toward the fight like the others did. While she fought, she noticed something strange about their leader.

He calmly surveyed the calamity in the crowd, and their eyes met. Lilae took pause when she saw his face in the shadows of his black cloak's hood. His head tilted as he looked at her, and she was sure she saw a smile stretch across his face. Lilae's heart pounded nearly out of her chest when she saw his gaze go from her to Pirin.

Lilae gasped, sensing that he was *not* like the others. She began to run toward him when he darted toward Pirin.

She blinked.

He was so fast that all she saw was the dust that he left behind. Her eyes tried to catch up as he swept through the crowd almost completely unseen, leaving dead bodies in his trail. Lilae tried to catch up with him to kill him, but it was too late.

"*Pirin, look out*!" Lilae shouted as loud as she could over the noise, but to her own ears it sounded like little more than a whisper. She started to run.

The leader was upon Pirin too fast and, with a wave of his hand, she watched him produce a glowing dagger that stabbed Pirin in the back. The blade went through his chest. Lilae's mouth opened to scream again, but her voice was stuck in the pit of her stomach like a lump of coal.

She gulped through the sharp pain in her throat, the tears sprouting without restraint. The man who had slewn the only father she knew had vanished; her eyes caught those of Pirin's. His eyes were locked on hers and then to his true daughters', as he fell to his knees in shock.

With a scream of anguish, something happened. Her body seemed to dash in flashes toward Pirin. The wind swept through her hair, and her eyes were dried by the speed at which she moved. She was upon him so quickly that she nearly crashed into him. She caught Pirin in her arms, and Jaiza ran over to meet them. Anic held Risa back as she screamed. She clutched her wound and tried to wrench free from his arms.

Lilae's face drained of all color as she looked down at Pirin's stab wound. She felt the tears drip and furiously wiped them off. She couldn't let Pirin see her cry, not now, but they kept falling. She moaned. Jaiza cried as well.

Pirin grabbed them by the backs of their heads and pulled them into him. "I love you, girls. Never forget it." He coughed.

Lilae and Jaiza nodded. Pirin wiped Jaiza's tears, and his eyes met Lilae's. He looked worried. He knew he was dying.

"Lilae." His voice came out hoarse. "You need to know."

Lilae leaned in closer. "What is it, Father?"

Pirin smiled weakly. "That's it, Lilae. I am your father. You always knew."

Lilae and Jaiza shared a look. Lilae faked a smile. "I know. You're like a father to me. You're the only father I've ever known." She tried to keep her voice steady.

Pirin grabbed the back of her neck and looked into her eyes. He was serious. "I am your *real* father, Lilae. You are my blood. You are my daughter. Your mother," he coughed, "is queen of the Black Throne. I loved her before she was forced to marry the king."

"Father?" Jaiza made a face of confusion as she listened.

He shook his head. "Forgive me, Jaiza. It's up to you now… to protect your sisters."

Jaiza nodded and closed her eyes. The soldiers were closing in. The noise intensified, and Lilae knew they were coming for her.

Pirin held tight to the back of Lilae's head. The blood began to come from his mouth but his eyes were full of eagerness. There was something important he needed to say. "Lilae, listen. You don't have to…" He was cut off by an arrow that went through his head.

Lilae stared in stunned silence at the pointed end of the arrow piercing Pirin's forehead.

Jaiza screamed.

Something snapped within Lilae's mind as Pirin's body slumped in her arms.

"No!" she growled in disbelief. She beat the ground with her fist. She stared at Pirin's lifeless body. She felt such grief that it left her paralyzed. That was, until a soldier took a jab at her with his sword.

With a feral cry, Lilae caught the sword's blade in her hands and yanked the sword from him. Her hand bled profusely as she took the hilt and rammed it into his mouth with all of her might. He choked and reached for her, and she took a wild swing with the back of her hand. Bones crushed in his face, and he fell over. She stomped his face and heard a crunching sound.

She looked up. She couldn't breathe. Her face grew hot, and she felt her voice trapped in her throat as she swallowed back a flood of tears. Pirin's lifeless body lay at her feet. Jaiza cried over him in anguish.

Lilae's heart was broken. Everything was gone. She screamed so loud that groups of fighters turned to stare at her. She felt her blood boil as she beheld the death and carnage all around her. Those streets had once been clean. Blood and dirt covered everything now.

Her eyes were wild with grief and changed from the brightest green to black. Everyone stopped everything as the sky darkened to the color of blood, and Lilae looked into the sky as though she pleaded for something. Her heart pounded.

She felt delirious. Her father was dead. He had been her real father all along, and they had taken him away.

"I want him back!" She screamed to the sky. *Bring him back!* Lilae felt the tears spilling down her cheeks.

The sky as it began to turn red. The air grew hot. They began to back away slowly as sparks and lights began to dance in the sky. Balls of fire fell like rain, and everyone ducked in fear. Villagers and soldiers alike began to run in every direction to avoid being hit by falling fire. There was a roar of painful cries, no longer caused by fighting, but from people being burnt alive.

The scene was of utter chaos and destruction, even more than caused by the imperial soldiers.

Anic called for Jaiza to run as he tried to drag Risa from her place on the ground. No one was safe. As Risa, Jaiza, and Anic ran faster for the forest boundaries, Lilae turned to face the rushing horsemen. There were grim looks on their sun-scorched faces. She met the eyes of the closest horseman with a more sinister look of her own. They had ruined her entire existence. She refused to let them get away with it.

She soon became very sensitive to everything around her; she could feel the vibration on the ground from the horses' loud trampling. Everything became too loud in Lilae's ears, and she felt slightly dizzy. Her blood nearly boiled. She tried to control that sensation, harness it.

Lilae didn't hear the screams, just faint whispers from afar as the ground became smothered in flames, surrounding her.

"No, Lilae. Not now! Not here…" The Winds pleaded with her. They sounded miserable.

"Why not? Whoever you are… Why didn't you save him? Why have you forsaken me?" Lilae ignored their pleas, shoving them to the back of her mind. She felt no pain as the fire began to lick at her feet and cover her. Her body began to lift from the ground, and she smiled with relief. Tears dripped from her face. It was as though she was meant to fly. Her bare feet had nearly left the ground when something snatched her from the sky.

Chains clamped around her as though from an invisible hand. Lilae didn't have a chance to see what had done such a thing before her head hit the ground. The fire was immediately extinguished, and the sky began to turn blue once more. Her head spun as she lay on her back, the sun bright in her eyes.

"*Lilae*!" She heard Anic's frantic yell for her. She shook her head groggily; she was losing her grip on consciousness.

"Anic," she called weakly.

The sun's rays were suddenly blocked by the man in a cloak. He stood over her then knelt down.

"*Now,*" he whispered down at her, "I've finally got you."

With her last moment of lucidity, Lilae heard Anic yell once more. Then she heard Risa and Jaiza's bloodcurdling screams.

PART TWO

CHAPTER 24

LILAE WOKE UP FEELING as though she'd been drowning and desperately needed air. Pitch black welcomed her, and she was wet. She realized that she was sitting in a puddle and could hear water dripping near her head. Her face was wet and itchy, and there was a terrible smell invading her nostrils.

She felt the fear rise when she couldn't decipher where she was. She was cold and disoriented. Her stomach was empty and had a deep ache. She felt as though she'd been out for days. Her head hurt. Her hand had been sliced, and it hurt, as well. Lilae heard faint crying somewhere close to her.

"Hello?" she whispered. Her voice cracked painfully. She tried to clear it, only to make it worse. She grimaced at the pain and stared into the darkness. She strained to see ahead of her. All that she could see was black. The air was foul and scarce. She hugged her arms to ward off the cold.

Eventually, her eyes slightly adjusted to the darkness. A swinging torch in the distance provided a small beam of light.

The weeping continued without reply.

"Who's there?" Her voice was raspy now. Then there was the sound of men coming down a flight of stairs. She crawled backwards to hide, her back pressed against a cold wet wall of some sort.

The crying stopped. Whoever had been crying sensed the danger, as well.

Lilae clutched her chest and tried to suppress the anxiety that made her heart beat too quickly. She heard them approaching her, yet she still couldn't see them. She stopped breathing for fear they would hear her.

The ground moved, and she slid over to the left side. She instantly realized that she was on some kind of ship. Lilae gasped when her face fell against what felt like cold bars. She felt frantically all around her and realized that she was in a cage. She tried to stand, and it was helpless; the cage boxed her in. She froze in a crouched stance when a flood of light nearly blinded her.

"Lord Dragnor," he called to the other man who was searching the darkness for something. "That's the one." He stood before her and pointed.

She tried to shield her eyes and see who it was that spoke, but the light was too bright in her face. She wondered what the source of the light was; she'd never seen a candle or anything produce such brightness.

He reached through the bars and grabbed her jaw, tilting her head to get a better look. She felt fear first, then rage. She wanted to rip out his eyes. Her jaw clenched and he noticed.

"Wait at the door," Dragnor said to the soldier.

"Yes, sir," he said and returned to the staircase down which they came.

Her face was released, and she moved away from the light. It followed her.

"What are you called?" Dragnor locked eyes with her. When she didn't respond, he broke the gaze and stepped back. "What is your name? Or are you deaf?"

"Who are you?" Lilae snapped back, but she realized what he was. A Shadow Elf.

The light began to dim slowly, giving her a better look at Dragnor. He was very thin and long, with perfect posture. She noticed that the light was coming from the palm of his hand. Her eyes met his as he paused looking her over.

"Who I am is of no concern. All you need to know is that your life will be cut very short if you don't do as I tell you." Dragnor bent down to her level on the floor.

Lilae trembled. She was afraid of his eyes. They were so dark that they were nearly black. The shape of his eyes was odd to her, as well; thin, with their corners turned down and the crease absent from his eyelids. His skin was dark like ash. He had long, straight, black hair that hung over his shoulders.

There was a tattoo across Dragnor's face, symbols that she'd never seen, stretching from one temple to the other. The tattoos were illuminated, as well, as if a light shone from inside his body.

Memories flooded Lilae's mind. She remembered the chains that had caught her. How impossible it had seemed, like they had come from nowhere and ripped her from the sky. Now, she understood. His was the last face she'd seen before blacking out that day. Lilae had watched him dart across the crowd like a shadow of death.

Lilae remembered the glowing dagger that he had withdrawn from his cloak, how it had penetrated Pirin's chest. Lilae gulped back new tears. The memories twisted her gut in agony.

"That show you put on in Lowen's Edge is all the proof I needed that you are The Flame. We've been waiting for you for a *very* long time." Dragnor stood and folded his hands behind him. "Wexcyn has great plans for you," he told her in a whisper.

Lilae withdrew from him, sitting in a corner. She pulled her legs into her chest and shook her head. "You killed him!" she cried. "If you try to put your hands on me," she said, wiping her cheek. "I will kill you. I swear it."

"Such empty threats are of no concern to me. You might live if you learn to hold your tongue."

Lilae refused to let him see the fear in her eyes, though she felt fear like never before. Dragnor raised his hand to examine the room, the light from his right hand slowly going over the darkness around them.

Lilae looked around, nervous about the silence. There was a row of cages filled with terrified girls who were all around her age.

Only she was alone; every other cage was stuffed with Parthan villagers.

"Jaiza? Risa?" she called out raggedly. Everyone turned to look at her. "Risa! Jaiza! Are you there?"

No one answered Lilae's plea.

"Where are my sisters?" She turned on Dragnor. Her face reddened with anger.

Lilae feared the worst. Anxiety took over. She remembered hearing their screams. She had failed them. She began to cry out with grief. She beat the bars with her hands as she howled through her tears. Just thinking that they were dead made her stomach twist into hundreds of knots.

They didn't have to fight with her. It was all her fault that they had ever been in danger. It was her fault that they were dead. The guilt ate away at her. It twisted and burned like hot coals. She didn't care about anything else in the world.

"Quiet!" Dragnor shouted at her. "I will not warn you again."

Lilae didn't feel too much concern for herself in that moment.

"*You killed them*!" she screamed at him and rushed to the bars of the cage. The impact shook the cage, and threads of light lit the room. Her glare cut into him.

Dragnor grinned. "Yes, little flame. Show me more of that divine power."

The lights danced around her, flashing around the entire room. The other girls gasped and scrambled toward the walls to get as far away from Lilae as possible.

Lilae no longer cared. She let the light shine around her body. She would no longer suppress it. The power was nearly blinding, thrilled to be free. It wrapped around her, making her look like a goddess. Her secret was out, and she wished Dragnor would try something. She pictured herself ripping his throat from his body, wiping that smug look off of his face. She wanted to pound his face into mush.

But Dragnor just looked at her with a small grin. It confused her that he seemed so self-satisfied. She had wanted to frighten him.

A second later, Lilae regretted her actions. Dragnor grabbed her neck through the bars, and his thin wiry fingers dug into her flesh. She felt his palm heat across her throat, and she felt something course through her veins, burning her from the inside out. Her eyes bulged. It felt as though he were ripping out her very soul.

Lilae felt those familiar powers that she had been keeping secret abandon her. She started to panic, willing them to stay put. She tried to harness them mentally, but Dragnor was stronger than she was. It was as if he had done this before, and Lilae was a mere novice. He held on tighter, and the power bubbled from her core. It flew to Lilae's veins, and she felt as if it were soaking out of her pores.

Lilae shook violently. She bucked and fought it, but Dragnor sucked her power into himself. Defenseless, she saw into the dark slits of his black eyes once more, and her entire body grew frigid. She saw evil in his eyes. Hate. Malice. And satisfaction that he had finally made her wish that she hadn't been born. The pain went into her very soul.

He released her. Lilae doubled over and squirmed violently, waiting for the intense pain to subside. It was like nothing she had ever experienced. She felt hollow. Only the pain remained. Everything else faded into the darkness.

"When we reach land, offer as many as you can to the Sisters," Dragnor ordered. "Sell the rest." He stared at her as she cried out in pain. He played with her flames, throwing them from one hand to the other, taunting her. Her face lay against sour-smelling water as she wept in misery. He looked to the soldier who waited silently by the door.

"Take this one directly to the emperor." Then they left, as the other girls' silence was filled with Lilae's agonizing cries.

CHAPTER 25

THEY TRAVELED FOR DAYS days along worn dirt paths. The sun was setting, and it had begun to grow colder. The valley was filled with thick forests that reached up the mountains and down to either side of the Silver River. It was a straight path to Tolrin, where the fairy colony was hidden. Ahead, Liam and the Order could see a clearing from the thick forest.

Liam rode Midnight, stuck in his own thoughts. He had withdrawn from the group ever since learning about Lilae. Her face was in the forefront of his mind. No one bothered him while he was in his reflective mood. Rowe and the others were too tired from the journey; the constant chatter from Wilem and Jorge filled every moment of the day.

Liam could only envision Lilae in danger. There was a bond there that made him feel as though he already knew her, and he wanted to protect her with everything he had. He knew he had to hurry and lighten his load. He was ready to meet her and deal with Wexcyn as a team.

Liam and the others approached the gates to the north of Kyril. It was sectioned off for the fairy territories. The Silver River ran through, breaking into hundreds of canals and brooks. The river glowed and shone beneath the crescent moon. The sky grew darker, but they couldn't afford to set up camp. There wasn't much time, and it was much too dangerous in this area.

The northern lands of Kyril were wild and full of beasts and mischievous folk. Dryads and nymphs could steal horses and belongings while you slept. At least the other side of the gate was guarded by Nani's kin. He urged Midnight forward and heard faint footsteps behind him.

Liam paused and turned to look behind him to see the pale, almost luminescent faces of Vars and Ved, the fairy sentries.

"Brothers," Liam called to them with a grin.

They both looked at him and returned the grin, their hands on the hilt of their swords. They looked similar, with short purple hair and slim faces that had soft, almost feminine features. Their eyes were friendly. Each wore the blue of their kingdom and light silver armor. They each carried a sword and a long bow with arrows made from the bark of their enchanted mother tree. Their wings glittered in the moonlight, and they were barely taller than Liam's chest.

"Brother," Ved spoke. He drew his sword which caught the light of the moon, making it shine. The fairy Enchant was similar to the Tryans', however, instead of making their weapons glow, it made them glitter.

Vars did the same and pointed his at Liam. They clinked blades and laughed.

"It's been awhile," Vars said as he approached Midnight, petting him.

Liam dismounted his horse and stood before them. The others waited quietly behind, watching. "Indeed, not more than a week at home, and I'm already back on the road."

Ved raised an eyebrow. "And what is it this time? Why do you travel with the Order?"

"Haven't you heard?" Liam sighed with a shrug. "The Realm Wars are brewing."

"Aye. We've more than heard." Ved nodded. "Two colonies have been rampaged by Shadow Elves already. You'll find there are more than just my brother and me patrolling the road to Tolrin these days."

Midnight lowered his head in bliss as Vars stroked his soft, black mane.

"And why have you come this way?" Ved asked.

Vars smirked, nudging his brother. "Everyone knows that where Liam goes, trouble follows."

Liam picked up that he was only half joking. "It's a long story." He held up his hands. "Trust me, you don't want to hear it all. Looks like I need to travel lighter, so I am dropping off my healing troupe and my soldiers. They will be glad to protect your people."

"*Protect* our people?" Vars tilted his head. "Like we need a bunch of career Tryan soldiers crowding our colony."

"Our forests are well equipped for keeping outsiders out. You know that." Ved tipped his head toward the darkness of the forest that surrounded them. "The other, smaller colonies, like Vickston and Terinton, weren't built as strategically as Tolrin."

Vars sighed. "I wouldn't take anything for granted anymore."

Liam knew the dangers of their wilderness. The Attguart Forest was one of the most dangerous places in their realm. He also knew that that wouldn't be enough to keep Shadow Elves away.

"I know, I know. You can protect yourselves, but it doesn't hurt to have extra help. Am I right?"

"Looks like *you'll* need the protection. There are many who support the rise of Wexcyn and the Forgotten Ones." Vars glanced at those who waited on their horses. Their faces were grim and covered in dirt and grime. Everyone looked tired.

Liam lifted a brow. It was surprising to hear a fairy sentry speak of the Forgotten Ones. "It seems they aren't quite forgotten."

Vars shrugged. "You forget our history. Fairies take pride in the world as a whole. Not just our realm. We are spread throughout each realm. We do not claim a realm anymore, Prince Liam. Our fallen Ancient will always serve as a reminder of the strength of our people. She may no longer be an Ancient, but she still watches over her people. Would you have forgotten Pyrii, if the Tryans had lost the war?"

Liam didn't reply. He knew how sensitive fairies were about their own Ancient. She had died, and yet an Ancient's energy could never be completely extinguished, and she had returned as what they now called their Mother Tree.

Liam had always found it interesting to read about the fairies. Tryan were all created with the same features. Black hair. Blue eyes. No variations. On the other hand, the humans and fairies were created with much more diversity. He found that beautiful. It was too bad that their Ancient had sacrificed herself to get rid of another evil Ancient in the Great War.

"Well," Ved cut in, relieving some of the tension. He motioned to the river. "You and your men better have a drink from the river."

Its glowing waters rushed calmly downhill, a beautiful sight at night.

"You can't sleep in our forests, so it's best that you replenish your energy now and continue traveling until you reach the city."

"Thank you. We greatly appreciate it." Liam motioned for the others to dismount.

The men didn't hesitate. They were all desperate for a drink.

"I'm serious, Liam. Do not stop. Do not sleep."

"I understand," Liam said with a nod. He walked to the river. When his hands entered the water, it was cool and instantly gave him energy. He cupped a handful of water and drank. The refreshing liquid entered his body and sent him into a euphoric state. It was as if his body had been given something it had been craving for years and was finally satisfied.

"Yes, fill a flask while you're at it. It'll keep your vitality at its maximum as you travel,'" Vars added.

Liam filled his water flask with the river's fluid. He stood and secured the flask in the bag tied to Midnight. All the while, the fairy sentries stared at him. "Well, it has been a pleasure. But we must press on."

Ved put a hand on Midnight's head, stopping him before he could take a step.

Liam looked to him, perplexed.

"Wait." Ved's face had become serious; it made Liam feel uneasy. Ved looked around as though checking that they were alone. He seemed on edge. Liam had never seen him behave in such a way.

The fairy sentry spoke in a whisper. "Be cautious on your journey. I cannot speak too much on it, but you are being hunted. Perhaps our queen will fill you in."

He checked for the hilt of his sword. He had known those fairies since he was a boy. You couldn't tell by looking at them, but they were thirty years older than Liam and still appeared to be his age.

Ved put a hand on Liam's shoulder. He drew closer to his ear. "Obviously, there are those who would wish to see you dead before you reach your destination."

"There is unrest in our world." Vars lifted himself into the air and motioned around him. "With the opening of The Barriers, everything will change."

"Do not forget that we are bound to this soil, we can feel when something is amiss."

"And we know something is coming," Ved finished.

"What is coming?" Liam raised an eyebrow.

"Something darker than you think," Ved said.

All traces of a smile left Liam's face, and he thought a moment about what they had said. He knew the Dark Nation of Nostfar was on the rise, but he somehow felt that what Ved alluded to was more sinister. He couldn't imagine what could be worse.

"Tell me what you mean."

They heard something crunch in the woods, and Vars and Ved's ears perked up as they listened. Then they both looked to Liam then to Sona and Rowe and began to return to their posts.

Vars and Ved shared a look. "We believe the Ancients are keeping something secret."

Liam tensed. "What?"

Sona walked up and put a hand on Liam's shoulder. "What's wrong?"

"Rumors," Vars said, walking backwards.

Ved nodded, but his look to Liam confirmed otherwise. "Just rumors."

He wished he could read the minds of others like his mother.

CHAPTER 26

"WELCOME TO AVIA'TORENA," A SOLDIER SAID TO LILAE AS HE UNLOCKED HER CAGE. THE RUSTY METAL DOOR CREAKED AS HE OPENED IT. "Your new home," he added with a sarcastic smile on his sun-darkened face. His large hand reached for hers.

It had been what felt like weeks, and Lilae was more than ready to leave that dreaded cage and the wretched smell of that room. She took his callused hand and climbed out of the cage. Her feet were bare as she stepped onto the wet, slippery deck.

The other prisoners watched as she was taken away from the filth. Her limbs ached from sitting in such an enclosed compartment for so long, but she walked behind the soldier, anxious to get away from the ship. She desperately craved fresh air.

Lilae squinted when she emerged from the low deck, the sun shining bright and hot onto her face. She took a deep breath of the crisp, clean air and let it out slowly. Her savory moment didn't last long. It ended when she saw Dragnor waiting for her above deck.

Seeing him in the daylight didn't make him appear any less sinister. Dragnor stood out amongst everyone else, and the soldiers seemed to avoid being close to him.

He wore a long dark cloak, its hood hanging behind him. His hands were folded before him, and his eyes pierced into hers. His gaze was so unsettling that she had to look away. She would never forget the pain he had caused her. Lilae still wasn't sure exactly what Dragnor had done, but she feared the worst. She had been too afraid to use her power, to see if it would still come if she called it forth. All she remembered was the pain.

"Shall I take her to the litter now?" the soldier asked Dragnor.

Dragnor nodded and turned to lead the way.

As she walked behind Dragnor, a troupe of soldiers surrounded her as though she were a dangerous wild cat. Lilae felt numb. Everyone stared at her as she followed them to the litter. It was a box-shaped device that had a cloth covering and four poles extended beneath it, two in the front and two in the back.

"Sit," Dragnor commanded.

Lilae sat down inside, and Dragnor joined her. She was unsure of what to do, so she sat completely still, afraid of what was next.

Lilae was surprised when the litter was slowly lifted by eight men and started to move down the path from the ship's dock.

There were tall tropical trees all around, their branches thin with large waxy-looking leaves. She saw fruit hanging from the trees, large melons like she'd never imagined. The sounds of animals and birds chirping all around them was deafeningly loud. The trail led up a steep hill that cut through the dense jungle.

After hours of lush jungle, the trail stopped before a gate that extended as tall as some of the trees. Lilae looked high up at the top of the gate and its sharp pointed edges.

At the clearing, Lilae saw that they were entering a highly populated city. Lilae beheld the lower land of the mysterious Avia'Torenan palace. The city was the size of four normal-sized kingdoms. This city was one that she couldn't have imagined in her dreams. She felt oddly excited. Something in the air made her hopeful.

Thousands of people walked in every direction. They filled the street. There were people in large groups laughing at puppet shows. Women danced to small bands in shadowed alleys to an audience of captivated men. Prepubescent children ran after one another with big smiles on their faces.

Lilae had thought that she was well traveled, that she had seen it all. She had never seen anything like this. Large four- to six-story homes and shops were clustered around the city. People had hung their clothes to dry from lines high above the ground.

Small gardens were situated around the streets, breaking through the chaos to provide a little space of beauty. Small children played in the streets with wooden or stone toys, and women congregated near the fountains. Their heads were covered in colorful silk scarves and jewels, and their babies were strapped to their backs.

The smells of freshly baked sticky buns tantalized Lilae's nostrils. She felt her stomach grumble. She and the other girls aboard ship had been served only stale biscuits and tree nuts. There had been an occasional bowl of gruel or porridge with scarce traces of potatoes. Lilae longed for a real meal.

She looked at the children who carried long sticks of grilled meat sold from carts along the street. She was mesmerized by the woman who carved lamb from a turning spit and served generous portions of the sliced meat to paying passersby on flatbread. Lilae looked away, tormented. She saw Dragnor watching her and looked out toward the city again.

Lilae leaned forward. "My god." The palace stood in the far distance. Like a piece of art from the museums of Halwan, the palace sat grandly upon a raised plateau. Squat in the center of the city, its towers reached high toward the clouds. Composed of gold and white stone, it had five tiers with statues and gargoyles built into gleaming golden siding. The sun fell behind it, making it appear like an enchanted place.

Lilae was amazed that there was a balcony that wrapped around each floor and had jeweled doors that caught the sun just right, making the entire palace shimmer as if magic surrounded it.

Could such a beautiful place be so bad? Lilae thought. She knew that looks could be deceiving. There was something about the people, though. They didn't look oppressed. They looked oddly… happy.

"Do not speak when you meet the emperor, unless I tell you to." Dragnor's voice broke Lilae from her thoughts.

Lilae turned to him. She scrunched up her nose in annoyance and forced a nod.

Dragnor sat across from her and observed her expression. She felt uncomfortable whenever he looked at her.

"You're afraid," he stated, his small eyes searched hers. "Rightfully so. You should fear me. I detest your very presence. It may have taken me eighteen years, but I've finally found you." His lips turned into a grin that betrayed the coldness in his eyes.

Lilae would love nothing more than to claw at his face.

"I give you credit, though," Dragnor nodded to her. "You try so hard to hide it, but I can see right through you. You cannot fool or beguile me. I know all about you. I've studied you for a long time. Out of all of the Chosen, you are the one *I* will use. You have put me behind on my plans. And trust me… You *will* pay for that with blood." He suddenly gave her a nod that resembled respect. "You've hidden quite well, but you cannot put off your punishment any longer."

Lilae gave him a curious frown. "Why do you hate me so much? What did I do to you?" She spoke so timidly, she didn't feel like herself. She was now uncertain of everything and felt fear all of the time.

Dragnor's grin faded. "You were born. That's why I hate you. You were born to ruin the uplifting of my people. Shadow Elves had to settle for the scraps of this beautiful world. While you worthless humans got to keep the cradle of civilization, my people had to migrate to Nostfar, the most desolate and unforgiving realm of this world." He leaned in closer to her. "And, I didn't tell you to speak."

Lilae looked down at her hands. Her heartbeat started to speed. Her cheeks burned with bottled-up rage. She was so frustrated. No one had ever limited her speaking her mind or opinions. Such domination over her would be difficult to accept.

"It seems that your death is not the will of my master, *yet*. However, if you give me an excuse, I will not hesitate. Nothing would give me more pleasure than to rid the world of your meddling. Whatever Elder hid you this long must have grown senile for leaving you unguarded. No matter. You are without power now and nothing more than a dirty human."

Lilae felt her face heat. This is what the other races thought of humans. Why such disdain? The humans had never harmed anyone.

"Now, let's discuss your purpose here." Dragnor lifted her chin so that she looked into his eyes again. "You are going to secure our claim over Eura."

"I'm not stupid. Why would I ever help you?" She pursed her lips, expecting to be struck across the face. She gulped as she was forced to look into those dark pupils. She shivered at his touch. His cold, thin fingers felt abnormal on her skin.

"That was your last outburst. Do you want to see what happens if you try that again?" He sneered, and Lilae noticed that two of his teeth were pointed like fangs.

There was silence between them. Her chest rose and fell as her breath quickened. She looked away as his thumb gently brushed her cheek and then glided over her lips. He pushed her to the other side of the small space. He moved away from her on his seat and looked out the window.

"I would like nothing more than to be rid of you. But it seems the alliance wants something from you. You will obey." His eyes shot to hers.

She wanted to ask questions, but she had been warned. She assumed that the alliance was Wexcyn and Inora. She wondered why Dragnor was taking her to Avia'Torena. She had already heard about the emperor throughout her travels, and she had studied Avia'Torenan history. The tales all spoke of the emperor as a tyrant who killed anyone who opposed his rule.

The anxiety continued to rise in her throat. They were getting closer and closer to what could quite possibly be the end of her life. She almost didn't feel the rocking of the litter as the men carried them along. She didn't want to meet him. He was responsible for all of the killing in Eura. No other king campaigned like the emperor.

"So this is what you will do. I have taken your power. Therefore, you will forget your role as the Flame."

Lilae slumped into her seat. It was true then. Her power was gone. She had tried to deny the fact that she could no longer feel it circulating within her. She felt like an empty shell. She fought the tears that threatened to sprout from her eyes. She would never let Dragnor see her cry. It took everything in her to uphold that vow.

"As princess of the Black Throne, you are now a war prisoner. There is something we want from Auroria, and hopefully they want you back enough to exchange with us. If not, you die, and we'll simply devise a way to take it from them. Clear?"

She nodded and yet her fingers clutched the cushion on the seat beneath her. She tried to keep a blank face, but she could feel her cheeks pale. Whatever they were trying to exchange must be extremely important. They wanted to use her. She wouldn't let them, no matter how much she was threatened. Wexcyn could not win this war.

"You follow my instructions… you live." He pointed a finger at her. "You stray from any of my instructions… you die a long, painful, death. And believe me; I know how to make you suffer, and I will take great pleasure in doing so." He looked off.

Lilae believed his every word. Still, she couldn't help letting her mind wander to all of the ways she could kill him. It was a habit. Pirin had taught her always to have at least three plans in mind.

"Good." He didn't speak another word the rest of the ride.

She feared what was next. Dragnor had literally revealed more to her in a manner of minutes than Delia ever did. She was a princess. She remembered Pirin revealing that her mother was queen of the Black Throne, and yet it didn't click what that meant. Lilae finally understood what it meant. Still, she couldn't see the king and queen still wanting her back after eighteen years. Why would they give away something of value for her life?

Lilae looked out the window, not really seeing anything. She was trapped in her thoughts. Delia had to know, and yet she steadily brought her closer and closer to enemy territory. She couldn't believe Delia. She wanted to yell at her for leaving them when they needed her the most. She wanted to pour out all of her sorrows, but above all, she wanted to hug her and never let her go.

Hours went by and yet the men never took a break as they carried the litter through the kingdom. They placed it on the ground in the palace's pristine courtyard. The stonework was impressive. The stones sparkled under the sunlight; Lilae was overwhelmed with amazement, and she hadn't even gotten inside the palace yet.

Then her thoughts returned to the emperor. Lilae imagined him as a dark, evil man with cold eyes and even colder fingers. She imagined him being like Dragnor. She didn't know how she would do what Dragnor wanted. She *had* to find a way out of this. She was still too numb to devise a plan. She still didn't really care.

Lilae had lost everything. What else was there to fight for?

The awaiting soldiers didn't waste any time pulling Lilae from the safety of the litter. Two men quickly dragged her to the palace. She barely had a chance to examine its immaculate beauty. Everything seemed to be jewel-encrusted and adorned with gold.

She went through a golden door and walked along marble floors; everything seemed to glitter, as if power pulsed within the very walls and floors. Lilae was surprised that such a wealthy place existed. She couldn't imagine why they warred with Partha when it seemed that they already had enough riches.

They stopped before an open entryway, and she heard talking inside. Lilae gulped. She was being led directly to the enemy. The man who had conquered more than half of Eura waited inside that room, but while Dragnor stopped before the door, she was quickly pulled the other way.

She sighed with relief. It was not her time to meet him just yet.

CHAPTER 27

EMPEROR KAVIEN STUDIED THE MAP. Eura was vast, and soon, it would all be his. He traced the path he would take his army or millions to conquer the rest of the world. Only the Black Throne of Auroria stood in his way. Their alliance with the Northwest of Eura was annoyingly strong. For years it had seemed impenetrable to his people.

He would find a way.

Artero, a general in his army, waited patiently. He offered advice when he saw fit and kept quiet when Kavien was in deep thought.

"How are the new recruits doing, Artero?"

"Splendidly, sir. They are faster learners than I expected. Of course, many are afraid, but we will break them of such a trivial emotion."

Kavien nodded, still studying the map. "Good. Very good." He knew it could be done. He wrote notes on a piece of parchment and sighed. "This is going to be a problem." Kavien pointed to a wide ocean positioned between Kyril and Eura. "How will the Tryans get over here? Sure, the fairies can fly, but they can't exactly carry the Tryans over the Cair Ocean, and no one would dare take ships onto those waters with all of The Barrier beasts."

Artero glanced at the map over Kavien's shoulder. "Fairies have airships. It can be done."

A servant entered the room and whispered something to the general. Kavien heard footsteps as someone entered the room and closed his eyes in annoyance.

"Emperor."

"Go away."

"Kavien," Dragnor began, clearing his throat. "This is important."

"That's *Emperor* Kavien to you. Do not forget your place, elf." Dragnor's voice only made Kavien more irritable. The Shadow Elf's presence always put him in a foul mood. His hate for him ran deep. "Make it quick." He didn't even give him the courtesy of turning to face him.

"You might want to pay attention… *Emperor* Kavien."

Kavien stood to his full height, taller than any man in the realm, and an imposing figure by anyone's standards. He was muscular, without an ounce of fat on his body. Grown men were too afraid to look directly into his face.

He turned around, and Dragnor entered the room with Sister Eloni. His scowl quickly dissipated, and he gave her a nod of respect. Most people would bow to her, but he was emperor; he bowed to no one.

Sister Eloni smiled and dipped slightly in returned respect. She glanced over his shoulder, and her smile widened. "Always preparing. So detail-oriented. I like that about you."

"It is my job, Sister."

She folded her arms before her, much like Dragnor was accustomed to doing. She eyed him for a moment. "Well, I have good news. I also have a request." The long draping sleeves of her purple robes billowed as she pointed to the door.

Kavien raised an eyebrow. "What is it now? More funding for your 'temples'? I thought you could turn sand into gold or something."

"Outside is Princess Lilae of Auroria. The Flame. Dragnor rid her of that title by removing her abilities."

Kavien's eyes narrowed. "What?"

She nodded. "You heard me correctly. Dragnor has been a good servant, and he has retrieved her for us."

Dragnor didn't flinch at being called a servant. His face never betrayed what he was really feeling. Perhaps it didn't bother him.

Kavien knew how powerful the Sisters were. He also knew about Dragnor's past with the woman. How she had trained him, in the Underworld.

"It may have taken him eighteen years to do it." Sister Eloni looked at Dragnor pointedly. Dragnor never met her eyes. "But he has been a success, nonetheless."

"Perfect," Kavien said, nodding. He walked over to his chair and sat down. "I want to see if this plan will actually work." He wrote orders on a sheet of scroll and sealed it with wax. "Take this to Haro. I will not negotiate with anyone but the new king of Auroria."

Sister Eloni smiled. "King Torek was a hard man who lived for far too long. Let's hope his son has more sense than to deny us what we want."

Kavien shrugged. "I don't care if he does. Either way, I will exterminate those Northerners."

"Ah, emperor, perhaps it is not wise to underestimate them. We must have faith in Wexcyn's wisdom. He has had thousands of years to devise this plan. Even he knows that while the Northerners are the purest of the humans, they should not be trifled with lightly. They haven't kept the North secure all of these years with just their wits. There is real power there."

Kavien watched Artero leave with the message. After some thought, he gave a nod. "If it fails, I march my men straight to the black gates. I want my realm, and I am tired of waiting for it."

Her smile widened. "Why, of course. No one would dare deny you such a thing."

Kavien tapped his fingertips on the tabletop as he thought. The princess was here. Just one of his many enemies, she was supposedly the most vicious of them all. "Where is the girl?"

"She is being taken away to be branded and cleaned as we speak. I wouldn't think of presenting her to you as she is right now."

"I want to see her immediately after she is cleaned."

Sister Eloni nodded. "Of course."

She looked down at him, and he realized how, even as a small woman, she carried herself with such confidence. She was the head of the Sisterhood. Not even he knew all of their secrets. Besides that, some would say that Sister Eloni was Wexcyn's greatest supporter. Some said she was one of the few who were powerful enough to help him out of the abyss, the only prison where the supernatural could be secured. Kavien knew it to be true.

If only he had managed to get Sister Eloni and the other Sisters into the North, their plan would have been much easier to execute. Now, they would have to hope that the young king was either wise enough to realize when his opponent was stronger, or naïve enough to fall for what they were devising. Either way, Kavien would be ready.

Sister Eloni stepped closer. She wiped a hand across his desk and checked for dust. "You know, the Aurorian king took four wives before he died. When will you take a wife, emperor?"

"I have no need for one."

"I hear that the princess is quite mesmerizing and pleasing to the eye."

"Have I ever been taken in by a woman? I have more important things on my mind."

Her friendly smile seemed to twist before his eyes. Her own green eyes darkened as she leaned forward. "Good. That's exactly what I wanted to hear. Now, I give you Eura, dear emperor. When all is done, you give me the girl. Do not spoil her. She must be pure. She must be clean."

CHAPTER 28

LILAE TRIED TO WRENCH FREE as they tried to brand her left shoulder. The soldiers pushed her to her knees.

She sucked in a ragged breath as two men had to hold her down. One even placed his booted foot on the back of her neck to keep her in place. She felt the steel and winced. It felt cold.

The brand didn't hold.

They tried again. She felt the rod press to her skin and the heat fizzled, absorbing into her body. "Ha!" Lilae laughed triumphantly.

Lilae braced herself as the guard lifted her up and slapped her. She bit her lip, tasting blood. She licked the blood, and her lips curled into a smile. "As my dead sister liked to say, *you* hit like a girl."

"Hold her down."

They pushed her back to the ground, and she cursed to herself when she saw the brander pull out a blade. "I'll etch it into her skin. That'll surely wipe that smirk off her face."

Lilae sucked in a breath and closed her eyes. She would not give them the satisfaction of her screams as he dug the sharp end across her shoulder. She blinked away tears, and the guard who had slapped her lifted her face up. "How's that? Better?"

She didn't say anything. She only imagined scrapping the skin off of his face with that knife.

"You men better hurry. The emperor will be waiting for her."

She was taken down a long hallway and a steep staircase. Paneled walls gave way to stone, and they finally reached the harem. All the while, Lilae cursed the lot of them in her head. They handled her roughly. It was as if they hated her as much as Dragnor, for some crime that she hadn't committed.

Even through the lingering pain of her branded shoulder, Lilae was impressed when she entered the massive room. She shut her mouth and simply took it all in. There were dark stone walls and smooth marble floors that shined. Bright green vines stretched along the wall, and elaborate flower arrangements were placed everywhere.

A large pool of clear blue water sat in the center of the room. Stone benches were situated throughout, surrounding the pool and standing against the walls. A pallet of pillows and billowy cushions sat on a raised floor near the rear of the room, where tall torches lit the shrine like an arrangement of art.

A beautiful cage, Lilae thought with a frown.

She had arrived just as the other girls were leaving. In two lines, they filed out of the room. They walked past her, their heads bowed, stealing glances at the new girl. Lilae counted a dozen of them.

She wondered if they were the emperor's servants, but she feared the worst. Lilae knew deep down inside that they were slaves and gulped at the thought of what purpose they served for the emperor.

Once the room was empty, the soldiers left her in the care of two young women who were cloaked in silk. The fabric was wrapped around their waists and draped over their chests, tied and secured at their right shoulders, displaying crescent-moon brands of their own. They both had long black hair that was braided into two braids twisted together and secured by a brass band.

Lilae stood there, unsure of what was expected. They smiled at her. They had bright gray eyes, the first friendly eyes Lilae had seen in a long time. She almost let herself trust them. She wondered if she would ever smile again.

They both reached for a hand and led her to a room where there was a smaller pool of steaming water. One of the girls poured a thick amber fluid into the hot water, instantly making the room smell sweet.

The girls worked at taking off Lilae's tattered nightgown. She stood nude, covering herself with her arms, shivering.

"Step in slowly," one of the women told her softly. Her accent was thicker than any Avia'Torenan she had heard so far.

Lilae did as she was told and slowly sat in the steaming water. It stung at first, nearly scalding her, but she got used to it quickly. It danced around her, deliciously hot as she closed her eyes at the soothing feel of it.

It was bliss to get clean again, but never had she bathed in such luxury. When she opened her eyes, she saw that, while one of the girls was pouring oil into the bath, the other was pouring a scented purple salt of some sort. They stirred it with their hands, and she felt instantly relaxed.

Lilae didn't want to think of what had happened before this moment, nor of what would happen after. She just wanted to enjoy this one good moment.

Each girl took one of her hands and began to scrub her arms. Lilae nearly moaned in delight as she let her head rest on the edge of the bath. She savored the sweet relaxing scents and the feel of the sponges they used on her. They scrubbed her everywhere and then poured jugs of fresh warm water over her to rinse. They thoroughly cleaned Lilae's long mass of hair and gently combed through it. She was rinsed once more.

Lilae was wrapped in similar attire, starting with a long piece of silk that was wrapped along her body and tied at her shoulder. It hung loose to her ankles. Her hair was braided similar to theirs, and they dusted her face and exposed flesh with gold-sparkled dust. She had no idea how she looked, but she was glad that she now smelled pleasant.

Once the girls were done with her, she was taken a long way from the harem. They went through corridors, through secret doorways, up a narrow stairwell, and finally to a plush carpeted hallway that led to a large set of double doors at the end of the hall. The uniformed guards watched her intently as she walked past. Their whispers followed behind her.

Lilae was used to whispers. She ignored them, focusing on what was behind those doors. She held her breath as the doors were pushed open by the guards.

To her surprise, there was a woman standing inside. She stood there with a friendly smile on her face and her hands folded before her as she watched Lilae enter. Lilae knew her face. It was an off color. Pale, with a slight purple hue, as if she was sickly. Lilae's eyes narrowed. She had seen this woman in Lowen's Edge. She had met her eyes at the gates of the Garden District.

She had a youthful face, yet her white hair gave the illusion of her being much older. Her hair reached the back of her ankles.

"Oh," the woman purred. "How magnificent you are." She walked around Lilae, examining her. Her eyes went up and down Lilae's body, and she nodded approval.

"Remarkable. Oh yes, you will do just fine. I cannot believe the elf ever doubted you." Her smile widened. "He wants you dead. I disagree. I see the good in all things. There is something positive to be found in every situation."

Lilae stared at the woman. She was unable to think of something to say. Was she like Dragnor? *Could* she speak to this woman?

The woman's green eyes sparkled. She laughed. "Oh, yes. How rude of me, child. I am Sister Eloni. I am the head of the Sisterhood of the Fallen. It is lovely to finally meet you."

Lilae felt awkward standing there as the woman gave a slight bow to her. She wanted so badly to ask what exactly the Sisterhood was and why they always took the girls in each village.

"Believe me, it has been quite the task searching for you." She shook her head as if she were annoyed by the thought. "Extremely tricky." Her smile returned.

All white teeth, and yet there was nothing in her eyes that said it was genuine. Sister Eloni's smile was one that Lilae wasn't sure was, in fact, friendly, or had something hidden behind it. Lilae wanted to trust that smile; but the nagging feeling in her stomach that she had grown to trust warned her not to. So, she stood there. She would listen, she would analyze, and then she would react.

It irritated Lilae that everyone seemed to think that she was naïve.

Lilae put on a blank face. She would fill that role… be less threatening…pretend to be as empty-headed as they assumed she was. For now.

"But all of the searching and waiting was well worth it." Sister Eloni stood before Lilae. She held her arms and looked into Lilae's eyes. "All right, I know you are probably scared sick. You're probably still grieving your loss and unsure of what treatment you will receive here." She kissed Lilae's forehead.

Lilae held her breath. She couldn't help it. She couldn't stop the words that spilled from her mouth. "Who are you *really,* and why are you touching me?"

Sister Eloni covered a giggle. "You are a funny child, aren't you?"

Lilae wasn't smiling.

"I am the only one in this empire who comes with good news. I want you to be treated like a princess. I want you to be pampered and spoiled. You will spend your days with the girls of the harem, and they will teach you the ways of Avia'Torena." She held Lilae's face in her hands.

Lilae shivered beneath her fingers. The woman was wearing high-heeled shoes. She was short, but her shoes made her almost as tall as Lilae. *Odd,* she thought. She tried to pull her face away. Sister Eloni only held her tighter.

"Eura must be united. So I want your brother to see that, although a prisoner, you are treated well. He must see our goodwill. Isn't that worth all of the trouble? Isn't this realm's safety and security the most important thing in these dark times?"

Lilae chewed her bottom lip, his brows furrowed as she nodded.

"Good girl. We will be allies, you and I. Let us unite Eura and face this new threat of Tryans and Silver Elves together. How does that sound, love?"

She was confused. Sister Eloni was right, Lilae was afraid; she *was* still grieving. She grew anxious as she thought about everything that had happened and what was yet to come. Then, Sister Eloni took her hand and placed her own above it.

"It is the right thing to do, Lilae." She looked down at Lilae's hands. They were still healing from her fight in Lowen's Edge. She had sliced her hand on a soldier's blade, and it had become infected from lack of care aboard the ship. Almost absentmindedly, Sister Eloni ran her finger along Lilae's palm, and the wound began to heal before her eyes. As if it took no effort at all, Sister Eloni looked off and sighed.

She scared Lilae. Lilae decided not to further antagonize her. This woman, who looked like barely more than a child, held power. Not just the power to heal, but power over Avia'Torena.

"But remember, Lilae, you don't really have a choice. After all, Dragnor has stolen your power. I'm afraid you are no longer of the Chosen class. You are nothing more than a silly girl who thinks she can question me. No Lilae, you will mind your tongue. You are a slave until your parents give us what we want." She pulled a stunned Lilae along by her newly healed hands. "Come, let's introduce you to your new master."

They walked across the room to a set of doors. Lilae glanced back at her with a frown. Sister Eloni simply smiled and pushed the door open slightly, then left the room.

Lilae stood there in silence for what felt like forever.

"Come in," a deep voice called.

Lilae gulped and hesitantly reached a hand out. She didn't want to meet the emperor. She wasn't ready. She wanted to turn and run, but she had nowhere to go. Instead, she pushed the door open all of the way and stepped inside.

It was some sort of study. There were large bookcases that stretched high to the vaulted ceiling. Long, squat tables lined the wall; piles of paper were scattered on the shiny, polished surfaces. Open flamed torches lit the room.

Lilae stepped from dark hardwood flooring onto plush ruby carpet. Her toes sunk into the soft fibers, and she smoothed her feet over it curiously. It was nice. She'd never felt anything like it.

A man stood in the shadows. She couldn't make out any of his features until he stepped into the dim light.

Lilae felt her eyes widen as she beheld the emperor. Her throat went dry. Her lips parted.

He leaned against a table with his arms folded in front of him "Well. Well. Well." He seemed pleased by what he saw before him. He stood to his full height and towered over her like no man had ever done.

She'd rarely seen a man as tall and muscular as the emperor. His face was unique. He appeared to be a mixture of the swarthy eastern folk and the pale westerner. The emperor's skin was a perfect olive color.

Lilae realized that she was staring in disbelief and checked herself. She looked away. He was *not* what she was expecting. She couldn't help glancing at him again.

He stepped closer, and she felt her body tense.

"Emperor Kavien." He gave a slight bow with his head. "Now, what is your name?"

"Lilae."

"So, finally, I meet the notorious Flame." He paused in front of her. "Oh, wait—you may no longer claim that title. No matter. You don't need such distractions anymore."

She flinched when he ran a finger along her bare shoulder and sniffed her hair.

"Splendid. They did warn me that you were pleasing to the eye. But no one told me you were this beautiful."

Lilae grew tense as he lingered near her neck. She could feel his warm breath on her exposed flesh. Having Kavien so close made her heart race. She waited silently, afraid to move.

Emperor Kavien took one last breath of her scent. "Here's how things are going to work," he said softly, pulling away from her. He held her by her shoulders, turning her to face him.

Lilae nearly gasped when she looked straight into his face. He was younger than she had envisioned and handsome… Handsome in a way that was frightening. He had striking gray eyes that made her heart quicken. Before that day, Lilae had never seen gray eyes before, and his seemed… abnormal.

They were such a bright gray that they were nearly all white. His hair looked soft. It was a short, wavy bronze with a shiny sheen. To Lilae, Kavien looked to be as near to perfection as the man from her dreams, and yet he was utterly different.

There was something else about him. Something that made her wish she could hide from his gaze.

"You are now mine. I own you, and you shall do as you are told. You will spend your days with the other harem girls and learn the ways of Avia'Torena. And hopefully, King Ayaden will meet my demands and come to Avia'Torena personally to fulfill them. Either way, you are mine, and you will do whatever pleases me. Forget whoever you were before this moment, for you are now my property."

Lilae looked away from his eyes. Her heart thumped in her chest. She tried to keep herself from blushing, but his presence made her feel out of control. She tried to focus on the open window that looked out to the city. The sky was so blue. The clouds were so white. Still, she couldn't help but glance back at him. She bit her bottom lip and looked away again. She had never felt so powerless. It seemed as though her body refused to listen to her orders.

Kavien smiled and used a long finger to turn her face to look at him again. "Pay attention, dear." His eyes searched hers, and she could feel herself holding her breath. "You needn't worry. I have a great many slaves, and I assure you, I treat them all quite well. However, there is no excuse for disobedience. You disobey me, and you *will* be disciplined."

Her lips trembled when she looked at him. Despite his calm voice and face, Lilae sensed something frightening from him.

"*Ah,* fear." He rubbed his cheek against hers and sighed. "I can smell it on you."

Lilae continued to look away. His presence made her mind all fuzzy.

Kavien smiled again, a handsome smile, yet it couldn't compete with the man's from her dreams. "Oh, Lilae," he said throatily. "It's such a pleasure to find that for a filthy Northerner, your beauty is without rival. I admit, I expected you to be a savage like your people, but it seems your travels may have refined you."

He grabbed her by the back of the neck and led her toward a large shiny door. There were figures of women with large headdresses ingrained into the gold. "You will be an excellent slave. I just know it."

Her feet lightly scrambled across the floor as he forced her forward. "I am going to keep a close eye on you, so I need you to be by my side."

Lilae looked at the large double doors in terror, and he removed his hand from the back of her neck. Her eyes grew large, fearing the worst, as the emperor pushed the doors open.

Inside was yet another massive room. There was a large ivory and gold canopied bed that sat high from the floor with plush furnishings. Beside it was a large chest adorned with rubies and a brass lock. A tiger skin rug lay before it; the tiger's head was still intact.

The stone walls were hung with colorful drapes and tapestries so expensive that she suddenly realized that she was standing at the doors of his private quarters. Lilae couldn't imagine sleeping in the same bed as the emperor, but she had a feeling that that was where the conversation was leading.

Lilae glanced at him, noticing that he was watching her reaction.

"Don't flatter yourself, slave. I assure you, I do not want you in that way." She shot a glance at him, expecting to see him smiling. Instead, he looked at her with a serious face, one that observed her own emotions. "I will keep a close watch on you until the Aurorian king sends word." Kavien led her toward the bed, and her eyes darted to his when he stopped her before the chest. He opened the lock and held the lid open for her.

Lilae's eyes widened. She realized that he wanted her to stay in the chest. There was nothing but a pillow and a quilt inside.

"Climb in. It's small, but it's perfect for my little treasure."

CHAPTER 29

KAVIEN WALKED THE OUTER corridor of his private quarters. He frowned at his thoughts. He was confused. Lilae wasn't what he expected. She wasn't what he was told.

He had been told since he was a boy about those evil Chosen, and yet he thought back to the look of fear in her eyes and felt as if he'd been lied to. She looked at him as if *he* was the monster.

He shook his head. He shook off that feeling. There was a plan. Kavien would stick to it. *But… the fear, in Lilae's innocent eyes.* It bothered him, even though he knew it shouldn't.

"*Are you becoming soft, Kavien*?" the voice asked. "*Are you going to let a little girl ruin our plans*?"

Kavien shook his head. He tensed. The voice had returned. He felt his body grow cold.

"Leave me alone," Kavien said through clenched teeth. "I told you. I can handle it without you."

He heard a low growl and fell back into the stone wall of his torchlit corridor. His pulse quickened.

"*I command you. You do not command me.*"

Kavien stood with his back to the wall, his mouth agape as a thick, foul-smelling smoke rose from the stone floor. Kavien wanted to run. There was nowhere to go. He could be reached, anywhere… at any time. Instead, he froze against the wall and waited for what he was sure was the end. Had he done enough to earn favor, or had his failings condemned him?

The black silhouette of a man emerged from the ground before him. He nearly reached the ceiling. He held a spear. He had no face, only eyes. He dripped black blood and shifted closer to Kavien, ever so slowly.

It was rare for Kavien to feel fear, but now he felt it encompass his body. Yellow eyes opened and glared at him. "*I grow stronger. Every day. When I rule this world, do you want me to remember you as a supporter or a traitor? You are my heir. Do not make me choose another.*"

Kavien held his breath. "You know I am at your command, my Lord." His words came out like a stutter, and he bowed his head in embarrassment.

The shadowy figure drifted closer and sniffed him. Kavien noticed how the figure smelled like sulfur and pitch. He grimaced and looked away. He couldn't bring himself to confront those eyes.

Just as quickly as he appeared, the shadowy figure was ripped from before him. Kavien came to his feet, relieved. It was unbelievable how strong Wexcyn was becoming. He needed to focus. He needed to follow through with the plan. If he did not, there would be no greater or more intimidating judge for his actions. Soon, Wexcyn would invade the Overworld, and all of their days would be dark.

Kavien smoothed his hair and breathed in relief. He regained his composure and resolve and made his way to the Temple of the Moon.

***

The Sisters were expecting him. Once Kavien reached the Temple of the Moon, four women, covered from head to toe in purple robes, met him at the stone gates. They opened the gates and led him into the quiet courtyard. Lines of women walked by, chanting a soft song that reminded him of the ladies in his village when he was a child.

The sun was setting, and the fragrant Yuvoria flowers filled the air with their toxins. Kavien breathed in deep their citrus-scented aroma. It instantly relaxed him as he followed the women along the black walkway.

The temple was an intimidating structure. It was perfectly square with large black windows and ivory stone walls. The outside was deceiving. The temple was much larger than it appeared. There were catacombs and tunnels underground that spread along the entire city. Beneath their feet waited thousands of Sisters, preparing.

Inside the large brass-barred double doors waited Sister Eloni.

She stood in the center of the silent entryway, her robes floating as she hovered above the ground. In public she would stay grounded, but in the privacy of her home, there was no need. She was not human. There was no need to pretend amongst her kind.

Kavien stepped inside, and the women closed the doors behind him, leaving him alone with their leader.

Sister Eloni floated over to him with excitement. She circled him, sniffing him. She groaned with pleasure. "He has been here, hasn't he?" she asked with a wide, white-toothed smile.

Kavien nodded with a grimace. He was annoyed that she continued to press her face to his clothes, breathing in Wexcyn's scent. He wanted to go back to the palace and burn the clothes.

She finally pulled back, clapped her hands with glee, and laughed. "Wonderful. I am so pleased." She came around to face him. "It seems my work is successful. He is getting stronger every day. It won't be long now."

"He is. Which brings me to ask you, where is your sense of urgency? Why isn't the Storm dead yet?"

"I would like to offer him to join us, first." She said it matter-of-factly. "He is one of the most powerful people in the world, after all. He can help us defeat the Silver Elves. It should not be hard. The Silver Elves dislike the Tryans as much as the Shadow Elves."

Kavien rolled his eyes. "We both know that won't happen. This Tryan prince needs to die. He cannot be allowed to make it to The Barrier. I would like Kyril's fate to be secured."

Sister Eloni smiled. "I can handle it. You will have one less realm to worry about. I assure you."

"I want you to pay him a visit. I want you to find him and kill him."

Sister Eloni's smile faded. She straightened herself up and looked at him. "I already have someone to take care of it. Either he will be brought to us as an ally… or he will be dead. We cannot lose."

Kavien gave her a hard look. "I want results."

"It isn't as easy as that, emperor. Such things take time and preparation. None of the last batch of girls was a sufficient vessel. I had to sell most of them in the city."

"I don't care. Use one of your own. You have plenty, don't you?"

"One of my own?" she repeated.

Kavien stepped closer, towering over her. He looked down into her green eyes. "You use humans like cattle. Why can't a few of your kind be sacrificed for our cause? It would be an honor for one of your girls, wouldn't it?"

She regarded him for a moment and finally nodded. "As you wish." She smiled again. "Look at you. Young Kavien is taking charge. I like it. I remember when you were just a boy. Dragnor had to whip you *good* a number of times." She laughed, and his glare silenced her. "I apologize. I only meant that he trained you quite well. You needed discipline. Everyone needs discipline. Look at you now. What respect you command just with your presence."

Kavien was losing his patience. There was nothing more he hated than to be reminded of his childhood. He could remember when Dragnor took him from his family just fine. Sometimes he wondered if he was really the lucky one or not.

"So quiet this evening," Sister Eloni said to him. She shrugged and turned toward the three dimly lit hallways behind her. "This way."

He followed her down the center hall. The ceiling suddenly vaulted high into the sky. He glanced into the other two halls as he passed by. He'd never been down either of them. For years, he had avoided visiting Sister Eloni. The things she did even made him uncomfortable. Now, there was no choice. There was so much pressure on him. Seeing Wexcyn reminded him that this was the time for action.

Sister Eloni pulled out a wand. It was made of bone. He wasn't sure what creature the bone came from, but it was thin and nothing fancy. One might look at it and think nothing of it. It was always handy and hidden in the folds of her sleeve. She swirled it as they went into the hall, sealing the entrance. She waved it again, and two young women quickly flew over to her from the other end.

They landed and bowed before her. They both lowered their hoods. With heads low, they spoke in unison. "Yes, honored Sister. You called?"

Sister Eloni stopped, and Kavien did the same.

"Names." Sister Eloni folded her arms before her.

"Tanvi."

"Adna."

He looked down at the young women. They were of low rank, merely apprentices. Their hair was chopped close to their scalps. Over the years, it would be allowed to grow as long as their ankles, displaying their advancement in the ranks.

Sister Eloni tapped both of their heads with her wand, and they came to their feet. They were now mindless. She glanced at Kavien, no trace of a smile on her face. "Which one?" she asked in a voice as cold as the air in that narrow hallway.

Kavien gulped. He did not like this part. He had no choice. He examined the girls. They levitated before him, their eyes glazed over with white clouds. They were both so young. He hated that they were little more than children, thirteen at the most. His shoulders slumped, and he nodded to the one on the right. Adna had perfect skin and full lips. Her beauty was against her this night.

Sister Eloni nodded. "Good choice." She waved the wand down, pointing its tip to the ground.

Tanvi rested her feet on the floor, and her eyes returned to green. She was awake. She looked at her friend and swallowed hard. She looked nervous.

"Take her, child. Bring her to the ceremony room, shut the drapes, light the candles." She paused. "You know what to do, right?"

Tanvi nodded.

"Good, go then." She motioned the girl forward.

Tanvi grabbed the hood of Adna's robes and pulled her along in the air. Like a kite, Adna's body floated along as her friend tugged her along.

"Wait," Sister Eloni called. Tanvi paused, horrified that they had changed their mind and would now use her as a vessel. She looked over her shoulder with large, frightened eyes.

"Try not to spill any of the blood onto the floor. I'd hate to lose even a drop."

The girl nodded. A look of alarm came to her face as what she would have to do settled into her mind.

"And lick the blade clean. That part is very important. All right?"

The girl nodded. Kavien was uncomfortable. He couldn't believe what he had asked that girl to do. He couldn't believe just how low he had stooped to please others.

"Good girl. It is your lucky day." Once she was down the hall and out of their sight, Sister Eloni looked back to Kavien. "And you, my boy. Go on, and wait in the Room of Calling. I'll bring you your results in about an hour. How's that for urgency?"

CHAPTER 30

THE SKY HAD BEEN DARK FOR DAYS. They were deep in the Attguart Jungle, the fairies' first line of defense against intruders. The trees were alert and watching.

No one had slept since they'd entered. Such a thing would have been suicide. The ground itself was alive. It heaved and rolled like waves. They remained on their horses, tense, hoping that they wouldn't be sucked in like quicksand.

Their only defense against the elements was the small troupe of fairy healers. Rowe and Nani were steady at Liam's side. Sona rode just behind, with the men and women of the Order. Tuvin tried to lighten the mood with his lute. He sat on his horse and played with his eyes closed. The melody only made them wish they were at home with their families.

It was pitch black in that jungle, but as long as Nani and the other fairies continued to light the way with their glowing wings, everyone would be fine.

Sting flies buzzed around them, waiting for a chance to rip into their exposed flesh. They craved a blood meal, and the scent of Tryan and fairy blood tantalized them. The sting flies had translucent wings that were lit much like Nani's. Their sharp tails were equipped to sting and suck the blood from their prey.

Liam batted them away, trying to see the dark path. The jungle that led to Tolrin was laced with a dark Enchant that was set to deter any strangers or unwanted guests. Liam hoped that Nani remembered the way home, for any wrong turn could lead them into an eternal nightmare or death.

"I never thought the fairy colony was in such a creepy place," Wilem mumbled in disappointment. "Look at this place. Where is the sun?"

"It's too dark here," Jorge whispered. His eyes struggled to see ahead of them, as he and Wilem rode close behind Liam. "It smells funny. I'm tired. I'm hungry. I don't like it."

"The fairies are protected by this forest," Liam explained. He dug in his saddle pack and handed Jorge a piece of dried meat. Jorge accepted it from across the horse and frowned at it.

"I want real food."

Wilem snorted a laugh.

"You have any more of those apples?" Jorge asked.

Liam sighed and looked over at Jorge. "No."

Jorge took a small bite of the meat and grimaced.

"Once we're in the colony, you'll see how beautiful their home is. It will be just the way you imagined it and more. I promise. We'll have tables full of delicious food prepared for us. Warm beds. Bubble baths."

Wilem made a face at Liam. "I'll believe it when I see it."

"I just want to get out of here alive. My mom always said the fairy village was only meant for fairies. Why exactly are we going there again?" Jorge asked, taking another bite of the meat.

Liam exchanged a look with Rowe.

Rowe chuckled. "You remind me of a certain someone." He grinned at Liam. "Always so cautious and worried. Don't worry, lad. We'll all make it there in one piece. You'll be running and playing in the sun soon enough."

Jorge looked skeptical but remained silent. He handed the rest of his meat to Wilem, who ate it in one bite. Liam started to laugh when he heard a whistling sound.

Nani paused. She held up a hand and listened. Liam tensed as he tried to see through the darkness ahead of them.

One of the fairy Clerics fell from the sky. Nani began flying backwards to Liam. Her wings flapped quickly, so fast that he could barely see them. The light of her wings went out, and Liam and Rowe heard her scream. An arrow shot through the darkness and sliced Nani across the face. The sound of her startled scream filled the forest.

Liam gasped and rode ahead. The Order and spread out into the darkness, making a circle that protected Liam and the heir to the Raeden throne. Liam blanched when he saw what had caused the sudden chaos. A wyvern flew above them. A Shadow Elf sat in its saddle. And behind that Shadow Elf, who grinned down at Liam, a swarm of wyverns lifted into the sky. Each had its own elf, and they held their bows pointed down at them.

"Nani!" Rowe shouted, and he and Liam both sprang from their horses.

Wilem and Jorge shivered as they listened to the screams as arrows were shot into the heads of the soldiers surrounding them. They rode closer to Liam, afraid to be alone while arrows zipped past them.

"I knew it!" Jorge exclaimed. "We *are* going to die!"

"Shut up! You'll lead the monsters right to us," Wilem ordered in a frantic whisper. He leaped from the horse as it was shot in the rear. The horse squealed, and Wilem pulled Jorge off just in time. The horse collapsed with a loud thud.

Rodev ran toward them. He waved his hands frantically. "Prince Liam! It's a trap! Go back. Go back!"

Liam and Rowe looked to each other. "No. I must get Nani." Liam continued to run. Rowe followed. The air was thick and putrid and pitch black. To their dismay, the ground felt slimy and squished beneath their boots.

"Something's out there, sir. Stay back," Rodev insisted as he came to stand with the other men in the Order. They all drew their swords.

Liam's heart raced. It grew silent, and Liam made his sword glow brighter. It emitted a yellow light, and he slowly moved it around to better see their surroundings.

Nani broke the silence, her wings buzzing, as she flew into Liam. He saw her small face bloodied by a thick gash in her cheek. He saw the terror in her eyes by a quick flash of light from an explosion erupting behind her.

Liam wrapped his arms around her as they fell to the ground.

"Wilem!" Nani called as she reached out to the frightened boys. "Run! Run!" She repeated frantically.

Rowe ducked down beside them. Arrows zipped past, and the flames from the explosion raced to burn them.

Liam had to think fast. "Sona!" He shouted and reached for her. She dove from her horse and rolled to him. The commotion was deafening, as the army scrambled to arm themselves and prepare for the threat.

Fire. The perfect revenge, since Vleta had killed scores of Shadow Elves with her own flames.

Rowe knelt down, his eyes wide from watching the approaching fire. Liam squeezed his eyes shut. There was a series of explosions all around them. Shards of broken tree branches flew past; one sharp piece slashed Liam's cheek before he covered them all in his shield. The bubble of energy encompassed them as the fire blazed all around.

Wilem and Jorge curled into balls to shield their heads. Sona stayed close to Rowe, looking up as the fire licked and fought to penetrate the shield.

The screams of those whom Liam missed tore at his very soul. His gut wrenched as he listened to those dying soldiers. There was nothing like the sounds of those being burnt alive. He would never be able to get those screams out of his head.

The others were lucky. They couldn't feel the heat blanketing them. Nani looked into Liam's face, channeling her energy to him so that he wouldn't pass out again. Liam lay back, his head against the muddy ground, as he tried to focus. He tried to calm his heartbeat and breathing. His energy was channeled into the shield, yet it was difficult to control.

Liam felt Nani's cool fingertips press into his temples and opened his eyes. Realization hit them all, and Nani felt her heart break when she saw the tears in Liam's eyes. They flowed silently as he thought of all the men and horses perishing in the fire as they sat there, safe from the danger. He tilted his head upward to look to where they left the horses and saw nothing but red and orange fire. The gold of the flames ravaged everything.

"Focus, Liam," Nani whispered, wincing as she started to feel the heat try to enter their shield. "Or we'll all die." Her voice cracked, and she nestled her head into his shoulder, hiding her own tears.

They sat like that for what seemed an eternity. The fire finally began to die down, and Liam was able to release the shield. He called a storm to quench the flames. He cursed himself for not being able to do both tasks at once. Otherwise, he could have saved some of his men.

They huddled together as the rain soaked them. Cold and shivering, they looked in awe at the destruction all around them. Midnight nuzzled Liam's shoulder. He was safe. He was the only horse that had survived. It was his bond with Liam that had shielded him during the fire. They were connected. A bond between a chosen animal and a Tryan lasted forever.

"What was that, Liam?" Nani asked, her face twisted in confusion.

Liam cupped his face in his hands as he sat there, utterly defeated. He looked at her with reddened eyes that were full of pain and hate.

"Wexcyn is behind all of this. Can't you all see that? Don't you all know what is happening?"

"Don't speak the name of the traitor, lest you to draw his attention." Everyone felt their bodies shudder as a voice called from the darkness. They all held their breaths in terror.

Liam could hear Jorge's soft cries. It grew even darker, until they could barely see each other anymore. A bitter cold wind swept through, stinging their faces.

As he welcomed whatever spoke, they heard a low growl. Then it sounded as if hundreds of feet walked toward them. Liam's resolve began to waver as he heard the sounds grow closer. He could barely see his own hand before his face and felt as if whatever was there could see him perfectly clearly.

"Liam," he heard Nani call softly. "Come back."

Liam stood his ground. His eyes narrowed as he tried to see what approached. The growl didn't sound like any animal or person he'd ever heard. It had an unnatural tone. He swallowed hard, and out of the darkness he saw a figure stand before him.

Liam's mouth opened as he looked up at the being. It was composed of nothing but shadows that flickered and reached out. It was as if many shadows had been combined to create this one being, and its eyes made Liam's skin crawl. What good was his sword against a shadow?

"Liam," Nani called again.

"Liam?" He heard Rowe's voice, and it seemed to be growing farther and farther away.

Liam looked down and gasped, seeing that his feet were still but that the ground passed by steadily beneath him. Liam looked up, dumbfounded.

"What are you?"

The being's face moved closer to Liam, and he couldn't help moving his head away. He smelled burnt flesh and sulfur, and it made his stomach twist.

"Elder Drefen." The being spoke in a low voice that sounded hollow and distant. "I would have been your guide, if your mother hadn't petitioned for your caretaking. It seems you are still ill-equipped for the task. Still, I have watched over you, from a distance."

Liam felt his voice catch in his throat. Drefen's face was like a nightmare, the faces of spirits shifting and looking back at him. He took a step back.

A real Elder. In its true form.

"We are death collectors. And soon there will be much death. We will separate the dead from the living as best we can. But the Elders are few now, and the dead are many. We fill this land now, for it is dying, along with everything in it."

The other Elders sniffed him, and he felt their hands touch him curiously. Their whispers to each other were too low to be understood but filled his ears. Their hands felt cold and sent violent shivers through his entire body.

"Not even the Ancients could have seen what is coming. Wexcyn has a great many weapons. One of his most sinister is upon us. She won't be easy to defeat."

"I don't understand." Liam hugged his arms to keep warm, as the other Elders started to back off. He still shivered, despite the warm night air. He wanted their hands off of him. "Who are you talking about?"

Silence.

"I already have to worry about Wexcyn and Inora. How can I face another enemy right now?"

"Do you think the Elders are the only beings free of the Underworld? The Underworld is open and rising to this world. Remember that whatever you face, it is because Wexcyn has put it there, to *slow* you down. Make it to The Barriers. Now."

Before Liam could ask more questions, the Elders faded into the darkness. He was left with a lot to think about as he walked back to the others.

CHAPTER 31

NANI COVERED HER FACE WITH her small hands. "They're dead! We cannot bring them back. Do you know what *shame* this will bring me?" Tears fell from her face.

Liam slunk down to his knees. Not only were the soldiers of the Order burnt to ashes, but so were the healing fairies. The stench of death had welcomed him as he stalked back from his discussion with Elder Drefen.

His cheeks were reddened, as were his eyes. Rowe sat silently at the edge of the clearing, glaring into the darkness of the jungle.

Wilem and Jorge stood near him, too afraid to relax.

Sona put a hand on his shoulder. "Liam."

He shrugged her hand off and came to his feet. He wiped his face of the wetness and looked up into the sky.

"Which way did they go?"

Sona frowned. "You don't mean to follow them?"

He gave her a look that made the color drain from her already pale face. "Who is going to stop me?"

Sona stepped back. "That's not the plan. Let's be reasonable. Nothing good will come of you following those Shadow Elves."

"That is the point. I want to punish them for what they've done. I want to teach them that nothing good will come to those who harm the people I care about."

Sona put her hands on her hips. "You're not thinking clearly, Liam."

He brushed past her. "I am thinking more clearly than I have in a long time. Stay with the children, if you are afraid."

Rowe came to his feet. He held his ax at his side. Liam watched him walk over and nodded in approval.

"Are you sure?" Liam asked.

"Let do this, Liam. Let's show those bastards who they are dealing with." His grip on his ax tightened. His eyes darkened. "I know what I have to do. Forget vows."

Liam looked into Rowe's face. He knew that look. He had seen that look in Rowe's eyes the night they were attacked years ago. The night Liam had seen Rowe do something… extraordinary.

All humor had drained from Rowe's eyes. The Order was his family. And they had just been murdered. Liam clicked his tongue, and Midnight strutted over.

Nani flew over, as well. "What are you doing?"

Liam met her eyes. It made his stomach twist into knots to see her in such grief. "Stay here. We will be right back."

Sona frowned at them. "They went east. Follow them, if you are so anxious to get yourselves killed."

Liam ignored her.

Rowe did as well. He rolled his shoulders. "Ready, Liam?"

Liam nodded and stood before Rowe. "Ready."

With a flick of his wrist, Liam brought up his enchanted barrier shield. It enclosed Liam and Rowe into its protective bubble, and he waited.

Rowe's Tryan glow brightened. It multiplied so much that rings of light began to run up and down his body. The light was so bright that Liam closed his eyes.

Rowe was a brute. He was extremely good at killing people with his bare hands and his ax. He was not one for flash or bragging, always hesitant to use more than necessary.

Rowe was proud to be a brute. However, Rowe was also a Legacy. His entire clan had died years before, passing centuries of Tryan abilities down to him.

Rowe was not one to be messed with.

Even behind his eyelids, Liam could see the light grow and grow and braced himself. And in an instant, their bodies were catapulted east by Rowe's light. Like lightning, they cut through the trees. Liam opened his eyes to see the landscape flash past him at such a speed that all he could really decipher were colors.

Green. Brown. Black. The dark jungle passed by as they sped miles ahead. He glanced back at Rowe to see him completely focused.

Liam looked ahead and readied himself. His jaw was set. He would make those elves pay for what they'd done. Perhaps now would be the time when he could finally see who was behind their plots. Who led them? Was their Chosen one in Kyril? He hoped it was so. He could already taste the satisfaction of killing the Shadow Elf named the Seer by prophecy.

His eyes widened when he saw light up ahead. Fire. Campfires.

"Slow down," Liam said quietly, and Rowe did just that.

Rowe's eyes opened, and, with a final burst of speed, he landed them right in the center of the Shadow Elf camp. They hadn't the time for Liam's usual meticulous planning. Liam had one thing on his mind: he wanted their blood.

Chaos and commotion rose to his ears as the Shadow Elves emerged from their tents in surprise.

Liam let the bubble dissolve, and his eyes went black. His sword glowed red. Rowe waited patiently behind him. He knew what Liam was doing, and he waited.

Liam called forth the lightning and grabbed it with his sword. A rope of currents extended from his sword like a terrifying whip. He swung it at them with a cry of rage, and the electricity shocked anyone in its path. Once he was done with the first round of elves, Rowe tightened his grip on his ax. His hawk-like glare caused the remaining elves to stumble if for but a second.

They tore through the camp like death itself. They were untouchable. Liam had lost all caution. His grief and rage fueled him as he swept through the hordes of elves with electric fury.

Bodies burned and convulsed beneath him. He stepped over corpses toward the command tent. *Who is behind this*? Liam wondered.

"You shall see," The Winds chimed.

Liam nearly stumbled at hearing the voices again. It had been so long. There was a quiet sense of relief to have them return.

The tent was close, and Liam felt the tension steadily rise. He heard the screams behind him as Rowe ripped through scores of elves with his enchanted ax. Liam knew Rowe could handle himself. His eyes were fixed on that canvas tent. The glow from inside promised him that he was finally about to find out who was sending those Shadow Elves to his realm.

What he saw when he stepped through the tent flaps made him stop mid-step.

"Oh," a woman said. "It's you."

Liam's jaw hung. He knew that woman. He had seen her before. In Oren. In the temples. She was a Sister.

She made a face. "Why aren't you dead yet?"

"Sister Eloni," he said in disbelief.

Sister Eloni smiled. He knew that smile. He had always thought that it was creepy. How right he was.

"The one and only," she curtsied. "At your service, dear prince." She stood to her full height, which wasn't much taller. She always wore those platform shoes. "Come to pledge your allegiance to Wexcyn, have you?"

Liam lifted his brow. "What are *you* doing here?"

She shook her head, that phony smile plastered to her face. "I'm not really here, dear prince. That would be most unwise."

He tensed as her image flickered. She stepped closer to him. Her purple robes shimmered in the dim light cast by the torches of the tent.

"I finished my work in Kyril years ago. I'm afraid that realm is doomed."

Liam couldn't help the bewildered look on his face.

"Has no one told you? Raeden… gone. Versan… gone. Holden… gone. And yes, Oren will die as well." Sister Eloni folded her hands before her. "It seems to me that you are chasing a victory that has already been claimed."

Liam narrowed his eyes. "You're lying."

She shrugged and turned away. "Believe what you want. Oren will be no more in a few days' time." She wiped her hand across a map that was stretched across a round table in the center of the tent. It glowed, and the drawn rivers trembled. The pictures of trees rustled, and the mountains became clouded with falling snow.

"What have you done?"

She didn't turn to him. "I have made the world as it should be. Soon, the races will be forced to deal with one another. In one land." She held up a single finger. "Under one god."

"Why?" Liam eyed the Shadow Elf soldiers who waited in each corner. Their thin eyes never left him. "What do *you* have to do with anything?"

Sister Eloni glanced over her shoulder. She no longer smiled. "To let the strong rise and the weak fall." She turned away. "I thought that was obvious. I thought you were the smart one. You have already lost. I have the Flame. She is mine to use as I please. The Seer is mine. The Steel, well, he is unimportant since the Silver Elves will all be destroyed shortly. The Inquisitor shall be mine one way or another. Which side do you choose? You can fight for me against the humans, or you can die with the rest of your people."

Was Sona right? Should he have stayed back? He wouldn't have known what he was up against otherwise. He felt worried. She had Lilae. His fists clenched at the thought of what that woman had done to her.

"Who are you?"

Sister Eloni turned back to him then. Her smile was wider than ever. White teeth flashed before him. "I am the bringer of change. I am the destroyer of worlds. Soon Eura will fall beneath my feet, just as Kyril already has."

Liam's mind raced. He had heard the name before. Liam readied himself. He could sense that something was about to happen.

"You must kill her..." the Winds whispered.

She isn't really here. How? Liam asked them.

"Can't you see that, soon, you and your friend will be the only Tryans left? Who will you lead in this war if you are the last? It makes sense to come and fight for me. I would be glad to use you. What do you say? The emperor wants you dead. But I see the good in all. I would keep you alive and fighting for us. Come, Liam." She reached out toward him.

Liam pulled away. He watched her long arm distastefully. She was evil, and he now knew whom he was up against. The knowledge didn't comfort him. Instead, it made his stomach knot. Many people were going to die.

"Take my hand, and I promise you all of the glory that comes from serving Wexcyn. Come with me back to Avia'Torena."

Liam closed his eyes. He took a breath, and, with a powerful surge of energy, he shot electric currents to all four Shadow Elf soldiers. They fell to the ground with a zapping sound. Their bodies were burnt from the inside out so quickly that they hadn't the chance to scream. When he opened his eyes, Sister Eloni was glaring at him. Her face was red with anger.

"You have my answer?" Liam glared back at her. He lifted his swords tip to her image.

She ignored it. "I'm coming for you."

He didn't wait for a response. Instead, he left the tent.

"And I'm coming for your mother. How does that sound?" she shouted back at him. "You will regret this. That was your final warning!"

He ignored her. He was focused. He had seen his enemy, and he had confronted her. He stalked through mounds of dead bodies to find Rowe in a bloody battle with the remaining Shadow Elves.

"Rowe, let's go."

Rowe looked up. Blood and sweat trailed down his face. "What? But I'm not done yet." He caught two rushing Shadow Elves by their hair with his large hands. He slammed their faces together so hard that their teeth crushed with the impact.

"We need to go. Now."

Rowe growled with frustration. "Not until they are all dead."

Liam nodded. "You'll get your wish. But we must leave now."

Rowe used the momentum of his spin out of the center to slash straight through the bellies of three elves. He gave Liam a dangerous look. "You better keep your word, Liam." Liam nodded. Sister Eloni needed to die. He had to find a way.

Bringer of change. Destroyer of worlds. He wracked his brain, thinking about those terms, when it came to him. Years of study had filled his mind with many prophecies. He had never expected to come face to face with the Ancient of the Bellen race.

Liam stood there as Rowe catapulted them through the forest. The world had no idea what was coming. They spent their days preparing for what the prophecies promised would be times of darkness and destruction.

Liam did not really see the trees and mountains flash by. He knew what no one else could have ever expected. Their worst nightmare was already there.

CHAPTER 32

SONA, NANI, AND THE BOYS all watched in silence as Liam and Rowe returned. Liam couldn't look Sona in the face. It was surprising that she didn't look disappointed, as he had expected. She looked angry.

Liam nuzzled Midnight and felt slightly more at ease.

Wilem walked over to him. "What happened?"

"Are you all right?" Jorge asked in a soft voice.

Liam tried to force a smile, but whenever he looked at them, he only felt more worried. His plans were crumbling. He no longer knew which direction to go, and, to make things more complicated, he was responsible for two children.

He put a hand on their shoulders and knelt down to their height.

Both of their innocent faces were frightened and concerned. He couldn't believe that, after everything that had happened, they were worried about him. It made him want to protect them even more. He sighed and looked into their eyes.

"I need you boys to be brave right now," Liam told them.

Wilem nodded. Surprisingly, Jorge did as well. He didn't question Liam like he normally did. "We can be brave," Wilem said.

Liam gave a side smile. "Good." His smile faded. He tried to think of how to say what he had planned without frightening the boys too much. He felt even more pressure when Nani buzzed over. She looked over curiously. Her eyes were red from crying.

Sona still waited over by a tree with her arms folded. She made it clear that she didn't want to hear anything Liam had to say. He knew he'd eventually have to make things right with her.

Rowe stood beside Liam. Everyone waited.

Liam looked up at Nani. His face was serious. "In the Great War, the fairies did something very important, something that united them with the Tryans. They eliminated a race that sought to suck the sacred power out of all fairies. This race kidnapped fairies for years and, stealing their life force, used it to fuel their own power, to make them live longer."

Nani landed on her feet and pulled her legs into her chest. She wrapped her arms around her legs and shook her head. "No, Liam. Please tell me you're mistaken."

Liam swallowed the lump in his throat. Wexcyn had returned with a vengeance. He would not leave anything to chance. The Mithrani were back. The Shadow Elves were on his side. Now, he had brought back another fallen race. The odds were no longer in their favor.

Rowe lifted a brow. "What did you see, Liam? I only saw elves. What are you talking about?"

Liam looked up. "I'm talking about a powerful race that uses the dark arts. Like we use the gifts of the Overworld, these women utilize the power of the Underworld. They have no men, and they have no need for any. They replenish their ranks by turning other women."

Rowe gave an exasperated sigh. "Great. Just great." He paced back and forth.

Wilem moved closer. His blue eyes were wide with wonder. "What are they, Liam?"

Liam looked through the trees to the moon. "Bellens." He looked back to Nani, whose eyes were filled with tears of horror.

CHAPTER 33

AFTER ONE NIGHT OF HER tiny prison, Lilae became enraged. She had tried to sleep, longing to see the man from her dreams. Maybe he would be there waiting for her, to comfort her. Sleep never came. Only quiet tears.

She wondered when Emperor Kavien would return. She hadn't heard him enter the room all night. She had kept quiet for long enough. She had waited. Somehow she didn't care anymore. She was tired of being trapped in there.

There was a simple cushion along the base of the chest. The chest was barely long enough for her to stretch out her legs. She beat the walls with her hands and feet.

Lilae hated enclosed spaces and felt the anxiety rise within her until she was nearly delirious with fright. She yelled and kicked until she was exhausted. No one heard her, or perhaps she was being ignored.

"Is anyone there?" She tried to find a hole to peer out of and discovered a tiny crease in the wood. She struggled to look through it. Squinting, she saw that the room was empty. She heard footsteps from afar and saw the large double doors open. Although her vision was blurred, she saw bare feet enter the room. She could tell that it was a woman. Her dress brushed her ankles as she crossed the room to stand before the chest.

Lilae heard the lock turn, and the chest opened with a creak. She looked up at the face of a woman who had a serious face, aged, but Lilae could tell that she had once been a beauty. The woman held a hand out to her.

"Thank you." Lilae pulled herself from the confines of that small space. Her knees were locked and every joint screamed at her.

She stretched carefully and looked around the empty room. Two torches lit the room by the large double doors.

"Don't waste time. Come on," the woman urged, motioning for Lilae to follow her.

"Who are you?"

She opened the large door and held it so Lilae could walk through into the quiet corridor. "Vasira," she answered. "I was assigned to you. I am to make sure you're taken care of. But, above all, to make sure you stay out of trouble."

Lilae's shoulders slumped. Had Dragnor really taken her power? She felt cheated. She had just started to understand it.

Is it even possible? All of those years wishing she was like everyone else. Now she felt foolish. She was defenseless. Powerless.

What trouble can I make now? Lilae thought. "I wouldn't worry about that."

Vasira raised an eyebrow as she looked back at her. "Good to hear it. Because I don't tolerate *any* foolishness. Especially from a foreigner." She scrunched up her nose disdainfully. "And let's get one thing straight." Vasira pointed at Lilae. Her eyes narrowed.

Lilae stared at her pointed finger.

"I am not your servant, maid, or anything of the sort. *You* are a slave, and you better come to terms with it right now. You understand?"

The woman talked to her like a child. Lilae nodded, annoyed. "And what do slaves do?"

"I can already tell you are going to be a pain." Vasira glared at her, putting her hands on her curvy hips. "You do *whatever* you are told. Now come. I don't have all day."

She and Lilae walked a long while through the lower palace corridors. Each turn presented a new maze-like hallway, quiet and dimly lit. It was obvious that only the servants traveled this route. The floors were made of older wood, unlike the polished marble and carpets she had seen when she first entered the palace.

There were stone walls and shorter ceilings. While the halls were mostly empty, she did see uniformed guards placed throughout. They all stared at her as she passed them by. Lilae reached the doors to the harem.

Inside the large room, Lilae could feel the heat and steam immediately upon opening the door. The smell of oils and fragrances filled her nostrils delightfully. Her first memory of that place had been pleasant. She looked for the women who had bathed and dressed her. They were nowhere in sight.

"Go on. Hurry up." Vasira firmly pushed Lilae forward. "Don't be shy."

Lilae slowly walked in. All eyes turned to her. The room became quiet.

"Get yourself acquainted with this place." Vasira then turned to leave. "I'll come back for you all soon."

Once the doors closed securely, an excited chatter arose all around her. The girls left their spots to swarm her. While most were openly curious, there were those who were cautious. She was different in appearance and mannerisms, and they were unsure of what to think about her.

Lilae found a spot on a bench. She drew her legs into her chest. This was where she would spend her day. At least she was outside of the uncomfortable wooden chest. Lilae wrapped her arms around her legs and rested her cheek against her knees. She didn't know how she would adjust to life as a slave.

She sighed. They were so jovial with each other. She was painfully alone. Lilae's heart was broken, and she hadn't any more tears left to grieve. She felt empty; so much so, that she barely cared what happened to her anymore.

It was warm inside from the steam of the bath, and Lilae missed the crisp air of Sabron, the village she had lived in before Partha. She forced the memory from her head. That was all in her past.

"Girl. What is your name?"

The voice startled her, and she jumped. She looked to the girl who spoke to her. She was beautiful, as were all of the girls of the harem. She had darker skin with a light brown undertone and wavy black hair that rested long over her right shoulder. Her gray eyes were similar to the emperor's and lined with kohl, making them stand out even more. Her lips were mauve and full. She was eerie in her beauty, mysterious, and Lilae found herself staring, rather than speaking.

"I'm trying to talk to you." Even her accent was alluring.

Lilae shook her head, unable to stop staring at the girl. "Sorry. I'm Lilae."

She smiled and sat next to her. "Rahki."

Lilae returned the smile, happy for a diversion from her depressing thoughts. She realized that the other girls had quieted and were drawing closer to listen to the exchange. "Hello, to you all."

Rahki giggled. "You talk funny." The other girls covered their lips as they joined in the giggling.

Lilae raised an eyebrow. "So do you."

Rahki giggled. "What land are you from?"

"Nowhere," Lilae said trying to mimic an Avia'Torenian accent.

"What do you mean? We are all from somewhere. Did you fall from the sky?"

"I guess you could say I came from Partha," Lilae explained with a deep sigh. She gave up the accent. "It was the last place I lived."

"Where is that?"

Lilae shrugged. "I don't know. West, I guess."

"In between Sabron and Glendale," another girl replied. She seemed slightly older, with a more serious face. "Have you never seen a map?"

"That's my sister."

Sister. Lilae nearly choked on new tears at seeing Jaiza and Risa's faces in her memory. Their cries haunted her. She pictured them being raped and killed. She nearly shook with sorrow. She squeezed her eyes shut. She had to rid her mind of those images.

No, she thought clenching her jaw. *No tears, not now. They are dead. Forget them, or you're dead, too.* She couldn't get over the fact that they were her real sisters and never knew it. Their cries of horror and pain made her feel ill, made her want to crawl into a ball and weep her eyes out until the pain was gone. *The pain will never leave…*

"Faira," the older girl added and went back to washing her long hair that fell nearly to her waist. She wore a thin gown that was soaked by the large bath. Lilae noticed that the material clung to her breasts; she could see right through it and looked away.

"I thought you were supposed to be Aurorian." Rahki hands went to Lilae's hair. She touched the golden-red mass curiously. "Yes, your hair color is definitely Northerner."

"Then why did you ask?" Lilae snapped. The girls all stared at her. She sighed, trying to soften her voice. They were curious. She had to try to be friendly. She needed to make friends with someone, anyone.

"I'm sorry. I guess I am from Auroria, originally. I do not remember it though. Where are you from?" Lilae asked softly, trying to overlook the fact that Rahki's attention was on her hair. It made her uncomfortable, but she craved such friendliness now more than ever. She needed something to keep her from slipping into a depression that she feared she'd never escape.

"We are from here. Avia'Torena. Well, from the northern desert actually, a city called Vor'Mavi."

"You were kidnapped, too?"

Rahki's brows furrowed. "Kidnapped?"

"Yes, did the emperor take you from your village?"

Rahki laughed then stopped when she realized that Lilae wasn't joking. The other girls were silent now, as they looked at her.

Rahki shook her head. "We weren't taken against our will, Lilae."

Lilae looked around at them all. Their beautiful, young faces were all serious as they looked back at her.

"We were selected for our beauty and our talents. Our fathers were elevated in status when we were chosen."

Rahki met Lilae's eyes then looked at Faira.

"It is an honor," another girl from the pool said.

"Yes, our families have much honor now."

"And gold coins," Faira added, wringing her hair of excess fluid.

Lilae swallowed and saw the others were nodding. She felt more of an outcast then.

Rahki touched her shoulder gently. "You were kidnapped?"

Lilae nodded.

"Sorry to hear that," Rahki said softly, her eyes looking down. Lilae was amazed at how long and black her eyelashes were. "That is unfortunate. Perhaps we can be your new family."

Lilae smiled. She liked the idea, however unlikely.

Faira shook her head. She examined Lilae She leaned back. "What are you?"

Rahki put a hand on Faira's leg. Lilae noticed the subtle gesture. Faira was telling her sister to keep quiet.

Lilae squinted and turned to face them again. "What was that? Why won't you let her speak?"

Rahki looked uncomfortable.

"Mind your business," Faira said quietly. She gave Lilae an off look.

Lilae was definitely interested now. She sat up straighter. "I'm here just like the rest of you. It is my business now."

Faira's lips turned up into a bitter smirk "We are more than just pretty faces. Now, tell me. What are you?"

Lilae didn't know how to answer that. Apparently she had many titles, and yet she still didn't know who or what she was. She was the girl responsible for her entire family's death.

"Never mind all of that." Rahki took Lilae's hand and helped her up.

"Rahki, you would touch a Northerner? Father would not be pleased."

Rahki frowned. "She is one of us now."

Lilae managed a weak smile. Her smile tried to hide the hurt that was bursting to get out. "Do not worry about me. I don't need anyone. I never did."

Even as she said those false words, Lilae thought of Risa, Jaiza, Lhana, and Pirin. Her guilt for getting them killed boiled within her stomach. At first, all she had wanted to do was cry. Now, she wanted to hurt someone.

The Shadow Elf that did this to her.

CHAPTER 34

RAHKI SPENT THE EVENING teaching Lilae about basic Avia'Torenan etiquette and behaviors. Such foreign practices were new to Lilae, and so she forced herself to pay attention. She needed something to keep her mind off of her thoughts of guilt and grief.

Lilae was in the hands of the enemy. So far, Dragnor was the only clear enemy to her; he had killed Pirin. Emperor Kavien was still a bit of a mystery, as well as Sister Eloni, but they were both responsible for the attack of Lowen's Edge. The Sisters had been there, and then the soldiers followed. She couldn't tell for certain who was in charge. Lilae could feel it in her bones that there was something more.

Lilae observed her surroundings. Her eyes were always searching. She reached for her necklace, to hold it for comfort, and gave an exasperated sigh. She kept forgetting that it was gone. It must have fallen off when she was captured. She missed it. She wished she hadn't taken it for granted.

Lilae needed to know exactly what she was dealing with. So far, she knew that the army was composed of gifted soldiers. She hadn't been able to tell exactly how many of the soldiers had special traits when Lowen's Edge was attacked, but she knew that the greater majority fought with enhanced skills.

It was amazing just how different the Avia'Torenians were from any other group of people she'd encountered during her travels. Lilae was used to watching people. She could tell that there was something strange about the Avia'Torenians.

Later that day, Vasira led them to a narrow dining hall. Lilae hoped that she would catch a glimpse of the emperor. He always managed to leave before she was taken away by Vasira and after she was returned. Lilae found herself growing desperate to see him.

The girls walked in a single file with their heads held high, as if they were proud to be slaves. Lilae was still confused by the honor those girls seemed to have by being chosen by the emperor.

Lilae followed behind silently, calculatingly. She would observe their mannerisms and customs and try to mimic them as best as she could to fit in. She held her head high like them and tried to walk as gracefully as they did. It was no use. Lilae was too tall. She stood out, no matter how hard she tried to blend. Anic was right. It was impossible for her to do so.

The dining hall was beautiful, small, but the walls were covered in colorful drapes. They all sat on pillows around a rectangular-shaped table that was low to the floor. Vasira sat on her knees at the head of the table. All eyes were on her, waiting for her to begin the meal. Once Vasira took her first bite of flatbread, the other girls all reached for food off of the platters.

Lilae was starving. She broke a piece of bread and stuffed it with shredded meat from a steaming bowl at the center of the table. The first bite was all too euphoric. She closed her eyes and moaned with delight.

The flavor was delicious, and her stomach thanked her for finally putting something of sustenance inside of it. She greedily ate all of her bread and meat, spooning fluffy rice and sauce into her mouth with each bite. She sat back on her heels and felt her stomach twist with pain then held her stomach and groaned.

"Slow down, little piggy," Rahki said. She nudged Lilae and handed her a cup of warm spiced tea.

Lilae nodded gratitude and blew the steam from the top of the cup. She drank slowly, and her stomach started to settle. It had been so long since she had really eaten that her stomach needed to get used to real food again. She was already full and just sat and watched the other girls eat. She looked at them all, feeling afraid of what the future would hold but still shaken up from Dragnor's assault on her powers.

As if he knew she was thinking about him, Dragnor entered the room, and everyone quieted, putting down their food and bowing their heads. Lilae didn't bow like the others. Instead, she tightened her grip on her spoon and glared at him.

What does he want? Lilae was still afraid. However, she had had enough time to think about how much she hated that elf. His eyes met hers. Then, he looked over the other girls.

"Faira," he called.

Faira stood with her head still bowed.

"Come. Emperor Kavien wishes to see you."

Faira left the room, walking past Dragnor, without glancing back.

Lilae tensed and leaned back as he stepped toward her. The other girls all turned to stare at her. Lilae held her breath. He seemed to suck all of the previous cheer out of the room.

Vasira glared at the both of them. "What do you think you are doing? You think you can just come in here any time you like, elf? You came for what you wanted, now go."

Dragnor ignored her. He stooped low before Lilae. "I hope you're enjoying being alive. Your time here is short. I will be pleased when you are no longer breathing our air."

Vasira slammed her hand on the table. "Get out, I said!" She threw her arm out, pointing to the door. "She is my charge now, and you may not threaten her whenever you like."

Dragnor swiftly came to his feet, and, like the wind, he swept across the room and backhanded Vasira across the face. She was knocked to the floor with a crash, spilling her soup onto her dress and the floor. Vasira turn red with rage. She remained silent, nonetheless. She held her face and glared at him, her chest heaving.

Dragnor lit a flame with his fingertips and grinned at Lilae. His grin held no humor. It was a taunt. He bowed to the other girls and left the room without another word.

Lilae slammed her spoon on the table and came to her feet. She trembled with anger. The other girls all stared at her, curious to see her next move. She started for Vasira, to help her up, and the older woman put out a hand.

"Sit down," she ordered.

Lilae withdrew and pursed her lips. "I was trying to help you."

Vasira stood and motioned for an attendant to bring her a towel. She used the towel to wipe the soup from her white dress. "I don't need your help. I need you to sit down, like I said."

Lilae shook her head with a grimace. She flopped back down. "What is wrong with you? I was trying to be nice to you."

Vasira ignored her. "Finish your meal, girls. We will take a walk through the gardens before bed. And you." She shot a glare at Lilae. "Will spend your evening in solitude… after you clean this mess."

Lilae's mouth parted. She pushed her food away and covered her face. Her face grew hot. Everyone stared at her. She wanted to run. She had nowhere to go. Rahki slid her hand onto Lilae's thigh and gave her a friendly squeeze. Lilae sniffled back tears. Rahki kept her eyes down on her food, but her hand offered comfort.

Lilae smiled weakly, watching Rahki. There would be but one she would let live when she found a way to burn that palace down.

AFTER DINNER, all of the girls left the room with Vasira. She looked back at Lilae.

"You will clean this mess. Take all of the serving platters, wash them, and put them away. Then, clean the floors until they shine. Only when everything is cleaned like it was before we arrived will you be allowed to retreat to the garden. There you will stay by the fountains until I come for you. Understood?"

Lilae nodded. Rahki offered a smile to her from behind Vasira's back. She didn't care any longer. She didn't want to show that woman that she was bothered or hurt by her unjust punishment. Her face showed no emotion, and Vasira smiled.

"Good. You better get started, slave." She left the room and had an attendant stay near to show her where the kitchens and the gardens were.

Vasira didn't know how easy her task was. Lilae had cleaned and scoured dishes before. She had spent her life cleaning and doing what Vasira obviously thought was menial work. Lilae took comfort in the familiar tasks. She took the food to the kitchen, dumped the remnants, and cleaned every porcelain dish until it was sparkling clean. It was an enjoyable moment, with her hands wet in the sudsy water.

She could almost hear Jaiza singing in the background. She was back home in a cozy cottage. Pirin had his feet up in front of the fire as he sharpened his tools and knives. Delia wrote quietly in her journal in her wicker chair in the corner. Risa danced to Jaiza's singing. Lhana clapped along to Risa's dancing and laughed at her silly moves. Lilae didn't notice that tears were falling, for she was smiling at the memory.

She wiped her nose with her sleeve. *Look at how weak I am now, father,* she thought to Pirin. She looked up, wondering if he heard her thoughts in the Underworld. *I cry all the time now.*

The scullery maid watched her from her small nook beside the door. She had a few moments off while Lilae did her job. The maid didn't taunt her, though. She just watched, as curious as anyone Lilae had ever met in her life. The maid was a pretty thing, but quieter than any girl Lilae ever knew.

Lilae smiled at the young girl and began to dry all of the dishes. The girl seemed surprised to have Lilae smile at her and eagerly returned the smile. She looked more Western than the other people of the palace. To think of it, all of the maids and servants looked a bit more Western. They had brighter brown hair and didn't have the same striking gray eyes. Lilae found that interesting. Perhaps all of the staff was slaves taken from Western kingdoms.

The girl got up from her nook and helped Lilae put away the dishes. She didn't speak a word to her, but her friendly eyes said it all. They worked in silence until they were done. The attendant from the dining room came for her and silently led her through the palace to the hall of open archways.

Lilae was giddy with excitement. It had been so long since she had seen the moon, since she'd been in the night air. The path to the lush palace gardens was stunning. It was made of the shiniest stones that reflected the light of the moon like mirrors. She almost felt free, as the breeze swept through her gown. Her hair was still braided but unruly wisps floated around her face as she walked the pathway.

To either side of her were beautiful bushes. They were thin, with large, blossoming white flowers that emitted a strong yet alluring fragrance. Lilae breathed in the citrus scent and immediately felt her mind grow cloudy. She paused and looked around. Everything looked more colorful, more vibrant. She reached for a white flower and sniffed closer. The attendant grabbed her and pulled her back onto the path.

Lilae looked at him defiantly. "What are you doing?"

The attendant didn't speak to her, but his eyes were full of warning. Lilae could read what his eyes tried to communicate. The flowers, they were dangerous. She felt drunk, like with Anic at The Blind Cow. She nodded that she understood, but she looked at him more closely. He had nice brown eyes, and skin that was a little paler than an Avia'Torenian's. She was right: the staff was all Western.

"What is your name?" she asked him, and he let her arm go. "Where are you from?"

He looked ashamed and started to walk away. Lilae wasn't about to let him get away. No one watched them, from what she could tell. She rushed to get in front of him and keep him from walking. He looked frightened, and his eyes darted from side to side.

Lilae grabbed his arms. He tensed. "What is it? Why won't you tell me?"

The man's eyes darkened. He looked sad. He shrugged and opened his mouth. Lilae felt sick. He had no tongue, only a short stub.

She let his arms go and took a step back. "I'm sorry." She knew better than to judge. He looked at her for a long while. There was hurt in his eyes. It was buried deep, but Lilae could see it. She felt her throat dry.

He looked away from her, and she felt guilty for having him reveal his secret. She followed. She would torment him no more. Lilae was right about the staff. She thought back to the scullery maid—she never spoke to her, either.

Are all of their tongues cut out? Lilae shuddered at the thought.

The attendant led her through a labyrinth of bushes and flower patches, each turn more intricately arranged than the last. Finally, he stopped at the fountains that Vasira spoke of and left her.

She sat on the edge of the fountain and leaned against the smooth stone side. Thoughtfully, she watched him walk away, realizing how quiet it was.

She should hate water by now, after being on that horrible ship for weeks, but she found herself drawn to the water of the fountain. It was so perfectly clear that she could see her reflection in the surface. She saw herself. It was shocking. She hadn't seen herself in a mirror in years. She didn't recognize the girl who stared back at her from the water. She looked sad, yet she was beautiful. Lilae shook her head and looked away.

It was an illusion… it had to be. She looked back and stared at her reflection. The flowers… they had altered her vision. She breathed and touched her face. The water began to ripple. Lilae tensed, feeling a cold chill run up her body. Something gripped her.

Lilae looked around. *Wexcyn*. She felt her blood grow cold.

"All alone, I see," a familiar voice called from behind her. Whatever had Lilae let go.

She stumbled backwards when she saw that Emperor Kavien had been looking over her shoulder. He was right behind her, so close that when she turned, she bumped her head into his chin. He caught her as she began to fall.

"And clumsy. Perhaps you shouldn't be left alone. You might kill yourself."

His hands were big. They were wrapped around her arms. He let go and took a step back. She moved away from him. She held her arms across her body, hugging herself. She watched him tensely, with big eyes.

He sat on the fountains bench, looking off into the garden. "Sit down."

Lilae hesitantly sat on the bench, as far from him as she could manage without falling off the edge.

There was silence between them for a long spell. The sounds of crickets and cicadas filled the tension. She could still smell the lingering aroma of those big flowers. She wanted to feel relaxed, but the emperor's presence made it impossible. She stole glances at him, yet he never looked at her. When he finally spoke, Lilae listened aptly.

"I come here every night, even when it rains. I come here to be alone, and what a surprise to find you here. I keep you near, but all I want is to be away from you."

Lilae looked down. "Why do you keep me?"

"I don't know. I like to do things right. I want something that your brother has, and I will bargain for it."

The mention of her brother was still odd to her. She decided against asking what the emperor wanted from her brother. She didn't know why he even spoke to her. She didn't want to ruin his civility with questions that could wait. She had traveled for eighteen years from Auroria. She figured she'd be waiting quite a while to meet this brother of hers.

"Tell me, Lilae," Kavien began. He spread his arms out around him. "Have you ever seen a collection of gardens as exquisite as mine?"

Lilae shook her head. She watched him. She was still taken by his looks. There was something about him that, despite their situation, drew her to him.

"When I first built this palace, I knew there had to be gardens at every turn. It was actually one of the more important things I wanted, over the golden siding and the crystal towers. You see, one needs such beauty to help them forget about the bloodshed." He seemed to be deep in thought.

Lilae noticed that he was more reflective than she thought he could be. He sighed and glanced at her.

"The gardens are beautiful. Don't you agree?"

Lilae nodded eagerly. It was nice to have him speak in such a calm manner. "Yes, they are."

"My mother used to plant flowers, in our little garden. I would help her sometimes. I was just a boy, and I enjoyed getting dirty more than anything. That is, besides being close to her. I'll never forget the first time I saw a beautiful, blossoming, red rose. Such a deep red and fragrant, it was the most glorious thing I'd ever seen."

She watched him look far off. She wanted to hear more about his mother. There was tenderness in his voice when he mentioned her. No one else had said anything about the emperor's mother. Lilae wondered where she was.

Kavien's head tilted at silent memories. His eyes took on a distant look. They darkened, and he clenched his jaw. "I also remember the first time I tried to touch one, and how the thorns drew blood."

Lilae didn't look away. She couldn't. She was intrigued by his face, voice, and his very presence.

"Things of beauty are often the things that can cause the most pain." He gave her a hard look that made her hold her breath. "You're going to make problems for me, aren't you, Lilae?"

Lilae shook her head. She calculated her words. "What could I do?" She spoke softly. "I am nothing now, right? You all keep reminding me."

Kavien nodded. "That's right." He looked away from her again, still nodding. "You are nothing." He said it in a low tone, as if he said it more to himself.

Lilae frowned. "What happens if this brother of mine, whom I've never met, refuses to give you what you ask for?" She wasn't sure where her bravery came from, but she had been musing over that question since the mention of her brother.

"You really need to ask that question?"

Lilae's shoulders slumped. "I suppose not."

"So you'd better hope he does what I ask." He cracked his knuckles and leaned back against the side of the fountain.

Vasira came around the corner and hurried over. "Forgive me, Master." She bowed low, placing her hands on the ground before her in the shape of a triangle. "The vile Northerner is a disobedient slave. I punished her and left her in solitude. I had no idea she would manage to bother you with her presence. Forgive me, I beg you."

Emperor Kavien stood. He smoothed out the wrinkle in his billowing white pants then looked down at Lilae. "Disobedient?" Kavien repeated. His bright gray eyes gave her a sharp look.

Vasira looked up from her position on the ground. "Indeed."

Lilae felt her ears heat with anger. She had done nothing wrong. Fairness and justice didn't seem to be a quality valued in this land. She clenched her fists until her nails drew blood in her palms, looking to Kavien expectantly.

He began to speak but stopped himself. For a second, Lilae thought he looked uncertain, but that thought flitted away before she could be sure of what it was. His face became like stone.

"Let Dragnor have her for a night."

Lilae stared at him, mouth agape. She glared at Vasira, expecting to see her self-satisfied smirk. To her surprise, even the older woman was stunned.

CHAPTER 35

"WELCOME," DRAGNOR SAID.

Lilae felt as if she would vomit. Her hands and forehead were wet with sweat. Her worst nightmare was being realized. The guards sat her in a cube-shaped room before the one being she hated most.

Vasira waited outside the door. She didn't need to. Dragnor was to have her for the night, but Lilae had a feeling that Vasira felt sorry for her.

Over the room's stench, she could smell Vasira's perfume waft through the barred window above the door. It was dark inside. Two high chandeliers stocked with thin black candles lit the space. Dragnor waited in the center of the room with his hands folded behind him. There was a fire crackling behind him and a wooden table that sat upright. A short table sat beside it that held shining tools lain neatly across a black stone.

Lilae swallowed. Her throat was dry. She now wished that she had pleaded with the emperor to change his mind, but that was not her way. She had grown so used to hiding her fears and hurt that she couldn't even bring herself to beg for her own safety. Now, as she waited before the grinning Shadow Elf, she wished she had thrown herself at Kavien's feet.

"Stand."

She came up from her knees and waited, shaking. He came over and stood before her. She couldn't bring herself to look into his eyes. His hand came from behind his back, and she stared at his glowing dagger. It was her first time seeing it so close up. It was sharp, like her own used to be. The glow was a muted blue that cast shadows across her face.

Still, Lilae refused to look up at him. Her heart raced. Dragnor brought the blade up before her eyes and grabbed the front of her gown. A little cry escaped her lips. Her lips quivered as he sliced the front of her gown with the dagger from her chest to her feet. Sliced down the middle, her garments fell to the floor around her ankles.

Stark naked, Lilae instinctively wrapped her arms around herself. He held her chin up, and she finally looked at him with hate in her eyes. Dragnor nodded to the guards and turned away from her, walking over to the upright table.

"Strap her down."

The guards picked her up and carried her over the table. She hadn't noticed before, but there were three sets of black leather straps on it that they secured across her body. A last strap went across her neck, keeping her head from moving. Lilae shook and closed her eyes. She couldn't bear to see those guards looking at her naked body. No man had ever seen her without clothes. Any shred of modesty and dignity she had had was now lost. Tears stung behind her eyes. She sucked in a breath.

Don't let him see you cry, Lilae ordered herself. She bit the inside of her lip instead.

Dragnor's cold hands were surprisingly smooth. He lightly ran a finger across her belly, and she opened her eyes. His eyes were closed as he touched her. He sighed and took his hand back. He stood there for a moment staring down at her and reached a hand behind the table. He turned a lever, and the table moved. It went backwards and lowered until Lilae was lying on her back, staring up at the black candles of the chandelier.

"Wait outside."

The guards left without a word, their heavy boots stamping on the stone floor. Lilae saw Vasira peek inside when they opened the door. Then, she heard it shut, and the finality was stifling. She felt she would scream in madness. She was alone with Dragnor.

"Alone. Finally," he said in a whisper.

Lilae tried to turn her head, but the straps prevented it. Dragnor leaned over her. She squirmed, trying to get away. He kissed her collarbone. She turned stone still. With a yelp, she jerked in shock as he bit the soft flesh of her breast. She looked down at the blood as it dripped down the side of her body. Mouth agape, her eyes shot to his face. Her blood dripped from his lips, and he licked it clean. Then he reached over and picked up a black sack and held it over her body.

"You think you're so beautiful, don't you?"

She shook her head hurriedly. "No. I don't."

He didn't smile at her response. He nodded with a stern look. "That's right. You aren't. You are hideous. Your looks cannot sway me. My sole intent is to cause you more pain than you've ever known." He put the black sack over her face and tied it shut across her neck.

The sudden darkness only intensified her anxiety. Now, she couldn't see what he was doing. She could only hear him reaching for something on the small table beside her. The anticipation was maddening.

"It is unfortunate that our time together is so short, but I shall make the most of it." She heard the tools clink together like a little bell. "Ever heard of High Jordanian?"

Lilae shook her head.

"Of course you haven't. Not only are you ugly, but you are dumb as well." She felt his cold hands smooth across her belly again. He wiped it with a cold wet cloth. "High Jordanian is an ancient text. It is the language of my people. But one such as myself has been trained in its mystical arts."

Lilae jumped when she felt something sharp pierce her flesh.

"What I am engraving in your skin cannot be removed. You will be linked to me until one of us dies. I will not tell you what it does. You'll just have to live with the uncertainty. But know this… I can invoke the spell whenever I please."

Lilae cried out. The sharp blade cut into her precisely, but the pain was far less precise. She shook. She wanted to break free and run. The nausea came back, and she was sure she would vomit all over herself and possibly choke on it, if she couldn't turn her head. She forced her dinner to stay down.

She tried to think of other things, of better times. To her surprise, the only face that came to mind was that of the man from her dreams. She gratefully accepted the image, trying to ignore the pain. He was like a savior. His face was perfect, unreal.

What was he? His glow was like that of something she would imagine dwelled in the Overworld. She kept his image in her head, and the pain began to subside. Silent tears flowed, and, under the black sack, she smiled. He was beautiful. Why wasn't he real? Blue eyes looked back at her, and she yearned to pass out, to be near him again in her dreams.

In that moment, Dragnor seemed to know her thoughts. There would be no escape from the pain. A hot, searing pain made her body buck on the table as he poured something much like acid across her body. He pulled the bag from over her face to delight in the sight of her suffering.

CHAPTER 36

AN ODD SENSATION crept up Liam's spine and made his skin tingle. He shuddered in Midnight's saddle.

The girl. He could feel her. He froze. Midnight noticed and stopped walking, as did everyone behind him.

"What is it, Liam?" Nani pointed ahead as she hovered beside him. "We're nearly there."

Liam felt a chill. *The Flame, she needed him.* He was certain of it. He looked around, unsure of what he could do. Her image came to his head.

There were tears in her eyes. He tensed. No look had ever made him more deeply sorrowful in his life. He wanted to drop everything and run to her.

"Liam?" Rowe called. Everyone watched him.

Liam looked at them. He nodded, still focusing on her face. "Sorry. Everything's all right. Let's proceed."

They nodded, and Midnight started down the hill again to the Valley of the Fae. He tightened his grip on Midnight's reigns. Someone was hurting her, he just knew it. The fairies could help him. They could get him to The Barrier faster than anyone.

Their arrival at Tolrin was a grim one. The fairy children spotted them once they reached the top of the hill, and an army bombarded them like a swarm of bees. They flew by with beaming smiles the instant Liam and the others reached the stronghold. They had all heard the tales of his journeys and abilities and wanted to see Liam display his power.

Their laughter only slightly eased Liam's mind as the stress of the journey began to fade away. Lilae's image clung to the forefront of his mind. Still, he would never get over the loss of the Order. Only Sona, Rowe, Nani, Midnight, Wilem, Jorge, and Liam had survived.

The Shadow Elves had nearly succeeded in killing them all. Even more unsettling was the encounter with the Elders. Just as he had been warned, he had come face to face with a fallen Ancient and the return of her people. All along, Sister Eloni, a woman who Liam had believed to be holy and good, had been on Wexcyn's side.

"Now that's more like it!" Willem was overcome with amazement. "You didn't tell me there were other kids here, Liam!" His eyes watched the fairy children hovering above them, curious and excited.

"I thought you weren't a kid, Wilem." Liam almost smiled. Wilem could do that to a person--make them smile, even when all of their thoughts were of gloom and doom.

Wilem shrugged. "I am a man, Liam… *but*… I can still play, can't I?"

Liam chuckled softly and nodded. "Of course."

Liam remembered the day when his mother had first taken him along on her visits to the other kingdoms of Kyril. Seeing the fairies all flying around their creatively constructed villages had always astounded him.

Queen Aria had always been there by his side, sheltering him yet exposing him to other cultures and ways of life. He was now proud to be there for Wilem's first encounter with the land of fairies.

They were led by a quad of fairy guides through the village, along a series of glittering stone bridges. Settled at the bottom of the mountain sat thousands of small huts and structures that were shrouded by trees and vines, like a village built *into* the jungle instead of by tearing it down.

Gold dust filled the air like an enchanted fog. Liam could even see the top of the Mother Tree where it stood, far away from the citadel. Hundreds of fairies flew around like hummingbirds, and Nani's face lit up as she gazed at her beloved homeland. Her smile warmed Liam's heart. Still, haunting thoughts kept him from the joy the others felt.

"It's amazing how unaffected these fairies seem to be," Rowe pointed out as they moved into the compound. "Not a sad or frightened face in sight."

"Let's hope we can keep it that way." Liam wanted nothing more than to protect his realm and everyone in it, but it seemed the Ancients expected much more of him. He had the entire world to look after.

"How likely is that? Their mortal enemies have returned."

Liam grimaced at the question. "I can try, can't I? Who else is going to protect them, if not me?"

Rowe shrugged. He had withdrawn ever since the soldiers and fairies died. He appeared to be apathetic; Liam knew he was only harboring anger and pain for later.

"I'm sorry. I just miss Cammie is all. I've probably missed the birth of my first child, for all we know."

Liam's face darkened. He reached out to put a hand on Rowe's shoulder.

Rowe shook his head and stepped back. He gave Liam a pained half smile. "It's okay. They're probably dead anyway, right?"

Liam swallowed a lump. Tears stung behind his eyes at hearing Rowe speak in such a way. "Don't say that." He wanted to say more, be more reassuring, but he knew the odds. Oren was probably gone already, his mother along with it. "When Yoska came to me, he told me that everything was fine. Let's not worry about things we have no proof of yet. I'm sure Cammie is well."

Rowe nodded but said nothing. They walked in silence as they followed the quad. Liam glanced at Rowe occasionally, noting the big man's expressionless face.

Their boots made loud steps as they came to the bridge highway. Each bridge crisscrossed above the many canals and streams that fed the Silver River. The waters glistened like jewels day and night, making the entire village seem flooded by magic. The quad led Liam and the others to a long hut that was sectioned into guest rooms set aside for special visitors.

The fairies were the most hospitable people Liam had ever encountered. He didn't have to lift a finger once he arrived in Tolrin. They cared for Midnight, led him to his quarters, opened the door, and lit the candles.

Liam, Sona, and Rowe put their things away as Nani went to sleep in the house of her parents and siblings. Wilem and Jorge were taken to rooms in a hut adjacent to Liam's. Liam removed his cloak. He groaned in relief as he fell backwards onto the bed. The mattress was made of straw and cotton stuffing, but at that moment, it felt better than any bed in the Orenian palace.

Liam felt as if he could sleep for days. He had just closed his eyes when he heard a soft tapping on the door.

"Yes?" he called weakly. He looked down toward the door. The door opened a crack. Liam sighed and covered his face. He was too exhausted for visitors. A red-haired fairy stuck her head in and then the door was opened fully to reveal three other girls. Liam quickly sat up, shaking his head to awaken himself.

The fairies flew into his room with heavy buckets of hot water and began filling the circular tub that was set into the floor. He raised an eyebrow and realized that they were preparing his bath. It was customary for royal and special visitors to be bathed by ladies of the royal compound. Afterwards, there would be a large feast for everyone in the village.

Two of the fairies took his hands and pulled him to his feet. Liam looked at them questioningly. He blushed as the fairy women began undressing him. Their giggles made him cover himself with his hands. Despite being pampered most of his life, he had never been treated like this by young women. They nodded to the bath, and he hurried to get into the hot water.

Despite his exhaustion, the hot water was welcome. They poured more sudsy water over him, the scent of peppermint filling his nostrils, instantly invigorating and energizing him. Liam felt more comfortable being underneath the suds and bubbles than having them stare at his body. Future king or not, he was still a bit bashful around women.

Liam started to fall asleep as they scrubbed his body. It had been weeks since he had had a proper bath. Cold rivers and lakes in the early dawn had been his baths lately. The girls cleaned and trimmed his fingernails. They washed his hair and massaged his scalp as they lathered the suds into dozens of bubbles.

Liam ducked into the water and emerged to find their smiling little faces staring at him. Again, he blushed.

"Nani is lucky to journey with a handsome prince," said the fairy with purple hair over giggles.

"Keyata!" one of the others scolded her in a whisper. She quickly covered her mouth in regret for speaking. The other girls' faces all turned red, surprised by Keyata's comment. Their eyes looked to him, anxious for his reaction.

He laughed, and they sighed in relief. "Thank you. Nani is a great girl."

"I know," Keyata smiled brightly. "Nani is my little sister."

Liam raised an eyebrow. "Really?"

"Yes, there are sixteen of us in the family." Her eyes were as green as Nani's, and he finally saw the resemblance. She even shared Nani's purple hair. However, Keyata's was shorter and cropped above her ears.

"She is a lucky girl. She's the only one born with the healing gift in our family."

"What were you born with?" He stood as the other girls lifted a large towel up for him. They wrapped it around his tall body, and Keyata stood as well.

"Not everyone is born with a power as special as Nani's," she explained to him. "I wasn't born with a gift. So, I was lucky to find work in the royal compound."

"You're ready, prince," another fairy informed him, flying back with her head bowed.

Keyata watched the others leave and whispered to him. "We've all heard so much about you. Show me something, please." She smiled up at him like an expectant child.

He knew he shouldn't reveal his power to everyone, so he decided to appease her with a small sample. Liam lifted his palm, a light glowing from within. Keyata's eyes grew wide as she watched him motion toward the water in the bath. He moved his hand upwards, and the water climbed higher and higher to the ceiling.

"Wow," Keyata whispered softly, and her voice caught in her throat when the water evaporated into the air. "The rumors are true." She beamed up at him.

Liam playfully pinched her cheek and walked from the room. Outside, the quad waited to lead him and the others into the royal compound.

Sona glanced at him and quickly looked away, her hair long and loose against her back. She was dressed in formal fairy attire. Her dress was short but sleek, in a sea green color that glistened like scales.

Rowe was dressed in one of the finest garbs Liam had ever seen him wear, and Wilem and Jorge both looked regal in their new clothing. Both boys looked proud in their fairy clothing. One could not tell from the way they skipped excitedly behind their fairy escorts that the boys hadn't slept in days.

The guards traveled down a cobblestone path that trailed to the center of the compound, where the banquet hall was found on a raised foundation, constructed of stained glass.

Inside, the banquet hall was much bigger than one might have thought from the look of its exterior. It seemed as though the entire colony of fairies was already seated in the floral decorated room. Hundreds of fairies watched as Liam and the others entered the room. They sat along rows of tables with glass tops and stone bases.

An assortment of colorful fruits and vegetable were piled high in intricately-woven baskets. The guests were taken to a table where Lady Evee and Lord Edwin sat upon ruby-embellished chairs that had high backs sculpted into bird's heads, their wings extending high above.

Liam bowed before the royal family, and they both smiled down at him.

"Prince Liam, it is our honor to host you on your journey," Lady Evee said, her voice as soft as a twinkling bell. "We have always supported the Orenian line, and we will always do so."

Liam and the others stood. He took her delicate hand and kissed her knuckles. He bowed his head.

"Thank you, dear queen. My mother and I value your colony's friendship and the aid of your people. I offer my condolences for your loss." He spoke of the Clerics who had died protecting the Order. She nodded but didn't say anything. She looked saddened by the memory.

Lord Edwin appeared to be over one hundred years old. It was rumored that his mind had left him. He sometimes forgot who he was and what he was doing. Still, he motioned for them to sit at the table beside them.

The table was long enough to fit thirty guests and set elaborately with smooth brass plates. Facing the grand hall, they had a view of the entire dining hall.

Sona sat next to Liam. Still, she pretended as though he didn't exist. She spoke to everyone around him, ignoring him whenever he made a comment. He had never felt more awkward in his life.

"You two are an adorable couple." Lady Evee smiled as she watched Sona. She tried to lighten the mood, but she had no idea that she had just increased the tension.

Liam cleared his throat and gave Lady Evee a slight nod of gratitude, faking a smile. If Sona wanted to ignore him, he would do the same.

Wilem and Jorge sat at the far end with smiles that could warm any heart. Liam missed being that young. He had had the perfect childhood, during which his every desire and wish had been fulfilled. He was amazed at how Wilem could still play and smile, even though his family had been killed.

The night went on, and they ate sweet breads and fruit, roasted vegetables and crushed chickpeas. Everything was spiced perfectly and delicious. It was so good that Liam barely noticed that the fairies didn't eat meat.

"When do you need the ship to be ready?" Lady Evee asked between bites of sweet bread.

Liam swallowed a small sip of wine and frowned at the taste. He pushed his cup away. "As soon as you can get it ready. Two days, perhaps?"

She thought a moment. "Certainly, it can be ready in two days."

"What ship?" Lord Edwin asked curiously. "There are ships here?"

Lady Evee smiled at Liam and drank from her goblet. She patted Edwin on the shoulder. "Eat your soup, honey, and you can go rest. Sound good?"

He nodded, yet his eyebrows were drawn in confusion. He stared at Liam so intently that Liam cleared his throat nervously and looked away.

"Thank you."

"So, you'll be sailing toward Eura?"

Liam nodded. "Yes, ma'am. I'll be alone from this point. I'd appreciate it if you'd look after the boys for me."

"Of course. Our own children are older than you now. It will be nice to have a child's laughter in the royal compound once again."

Lord Edwin leaned over the table to get a good look at Liam. "Things must be getting serious."

"Nothing for you to worry about, sir," Liam replied.

"That Wexcyn is up to no good." Lord Edwin pursed his lips and shook his head. "You know, I'm surprised he didn't come sooner. I would have looked quite spiffy in my fairy armor, standing ready to fight some nasty Shadow Elves." He looked off as if envisioning what he spoke about. He moved his hands as if wielding a sword and chuckled. "I'd sure like to slay a couple of those Bellens, too. Just lop their heads off. That's how it's done, my boy!"

Liam started to bite into a sweet potato and paused. He was surprised by Edwin's remark. As far as he knew, only a few were aware of who was really to blame for all the death and destruction. As far as he knew, no one had known about the Bellens. He wondered if Nani had said something. His eyes searched for hers and saw that she was laughing with a group of young ladies.

Lady Evee grew quiet as well, uncomfortable with the turn of conversation.

"I commend you for trying to protect us." Edwin looked squarely into Liam's face. His eyes grew serious. "But what can a Tryan and fairies really do against an Ancient? What chance do we really have?"

Liam began to speak, but Edwin cut him off. His stomach began to feel unsettled by Edwin's change of tone. The old man was serious. He was lucid.

"Wexcyn knows the ins and outs of war. You think yourself a scholar, but you have no idea just how bad the Great War was. Wexcyn will cheat and lie. I can promise you that."

Liam raised an eyebrow. He wiped his mouth with a cloth napkin and sat back in his chair, stunned by what he was hearing.

Lord Edwin grinned. "You look surprised. Why? Did you really think he would follow the rules made by his enemies? Wexcyn hates Telryd. You know why? Because he is just as powerful as him, and Wexcyn feels threatened."

"But, if he cheats, then the Ancients will step in." Liam turned his full attention to Lord Edwin. He tuned everything else out.

"Ah, yes. He is probably counting on it. What other way to bring the other Ancients out of the comfort of their homes to *destroy* them?"

Lady Evee cleared her throat. Lord Edwin leaned closer over the table toward Liam. "Wexcyn will use any tactic to secure his position. You're sorely out of your league. Wexcyn will use others to do his bidding, and he will influence good people to do *very* bad things."

Edwin's words were making sense. Liam sat up straight in his chair and listened. With the knowledge he had just uncovered about the Bellens, he knew firsthand that Wexcyn had already gone against the rules. He had brought back a race that was not his own, just to do his dirty work.

Edwin pointed at him. His thick white eyebrows were furrowed. "I can guarantee you, my boy, when we are at our weakest, that's when Wexcyn will make himself known." He wiggled his finger. "The world will tremble at his rage. He wants revenge, and there's nothing we can do to stop him from getting it."

Liam realized that Vars and Ved were right. The fairies were more versed in history. They all knew what was happening. Only the Tryans were ignorant of what was coming.

Lady Evee stood and began gently helping Edwin up. "Come, darling, it's time for bed."

Edwin slammed his fist on the table. "I'm not a child!" he growled, and everyone grew silent, staring at him. Edwin didn't seem to care. "Listen to me, Liam." Edwin leaned close to Liam's face. "Do you know what will happen when Wexcyn walks this world?"

Liam felt the blood drain from his face. His eyes widened.

"It is when the Underworld becomes one with ours." He seemed desperate for Liam to see that he knew what he was talking about. "Understand?"

Liam watched Edwin's eyes as they bore into his own and nodded. "Lord Edwin, how do you know all of this?"

Lord Edwin smiled an eerie smile and sat back in his chair. "Once upon a time, I was prone to what you now call prophecies. I used to call them dreams. That was before those dreams started coming true. Before I stopped knowing what was real and what was not."

All of the talk about Wexcyn had made him lose his appetite. Liam pushed his plate away and downed his goblet of wine.

Edwin suddenly grew jovial again, and it felt as though a dark cloud had moved from above them. Liam looked over the crowd. Everyone was happy and going about their lives as though nothing was wrong.

He envisioned what this village would be like once Wexcyn paid a visit. The chaos would be devastating, and the thought of any of those joyful fairies dying made him more anxious to hurry and join the Flame.

Liam felt such an intense emptiness without her, and they hadn't even met in real life yet. He wondered if the dreams counted.

Liam sat there in deep contemplation for the rest of the evening. He needed direction. He needed someone who was around during the Great War to help him. If only someone like that still lived.

Looking over to Wilem, Liam froze. The boy was standing in his chair, telling a story to the fairy children. They all watched aptly, their eyes big with wonder. The talisman hung from Wilem's neck.

Vleta. He needed to speak to the dragon.

CHAPTER 37

THE SOUND OF WEEPING WOKE woke Kavien. His eyes opened, and he rolled onto his back, listening to Lilae's soft sobs. Maybe it was a mistake keeping her so close. He wanted her to be closer. He hadn't expected her to be so beautiful. He hadn't expected her to be so calm, so tame. She was nothing like he had imagined. For some reason, he wanted more of her than he was allowed, and had to resist.

"That is right. Resist. She is the enemy. Do not forget that."

Kavien squeezed his eyes shut. He wasn't in the mood to be controlled.

I can do this on my own. I do not need you coaching me!

"You are mine. Your will is unimportant."

He tried to drown out the voice with his own. He sang inside his head, hoping the intruder would shut up. He couldn't let Wexcyn gain control. Not again. He was a terrible person and did terrible things when Wexcyn took over.

"Let her cry. She deserves it. Your punishment was just what she needed to keep her down."

He sat up and kicked the chest. "Shut up!"

The sobbing ceased.

Kavien sighed, raking his hand through his hair. He hadn't meant to say that to Lilae. He almost reached down to open the lid of the chest. He withdrew his hand. Still, he could never tell her that or show more than a little kindness at any given time. He felt physically sick that he had let Dragnor hurt her. He had had no choice.

He would never forget the day he first laid eyes on Lilae. Kavien would have never expected to feel what he did now. Her image haunted his every waking moment. Those green eyes stared back at him in his sleep. That soft creamy white skin. Her brown freckles.

Kavien longed to run his hand through that long silky red hair. His pulse began to quicken, just thinking about how close she was. Inside that chest, by his bed; he wanted to open the lid and just look at her… to touch her.

His pulse beat loudly in his ears. He grew hot. He stormed from the room. Kavien didn't stop until he was out of the palace and far from her sweet scent. He already had enough to drive him mad. He had to get her out of his head. She suffered because of him.

He marched through the palace; everyone bowed to him as he passed. He ignored them. Every day was the same. No one wanted to look him in the eyes. They all feared him, as if he were as foreign as Dragnor.

Kavien was cursed. He was an abomination, full of demons that haunted his every waking moment. His anger started to rise at those thoughts.

Kavien stopped at his army's training grounds. He ripped off his shirt and grabbed a sword from the weapon rack. He rolled his shoulders and stood at the center of the training circle. The men all quieted when they saw him, backing away behind the wooden fence that encircled the training grounds. They lowered their eyes to the dusty, sun-scorched ground. No one wanted to accept his challenge.

"Come on."

The soldiers were all afraid of him. They had seen what he could do in battle.

"Who wants to practice?" Kavien's eyes slowly surveyed the crowd of soldiers. They were all well-built men with years of training and experience.

Cowards, the voice hissed in his head.

Kavien's grin faded. "Someone had better step up, or it's off to the dungeons with *all* of you!"

The men grumbled, looking at one another in apprehension. One of the captains stood up for his men. He selected a sword from the rack and took his place before the emperor.

Their eyes met and Kavien nodded. "Artero."

"Be fair this time, emperor," Artero replied. "We are but men." He felt no shame in admitting such a fact, even in the presence of his men. They all felt the same. "We are no match for you."

Kavien raised an eyebrow at the statement. Then he smirked, yet they could never tell that his eyes were full of pain. Those men would never understand. Kavien feared that no one would. He wasn't blessed with godlike powers. He was cursed.

"As you wish, captain." Kavien took a step back, and his body vanished before them.

rtero gulped. His eyes searched frantically. He held his sword up, anticipating a mortal blow to come at him.

"You better use more than your eyes, captain. How about you turn on some of that Reach of yours? It's the only way to catch a Silver Elf in battle."

Artero turned quickly toward the voice and met Kavien's sword with his own. He was hesitant, unsure if Kavien were testing him or teasing him. Reach was used to pull an opponent to oneself.

How could he use it? He'd have to… *see* his opponent first. Artero's eyes widened. Maybe there was a method to Kavien's madness. Artero's eyes blinked, and, with his free hand, he Reached.

To his surprise, he could feel Kavien, even though he couldn't see him. He cringed at what he was about to do, but had he any choice? He pulled Kavien toward him… An invisible body slammed into him with such force that Artero was knocked to the ground.

Kavien reappeared, his eyes glowing silver and back to their normal gray. "Good man!"

"This isn't fair," Artero protested, his face reddening. He was breathing heavily with fear already; he didn't want to die that day.

Kavien's intentions weren't to humiliate the man. He reached a hand out to Artero, helping the man up.

"Yes. This I know," he admitted. "But the Silver Elves can vanish before you can blink."

Then his body seemed to fly from man to man as he took their weapons before they could understand what was happening. He dropped their weapons in a pile on the ground.

"You see, the Shadow Elves can dart faster than a cat and spit venom. The Tryans..." Kavien's grin widened; their power was his favorite. He gripped the hilt of his own sword. It began to glow red. He stared down at the light as it illuminated his bronzed face. "They can enchant their weapons, making theirs more powerful than any in the entire world. Such power could cut right through your armor," he explained, his voice lowering as he looked into the light, feeling the power radiating throughout his entire body and into the sword.

His shoulders slumped. The men were staring at him in utter shock. Their jaws had dropped. "I possess the main skill of each of the races, and I will train you men to fight against them all."

Kavien walked to the gate. With expert Agility, he stepped onto the gate and walked it like a tightrope. He looked out at the masses. These men were all gifted. They were all selected for having inherited special abilities.

Kavien didn't conquer lands to acquire slaves; he didn't take girls from their homes to make them whores in his harem. He wanted people to think that, but he wasn't sure if the truth was more intimidation or less. Kavien was recruiting men and women, powerful ones.

Before him was a collection of well-organized men each of whom held a very special talent. These were talents that the world hadn't seen in thousands of years. He was anxious to remind the world of the power of his people. Kavien looked them over. The sun blazed, and he was already dripping with sweat. He ran his fingers through his hair and sighed.

"You see men: the Realm Wars are not going to be fair. Because the world is not fair."

The men finally understood, but that didn't make them any less fearful.

CHAPTER 38

"WHAT WOULD I DO WITHOUT YOU, Faira?" Kavien asked as Faira sat before him. Her amber eyes looked up at him, and she smiled.

"You would probably go insane," Faira replied with a laugh.

Kavien returned her smile and leaned back in his chair. She massaged his feet, and his entire body felt at peace. He took a sip of cold pineapple juice and glanced out the large cutouts in the clay wall. It was going to rain. He looked forward to its sweet smell.

"Can I ask you something, master?" Faira dipped a cloth into a hot basin of scented water. She wrapped the cloth around his feet and sat back on her heels.

Kavien glanced down at her. "What is it?"

Faira met his eyes. "My sister and I, we've been with you for five years now."

He nodded. "Yes…" He sighed inwardly. He could already tell by the look in her kohl-lined brown eyes what she was thinking. Faira was a needy one, but Kavien didn't mind. He enjoyed being needed.

"We've served you well, haven't we?"

"Of course." He pinched her cheek and sat back in his chair.

She looked troubled. "Why have you chosen Lilae?"

Kavien sighed. He had tried to keep her out of his head. He knew there was nothing he could do. King Ayaden was already heading their way. Soon he would have Auroria. Soon Lilae would have to die. He wished he'd never promised her to Sister Eloni. He dreaded thinking of what the Bellen would do to her.

"It wasn't my choice. You know this. Why do you ask?"

Faira shook her head. "She doesn't fit in. You chose us for our talents and beauty. However, we do more for you than people think.

We live with the way people look down on us in silence. We don't protest against the way people call us whores, when we are not. She is a Northerner and yet you keep her close to you… in your private quarters, which none of us have even seen. It doesn't seem fair. I would happily give myself to you, if that's what you wanted."

Kavien lifted her chin and leaned in close to her. "Are you jealous, Faira?"

A sad look came to her eyes. "Yes."

He sat back again, and she rested her head on his lap. He watched her as she hugged his legs and came up to sit in his lap.

She looked him directly in the eyes. "She will take you away from us."

He moved her hands from his chest, and she clung to him. "Stop it, Faira. This is nonsense."

"Is it? Why won't you tell me? Can you imagine how it feels to be a person of power yet thought to be nothing more than a slave?"

Kavien didn't answer. He did know how it felt to be a person of power, yet people feared him. They thought of him as a tyrant, an oppressor, a murderer. He wished he was more than those things. He had no choice but to be who he was born to be.

"Focus…"

"My sister and I were the first in our family to be born with a skill. We were practically worshiped in our village, and now… look at us. How is this fair?"

"Enough, Faira." Kavien put his hands to his temples. She wasn't helping him anymore. His feeling of relaxation had disappeared. He lifted her off of his lap, peeled the cloth off his feet, and stood before her. He looked away when he saw the tears in her eyes.

"You don't get it. You brought us here and made us fall in love with you, and now… you're going to abandon us, for *her*. How is that fair? Something is not right about her."

Kavien shot a glance at her. "What do you mean?"

"Her power… it is frightening. I've never seen *anything* like it."

Kavien's shoulders slumped. That was obvious. She was the Flame. She had immense power. He sat up taller. *But wait,* he thought. *Dragnor was supposed to have taken her power… How could Faira still see it?*

"But what is she like?"

"She is a Northerner. What else do you need to know?"

"Leave." He turned away.

She didn't budge. "Why? What did I say?" She tilted her head as she looked at him.

"I said leave!"

His tone made her jump. She scrambled to her feet and collected the basin and cloth. She hurried from the room without another word.

Once she closed the doors behind her, Kavien walked over to the cutout in the wall and looked over his gardens. Even though Faira had failed to give him an idea of what Lilae was really like, she had just revealed something he hadn't even anticipated.

She was the best Seeker in Avia'Torena. He had brought her along on recruiting missions, and she had always found him the best soldiers with skills. She had seen the Flame's power. There was a clue in there somewhere. He would figure out Lilae's mystery. He would just have to find out what he wanted, himself.

Over his shoulder, to the west, stood red mountains and the sprawling desert that rose and fell like waves. Kavien stood there stoically. He watched the picturesque sunset quietly but his mind raced. Everything was about to change and yet he wasn't sure what he was doing. He didn't even know why he was so affected by Lilae. He had tried to convince himself that she was just another girl. It wasn't working…

That night, Kavien had her washed and dressed and brought to his private dining area. When they sat on the large plush cushions on the floor at separate ends of the short black table, she avoided his stare and busied herself with watching the attendants bring out platters of steaming food.

The room was decorated with drapes that billowed in the warm night breeze. The rain provided a soft melody in the background. Candles set upon tall pedestals bathed the room in a dim light. Such an unexpected invitation for her to join him had resulted in a look of surprise on her face, and he loved watching her each expression. Obviously, Lilae had no idea how much he thought about her. Perhaps it was best that she remain oblivious to how vulnerable she made him.

Kavien broke the silence. "Are you as innocent as you look?" He made his face unreadable. His voice would reveal nothing of the turmoil he felt. He took a piece of black bread and dipped it into the dish filled with creamy paste. He took a bite and watched her reaction. She stared at him with wide eyes.

Lilae shifted uneasily on her cushion. "What do you mean?"

He chewed his bread for a moment. He drank a long swig from his cup. He let her squirm a little longer as he savored the taste of the red berry wine. "I think you know. Let's not pretend to be dumb. It's not becoming of you."

Lilae glared at him, and his smile grew. It wasn't the reaction he had expected. She was deliciously full of surprises. *More,* he thought. *Show me more.*

"I am a virgin, if that's what you are asking." She said it in a matter of fact tone, trying to hide her apprehension.

He detected her fear. Her breaths were shallow, as if she half expected him to pounce on her at any moment. Kavien silently examined her face. He almost laughed at Lilae's feigned bravery. She wasn't good at hiding her emotions. It was endearing.

"Thank you." He drank more wine. "That's all I wanted to know. See? Simple isn't it? I ask the questions, you answer them, no one gets hurt."

"You don't intend to kill me?"

"Why would I do that?"

There was silence between them. She stared at him, unblinking.

"What use would you be to me if you're dead?" He waved a piece of bread around.

"What use am I to you alive?" Lilae made a face. "I'm not as stupid as everyone seems to think. You're hiding something."

His eyes darkened, and any shred of friendliness faded from his face. She didn't know. She couldn't know. Could she?

Lilae challenged him with a look, despite her fear. His smile returned. Kavien had never met someone who vexed him so. She was an anomaly to him, and he was determined to figure her out. He needed to learn her past, her secrets, and use them somehow.

"Go on," he motioned to the food before them. "Eat."

"Why are you doing this? Why can't you let me go? You already have my powers. What threat am I to you now?"

"That would be too easy." He drank the last of his wine and held his cup up for the servant. The woman filled the cup from a large vase and stepped back toward the door. "You deserve to suffer." His mind went back to all of the things he had been taught growing up about the Chosen class. He wasn't so sure he believed those teachings anymore.

Lilae held her hands out. "But why? What have I done to harm you?"

"You were born to interfere with my rule. I seek to unite the races under one rule. My rule."

"What?"

"You'll understand soon enough."

"Understand?" Lilae's brows drew in. "You can't rule everybody. That's absurd. Why would you even want to?"

Kavien paused from reaching for his cup. She had questioned him. He was on his feet so quickly that she fell backwards onto the floor. He grabbed her by the throat and pulled her close to his face.

"And why can't I?"

Her face grew red. She desperately grabbed his wrists, trying to wrench free.

"Let's remember something. I have *you,* and there's nothing you can do about it."

She squirmed and struggled to breathe. His eyes widened, and he let her go. He sat back on his heels, watching Lilae catch her breath. Her hair shifted from red to gold, like ripples on water. "Hasn't anyone taught you about speaking out of turn?" He watched the beautiful change of colors.

Lilae's eyes watering. "Yes. Dragnor."

Kavien felt really guilty then. He couldn't believe how much Dragnor influenced his actions. He had tried to be different from

Dragnor. That elf had caused him enough pain. He hated how he was doing the same thing to Lilae.

"Well." He cleared his throat. "Let me explain something to you, Lilae." He spoke softly. Lilae looked up curiously. He waited for her breathing to return to normal. "My people have waited a long time to be returned to power. I have secured such power for them. Once we were the strongest of the races, and finally we can feel proud that we are so, again. The humans can benefit from my rule. I treat them well, don't you agree?"

He looked at her, and his eyes narrowed at the look on her face. Her face was screwed up in confusion.

"Wait… What?"

Kavien made a face. "Which part don't you get?"

She sat up a little. "You said your people, and then you spoke of humans as if they were separate."

It hit him. He stared at her, mouth agape. Lilae didn't know. He shook his head. *How could she not know?*

Kavien composed himself and sat back on his cushion, waiting patiently for Lilae to sit back up. She returned to her seat, never taking her eyes off of him. He didn't even know how to begin.

She knew nothing. He should have felt pleased with himself for a perfectly executed plan, but she was supposed to be the Flame. How could no one have told her that they were mortal enemies? Kavien almost didn't say anything. He didn't really want to be her enemy, but there was no way he could keep that from her.

Lilae had to know. Maybe then, she would understand. He was named. Perhaps she would figure out what he was going through. He looked at her for a long time. Even with a frown on her face, he found her incredibly pretty. He sighed. His shoulders slumped, and he sat back against his cushioned back rest.

"You really didn't know that you are now in the first Mithrani kingdom since the Great War? That we have conquered most of the human realm with little to no opposition?"

Her face lost all color. Kavien waited in anticipation. Maybe her ignorance was why she wasn't what Dragnor had told him she would be. She never knew. Perhaps now, he would see her true colors. He just waited for her to change, to become the villainous beast he had envisioned her to be.

"You," she began and paused to swallow, "are the Cursed one then?"

Kavien hid the wash of sadness he felt at hearing his title. The prophecies couldn't have been more accurate in his naming. It was the tenderness in her voice that caught him off guard. The empathy in her eyes stirred his deep feelings of regret.

He knew it. She was not what Dragnor or Wexcyn had told him she would be.

Kavien breathed in. He looked down at his lap. He had no appetite. He knew she watched him, and he felt afraid to meet her eyes…

The memory of the first time Wexcyn had invaded his mind returned. Kavien's mother had put her hand on his shoulder. Kavien was young again, a boy of only four. He had just killed his cat, Jinx. He had screamed and wept as he'd used all of his strength to crush the cat's throat. The look in Jinx's eyes would haunt him forever. He hadn't meant to. He didn't even *want* to.

The voice had made him do it. His curse. He'd cried that day until his eyes were raw. She'd knelt down and hugged him tight. He could still smell the rosemary oil she used in her hair. It was the most pleasant smell and calmed him. He had loved that cat. He used to smooth its white fur as he fell asleep at night in his little bed beside his mother's. *How could he kill it?* His heart had wept, but his mind had rejoiced at his success.

"Good job, my boy," it had kept saying. He'd hated the voice, even then. He didn't know whose voice it was until Dragnor stole him from his mother's small home in the south of Eura. Back then, there were only a couple thousand Mithrani, the descendants of the four

Mithrani people who survived the Great War and the creation of The Barriers. They'd lived simply. They'd kept to themselves.

Hidden in the goblin city, the Mithrani had never wanted another war. Wexcyn, however, couldn't have cared less what they wanted. He would have his war, through Kavien. Now there were millions of Mithrani, thriving and blending with the humans the way no other race could…

Kavien looked up at Lilae in horror. There were tears trailing down his face. She was watching him, her mouth agape. Her eyes were sad.

Kavien roughly wiped his face. He cleared his throat and hardened his voice. "You were born to kill me. Do you understand what that means?"

Lilae shook her head. She spoke softly. "I don't. I never did understand it. I used to follow the law of The Winds. I would only kill those who deserved it. You killed millions of people with your armies. The humans don't even know what you are. I have seen countless horrors in my life. Results of what *you* did. But knowing what you are, the Cursed, I can't help but wonder… *do* you deserve to die by my hands? Are any of those actions your own?"

The question made his eyes widen. He almost came to his feet. He could have kissed her with joy right then. She understood. *No.* He shook his head. She couldn't. It was a trick. It had to be. He couldn't hope for more.

"What games are you playing?" Wexcyn chimed.

Kavien winced. He could never have more than a few minutes to himself. He growled and came to his feet.

"Take her away," he said while walking to the window. He needed air—just a moment of peace. Just to get away from her eyes would be a blessing. She was weakening him.

Vasira pulled her up. She walked along with a questioning look on her face. When the door was closed behind her, Kavien stood there for a while, contemplating what had just happened. She had just disproved everything he'd been told.

He had been lied to since childhood. He needed to figure out what he would do with her. As unsettling as what he had learned was, it didn't matter.

Kavien had made his decision the moment he'd laid eyes on her.

CHAPTER 39

LILAE WAS TAKEN FROM THE ROOM. She was confused by what she had just seen. Emperor Kavien was a big man, a big *Mithrani* man. He had conquered nearly all of Eura, and yet she was certain she saw regret in his eyes. There was a deep pain in his eyes, a silent suffering that made Lilae feel uneasy.

She was afraid that she would never understand that man. One moment, he was choking her; the next, he spoke tenderly and actually shed tears. The Cursed. She couldn't believe it. She'd been there for months already,y and she would never have guessed that he was the Chosen of the Mithrani. Were the Mithrani so different that she couldn't tell them apart from humans? Darker skin, bright gray eyes, larger bodies—these were the only things Lilae could differentiate. She wondered what skills they had.

Wexcyn's greatest weapon. Kavien proved to be far more complex than she could have imagined. Still, his eyes never ceased to make her feel breathless. She hated to see tears in those eyes.

Ugh, she thought in annoyance. *How could I feel sorry for him? He will kill me the first chance he gets.*

Her stomach itched. Whatever Dragnor carved into her skin bothered her. She spent hours in the harem baths, staring at it, trying to make sense of it. Black symbols were spread across her white flesh. It made her worry every time she thought about it. Dragnor had warned her that he could evoke the spell whenever he wanted. Recalling that long night with Dragnor kept her awake in terror most nights.

"What did you do now?" Vasira's gray eyes bore into her own. *Mithrani woman.*

Lilae rolled her eyes. She would not speak to that woman. She was responsible for her unjust punishment.

Vasira pursued. "The emperor looked quite upset. What did he say to you?

Lilae pursed her lips, looking ahead. Vasira stopped abruptly and turned on her.

"You answer me."

Lilae stared at her blankly. She tilted her head and blinked, showing the older woman that her words meant nothing to her.

Vasira examined her eyes and pulled back with an exasperated sigh. "Have it your way. Be stubborn while I try to help you. Makes no difference to me." She stormed ahead.

Lilae frowned. "Help me?" she called after her. "You've done nothing but cause me pain. I don't trust you."

Vasira didn't turn back around. She did slow her pace, however, and Lilae caught up to her. She gave Lilae a sidelong glance. "I never expected the emperor to send you to that elf. Let's get that clear. He's never done anything like that." Her eyes read true. "Tell me, what did the emperor say? Why was he upset?"

Lilae wasn't sure she trusted Vasira. She never gave Lilae a moment of kindness before, why would she care now?

Lilae spoke cautiously. "He seemed sad. Regretful. I can't explain it."

Vasira lifted a skeptical brow. "Sad?"

"Yes. Sad. Something is bothering him. Why do you care?"

Vasira laughed then. "I cannot believe such a thing. I've never seen Emperor Kavien sad. Perhaps that is what he wants you to think."

Lilae never thought of that. What would be his reason for manipulating her? Then Delia's words came back to her.

It's not that they want you dead, necessarily. They want something from you.

"Maybe." Lilae felt defeated. She had almost believed Kavien.

"Is that what you think? Do you think he was being sincere?"

Lilae thought a moment. "I do. But you know him better than I. Vasira, what will happen to me?"

Vasira turned to her. "Nothing good. Unless you try to be as unthreatening as possible."

Lilae rolled her eyes. "Why do people keep saying that? How am I a threat?"

Vasira shrugged. "How am I supposed to know? You must be someone special or important, to be kept so close to the emperor. That Dragnor, though. My god, he *hates* you. Trust me, I've been around for a long time, and I know that Dragnor influences the emperor. Don't let him convince the emperor to get rid of you. I'd say you're much safer close to the emperor." She turned a corner with a smirk. "But what do I know?"

They reached the gardens, and Lilae felt a chill run up and down her body when she saw Sister Eloni waiting by the fountains at the beginning of the garden.

Vasira froze. She put a hand out to Lilae as she gave a low bow. Lilae hurried and followed suit.

"Ah, Lilae." Sister Eloni smiled big with her arms extended out toward Lilae. "Come."

Lilae hesitated and stood tall. She did not want to be anywhere near her. She shook her head and looked at Vasira.

"I said come."

Lilae went closer to the strange woman and stood before her awkwardly. She didn't know what to do with her hands or where to look.

"I can stay, if you're not going to require Lilae for long, honored Sister," Vasira said, still bowed.

Sister Eloni waved her off. "I can return her once I'm ready. Now, run along."

Lilae and Vasira exchanged glances, and, for the first time, Lilae wondered if she had found an ally in that woman. Perhaps getting Lilae sent to Dragnor had changed how Vasira felt about her. Nonetheless, she was left alone with someone with whom she really didn't feel comfortable.

Lilae shivered as Sister Eloni put both of her hands on Lilae's face, cupping her cheeks. She frowned. She would never get used to people just touching her whenever they wanted.

"Oh, child, you're filling out. I am glad to know the emperor has you well fed. You were nothing more than a twig when you arrived." She laughed lightly as she put her hands on either side of Lilae's waist.

Lilae cringed and shrunk away from her hands. Sister Eloni's smile flickered when Lilae stepped away from her. "Something wrong?"

Lilae shook her head. "No. Everything's fine." Everything wasn't fine. She was sure she sensed evil coming from that woman. It was a look in her eyes. If Lilae looked deep enough, she could see a glint of insanity in Sister Eloni's eyes.

Sister Eloni didn't seem convinced. She stared at Lilae for a moment then grabbed a fistful of her hair. "Your hair… It turned gold just now. Why does it do that?"

Lilae hadn't realized what she had done. She could never hide her emotions. Her anger was showing. She wished she had her cloak, to cover it. "It does that sometimes when I'm happy."

Sister Eloni gave her a look as if she didn't believe her. "Happy, Lilae? What are you happy about?"

Lilae didn't like Sister Eloni holding her hair like that. The woman was pulling it, making her scalp sore, and there was an iciness to the woman's voice that Lilae wasn't used to hearing. "I hear my brother, the king of Auroria, arrives soon. I am anxious to meet him."

Sister Eloni nodded, but Lilae could tell that she still wasn't convinced. Sister Eloni flicked her wrist, and, before Lilae could blink, she caught something in her small hand.

A stick. No, it was a long, thin bone. Sister Eloni turned her back. Her long hair brushed the back of her heels.

"And what will you say to him? I trust you'll tell him how well you've been treated. I'm sure you'll convince him that an alliance between Avia'Torena and Auroria is a wise choice." She straightened her shoulders and looked up at the moon. "The only choice. You see, it is best for the humans. We will protect them from the other races. Will you do that for me? Convince him of this?"

Lilae nodded, slowly. "I will," she lied. She would do no such thing. If it was the last thing she did, she would tell her brother the truth. She would honor the dead and protect the living, even if she died for it.

The woman nodded slowly, giving Lilae a hard look. "Do I look like I am stupid to you, Lilae?"

Lilae stiffened. Her tone had changed. There wasn't a shred of kindness.

"What do you think you are doing with the emperor? He is mine. You are mine. I will not have you distracting him."

Lilae's hair burned red. She felt something inside spark.

Sister Eloni watched her. "I knew it." She reached for Lilae's hair again.

Lilae had had enough. She blocked her hand. She swept her other hand across the Sister's throat. Lilae's face reddened. She glared down at the stunned woman. Something warned her that she had just made a mistake. Somehow, Lilae didn't care. She would take the punishment.

Sister Eloni glared back at Lilae. Then her lips curled into a malicious smile. She lifted whatever was in her hand toward Lilae, and a haze of light radiated from it. Lilae's eyes widened. She turned to run.

A jagged purple light shot from the stick. It struck Lilae right in her chest. Lilae screamed. Her hands flew up to her chest to block whatever it was that had stung at her heart.

Sister Eloni's smile turned maniacal. "I don't trust you, Lilae. I want a guarantee that you will do what you are told. I find that pain is usually the best solution, next to kindness. But I can see that you are a sneaky little bitch. You think you can lie to my face?"

Lilae's body was lifted into the air by the light that cut into her core.

Sister Eloni took deliberate steps closer as Lilae flailed in the air. "I tried to be nice to you. I really did. I thought that maybe we could be allies. Dragnor was right. You should have been killed a long time ago. But no matter, this will surely rip any rebellious spirit out of your body." She spoke words that Lilae didn't understand.

The light sent colors all around the garden. It was beautiful, and yet Lilae felt as if she was dying.

The pain shot through her, sending every vein and artery into a screaming torrent. Lilae gagged on her own blood. Her fear intensified as she wondered where the blood was coming from. She saw Sister Eloni below her and reached for her. Lilae wanted to kill her. If only she knew how.

She called her power. When it didn't respond, her hopes were dashed. The power was truly gone.

Sister Eloni covered her mouth with her other hand, suppressing a laugh. "What are you going to do? You have no power here. You will do as I tell you, or you can die right now for all I care. And I will eat your remains for dinner with a large mug of your blood." Her lips curled into a cruel smile. "And I will enjoy your youth for an eternity."

Lilae's mind raced. She felt nothing but pain. The sound of her own screams was deafening in her ears. Her ears actually pulsated with the rush of blood. Her face felt hot. She thought she might explode, not knowing if she could stand the pain any longer. Her body felt as if it might break apart.

Lilae saw something approach out of the corner of her eye. A dark shadow. *Dragnor,* she thought with tears in her eyes. *How could it get any worse?*

She fell to the ground. The light from Sister Eloni's stick instantly faded. Lilae choked on her own blood. She coughed and struggled to breathe. She clawed the ground and tried to pull herself up.

She glanced up. Kavien held Sister Eloni up by her throat. The woman's eyes bulged. The look in his eyes made Lilae suck in a breath. There was tension in his arms as his muscles bulged with his strength. He tossed that woman far into the garden where she fell with a crash into a bed of roses.

Lilae crawled away, fearing the woman's retaliation. She sniffled and climbed onto the fountain stairs.

Kavien stood there, his hands balled into fists as Sister Eloni popped back onto her feet. She flew at him, her magic stick pointed at him, a determined look on her reddened face.

Kavien didn't move.

Her white hair was wild now and flapped all around her face. Her glare darkened, and she aimed and shot Kavien with a massive blast of light.

Lilae shielded her eyes and ducked. A loud popping sound made her jump. The air flew all around as if a tornado was brewing.

Peeking between her fingers, Lilae saw the blast bounce off of Kavien's body and return to its sender. Sister Eloni screamed, and her own power knocked her down again. He towered over the fallen woman. She looked up at him in anger. A glint of fear passed through her eyes and disappeared, but Lilae caught it.

"You may not harm her. If you put another finger on her, I will kill you." His voice was calm, yet there was no mistaking how serious he was. He shared a long hard look at Sister Eloni.

Finally, she nodded, still shaking. She panted and climbed to her feet. She turned and flew away. Lilae watched her body disappear into the darkness.

Lilae waited. She was too afraid to breathe too loudly. She was confused by what had just happened. Kavien had just saved her life.

He turned and came directly over to her. Kavien avoided her eyes, but his face was troubled. He picked her up with both arms and carried her away. Her blood stained his shirt, but he didn't seem to care. He held her to him and walked toward the palace.

Lilae didn't know what else to do. She buried her face in his shoulder and finally breathed with relief.

CHAPTER 40

SONA STILL REFUSED TO SPEAK to Liam. He suffered her silence with a fake smile. He would have to apologize, but still, he didn't think he had done anything wrong. Liam drank a special honey drink that the fairies had prepared for him. Wilem and Jorge drank theirs, as well. The sugar made them smile and bounce with excitement.

"Let's play hero ball!" Wilem jumped up and down in front of Liam.

Jorge laughed, tugging on Liam's sleeve. "Come on, Liam. *Please*."

Liam stood and rustled Jorge's hair. "Maybe later, Jorge. Wilem and I have some business to attend to."

Jorge frowned. "Business? I'm coming, too."

Liam smiled warmly. "Sure, you can come along."

Wilem drank all of his juice and wiped his mouth. "Are we going on another adventure, Liam?" He grinned.

Liam hugged Wilem. "Not today. Soon. Right now we need you to summon Vleta. We can go to the wheat field, where she won't scare the fairies."

Wilem grinned. "Great! I've been wanting to play with her again! Can we take her for a ride along the valley? I want to get a better look at the Mother Tree."

"She's not a toy, Wilem. She is a very dangerous weapon."

"But she was so much fun to fly," Wilem grumbled. He lowered his head in disappointment and followed behind.

Jorge caught up to Liam. "I agree with you, Prince Liam. That dragon is dangerous."

Liam gave him a sidelong gaze. Jorge really did remind him of himself at that age. Wilem reminded him a lot of Rowe.

"I will take you to see the Mother Tree. I promise. I just need to ask Vleta a few things so that I can complete my quest."

"Are you taking us on your quest, Liam?"

Liam looked to Wilem, then to Jorge. "No. You will be much safer here, with the fairies. There's food and safety here. But don't worry. I'll come back for you. I promise."

"If you're still alive."

Liam paused at the sadness in the boy's voice.

Liam hugged Wilem. "I'm not going to die. Don't you worry yourself with such things."

Wilem pulled away and looked to Liam with tear-filled eyes. "Everyone dies." He sniffled. "Everyone *I* love, anyway."

Liam felt bad for him. Wilem was such a cheerful boy that one could almost forget he had lost his entire family line. He remembered all of the bodies scattered around the Raeden palace.

"I'm going to be all right, Wilem. Trust me."

Wilem didn't respond. He walked quietly along the cobblestone path as they made their way out of the colony square toward the expansive wheat fields. His eyes brightened a little when he saw the tall golden wheat that stretched far into the horizon. The sky was the most perfect blue, with scattered puffy white clouds.

Liam closed his eyes. It was nice to have the sun shine on his face again. Those days in the Attguart Jungle had been extremely tough for more than one reason. The only comfort he could take from that journey was his having managed to save the boys and his friends. The other soldiers in the Order were in the Underworld now. He hoped they had made the journey safely.

Jorge beamed. He started to run through the field with his arms outstretched. His energy seemed to bring Wilem out of his grim mood once again. Liam smiled. "Call Vleta for me, and you boys can play. Once I'm done talking to her, you can give her a ride. How does that sound?"

Wilem didn't hesitate. He pulled the necklace off and held the talisman out with his right hand. "Vleta. Wilem of Raeden summons you," he said confidently. The glow reached out, and along its rays came the large black dragon.

Vleta was a majestic, massive creature. Her scales shone beneath the sunlight, and her eyes looked them all over. There was an ancient wisdom in her eyes; one could see it just from looking at her. If she were a woman, she would have surely been a queen. Her long neck reached down and went close to Liam's face.

"It is about time that you have summoned me," she said in an unreadable tone.

Liam waved the boys off. "Go on. I'll call you when I am done."

"Do you think I was created to just sit in that talisman? I know what has been happening. Many people have died, and I could have protected you." Liam swallowed as Vleta scolded him. The moment reminded him of Lady Cardeli's being angry about Liam's playing in the mazes all night. This was much more serious than that, however.

"Well," she pursued, "what do you have to say for yourself, Storm?"

Liam sighed. He held his hands out. "They caught us off guard. I would have summoned you if I'd known what was going to happen."

"And running off for revenge like that? How do you explain that? You are an important person. We cannot afford to have you die for such foolishness."

"It wasn't foolish to me. My men were killed. My healing troupe was killed."

"And so you thought you would just run off and join them in the Underworld?"

Liam pursed his lips. He let out a long sigh and calmed his temper. "I know, but I had to find out who was behind all of this."

Vleta stood tall. She towered over him, her head blocking the sun. "I could have told you that."

Liam's mouth parted. "What? You knew?"

Vleta gave a nod. "I did." She tapped a talon on the ground. Even though it was an inappropriate time, Liam almost laughed. Right at that moment, Liam thought of how much Vleta reminded him of Lady Cardelia.

Liam looked up at her. "I've never been in possession of something as valuable as you, Vleta. I thought it wise to keep you hidden. I didn't know."

"No use fretting over the past now. What's done is done. I only wanted you to know that I am a weapon, a tool, a guide. You have me. Now use me. What would you like to know? I know that's why you are here."

"The Bellens. How can I stop them?"

"The Bellens are a nuisance. They have hidden for centuries. The Shadow Elves crave nothing more than revenge on their brothers, the Silver Elves. The Mithrani have numbers greater than anyone knows. They have infiltrated the human world and blend so well that the humans have no idea that they are even there. And then, dear boy, you have their leader… the Cursed. His power is so great that he can destroy the world, if given the right motivation."

Liam settled onto the ground near where Vleta rested on her belly. "What do you mean by that? Isn't he motivated already?" Liam looked over his shoulder. He could hear Wilem and Jorge laughing and playing.

"He can be swayed either way. He can be an enemy, or he can be an ally. It depends on whose influence over him will be strongest."

Liam shook his head. "I don't understand that."

"The girl. She will. It is her duty."

"The Flame… Lilae?" Liam perked up at the mention of the girl from his dreams.

Vleta gave a little nod. "Yes. She is his prisoner. She has the power to have him switch sides."

"I don't like the sound of that. She is in danger." He balled up his fist, thinking of Lilae being the prisoner of their enemy. "I have to rescue her."

Vleta sat up. "You don't."

Liam raked his fingers through his hair. "Why?"

"Because that is not your journey. She has to get out of it herself. You, my friend, simply have to make it to The Barriers. That is where you will meet the Guardians, and they are the last link to the Ancients since they closed the Overworld. They will tell you what must be done. And then, the real journey begins, and we can only hope the Flame will be alive to join you."

Liam felt sick. He hadn't met her yet, but he already felt so connected with her. He cared about her. He didn't know how he would continue without her.

"You care for her. I can tell. That says something about your character."

Liam looked embarrassed. He looked around to make sure no one heard what was just said. He still feared what Sona would think about it all. "I dream about her," he spoke softly. He pictured her face.

"And she dreams of you."

Liam cleared his throat. "What of the others? Am I to go to The Barriers alone? We've heard nothing from the other Chosen."

Vleta's golden eyes stared at him. "The Inquisitor is here."

Liam shot a look at her. "What?" He was stunned.

"Has been the whole time."

Liam looked confused. "Who is it?"

Vleta seemed to think a moment. "I can't imagine why they wouldn't tell you." She made a clicking noise in her throat. "Perhaps they don't know who they are yet. Perhaps they are spies."

He pushed himself up and looked around for Wilem and Jorge. "A spy. One of the fairies? Or one of my friends?"

Vleta stretched her wings. They blocked all light from shining on him. "It is a friend. Or an enemy. I am not sure which, yet."

"Wilem! Jorge! Come back now." He called to them. He needed to find out who the Inquisitor was, immediately.

"Get to The Barriers. Do it quickly. We don't have much time left. I can feel Kyril dying."

Liam nodded. He was ready for action. "Thank you, Vleta. I will do my best."

The boys ran over. They had sticks of wheat in their hair as if they'd been rolling around in the field. They panted as they stopped before him, their faces flushed from whatever game they had been playing. Liam had to make it to The Barriers. For them. For everyone in the realm.

Wilem smiled up at Vleta. "Hello."

It almost appeared that she smiled back. "Hello, master. Would you like to take a ride?"

Wilem jumped up and down with glee. "Yes! Come on, Jorge!" He ran over to climb onto her back.

Jorge grumbled but did what his young master commanded. Once he was on top, he wrapped his arm around Wilem's waist, as Wilem held onto Vleta's neck.

Liam waved at them as they took off. He laughed at the look on Jorge's face. They were lifted into the air and went high into the sky. He stood there for a moment then his smile faded.

There was much to do. The Barriers weren't that far from Tolrin, but now he had to worry about one of his friends possibly betraying him. It left him feeling exposed. He had no way of figuring out which one it was.

CHAPTER 41

NANI LED LIAM, WILEM, AND JORGE to the Mother Tree square. It was a bustling citadel made of white stone with a large tree in the center.

The Mother Tree reached high into the sky and shaded the entire massive citadel with its branches and leaves. Pixies buzzed around in droves, looking like nothing more than tiny beads of light. A thick, sparkling haze clung to the area. Wilem and Jorge were afraid to step into the haze.

"What if I breathe it in?" Jorge asked. "Will it hurt?"

Nani giggled. "Of course not. The air is pure. Come on in. Just step into the citadel, and you'll see what I mean."

Liam grinned. He couldn't wait to show the boys what happened once one breathed in the air of the Mother Tree. He stepped onto the white stone steps of the citadel and breathed deep. Wilem and Jorge followed his example. Fairies smiled at them as they entered their sacred circle, flying off into the different buildings of the square.

There were child fairies going to school in the large building toward the back. There were other fairies visiting the shops or talking to the tree with their hands pressed to her trunk. They asked for guidance, they prayed, they offered blessings to it. Liam waited for the boys to breathe. Nani laughed and flew up higher. Liam took Wilem and Jorge's hand.

"Come on, boys!" He bent his knees and leapt into the air.

Wilem and Jorge both yelped when they felt themselves being lifted into the air. Jorge held onto Liam as if he might die if he let go. Wilem's eyes widened. And then, he cheered, taking his hand out of Liam's.

"How's it feel boys? To fly…" Liam asked as he chased Nani, who zipped in and out of the crowd.

"This is amazing!" Wilem went higher and higher.

Liam held his hands out. "Not too high, Wilem. You will fall if you leave the Mother Tree's haze."

"Oh! Okay!" Wilem came back down a little.

Liam flew toward Nani. She beamed at him. "I knew they would love it here. Thank you, my friend."

Nani nodded. "Anything for you, Liam. I do love those boys. I am glad we were able to rescue them, if no one else. The other fairies are quite taken by them, as well. It is rare that we ever see Tryan children. The others find them very interesting."

Liam smiled warmly. "It is the same way I felt when I first met you, Nani. On my first trip to Tolrin. They always said you would be my Cleric one day." He settled down on the ground near the Mother Tree. "I thought there was nothing more outstanding than to have my own personal fairy."

Nani landed beside him. She put her hand on her narrow hips. Her purple hair was brushed down now, yet it was as wild as ever. Wisps of it still clung to her face, but she didn't seem to mind. "It's almost as if we were betrothed, Liam," she teased with a grin.

Liam laughed. Nani couldn't be his enemy. It wasn't possible. There wasn't a malevolent bone in her body. "You'll make a good bride to a nice fairy man. Perhaps Vars or Ved?"

She made a face. "Gross. They are ancient! I'm your age, Liam."

Liam laughed harder. He held his stomach. "Sure, you're my age for now. But you'll live much longer than I. When you're a hundred years old, you won't remember who I was."

Nani's smile faded. She turned awa, toward the Mother Tree. "Don't speak like that, Liam. You'll live as long as I. I'll never let you die. I'll feed my very essence to you through my power, to let you live. I won't see you dead. I won't." Her voice cracked.

Liam sighed. Her words were touching. He wrapped his arms around her, hugging her back to him. "I didn't mean anything by that comment. You're right. We'll grow old together." He looked around at her face. She gave him a sidelong glance. "But you'll still be beautiful, and I'll be nothing more than a shriveled up old man with saggy skin and a walking stick."

Nani couldn't help but laugh. She pinched his check. Her eyes sparkled. "You'll always be the most handsome man to me. For a Tryan, of course."

"Of course." Liam nodded with a wink.

"Come, get the Mother Tree's blessing." Nani motioned him forward. "The ships should be ready by tomorrow."

"Oh, that's good. I'll hate to leave Tolrin, but I am ready to make it to The Barriers."

"Don't worry. We'll make it on time."

"You're really not afraid, are you, Nani?"

She shook her head. "No. I'm not." She winked at him then. "Take off your boots here." She pointed to the trench cut out for shoes. She slipped off her thigh-high boots and put them inside. Liam did the same and put his boots in beside hers and the others'. He looked up to see Wilem and Jorge playing with fairy children who were on a break from school.

Liam and Nani stepped off of the stone floor and down the stairs until their feet touched the smooth dirt that provided sustenance for the tree. Her roots were large and stretched out on all sides. Liam looked at it in awe. To think, this was created by their Ancients' energy. Her sacrifice had become a powerful monument for her people.

A pixie landed on his nose. Liam gasped. He could see a tiny, smiling face surrounded by short, curly blonde hair. Liam wiggled his nose. It tickled.

"Oh, it's Allie," Nani said with delight. "Hello, Allie," she spoke to the pixie. She looked to Liam. "She likes you. Figures." She shooed Allie away. "Sorry, Allie. Liam is here to be blessed. No time to waste."

Allie giggled and flew away with a swarm of pixies that seemed to race around the tree and up into the branches and leaves. Liam's eyes watched her with wonder until she disappeared.

He followed Nani into the shade of the Mother Tree. There was a low hum that came from her. The tree was alive and aware. He got on his knees and pressed his hands onto her bark. She spoke.

"Oh, what have we here? The prophecies never lie," she said to him. "I am happy that you have come to see me. A blessing, shall we?"

Liam felt nervous. The tree spoke to him through his link with it. Its voice made his bones rattle, but the sensation was like an itch that he couldn't scratch. He looked to Nani and gasped. He couldn't see her. No one was there any longer.

"Don't panic. They are all still there. This moment is for you and me. And you and me only. Now, which blessing would you like?"

Liam thought very carefully. He could ask for vitality, to keep his strength up on the journey. Or he could ask for a number of other things. The decision was too difficult.

"Let me make it easy for you. I grant you the blessing of protection."

Liam looked up. "Protection?"

He could feel the Mother Tree smile. "Yes. You need it. Many want you dead. But it is only good for one time. So please, be careful. This blessing is not to be squandered, but I can tell you are a smart man. Good luck on your journey."

The link was broken. Liam breathed in deeply. Everyone had returned. Nani sat beside him, cross-legged. She watched his face. Liam began to speak, and Nani held her hand up to silence him.

"Don't tell me which blessing you received. It is for only you to know." A loud bell rang, and she came to her feet. "Let's gather the boys. The children need to return to their studies."

Liam followed suit and stood. They walked over to retrieve their shoes. He couldn't stop thinking about his blessing. He already knew that he would face dangers that he'd never even dreamed of, but the reality overwhelmed him. Even the Mother Tree knew of the danger. He thanked her silently, looking over his shoulder. The tree seemed to glow with acknowledgement of his gratitude.

AT DINNER, LIAM WAS BOTHER BY what the Mother Tree had told him. He looked over at his friends. Rowe sat next to him. Nani and the boys sat at a table near him with her large family. They looked so happy.

Sona sat across from him. She made it clear that it wasn't by choice. Still, she refused to speak to him. She was being so stubborn, it made Liam's stomach twist with worry. He feared he had caused irreparable damage to their relationship.

Liam stared at her now, urging her to just look at him. She kept her eyes down with an apathetic look on her face. She gingerly ate off her plate. She paused, her fork clutched in her hand.

Instead of meeting his pleading eyes, she got up and excused herself from the table. Liam frowned as he watched her leave the dining hall. Lady Evee placed a hand on his and gave it a little squeeze.

"She wants you to go after her."

Liam looked at her skeptically. "I doubt it." He slouched in his seat and watched her go out the door.

Lady Evee smiled knowingly. "Women don't always make sense, dear prince. It is the sole duty of a man to figure out our mysteries. Let me save you some trouble. Trust me. She wants you to go after her. Go on. Deal with whatever squabble you've had."

Liam groaned. He wasn't sure he would even know what to say. A wind swept in. It was loud, but the fairies simply paused and listened, then went back to talking and eating.

Liam, however, tensed. The hairs on the back of his neck stood, and he felt the air grow cold. He wasn't the only one to sense that something was wrong. He watched Rowe's face and saw that he stared down the hall to the doorway. The wind swept in again through the open-aired ceiling that was made of woven vines and flowers.

There was a loud crashing sound from outside, and everyone jumped with fright. Then, there was complete silence as they all listened.

Liam, Rowe, and Nani were on their feet in an instant along with their guards, who drew their weapons. Wilem and Jorge rushed over to him for protection. He looked down at them, his face full of concern, and motioned for them to quiet.

"Where's Sona?" Rowe broke the silence. He looked around while Liam motioned for Lady Evee and Lord Edwin to remain seated.

"We'll check it out. Stay here!" Liam hopped over the table, and the others followed him as they rushed down the aisle to the doors. The assembled fairies were frightened. They clung to each other, their whispers elevating with fear. None of them were used to such a disruption from their routines and traditions. That look in their eyes—that fear—made Liam cringe.

They dashed through the doors and out into the darkness. All of the hanging lanterns and glowing flowers had lost their light. Only the moon shed a small amount of light onto the fairy village. Its light reflected off the canals of water and the streams that cut through the center of town.

Something felt very wrong. There was a warning in the pit of his stomach. It was so intense that Liam felt queasy. Sweat dripped down his neck and soaked his collar. His eyes scanned the dark scene.

Where are you? Liam asked The Winds. They were usually there to let him know exactly what there was to be cautious of, what to fear. *How can you abandon me now*?

Liam held a hand up for Rowe and Nani to stop. "Wait," he whispered. He heard something. His eyes widened.

"Sona!" Liam ran out toward her. He stopped abruptly.

Liam thought he saw her standing by a cherry blossom tree, watching them from the darkness. He felt his stomach drop. She didn't look like herself. Something on her face terrified him. The way she looked at them…

He gulped, almost afraid to take a step toward her. Then, she was gone.

Rowe squinted as he followed Liam's line of sight. "Where is she?"

Nani flew closer. Her eyes searched frantically. She looked at Liam, confused. "No one's there, Liam. You saw her?"

Liam's shoulders slumped. He looked in the direction that he had seen her, his mouth open in disbelief. Then, he grew confused. "I could have sworn…," he began and was interrupted by another loud blast.

This time, they saw where it came from and heard Sona's scream. The guests' huts burst into flames, and Liam was quick to pull a wave of water from the nearest canal. He raised his hands and flung the water into the hut. Nani was at the door before Rowe and Liam could run across the bridge.

Another explosion. The hut continued to roll in flames. The heat nearly blinded them. He coughed and pulled another wave of water from the canal and swung it onto the burning hay and beams.

As soon as the flames died down, Nani disappeared into the hut. Liam ran as fast as he could. The water had quenched most of the flames, but he feared that Sona had been hurt. He dashed into the smoking building, and his eyes were met with dust and heat. The smoke made his eyes water and burn, but he wouldn't stop until he got Sona out of there.

"Nani! Sona!" Rowe called. He flung furniture out of the way, heading to Sona's room.

"I got her!" Nani yelled. She had Sona by her armpits, carrying her toward the fresh air.

Liam stepped aside as Nani flew out the doorway. She pulled Sona to the bank of the stream and sat above her. Liam ran out, his forehead dripping with sweat.

"Is she all right?" he blurted, but Nani raised a hand for him to quiet.

Her eyes closed as she focused her energy on healing Sona. She was alive but seemed to be unconscious. Liam dropped to his knees, watching Sona's face for any signs of movement. He looked around, wondering who had done such a thing. Who had set the huts on fire?

They all gasped when Sona shot up. She roughly pushed Nani off of her and held her head. Her eyes were squeezed closed, and she seemed in pain.

Nani glared at Sona as she came to her knees. "Why did you do that?" Nani shouted at her. "I was trying to help you!"

Sona glanced at her, waiting for her vision to clear. "What happened?" she asked drowsily.

Nani's face softened when she realized that Sona was obviously disoriented.

Liam put a hand on Sona's back. "You feel okay? Do you know who did this?"

Sona shook her head. "No," she replied simply. She squeezed her eyes shut and cursed under her breath.

Liam frowned, looking to Rowe, who was equally perplexed. They were all disappointed by her response, hoping to learn more. "Can you stand?"

"I think so." Sona took his hand and stood with him. She took his hand and led him away from Nani and Rowe.

Sona leaned close to his ear. "The Elders tried to take me." She spoke so low that no one but Liam could hear her confession. He stared down at her. "I was trying to defend myself. Do not tell the others."

He didn't know what to make of it. Drefen had told him that they do not kill. What were they doing then? The Elders were supposed to be on their side. He knew then that he should be wary of whom he trusted.

"Protect me, Liam." Sona spoke softly, and he saw vulnerability in her eyes for the first time since he'd known her. She looked up at him pleadingly, and he saw that she was genuinely fearful for her life.

Liam nodded. "I will, Sona. I won't let anything happen to you." He held her close and thought deeply. She buried her face in his chest as his gaze roamed the colony. The fairies began to leave the banquet hall to see what was happening.

Lady Evee flew to him with a face full of worry. "What is going on?"

Liam held onto Sona. "Everything is fine. It was an accident." He looked down at Sona, who hid her eyes from the fairy. "I don't think any of you are to worry, but I think it's best if we leave in the morning. The sooner I am gone, the better it will be for everyone."

"I'm coming, too," Sona chimed.

"And I," Nani blurted, eavesdropping.

"You know I'm not letting you go without me, either," Rowe added.

Liam shook his head. "No, I can't put you in danger anymore."

"You're not getting rid of us, Liam, so just give it up," Rowe told him with a smile. "We'll pester you until the end of time."

"Very well," Liam said. "At least I know you guys won't slow me down. But it's not going to be easy."

"Watching you show off all the time won't be easy, either," Nani joked, trying to ease the tension.

Liam forced a half-smile. He put an arm around Sona's shoulders and hugged her close to his side.

Lady Evee settled on the ground. "So it's settled. The ship will be ready at dawn."

"Great. Thank you." Liam was anxious to get going. "Our rooms are quite a mess now. Are there other quarters for us?"

Lady Evee nodded. "Yes, you can stay in the guest rooms in the palace."

"No. We should probably be away from you and the king. If something else happens, we don't want you to get caught in the crossfire."

"Fine. I'm sure we can find three rooms in the village."

"Two," Liam interjected. "Sona will stay with me."

CHAPTER 42

SONA HID HER SMILE as they followed Lady Evee to rooms that were spread out around the colony. Once inside with the doors closed, Liam slumped onto a chair. He had had enough action and excitement and could only feel the intense fatigue he'd been suppressing for weeks.

Sona stood at the door, her back pressed against it as she watched him. She began to unbutton her shirt and kick her boots off. Her feet touched the cold floor, and he heard nothing.

Liam's eyes were closed, and she could tell that he was worrying. *Such a worrisome young man,* she thought to herself as she watched him. *But he's a good man.*

When Liam opened his eyes, Sona was standing before him in the dark, and he could see her pale naked body illuminated by the light that spilled from the open window. The light of the moon was faint but enough to provide a muddled view of her flawless body.

He couldn't help taking her all in before his eyes looked up to hers. She had a small smile on her face.

"You still love me, Liam. Don't you? No one else can protect me like you do. No one makes me feel the way that you do." She spoke in a voice that was soft and sultry.

Liam shifted uneasily in his seat and tried to avoid looking at her. His body responded before his mind could react. She walked closer slowly, letting him relish watching her naked breasts. Sona smiled a seductive smile that urged him to touch her. He held his breath.

That's right Liam, Sona urged. *Don't fight it.*

She took his hand and gave it a tug. He stood before her, and she pressed her breasts into his chest, looking up at him. As she captured his attention, she unbraided her long black hair so that it fell right above her smooth buttocks.

She tilted her head back as she looked at him and rolled her neck so that he would look at her creamy, white throat. Then she opened his shirt and kissed his chest. She smiled mischievously, and Liam gulped as she began unbuttoning his pants.

"Sona," he began, his voice coming out cracked and uneven. She put a long finger to his mouth to shush him.

"We might die tomorrow Liam," she said, trying to sound as sad as she could. "Don't you want to feel what it's like to be with me first?"

Liam remained silent. She felt his heart racing.

"It's okay Liam, don't fight it. We both want to. No one would know."

"Sona," he began again, almost pleadingly.

"I'm a pure, Liam," she told him in a soft voice, and he felt his face blanch. "I saved myself for you… Don't let me die a virgin." She batted her long dark lashes as she looked up at him. Her eyes welled.

His face instantly saddened. *Works every time,* she thought, gently closing her eyes so that the tears would fall down her flawless cheeks.

"You're not going to die," he assured her. It made him sad to hear her speak in that way. He wanted to hold her.

That's it. Wrap me in your arms.

Liam hugged her gently, careful not to look at her buttocks as she buried her face in his chest.

"I feel safe with you, Liam. Always have. I can fight and all but that life isn't enough. We all need love to fight for… Don't we?"

Liam nodded. His voice caught in his throat as she put her arms around his neck.

She smiled and pulled him along silently, leading him to the bed. She pushed him onto his back and slid her hand up his shirt. She felt the soft hair on his chest and kissed his navel. Liam swallowed and stared at the ceiling as she pulled his pants off.

"Sona," he called to her. She leapt on top of him and covered his mouth. "I can't do this."

Enough of this, she growled to herself.

Sona reached a hand out to him. She touched his face, releasing her Charm, her most secret ability. "Shut up, Liam," she warned softly, and he looked at her in surprise. She kissed his neck and collarbone, and he lay back in bliss.

His inhibitions were dissolved. Finally, her Charm was working again. She had been perplexed as to why it hadn't been working as well, lately. He used to be in the palm of her hand. She worried that she was losing her touch. *No, that couldn't be*. Sona had been Charming for years.

She was the puppet or… a favorite toy.

Rowe was the same, so easily manipulated. That Nani, though. She frowned. She couldn't Charm that fairy no matter how hard she tried. It was harder with women, and it seemed to be impossible with fairies. The fairy hated her. But any man could be hers.

Except… *him*. She shuddered at the thought of him, glancing over her shoulder as if he might be hiding in the wardrobe or watching her from the window. Her blood turned cold at the very thought of him.

She closed her eyes. *No,* he *can't be here. He's miles and miles away,* she tried to reassure herself. She looked down at Liam. She had to remain focused.

Sona gently bit Liam's earlobe and he couldn't control himself. He was hers. She released more power. She would not let him deny her. He gasped as her power shot into him. His eyes widened, his pupil's dilated, and he was no longer able to resist.

Liam grabbed her by the back of her head and kissed her. He lifted her up and tossed her onto the spot beside him. He climbed onto her and ravenously kissed her, as his hands parted her legs. Sona moaned with delight. She was breathless. She was weakened by the amount of power she had used. But Liam was hers now.

"Yes, Liam," she urged. "Don't hold back."

Liam ignored her words, overtaken by his lust for her. Her Charm was strong. His will was no longer his own.

"I love you," she whispered inaudibly. She meant those words, but love had nothing to do with this. Her eyes widened with shock, and she cried out as he broke the seal of her virginity.

He covered her mouth with his hand to smother her cries of pleasure. He didn't want the whole of Tolrin to hear them. Sona clutched him close to her and closed her eyes. He was all she'd ever wanted. Even still, she knew she'd never truly have him. She knew that, the next day, she would lose him forever.

CHAPTER 43

DRAGNOR ABSENTLY TRACED the elaborate embellishing on the bookcase with his long finger. His mind soared with ideas. There were so many ways to torture a person, and he was skilled in the majority of them.

Lilae deserved to suffer. She was only partly the reason he had been brought back to this world, but she had cost him valuable time. All of those years searching for her had been wasted; he could have been petitioning the secret sects of the world during that time and bringing their dark powers to the side of his master.

He would venture out into the world and do what he was summoned for, but not before he administered his punishment to the girl. She'd only had a small taste of what he really wanted to do to her.

Dragnor could not wait to spend hours on Lilae. Soon, pain would be all she knew, and he would teach her well. He licked his lips at the thought. He promised himself that he would not let his rage get in the way.

Kavien entered the study and sighed in annoyance. He seemed exhausted. The emperor spent most of his days training and planning. Dragnor was at least satisfied that Kavien had sent different sectors of the army ahead, to occupy every city and kingdom that led to the next territory they were to conquer. They had campaigned for years, gathering soldiers and slaves, and soon all of their hard work would be rewarded.

"What do you want?" Kavien slumped into his oversized chair and leaned back. The candlelight flickered off of the shadows of his face. He massaged his temples.

"I've been patient for long enough. I want to invoke the spell," Dragnor replied calmly. He made sure that his eyes weren't challenging. Kavien's wrath was something he could not afford.

Kavien's eyes opened, and he regarded Dragnor with disdain. "I've heard enough of this. I've told you already. You cannot do that to Lilae until we meet with her brother. We cannot drive her mad just before the king arrives."

Dragnor almost balled up his fists. Kavien was a necessary evil. As much as he hated to admit it, he needed Kavien. Kavien was his first victory. He had stolen him as a child. His mother wasn't as clever as the Elder who protected Lilae. Kavien had never had a chance. Dragnor had broken him, beaten him, and trained him, and still, Kavien was rebellious. Dragnor needed to remedy that, immediately.

He heaved a sigh. "I will invoke the spel,l Kavien, whether you agree or not."

Kavien's face turned ashen. "You wouldn't dare go against my orders."

Dragnor eyed him skeptically. "What are you playing at, Kavien? You cannot really expect us to let you keep her."

"No. Do I have to say it again for you to get it? *No.*"

Dragnor's mouth twitched. He almost snarled. Instead, his face remained expressionless. He drew his cloak, his face shrouded in darkness.

"Can I have nothing for myself?" Kavien was worried.

"We've given you everything. All of Eura will be yours. You cannot really be this selfish. The girl was always meant to be bait. Nothing more."

"Don't do it, Dragnor. Don't hurt her."

"You threaten the alliance between the Mithrani and the Shadow Elves. The Seer will not settle for scraps. The Seer is gathering armies from the seven tribes of Nostfar. Would you rather we march those armies on Avia'Torena. Think, Kavien. The Maloji, the Kavarti, the Night Wisps—do I have to go on? The Seer commands them all."

Kavien closed his eyes. He'd rather not think about the Seer.

"Right now The Seer is on your side, which is the only reason I am even here. You even think to betray us, and you'll have no one. We'll wipe out your Mithrani and the humans before you can blink. We don't need you."

Kavien stood. "Threats? Is that what you came here for, Dragnor?" He took calm steps toward the Shadow Elf. "I will not insult your people because Wexcyn sees fit to ally himself with Inora. But do not think that I will hesitate to kill you if you threaten me again. You can be replaced."

Dragnor grinned. "Really?" Dragnor didn't flinch. He simply tilted his head up to look Kavien in the eye. Kavien felt the room grow oddly colder. "I'd think that statement over a bit if I were you. I am Dragnor, son of Malikar, the first king of Jordan, and I was born over a thousand years ago. I was killing Silver Elves and Tryans before you were even thought of. I have been brought back from the Underworld. Do you think death frightens me?" His grin faded into a snarl. "I think you should be afraid, for, if I die, I *will* take you with me." He stepped around Kavien, who stood there like stone.

Kavien turned his head to watch Dragnor walk toward the double doors. Dragnor's fingers lit up with flames. "I have taken the girl's power." He lit every candle in the room and sucked the flames back into his fingertips. "Remember who sent me, and perhaps I won't have to take yours, as well. I'll win this war on my own, with the power of all of the Chosen, if I have to." He looked over his shoulder and gave Kavien a pointed glare. "You think you know it all, don't you? You forget that *I* put you on the throne." He shook his head. "Do you really think I came here to ask your permission? You are nothing but a puppet. The spell will secure our victory. Don't think I haven't noticed how you have fallen for her. She is not yours to have, Kavien."

Kavien lifted an eyebrow and watched Dragnor leave the room. The bone-chilling cold he felt left when the doors slammed shut.

CHAPTER 44

THE TIGERS BOWED BEFORE HIM. The lions did, as well. They were caged, and yet they were calm. Kavien was their master. They were his pets. He rubbed Gigi's head, and she purred. A giant Vendi lion that stood nearly eight feet tall and weighed tons purred.

Kavien tossed a slab of meat into each cage. Human meat. The blood dripped as he slung the chunks to them. They ate it greedily, not pausing to savor the flavor. Kavien knelt down and watched them. They were vicious animals, but to him they were as tame as kittens. They devoured the body of his latest kill.

He had left the torturing to Dragnor; it was the Shadow Elf's favorite pastime and had forced the information he needed out of the victim. Kavien, however, had ended the man's life. He didn't even have to lift a finger. And now, he was being digested in the bellies of Kavien's beasts.

An Aurorian spy.

Kavien still couldn't believe that people thought he would be stupid enough to let a spy go unnoticed. He had his ways. Ways that no one knew about. The only perso, who had known about his… "special skills" had been his mother.

Dragnor had taken his mother from him, the only person to ever truly care about him.

"What are you doing?" Kavien asked quietly. His face was serious as he stared out at nothing.

The lions and tigers licked their talons and lay down, satisfied.

"Why are you here? What do you want?" The woman's voice came to him from far, far away. Her voice was shaking. He had surprised her.

"I want to know why you're stalling." Kavien came to his feet and watched her. She lay in bed beside *him*. Kavien sneered. "You are a whore. You're not supposed to be pleasuring him. Do I have to remind you of your duty?"

She sat up cautiously, pulling the blankets up to cover her breasts. Her blue eyes searched the small room that she was in. She searched in vain. He was thousands of miles away, and yet he could talk to her, and he could touch her.

He could hurt her. He didn't want to wake the sleeping man beside her, so he twisted her liver, making her hide a wail with her hand. Tears poured from her eyes as she endured the agony.

Kavien's face relaxed, and he released his hold over her. She rolled off the bed to the floor. Naked and covered in blood and tears. He lifted an eyebrow.

"Why are you bleeding?"

She glared at nothing. "Why do you care?"

"Oh. I see." Kavien realized where the blood had come from. *She had been a virgin. How ironic.*

"I'll take care of it. I promise," she vowed quietly, pleadingly.

Kavien waited. He wanted to torture her with his silence. He wanted her to guess and wonder what his next move would be, where the pain would come from. He decided she had had enough. He knew she would complete her task. She would keep her word.

"You better do it quickly, before I start to doubt your loyalty," Kavien whispered dangerously. "Or I will return to you when you least expect it and cut your life line. Do you think my father will enjoy seeing you in the Underworld?"

She shook her head vigorously. "I'll do it. I swear."

He exited her mind and returned to his animal compound. The cats were sleeping. Kavien watched them for a moment. He was in a foul mood. His mind returned to its favorite subject… Lilae. She would be in her chest now, the cage he had had built specifically for her, sleeping peacefully.

Maybe I should disrupt that peace, Kavien thought, and strolled from the compound into the warm night air.

***

Lilae lay there in the darkness. She was cramped and uncomfortable. Sweat pooled between her breasts, and her limbs were slick with perspiration, as well. She had to find a way out. She hadn't seen Kavien in days. She was beginning to think that he hated her as much as Dragnor.

But he saved me from Sister Eloni, she reasoned miserably. She couldn't make sense of it.

She had gone over countless ideas and schemes, and they all were worthless. Escape didn't seem possible. Lilae had walked the halls with Vasira every day and seen hundreds of soldiers and guards stationed in various places around the massive palace. Every day they stood guard over every exit. Every day, they watched her.

She held her breath. She heard Kavien's footsteps as he entered the room. He closed the large double doors behind him. She heard the lock click.

Lilae gulped, shifting closer to the back of the chest. His footsteps drew closer, his boots clanking on the marble floor. He stopped right before the chest, his form blocking the light. Her heart began to thump. Was this it? Did he finally come to kill her?

She readied herself. She would fight, even though it was futile. Pirin had taught her to never surrender. *Never back down*. She would honor his memory.

The chest lock clicked open. The lid creaked as he lifted it, dim light filling the darkness that had protected her. His eyes. They looked in at her… sadly.

Lilae was afraid to breathe. She was too terrified to move. To her surprise, he reached in and lifted her out. He held her tenderly, like a child, as if he were afraid to harm her. Lilae was still frozen. She didn't know if she should speak or act. He carried her to his bed.

Did he mean to claim her innocence? The innocence he had made sure she told him about? Months had gone by, and, to Lilae's surprise, he had never forced himself upon her. Even more surprising, he had never brought any of the girls to his room.

Kavien laid her on his plush bed; the down-filled covering sank in as she was placed on it. He leaned over her and gently smoothed her chin. Lilae's mouth parted as she looked into his gray eyes. They didn't look evil in that moment. She couldn't make sense of it. Kavien was two different people. She never knew which one he would be at any given moment.

Her chest heaved softly, and he put a hand on her bosom, not in a way that made her uncomfortable but in a soothing, calming manner. Her breathing began to slow. Kavien's eyes never moved from hers.

Lilae knew she should strike. He seemed unguarded. She was afraid. Something wasn't right!

When Kavien leaned in, Lilae didn't resist. She didn't know what she was doing. He was ridiculously, sickeningly attractive. His lips lingered softly above hers. His lips were soft and full. He smelled of mint and sweat. It was intoxicating. Her breathing quickened again. Her blood was rushing.

What is going on? Lilae screamed at herself. This could possibly be her chance. The chance she had prayed for. Kavien was… weakened. Instead, she surrendered to his kiss, her first *real* kiss.

She didn't want to run. Kavien cupped her head in his large hands as he devoured her mouth. Lilae felt blood rush to places she never knew could be awakened. She squirmed beneath him. Escape. It jumped into her mind, and she pushed it away.

His tongue invaded her mouth, but she welcomed it. He tasted delicious. She was breathless. Lilae wrapped her arms around his neck. And then, he withdrew. He looked into her eyes again.

Lilae gasped. For a moment, he looked as afraid as she. The moment of silence seemed to last forever, as both of them desperately wondered what was happening. He was the enemy, and he felt the same way about her.

She felt hopelessly abandoned when he simply lay down beside her. He pushed her onto her side and wrapped his arms around her. Lilae saw him wave his hand, and, to her surprise, all of the candles and torches were put out. Then, he fell asleep like that… holding her.

CHAPTER 45

FOUR MONTHS IN AVIA'TORENA had changed her. Lilae and all of the other girls of the harem were led to the expansive banquet hall at dusk. Each girl was scantily clad in sheer silk, a special gown for this night, with gold sashes tied at their waists. The halls were lit especially bright with petals of flowers festively scattered all around.

Lilae stood out, even though her skin had been bronzed by the scorching sun of the land. Nevertheless, the burning desire for revenge remained. She would occasionally see Dragnor stalking through the palace. He would scowl at her, and she would lower her eyes. She'd never feared someone so much in her entire life. The nightmares threatened to drive her insane; she had to kill that Shadow Elf.

The nightmares had lessened since she had been let of the box and was free to sleep at Kavien's side each night.

Each of the harem girls had their hair braided the same way: two long braids secured by golden bows at the ends. Lilae had her hair long and loose, as Kavien liked it. A sheer silk scarf extended across her face and hair, shrouding her. They were led to a platform that had a grand canopy over it; four brass posts extended upwards to hold a stretched sheet of silk.

They were all seated in the same pose, on their knees with their legs stretched underneath. They were to sit up straight and place their palms on their thighs. A guard sat post at each corner of the platform, stoic and silent.

"Straighten your back," Rahki whispered to Lilae and demonstrated how they should sit. "The emperor wants us to look our best."

Lilae sat up straight and looked over the assortment of decorations with curiosity. There were spreads of food laid out on long dark wooden tables that were covered in dark red cloths. The tables were low to the floor, colorful pillows set out around them for seating of the guests. The food was fresh, steam rising off the platters.

The room was dimly lit with torches and tall candelabras on pillars. Lilae was intrigued by what to expect from this peculiar night. She was also famished. The smell of roasted meats wafted into the room as the servers entered.

Her mouth watered and her stomach grumbled when she saw the legs of lamb and whole chickens on platters being carried on the shoulders of young men and women. Suckling pig was carried in, as well, along with freshly baked flatbread.

Rahki saw Lilae's eyes following the food. "Don't worry. They will feed us."

Lilae continued to stare, seeing the bare-chested men and barely-draped women set the platters at the centers of each table. They walked and moved with choreographed precision. Like Lilae and the harem girls, they were dusted in gold powder, their skin glistening underneath the soft glow of the candlelight.

The guards pulled the sheer satin sheet of the canopy down, hiding the girls behind it. Lilae watched through the sheet as the festivities began.

They heard the boisterous guests enter the room, walking in with their heads held high in their most expensive finery. The women had long gold necklaces hanging crisscrossed across their cleavage and a ring on each finger. The men also wore jewels on their fingers and sashes across their chest with golden pins.

"My guests," the emperor said in his booming voice.

Lilae sat up straighter. Kavien's presence excited her more than she thought was possible. He had been gentler than ever since that night that he saved her from Sister Eloni.

He had cleaned the blood off her, and it had been a tender moment that had begun a different relationship between them of unspoken adoration, and

Everyone cheered.

"Welcome to my birthday of twenty years and five!"

More loud cheering.

"Sit. The feast is about to begin!"

Lilae wished that she could see the festivities. She inched forward to try for a better look, hoping to catch a glimpse of the emperor.

"I hope the duke of Avia'Torena doesn't pick me," Rahki said. She nervously wound the end of her skirt around her fingers. "Don't make eye contact or he may pick you," she warned Lilae.

Lilae frowned, sitting back on her heels. "What do you mean 'pick me'?"

"Calm down. You worry too much," Faira replied rolling her eyes. "They only come over to feed us. It's just that the duke always tries to take it a step further. He is a dirty man. Just keep your ridiculous red head down, and he'll leave you alone." Faira turned away and straightened her back. "You really don't know anything."

Rahki frowned. "Why so harsh, Faira? Lilae was only curious." Rahki put a hand on Lilae's shoulder.

Lilae shrugged it off. "I've heard worse."

"Don't worry, Lilae," Rahki said. "It'll be over soon."

Lilae sat back on her heels. Her shoulders slumped. She was still confused by the entire arrangement. Faira's words however, caused her much trepidation. The young woman continuously questioned why Lilae was there, as if she were of some value other than what she appeared to be. She gave up trying to see what was going on at Kavien's birthday celebration and observed the other girls.

There was something about them that she hadn't noticed before. She had always thought it odd that Kavien never brought the girls to his room at night. She had always wondered if he bedded them elsewhere, but now she wondered if he slept with them at all. Her eyes widened with a sudden realization, as she watched the others stare calculatingly at the guests.

My god, Lilae thought. *They're all gifted! Why didn't I notice before?*

Lilae's mouth hung open as she watched them. *How clever,* Lilae thought. The emperor seemed to keep those with power around him.

In light of this, everything she thought she knew seemed to be a ploy.

They sat quietly while the guests ate and drank themselves into intoxication. Once they had had their fill, the girls were presented to them, as the curtains were drawn. Lilae was surprised that the men and women were expected to feed them. Lilae and the other girls had to sit with their hands down as food was brought to their mouths.

She'd never seen anything like it. A man stood before her with a small plate of food stacked high. He had large gray eyes and black hair like the other Mithrani men she'd seen. He fed her thin slices of lamb, his fingertips brushing her tongue with each piece.

Lilae felt uncomfortable; she could tell he wanted her tongue to lick from his fingers. She was too starved to protest; she ate everything he offered. Her eyes kept looking sidelong at the other girls, seeing that they were extremely focused on the guests.

Her face was turned to the man who fed her. He held her head back, and she looked into his eyes as he poured wine into her mouth. She sat silently as he wiped her chin with his hand. His grin grew, and he suddenly grabbed her face. She toppled over as he held her tightly, his thumbs gripping her cheeks together.

Lilae frowned, her eyebrows scrunched in annoyance. Her cheeks reddened with embarrassment. She wanted to push him away, but she knew where that would lead her. She bit her lip as she waited for him to finish adoring her. She cried out in pain as he grabbed her nipple through her silken dress and twisted it.

"Looks like the duke fancies that one," a guest chuckled as he ran a knuckle up Rahki's forearm. "Where did *she* come from?"

"Exotic, this one," the duke said, his eyes locked with Lilae's as though in a trance.

Lilae was furious, but she immediately looked away, remembering Rahki's advice. The Duke of Avia'Torena had obviously taken an interest in her. She was ready to snap his neck, if only she had the chance. She almost reached out and slapped him, but she forced herself to keep her hands at her sides.

Kavien approached from the crowds of guests with a golden goblet. Lilae looked up pleadingly at him.

Noticing her look, he spoke to the duke. "This one is mine. Stay away from her."

The duke nodded, bowing in apology. His face flushed. "Absolutely, Emperor Kavien. My apologies."

"All right, everyone," Kavien called, and Lilae noticed how they looked at him. He stood at least two feet over the other men with his muscular body showing through his regal garments. "Settle down. Dessert will soon be served."

Kavien kissed Lilae's forehead, and she felt her heart soar. There was something about his touch that made her feel disoriented. It was toxic. Yet oddly she found herself craving it.

The guests retreated begrudgingly, and the other girls all fixed themselves. Some of them had had their sashes loosened and their upper halves exposed.

Lilae knew what she had to do. She scratched at her belly. The symbols Dragnor had tattooed onto her itched. She ignored the annoying itch and focused on how much she was sickened by this place. She balled her fists, glaring after the guests as they followed the emperor from the pavilion. She couldn't let herself be absorbed in this world. It was not her world. She had bigger things to do.

"Come girls," Vasira called, and they came to their feet to file out after her.

Lilae followed behind the group. She looked over her shoulder at the party and saw that there were girls dancing in shimmering skirts and scarves. The girls had mounds of jewelry and very little clothing as they danced in unison to the musicians who sat on a colorful rug in the corner of the room with their lap drums and flutes. The girls' faces were covered from beneath their eyes to their necks with thin silk; their eyes were heavily traced with black liner.

Lilae saw Kavien sit upon a large embroidered cushion on the floor and drink from his goblet, his eyes not on the dancing girls but watching Lilae as she left the room. She almost felt sorry for him, for what she was about to do. Something told her to not worry. It was her time to escape.

She was careful to stay far behind the others and wait for the group to turn the corner. She silently pressed her back against the wall and listened for the guards. She scratched at her belly again. She hated how much the writing that Dragnor had engraved on her flesh irritated her, both physically and mentally. The constant itching was more than an annoyance. She wanted to kill him and be free of it.

No one noticed that she had left the line. Lilae ran as fast as she could down the hallway. She had taken note of the exits. Still, she would have to be stealthy in her escape.

All Lilae needed was a weapon. She noticed that the guards all came in pairs, so she would just have to kill both before either could alert anyone. She ran lightly, her feet softly padding the ground so that no one would hear her. Her heart beat rapidly, and her hands began to sweat with anticipation. She stopped abruptly when she heard the heavy footsteps of boots on the wooden hallway floor.

This was her chance. She waited silently around the corner for the two to pass her. She looked around to make sure no one else was coming and then quickly turned the corner behind the men. She only hoped her strength was the same. She tried to muster enough courage to go through with her plan, which only consisted of killing those two men and getting to the exit. She quickly came up behind the guards and yanked a knife from one of their belts.

They turned in surprise, their hands immediately going to the hilt of their swords. Lilae quickly slashed the blade across one of their throats. She withdrew the knife so fast that, before the other could draw his sword, she covered his mouth with one hand and went to slit his throat with the other. He shocked her when he grabbed her wrist and yanked her around.

Lilae flew into the wall, slamming her side hard against the stone. She grunted and tried to use her Evasion. She scrambled to her feet before he could come at her again, and the guard caught her with one hand and slammed her into the wall once more.

He countered her Evasion.

What is this? Lilae paused her attack, feeling the pain of being tossed around like a rag doll.

What skill could counter hers so easily?

She didn't understand the Mithrani; their powers were much like the humans', but she wasn't sure what else they could do. Worry filled her mind and body, making her freeze. She thought back to the man who had almost raped her in Lowen's Edge. He had overpowered her with his strength.

"What do you think you're doing?" the guard growled, his bright gray eyes glaring at her as he readied his sword.

She was on her feet, the knife held ready, as they stared at each other. Lilae was unsure of what she could do now. The knife was no match for his sword, and he could counter her abilities. This wasn't going the way she had imagined it in her head. She couldn't believe she had been so sloppy.

She looked around nervously, hoping that maybe she could still run. He lunged at her, and she sidestepped him. She took the chance to stab him, but his body was so hard with muscles that the knife barely did any damage. She sucked in a breath as he turned around, pulling the knife free. His eyes were furious.

Lilae turned and ran. He chased her, yelling for the other guards, and she knew that she had failed. She only hoped that a miracle would happen. She was faster than the guards and crossed more ground before they could catch up. She grinned when she saw the corridor ending at a large set of double doors. She quickened her speed. The door was finally within her reach.

She grunted. Her eyes widened as someone stepped before her. It was as if he came out of the shadows. She gasped when she looked up at Dragnor's face. To her shock and utter terror, when he looked at her face, he simply smiled.

"I barely began to evoke the spell and look, *you've* come to me," he said as he leaned toward her. "And what's this?" He looked at the guards who were chasing her. Lilae felt her stomach collapse. Dragnor's smile widened. "You've been very naughty, Lilae. Very naughty indeed."

Lilae's heart sank into her stomach, and she felt queasy. She already anticipated the pain. Sure enough, with one touch he sent what felt like shards of glass throughout her body. She collapsed to her knees and screamed. She wanted to fight the pain, but it was too strong. Tears fell from the corners of her eyes as she squeezed them shut, trying to block out the agony she felt. How foolish she had been to think she could escape.

"You will pay for this," Dragnor hissed.

The guards caught up and grabbed her. She could barely keep track of where they took her as the pain slowly subsided. They took her deeper into the palace than she had ever been. She fought and kicked, yelling the entire way. Her nails scratched the skin on one guard's neck, and he tightened his grip on her wrist.

Lilae shook her head when she saw where they were taking her. "No. Please."

The stairwell landed at the dungeons. It was dimly lit, and the air was stale and smelled of excrement and burning flesh. She felt her dinner almost back up in her throat.

The floor was slippery with dark liquid that Lilae knew was either water or blood. Dragnor led the way past the holding cells. The cells were barred, and in each sat a few unlucky folk. They were skinny, miserable, and barely clinging to life.

"Murderers and rapist dwell here," Dragnor informed her. "And tonight, you shall join them in their putrid cells."

"Please," Lilae pleaded. She felt foolish to think that she could actually escape on her own. Her mind went to what Kavien had said about what Dragnor would do to her. The thought of rats nibbling on her made her shudder.

Dragnor ignored her. "I can't pretend that I am displeased by your disobedience. On the contrary, I am thrilled that you have done this." He glanced back at her as he went through a narrow doorway. "The Ancients made you resilient in more ways than one. But you've finally showed your true colors, and Kavien will now see how much of a nuisance you really are."

Lilae took note of the torture devises as they went deeper into the large room. Memories of her night with Dragnor resurfaced, and she fought the guards again. Dragnor barely took notice.

Her belly itched.

"Did you make me come to you through some trickery?"

Dragnor grinned. "You're learning. Good girl. I did. It was a test, and my dear, you've passed."

"It's not true," Lilae whispered as her face paled. She refused to believe that she was tricked. "You cannot control me! I ran because I wanted to!"

He laughed then, holding his stomach as if what she had just said was hilarious. "Oh, I don't think so. I know about you and the emperor."

Lilae shook her head. She tried to reach up to claw at his face. "You know nothing! My will is my own."

Dragnor's smile faded. "Not anymore. You are mine." He leaned close to her face and grabbed her cheeks. His breath was rancid. He licked her lips.

"You've been lucky until now," he continued in a low voice. "If it were up to me, I would have engraved High Jordanian over every inch of your body and kept you as my pet for the rest of eternity." Dragnor's eyes met hers. "Tonight, I will do just that. But first, you must be punished."

Lilae felt her cheeks tingle, and she tried to keep from vomiting. She was terrified. Her entire body shook.

Dragnor motioned toward a device of shackles that hung from the ceiling.

The guards clamped Lilae's wrists into the cold metal shackles, and she stood on a square-shaped platform. She looked at Dragnor, her eyes pleading, but he moved so quickly that she only saw the air slightly waver at his speed. He appeared before her, and she winced when he slapped her face. The back of his hand struck her so hard that she felt blood squirt from her mouth.

Lilae squeezed her eyes shut as she turned to face him. Her neck was sore from the impact of his slap. Her head spun, her left eye stung. She surprised him when she spit the blood onto his face. Her cheek throbbed, but she felt her pulse race with rage.

For months, Lilae had been too afraid to try to use her power. Now, she called it. Desperately, she reached inside to that secret place where her power used to hide.

Nothing. No response.

Dragnor raised his hand to strike her again, his eyes wild with anger, but resisted. He shook his head, his nostrils flaring. A guard approached with a long, thin, black whip.

"I want to do it myself," Dragnor growled like a beast. He snatched the whip from the guard, who bowed his head and stepped away. Dragnor's eyes narrowed, and he held the whip's handle close to Lilae's reddened face. She breathed quickly as she looked at the long thin leather.

"I told you that you will pay." Dragnor stepped back and whipped her directly across her face.

Lilae was shocked that he would do such a thing. The pain seared through her eye and cheek. A vessel burst in her left eye, spilling blood down her face and into her mouth, and she continued to scream.

Dragnor was silent as he took a few steps around to the back of her, and Lilae closed her eyes, bracing herself.

Lilae thought that being whipped across the face was the worst, but the first lash on her back stunned her into silence. She would have screamed, but her voice was caught in her throat. By the third lashing, she screamed again, unable to hold back. She felt his anger all too clearly. With each strike, she was sure it would be the last.

After the twentieth lashing, all of her weight was supported by the shackles as she drifted into the darkness.

LILAE WOKE UP TO MORE PAIN. She was lying face down. Her arms were strapped to her sides, and she realized that she was back on Dragnor's table.

A sharp sting assaulted her sore, bloodied back as Dragnor returned to his work of carving those symbols into her skin. Her eyes popped open.

"Good afternoon, Lilae."

Lilae's eyes stared at the wall. She could only move her head an inch. Her sore cheek was pressed to the coarse wood of the table. She began to hyperventilate. "Stop, please. Take me back to Kavien!"

His grin widened. "You aren't such a quick learner after all. You really think I care what Kavien thinks? He isn't what you think. I trained him. He is my protégé. You think he is falling for you? It is a trick, trust me. Kavien cannot love. He can only conquer."

Lilae felt tears trail down her face. "I don't believe you. You are a liar." She spoke in a whisper. Dragnor's words hurt more than she thought they would. She wouldn't believe what he was saying about Kavien. She had seen his other side. He was good. She knew it.

Dragnor stopped his work and came around to put his face next to hers. "Let's test this new spell out, shall we?" Lilae tensed. She felt her flesh begin to burn. Dragnor wiggled his finger in the air next to her ear and recited words. Lilae felt her breathing slow. The air was sucked from her lungs. Her eyes widened. She panicked.

"Stop! I can't breathe!" Her restraints were stifling. She couldn't even get enough air to scream for help.

Dragnor grinned. "That is the point."

Lilae's body bucked, and she felt her lungs burn as if she were drowning. It was no use. Before long, the lack of oxygen made her pass out.

Lilae was sure she was dead this time. She only hoped the man from her dreams would be there to welcome her. She couldn't believe Kavien didn't come for her.

CHAPTER 46

LILAE OPENED HER EYES to the empty surroundings in the torture chamber.

Vasira squeezed her nose closed to keep the stench out. She looked at Lilae distastefully.

"Are you trying to get yourself killed?" She unclamped Lilae's shackles.

Lilae's knees were weak. She wobbled to the ground, and Vasira scowled down at her.

"You couldn't just keep your mouth shut and obey orders." She screamed at Lilae, her voice echoing off of the dungeon walls.

Lilae felt queasy and swallowed hard to not vomit. She noticed that her hands were in small puddles of her own blood, and the pain came back to her. Her entire body throbbed, and she'd started to weep again. She barely heard Vasira's complaints. She would never forget that horrible night.

Vasira growled and grabbed Lilae by her armpits.

"Someone help me!" she ordered the nearest guard. Lilae was exhausted as they led her to the harem.

Rahki and Faira rushed to Lilae once Vasira and the guard left her inside the entrance to the harem. They both ducked under an arm, draping her around their shoulders. They helped her walk to a small room near the bath house and a table with tightly-tucked linens wrapped around it.

Rahki and Faira helped Lilae lie on her stomach. She laid there, her cheek pressed against the linens, utterly broken, and the sisters knew it. Tears sprouted anew as Lilae squeezed her eyes shut. Her entire body screamed with burning, pulsing pain.

Rahki covered her mouth as Faira peeled Lilae's satin garments from her body. The welts were large and gruesome. Bloody, red cuts were scattered from across her shoulder to her lower back and buttocks. Lilae felt so ashamed; she knew they were staring at her.

"Faira," Rahki called in a cracked voice. "Ask the slaves for some clove oil, salves, and some bandages."

Faira stood stiff, staring at Lilae's back in disbelief. Even her lower eyelids filled with moisture at the sight of such barbarity.

Rahki became impatient with her sister. "Faira!"

Faira nodded hurriedly and rushed from the room.

"I'm so sorry this happened to you, Lilae," Rahki said solemnly. She bent down to her knees and tenderly smoothed Lilae's hair. "But what made you think you could escape the imperial palace?"

Lilae was silent. She sniffled and turned her head away from Rahki's eyes.

Rahki shook her head. "The emperor favors you. You should just accept your new place before he loses interest. Would you rather live in the dungeon? Or even worse, do you want him to have you killed?"

Silence. Lilae missed her family more than anything at that moment. They had died because of her, and she tarnished their memory with her weakness. What would Delia think? She was weeping there like a defenseless little child. Had she ever been less powerful?

"Just leave me alone," Lilae answered between sobs.

Rahki didn't budge. "No," she replied softly and hugged her, careful to not disturb Lilae's wounds. She snuggled Lilae's tangled hair. "I will not leave you alone."

Lilae sighed and wiped her nose. She lifted her head, resting on one arm, and stared at Rahki. Her exotic face was full of concern and empathy.

"Why are you helping me?" Lilae's face was wet with tears, her left cheek red from being struck. "I mean, you don't really know me!"

Rahki wiped Lilae's face with a smooth thumb. "I know how you feel, Lilae. While most of the girls are happy to be chosen to live in the imperial palace and have this lavish, carefree life, I never wanted to come."

Lilae raised an eyebrow, listening.

"Granted, I was not physically forced. But, how could I disobey my father and bring shame to my family's name?"

Lilae wiped her nose again and rested her head on the table.

"I had a love once," Rahki told her, as she looked behind her to make sure Faira wasn't listening.

Lilae almost laughed at the word. *Love…* didn't exist in her world.

Rahki smiled, almost bitterly. "He was a soldier with over a thousand gold coins to buy my hand, but still, he wasn't good enough in my father's eyes." She looked at Lilae pointedly. "Now, I'm stuck here serving the emperor, and my beloved Sethi is married to another girl." Lilae saw a tear escape her eye as Faira returned with the supplies.

Rahki quickly wiped her face with her hand and took the tray of materials from Faira. She applied the thick paste generously onto Lilae's cuts.

Something about what Rahki said caused Lilae to suck up all of her tears. She couldn't help remembering how Pirin had said that tears were for the weak. In battle, there is always a strategy, a maneuver to victory. Those who simply retreat or accept a fate other than victory were weak.

Lilae was *not* weak. She would get her revenge one way or another. She glanced up at Rahki with a curious look.

"Was he human, Rahki? Is that why your parents wouldn't let you be with him?"

Rahki swallowed hard. "Yes."

Lilae nodded. "What is it like, to be Mithrani?"

"So, you know."

"I do. The emperor told me."

"Most of the people in the empire are Mithrani or of mixed race. Many of the soldiers in the army are of mixed race. That is why they have both human and Mithrani skills. But to answer your question, it is stifling. Especially for the women. We have such harsh constraints. We are a growing race, and I'm sorry, Lilae, but your people won't survive. Bellens, Mithrani, Shadow Elves, and beasts. I could tell you these things, but you still haven't even begun to understand what secrets lie in the Empire." Rahki pulled away and lowered her eyes.

Lilae nodded. "Thank you, Rahki. For the truth."

CHAPTER 47

THE SUN BLAZED DOWN on them as they boarded the ship. All of the fairies of Tolrin were assembled to watch as Liam, Nani, Rowe, and Sona joined a few fairies on the small white ship. Its sails were a bright white and set high above the decks, billowing out with the wind.

Liam waved at the fairies. "I can't thank you enough, Lady Evee. I really appreciate your hospitality. I cannot wait to come back here when everything is back to normal."

She nodded with a sweet smile then took his hand in her own small grasp. "Please be safe."

He kissed the back of her hand. "You do the same, and make sure young King Wilem and Jorge stay out of trouble."

Lady Evee looked back at the boys who watched with anticipation. Wilem looked ready to run after him, his eyes glossy. Liam couldn't believe that, after only a month, he had grown to care for those boys. He felt bad for abandoning them, but it was for the best. They would be safe with the fairies.

"I'm sure they'll have lots of fun. There's so much here for young children. I've noticed that they are quite taken by the Mother Tree. Perhaps they can join the other children and attend our school in the citadel." Lady Evee jumped into the air, startled when Wilem ran past her. She covered her heart and smiled as Wilem clung to Liam's waist, hugging him tightly.

Liam didn't know what to say. He feared his voice would waver if he tried to speak. Instead, he ruffled Wilem's hair and hugged him back.

When Wilem pulled away, his face was wet from tears. "You're really going to just run off and save the world without me?"

Liam gave a side smile. "I wish you could come, Wilem, but it's just not safe. One day you'll have an adventure of your own."

Wilem grinned. "You think so?"

Liam pinched his cheek. "I know so. One day, you and Jorge will be young men, and you'll be off to begin an adventure of your own."

Wilem shook his head. "Jorge is a coward," he whispered. "I need brave friends like that big Tryan over there. Yeah, I need a friend like Rowe."

Liam chuckled. "You forget that it was Jorge who hid you and saved your life," he reminded Wilem. "One day, I bet he'll be bigger than you and braver than Rowe. You stick to those who are your true friends."

Wilem nodded. "You're right." He unlatched his talisman and held it out to Liam. "Take Vleta with you. She'll keep you safe." The talisman caught the light of the sun, and Wilem squinted up at Liam.

Liam was speechless. He looked down at the talisman and then to Wilem. Wilem put it in his hand and closed Liam's fingers over it.

"Just remember," his face grew serious. "I am only letting you *borrow* her. You better bring her back, or my adventure will be to hunt you down."

Liam laughed loudly and hugged Wilem again. He put the talisman's necklace over Wilem's neck and squeezed his nose playfully. "Thank you, Wilem, for the offer, but Vleta is yours. She will protect you while I am away."

Wilem held onto the gold talisman as it dangled above his chest. He nodded and smiled up at Liam. "See you soon, Liam."

"Soon, Wilem," Liam replied and turned to join the others.

He watched the boy return to his friend and felt sadness in his heart. Wilem had touched his heart, and he would never forget his innocent gesture. Liam waved at them, and the ship was ready to set sail.

Liam held onto the railings as the ship shifted its position. All of the fairies moved out of the way as the ship was lifted from the ground into the air. The sails puffed, and the wings below were outstretched. There was nothing like traveling by fairy ship. They could cover land and sea, and he was hopeful that they would make it to the Flame fast enough.

He avoided glancing back at Sona, even though he could feel her eyes on him. He sighed, watching the fairies and the remainder of his army grow smaller and smaller as they went higher into the beautiful blue sky.

Liam knew he had made a mistake with Sona and cursed himself for being so reckless. Despite his best efforts, he hadn't been able to resist. When he woke up that morning, Sona had been gone. She had left him with a guilty conscience and a pain in the pit of his stomach.

He looked over his shoulder to see her standing there. Her face was emotionless as their eyes met. She shook her head and turned away. Liam could feel it. Something wasn't right. Even as they flew above the Kyril realm, he knew things would never be the same.

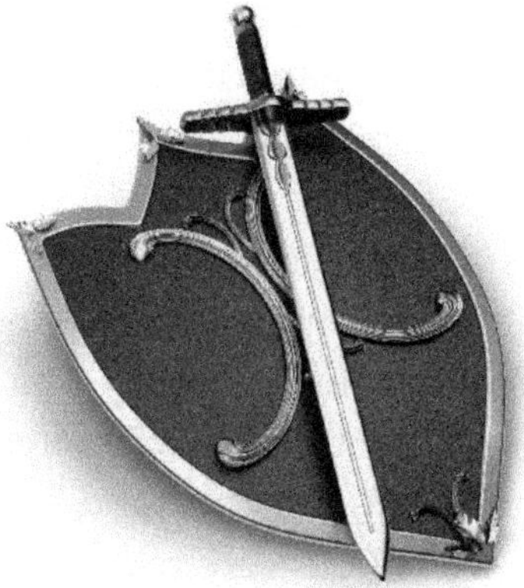

AFTER HOURS OF SAILING, SONA grabbed Liam's arm and tried to pull him to her. He snatched his arm from her grasp and turned on her. He was done being manipulated. He still felt guilty for sleeping with her and couldn't even look at her the same way. He almost despised her more, because, oddly enough, he hadn't wanted to do it. She had seduced him somehow, and he couldn't quite make sense of it yet.

"Liam, stop. Please, I need to tell you something."

"I'm sorry. I don't want to talk right now." Liam pushed her away gently.

"I see. You can't talk to me now. Why? After all we've been through."

Liam looked out at the sky. It was dark, and he felt his stomach twist into knots. There was a storm brewing, and it was not of his doing. He was worried that something would happen to the ship. She tugged on his belt loop.

"This is not the time. We can talk about this when we land." They stood on deck of the ship as night fell, and the sea rolled beneath them.

She slapped him, and his mouth fell open.

"What's wrong with you?" He roughly grabbed her wrist.

"I'm trying to tell you something," she replied angrily. "But you are so self-absorbed that you can't even listen to the most important information I could ever give you."

Liam rolled his eyes. "What is it? Tell me, Sona. What is so blasted important that it cannot wait?" he pursued skeptically. "Go on, I'm listening."

Sona stared at him with her mouth open. She couldn't believe how he'd talked to her. "Once I thought I'd always love you, Liam. But you're cruel, heartless, and feel nothing!"

Liam huffed. "Enough of this! You are the one who is cold. All these years, I thought you were just damaged by your overpowering father, that deep down inside you were really a loving person. I was wrong." He tried to stress those words to her as best as he could. He hated to hurt her, but it needed to be said. He lowered his voice and pulled her aside. Looking into her eyes was difficult. Her power over him was gone. "I saw something that night we were together. Can you explain to me what that was?"

Everyone stared now, overhearing their conversation.

"You make me look like a fool, Liam," Sona spat but tears rolled down her face. "But you are the biggest fool of them all." She moved closer to him. "What you saw was my love for you. I would have changed for you!"

Liam shook his head. "I'm sorry, but I don't want to do this anymore. It just doesn't feel right." His own eyes became glossy. He didn't want to hurt he,r but he had to tell her the truth.

He sounded sincere to her, but it wasn't enough. It was too late.

The hurt left her eyes. She reached out and stroked his cheek once more, and Liam raised an eyebrow, confused by the change in her. Sona leaned in close to him, looking deep into his blue eyes.

"When we were children, I saved your life," she whispered.

"And I appreciate that. I've saved yours, as well. Many times. But what does that have to do with anything?"

"Well, my father beat me nearly senseless." Tears welled in her eyes.

"What?" Now she wasn't making any sense.

Her tone turned icy. "He beat me because I was born to kill you. I should have let you die then, and it wouldn't hurt so much to do it right now."

Before Liam could react, Sona stabbed him deep in his chest. Her shiny white teeth flashed in an insane smile as she thrust the dagger deeper and deeper.

Liam's eyes widened, and his voice caught in his throat. An odd, stinging sensation, like nothing he'd ever felt, overcame him. He watched his blood seep out onto Sona's white hands. There was a squishing sound as she withdrew her dagger. The dagger glowed blue, and he finally understood. It was exactly like the daggers that the Shadow Elves always were equipped with. Her betrayal was too extreme to comprehend.

Liam flushed, his words unable to escape his lips, and he reached for her. She stared at him as he tried to grab her, watching the pain she saw in his face. She looked curiously at him, her smile fading. His eyes became full of tears as he tried to catch his breath.

Her voice was too soft for him to hear her. "I had to." She shook her head. She pushed him as hard as she could, and he stumbled overboard.

Her eyes were wild with a mixture of emotion as she watched his body fall. Thunder broke out, and the sky began to churn. As Liam's body fell, lightning struck all around uncontrollably.

"Liam!" Nani wailed.

Rowe yelled, and Sona quickly shoved aside her guilt. She had had to do it, and it was done now. There was no turning back. Before Rowe could reach her with his sword, a black wyvern darted through the sky.

"Hurry, you stupid beast!" Sona said through clenched teeth. She watched anxiously as Rowe charged toward her. The wyvern reached her, and she quickly mounted its saddle. She and the beast took off into the sky and vanished into the storm clouds.

"Traitor!" Rowe shouted angrily after her. He ran to look over the ship's railing where Liam had fallen. Before he could reach the ship's side, Sona reappeared from the clouds to cause them one last obstacle. One that she hoped would forever end their quest.

Sona used her blue dagger to send a powerful blast of light into the deck. The light burned through the ship's wood and cut through to the bottom, causing the ship to split in two.

She had used lightning. Liam's lightning.

"No," Rowe said breathlessly.

What followed was chaos all around. The fairies all began to flee the falling ship and the raging storm. Nani saw Rowe scramble to find his footing on the sinking ship as it tilted quickly toward the water. She grabbed him, pulling him into the air with her.

"I have to find Liam!" Rowe yelled at her, fighting her grasp. He strained to get away from her, to jump into those dark, fierce waves.

"Hold still, Rowe!" Nani shouted back. "You cannot swim in those waves! There are creatures in there that would gladly eat you. We will look together."

Liam had fallen for what seemed forever until he had finally crashed into the icy black sea. He was still awestruck as his body sank into the water. The waves fought for him, and he didn't have the energy or care to fight back. They tumbled and smothered him, pushing him farther and farther into the watery abyss.

Liam thought of nothing but Sona's face as she stabbed him. He suddenly realized just how far her betrayal reached. She had been on Wexcyn's side the entire time, constantly working her plot to slow them down or end their lives.

Her betrayal went deeper than she could have known.

CHAPTER 48

NANI WAS EXHAUSTED. She had carried Rowe for miles and finally set him on the black sands of the beach that surrounded The Barrier. He was heavy, and, after such a long flight, Nani collapsed to the ground. Her cheek pressed into the sand, the grains molding to her face and embedding into her skin.

Rowe hurried over to her. "Nani!" he called. He didn't know what he would do if he lost her, as well.

She moaned as he rolled her over onto her back. She winced at the pain in her arms from carrying him.

"Are you all right?"

Nani nodded weakly. "Yes, I'm fine." She took his hand as he helped her sit up. She stretched her arms and legs and pulled her legs close, hugging them. "Oh, Liam," she sighed, her heart aching like never before. She looked out to the ocean, her eyes stinging with wetness.

Rowe scooted close to her and wrapped his arm around her. She turned to him, those tears finally bursting free.

"*How could she*?" Nani screamed. She sobbed into his chest, and Rowe had to wipe his own face.

Rowe had just lost his best friend. He had set out on the journey, knowing how dangerous it was, but he had vowed to not let anything happen to Liam. He had failed.

Nani's shoulders gently bounced with her soft sobs. Rowe smoothed her hair and watched as the red sun began to rise. They had flown all throughout the night searching for Liam, until Nani could go on no longer. They had seen nothing but water and rain.

Nani suddenly sat up; her eyes narrowed as she looked into the sky. "I will rip her eyes out when I find her. I always knew there was something wrong with that filthy whore!"

Rowe's jaw was clenched. He couldn't get Liam's face out of his head. He had seen the look of shock and pain. It had morphed into sorrow at seeing someone he thought cared about him hurt him. The look in Liam's eyes made Rowe's stomach churn with grief. He hadn't stopped Sona in time. Nothing more than revenge would distract him from the grief he felt.

He slammed his fist into the sand and growled, "I'm with you Nani. We will hunt her down, together."

"How could she do that?"

"I really believed that she loved him. She fooled us all."

Nani snorted. "She didn't fool me!" Nani felt a chill run up her spine and shivered as she looked up. They heard loud swooshing sounds; in the sky, they saw wyverns flying all around them that seemed to have come out of nowhere, perhaps from the jungle or the clouds. Nani and Rowe were completely exhausted and caught off guard.

They were on their feet in an instant, and Rowe realized he didn't have his ax or his sword. All he had was a knife in his boot and a dagger in his belt. Nani clung to him like a frightened child. They both felt a wave of dread come over them when they noticed that riding each wyvern was a fully equipped Shadow Elf, and they were flying straight for them.

"Rowe," Nani called in a frightened little voice.

He held her close. "They're waiting for us. We'll go on for Liam. I kill, you heal. Got that, Nani?"

Nani swallowed a lump in her throat but nodded, as she watched the elves line up and block their path. "Yes. I am with you. For Liam."

NANI SQUEEZED HER EYES SHUT. She didn't want to believe what she was seeing. Rowe shook her roughly. He stopped shaking her to catch a Shadow Elf by his wrist and break it in half. He punched the elf square in the face and knocked him out. Rowe was never one to leave an enemy alive. He picked up the elf's head and snapped it with his hands.

With a battle cry, another Shadow Elf almost flew into Rowe while he was turned away. Rowe came to his feet, and he backhanded it in the face with his fist, shattering the elf's jaw. Teeth flew along with the elf's saliva and fell to the muddy jungle floor. Rowe kicked it in the head as it tried to get up.

"Nani! Get up!" He yelled at her again. His voice was hoarse, but all she heard was the commotion all around. She couldn't believe what was happening. As they had tried to flee the wyverns, Nani and Rowe had stumbled upon something neither could believe. They were in the middle of an attack. The Shadow Elf army was killing its brethren. Helpless Shadow Elf women and children screamed and ran, and it became apparent that not all Shadow Elves were on the same side.

Nani whimpered, too afraid to open her eyes. She heard footsteps draw closer, screams radiating all around. She could feel the heat drawing closer and squealed when Rowe picked her up.

Her wings had been damaged by a sharp dagger, and she had almost been killed by an elf. She had never felt so helpless before in her entire life.

What was she if she couldn't even fly away to save her own life?

Rowe flung her small body over his shoulder as if she was a child, and she felt the vibrations on the ground as he ran with her.

She peeked, seeing only dead branches and darkness. She was glad that they were running away from the fire and death, but it felt as if it were following them. It was as if death chased them, right on Rowe's heels. His tight muscles were hard beneath Nani's stomach, the smell of sweat strong in her nostrils. She wished she could fly.

"Where are we going?" she asked softly, afraid that, if she spoke too loudly, Wexcyn would take notice and head their way.

"*Shh,*" he whispered, and she understood. He suddenly stopped, ducking to the forest's floor.

Nani opened her eyes wide then searched the darkness for what made Rowe stop so abruptly. They crept close to a tree trunk and waited as silently as they could. Rowe was still shirtless and covered in blood. Nani wanted to touch him, to heal him. At least she still had that part of herself intact. But the light would draw attention to them as they hid.

Rowe had a hand on her thigh, to keep her still. As she pressed her lips together, she heard footsteps crackling along fallen branches and crunching on leaves.

She saw a flash of red flicker by and sucked in a deep breath. She wished Liam was there to save the day, like he used to.

But Liam was dead. No matter what the Shadow Elves were convinced of, she had seen him stabbed by the woman who had claimed to love him. Nani had watched helplessly as he had fallen overboard into the raging black sea. That hole in her heart would never be filled. She would never stop missing him.

Rowe tensed and Nani nearly screamed when a beast hovered above them in the tree. It was red and large but resembled a snake. Its yellow eyes were merely slits, and it sniffed with its nostrils which were only holes in the center of its head.

Nani held her breath, knowing that a single sound would alert the creature of their presence. They watched as a Shadow Elf man stepped through the forest, searching got them. Nani's heart turned to stone, and her blood boiled with rage. He walked carefully, his dagger lit, as he searched for his prey.

He called the beast and, with a loud noise, it jumped from the tree. Nani noticed that it had three sets of hairy legs and shivered. It ran to the Shadow Elf and followed him away from them.

When the elf was out of sight, Nani slowly came to her feet. Rowe followed her example and hugged her.

"We made it," he whispered with relief. They had narrowly escaped the Shadow Elves. Rowe was impressive. With only his two weapons, he had managed to kill many and save Nani from being torn to shreds.

"Ah, there you are." The Shadow Elf appeared behind them, and they both gasped. The beast had its eyes locked on Nani, and she gulped.

Two more Shadow Elves approached from either side, and Rowe balled up his fist. He had lost his weapons. They had been buried in the dead bodies of two Shadow Elves as they made their hasty escape.

Nani knew it was up to her to do something. She couldn't lose Rowe, and the thought of what torture they would experience if they were captured made her blood curdle. She'd never used her powers on anything but healing and regenerating. But she hated those evil elves.

The Shadow Elf looked at her amused. "What are you doing?" he asked as Nani stood there.

"Do it. Go on… You know what to do," voices said in unison.

Nani flushed. "Who are you?"

"The Winds."

Nani began to change. Something ignited within her, and she finally understood. She always knew her bond with Liam was special.

Nani stood in a blaze of smoke. It came from her feet and up her body, taking her healing ability with it. It took her healing gift and replaced it with another. She couldn't hold both powers at once. Her choice at that moment was to exchange her healing power.

She exchanged it for a deadly power. Her hair went white, and her eyes went gold with light.

She began collecting light and energy from the plants around them. She balled all of that energy up and into her body and out through her fingers. The result was a force so strong that Nani felt her body warm; sweat collected all over her.

The Shadow Elves finally understood what Nani was doing and began to charge at her.

Broken wings and half as tall as them, Nani looked like a goddess of horrors as a surge of black and blue light was freed from her fingers like a flood of knives. The elves were defenseless. Their screams were cut off when their bodies caught fire and light ripped at their throats. It was almost instantaneous as the bodies dissipated into a thousand pieces of bone and guts. Ashes flittered into the air like tiny lights.

The beast curled into a ball like a frightened child and seeped into the soil, vanishing. Nani stood there, spent of energy yet full of satisfaction. She took a moment to change back to her healing stance and fell to the ground, utterly exhausted.

Her hair returned to purple, and her eyes changed from gold to gray in an instant. She'd never used her Death Stance before. She came out of the fog of her mind when Rowe shook her.

"Nani, you okay?" Rowe finally let her eyes meet his. "That was amazing! I didn't know you could do that!"

Nani didn't know why, but she surprised herself when she felt the tears finally pour. "I told you, Rowe," she said through tears. She smiled then. "I am *not* just a Cleric."

"*You are* the *Inquisitor*," The Winds whispered. "You are ready."

CHAPTER 49

LILAE'S HEART PUMPED WITH poorly hidden anxiety. She stood before the mirror in a dress that would have made even Jaiza and Risa blush. Eastern fashion tended to be more revealing, but this was ridiculous.

Her bosom looked to be seconds away from spilling out of the dress. The only thing that provided some coverage of her cleavage was layers of thin gold necklaces and crystals. The silk dress was red and clung to every curve of her body. Her entire body had been dusted with a sparkling powder, and her arms had been drawn on with black ink, depicting various designs that made her hands and arms look like murals.

Lilae didn't recognize herself as she gawked at her reflection. Her hair looked more gold than ever beneath an elegant golden circlet that was secured with pins to the top of her head. Her eyes were stained red. She had soaked for what seemed days, cleansing her of any impurities or dirt. Then she had been scrubbed raw, then soaked again and subsequently scrubbed once more. Finally, she had been slathered with thick cream and scented oils.

The process had been daunting, leaving her with her thoughts of fear. She had been so optimistic, and now, she feared that something was going to go wrong.

King Ayaden, her brother, was here.

Lilae was finally summoned. She felt faint as she followed Vasira out of the room. A trail of twelve beautiful young girls followed behind her, lifting the long train of her dress. She was seated on a gold pallet and carried by strong men in crisp white pants and glistening exposed muscles.

Not only was there a grand orchestra in the main hall, there were smaller rooms along the outer walls of the room with smaller bands. There were also acrobats and performers, dancers and magicians.

All of this to convince the Aurorians to surrender.

She and Kavien were seated on a raised cushion on top of a pedestal at the head of the hall, and people were positioned to view the meeting with the notorious king of the North.

An announcer stepped forward and dropped a scroll before reciting from it.

"King Ayaden of Auroria, Lord of the North and King of the Black Throne."

Lilae gasped, her smile transforming into a look of bewilderment.

Her eyes met his, and she nearly stumbled from the pedestal. He had her same red hair, yet his was cut very short. His green eyes were the same, as well. It was like looking at the male version of herself. She wondered if he knew that they didn't share the same father.

"Welcome, King Ayaden," Kavien said with a smile. "It is a pleasure to host you in my fine Empire."

King Ayaden gave a bow of respect. "It is funny, though, only a year ago you were threatening my kingdom, and now we are exchanging pleasantries."

Kavien nodded but didn't show any signs that he took offense. He was cordial. "Amazing what can happen in a year, isn't it?"

"It is fortunate that you've found my sister." He bowed to her. Lilae couldn't help but notice the look of skepticism on his face.

Brother, Lilae thought. She yearned to hug him. She knew she needed to speak to him in private. She had to warn him. Lilae looked from Kavien to Ayaden. Ayaden was looking her over more carefully this time, before turning away. For some reason she got the feeling that he wasn't convinced of who she was.

"May I present you with gifts, for your gracious reception toward my Guard and me?" King Ayaden extended his hands out as chests upon chests were marched down the aisle.

"Twelve boxes of gold. Eleven crates of Northern fire stones. Ten Aurorian crystals. Nine pixies from the frozen plains of Gordanere. Eight Ordinivan giant eggs…" And he went on and on with gifts that were beautiful, and yet Lilae had no idea what most were. She was preoccupied with staring at her brother, amazed by the resemblance.

"…and one enchanted mirror, created by Inora herself for Ancient Telryd as a peace offering in the Realm Wars. I hope you accept these gifts with the same regard."

Kavien finally cracked another charming smile. "I do. Avia'Torena thanks you."

King Ayaden nodded and began to walk away. He had a haughty air about him, as if, despite the occasion and Kavien's threat to his nation, he felt that Kavien was somehow beneath him.

"But…" Kavien said, causing Ayaden to pause.

King Ayaden looked back with furrowed eyebrows.

"What of the Talisman of Osmund?"

King Ayaden's face flushed.

Lilae felt nervous about this sudden question. It seemed to change the mood between the two powerful men.

King Ayaden spoke slowly. "You can't expect me to give you everything, can you?"

Kavien's smile widened. "Of course not. I just wanted to make sure you actually had it. Knowing that you do, I am satisfied. You may go now."

King Ayaden looked surprised. Kavien had outsmarted him somehow. Lilae needed to know what this talisman was. Was that what he wanted? A talisman?

King Ayaden walked away, trying to keep his composure as best as he could. He was good, obviously trained well in royal etiquette, but Lilae had heard the exchange that most of the court had not been close enough to eavesdrop on. It had been tense.

Lilae watched her brother walk away. She wanted to rush after him and ask questions. She wanted to meet her mother. She needed someone to bond with to fulfill the void of grief that Pirin and the twins had left. She even missed Lhana. Anic's final scream still haunted her.

King Ayaden finally stopped in his private section, and their eyes met again. Lilae could see it on his face. He didn't believe she was his sister. It hurt. That was exactly what she feared would happen when she finally got the chance to meet her mother. How could her real family know? She had been taken as a newborn, barely an hour into her birth.

She strengthened her resolve. One way or another, she would get to him. She would warn him, even if it meant losing Kavien's affection.

CHAPTER 50

"NICE ACTRESS YOU'VE FOUND. How did you do it?" King Ayaden sneered at Kavien.

Kavien knew that he was bitter for having been outsmarted into revealing where the human talisman was.

"Red hair. Green eyes. Even the Osmund mark on her left shoulder. What an insult, since you've carved your brand into her right arm. And what were those other symbols?"

"It is of no concern. She is in good health, as promised. And technically she is mine now. Unless you hand over the Talisman. She's more Avia'Torenian than she ever was Aurorian, and she is not an actress."

"It doesn't matter anymore, does it? I'll pretend that she is my sister to keep you and your band of dogs out of my territory."

Kavien mocked a look of surprise. "Dogs?" He grinned wickedly. "I have millions of gifted soldiers that are ready to raid your lands at my command. They may be beasts, yes, but they'd slice through your army in seconds if I set them loose."

Ayaden frowned. "You're a fool."

Kavien shook his head. "And so the insults continue. Shall we forget treaties, alliances, and so forth and give the whole bloody war a try? So I can massacre every living creature north of Sabron?"

Ayaden held his shoulders up defiantly. "A man can voice his opinion here, can't he? I simply want you to know that I am not easily fooled."

Kavien raised an eyebrow. "Is that what that was? Well, I think you're the fool, Ayaden. The girl has been hiding for eighteen years. We could have killed her, but, like civilized people, we decided to try diplomacy first. Of course, my terms still stand. Naturally, you'll be stripped of your title as king, for there are no kings in Eura anymore. There is only one head of authority to rule all men… Me. Sure, you can still govern Auroria, however you will govern with my rules as Duke of the North."

"What is this Duke nonsense?"

"It is the highest title given in Avia'Torena." Kavien smiled. "Why, aren't I generous?"

"Like Elahe himself," Ayaden said under his breath.

"As Duke of Auroria, you will be protector of the Northern territory and execute my laws. Nothing shall change. Your people can still be free to live their lives as they see fit. However, you'll pay my taxes and open your gates to the Sisterhood."

Ayaden's eyes widened. "That wasn't part of the deal!"

Kavien shrugged. "It is now, Duke. You no longer have a say against my rules."

Ayaden's face turned red, and Kavien went on, pacing now.

"As I was saying… you'll allow the Sisters of the Fallen into the north, where they will set up monasteries. Of course, every child born with a special trait shall be sent to the monasteries as they are here. There they will be trained to serve."

Ayaden's face went from red to white, and Kavien smiled. Just like his sister, he couldn't hide his emotions. He did, however, nod. "We shall obey your terms, your imperial majesty," he agreed through clenched teeth.

Kavien clamped a heavy hand on Ayaden's shoulder. He may have looked gangly, but the young man was as toned as steel. Perhaps his sword wasn't just for show. "Good man. Your people will be grateful to still have their heads."

Ayaden's face softened slightly. "My sister, I will be taking her home immediately."

Kavien tensed. It was time to follow through. "After you give me the Talisman. It was created to protect the humans, and I will be its protector now."

Ayaden shook his head and glanced toward the door that led back into the grand reception hall. "And if I told you that I didn't have it?"

Kavien's face hardened. "Then we would no longer have a deal. And you will be considered an enemy."

Ayaden looked at him and understood his meaning. "Good thing I didn't say that. I know where it is, and if she is really my sister, then she has had the talisman the entire time." He grinned, and then, with a bow, he walked away.

Kavien watched Ayaden leave the room and head directly toward Lilae. She stood there, taller than most of the people around her, surrounded by attendants, personal guards, and diplomats. Her eyes went to Ayaden and he saw her fumble with the sash of her dress.

Lilae hair went from gold to red. Kavien glared at Ayaden. *He'd better deliver the talisman, or there would be blood covering that entire room.* He nodded toward Dragnor, and Dragnor slinked into the crowd.

King Ayaden went to his guards. He spoke in whispers and turned toward Lilae. Kavien stiffened. She didn't hesitate in hugging him. Even Ayaden was stunned by her actions. Kavien began to walk over, sensing something was wrong. Lilae's eyes glided to his, and her face was pale as ever. He knew that look. She had just done something. She had just betrayed him.

King Ayaden pulled away from Lilae and motioned for his men. Kavien's jaw tensed and he started to push his way through the crowd. He would kill the Aurorian king. He could not let him leave.

King Ayaden, however, took off his cape. He drew his sword. Every man in the room drew their swords with him. Lilae stumbled backwards. Kavien stopped in his steps. King Ayaden Split. Kavien felt the color drain from his face. This was something he had never seen before: one of the rarest skills to exist in humans.

The Aurorian king's body multiplied a dozen times until red hair and shining white swords filled the room. Ayaden and his troupe of men started to kill every Avia'Torenan man. Kavien watched in stunned silence as the blood of his men sprayed into the air. Women and delegates ran screaming.

It was chaos in the ballroom. People trampled each other to reach the doors. This was not what Kavien had been expecting. He had intended on causing a scene. Whatever Lilae had said to Ayaden had alerted her brother to his plan.

Kavien's eyes went to Ayaden, who was escaping, while his men and copies of himself did all of the fighting. Fury rose within his veins.

He glared over at Lilae. She was leaning over, reaching for a fallen sword. His eyes widened. She could not be allowed to take a sword. Kavien outstretched his arms, and an inaudible blast of power exploded from his body. Everyone in the room doubled over in pain. Men, women, he didn't care. Their faces became covered in black veins that choked them. Every copy of Ayaden disappeared, obviously called back to him.

Kavien cursed under his breath. Lilae was still standing. She searched under the bodies for that sword. He ran over to her and grabbed her by her hair, slinging her to the ground.

"How could you? This was to save lives. Now I'm going to have to kill every Aurorian in the realm!" he shouted into her face. She didn't know how much this would cost him. Lilae tried to wrench free.

"I did what I had to. You would have killed them anyway. At least now, the humans will have a chance." She glared into his eyes. "Are you going to kill me now?"

"No, Lilae. I will not kill you. I free myself from you. You will belong to Dragnor now," he growled at her, flinging her across the room. He wasn't sure if he meant what he said. A part of him still cared about her, but the bigger part was furious and expecting the worst from Wexcyn. His life meant more than hers.

Dragnor darted over to her body. "No, let the guards take her. This way," he shouted to the elf while drawing his sword. He took off after King Ayaden, who couldn't possibly get away. There would be squads of Mithrani soldiers swarming the palace and courtyard. The noise stopped behind them once they were outside.

Kavien skidded to a stop. Outside was quiet. King Ayaden held a glowing orb. He looked back at the emperor. Kavien thought of all the gifts that Ayaden had just given him. They had been taken back. The North was full of secret treasures. He recognized the orb. He stepped back, putting an arm out to stop Dragnor as well.

Ayaden grinned. "Well, this was a nice little evening. A bit short, but nice nonetheless. I have learned a lot about you and your plans, and I believe you now," he said letting the orb float in the air beside his head. It had a soft blue glow and hovered in the air as if it had a mind of its own. He nodded to the palace. "She is a true Aurorian, through and through."

"She'll be dead by morning," Kavien told him.

Ayaden shrugged. "A true Aurorian will sacrifice themselves for the lives of others. We will make monuments in her honor."

"Sure, you do that. I'll deliver her head to the Black Gates."

Ayaden chuckled. "Just try. You'll never make it over the frozen plains."

Kavien tightened his grip on his sword. He knew there was nothing he could do. The orb was like a bomb. It could level the entire palace.

"You do know I will come for you."

Ayaden nodded. "Sure, you will try. There's a reason we Northerners keep to ourselves. Perhaps one day you'll see for yourself. Though I doubt you'll live to tell the tale."

"Let me kill him," Dragnor hissed into Kavien's ear.

Kavien held a hand out to silence Dragnor. "In time."

"You can try." King Ayaden had to have the last word. Kavien hadn't met someone as cocky as he was. He nodded and watched him be sucked away by the orb. He would be returned to the orb's twin, wherever it was hidden and far from Kavien's reach. He realized that he was grinding his teeth and looked to Dragnor.

"She is mine now, right?" Dragnor asked knowingly.

Kavien shook his head. "No, she is mine. I will deal with her, and don't worry. She will regret what she has done this night."

Dragnor nodded. He smiled with a mischievous look in his eye. "I've trained you well. Show her pain that she will never forget. Just promise me you'll let me watch as you sever her head. I want to deliver it to the Black Gates myself. I've been there once. I can go again."

Kavien nodded, stalking back into the palace. "I have a better idea. I think it's time you visit the wise man." Finally, Kavien was thinking clearly. He had a plan.

"Good boy…"

Dragnor raised an eyebrow. "Who?"

Kavien glanced back. Memories flooded his mind.

"The wise man of the Goblin City."

CHAPTER 51

LIAM COULD FEEL THE PRESENCE of someone standing over him. He rolled over in the soft grass and there she was. Lilae stood there, the sun shining behind her. She looked down at him in wonder and shyness. He sat up and looked around. He was back in his dream world.

He spun around to Lilae. He felt his chest. The stab wound was gone. Sona had dug that dagger deep into his heart.

He finally began to make sense of where they were. The Overworld. He turned to Lilae, and she looked up at him yearningly. It had been so long since they had seen each other. He wanted to smooth her soft cheek with his thumb and kiss her pouty lips. Then, he remembered. He had to get to her as fast as possible. He had no idea how long he was out.

Liam couldn't let Sona and Wexcyn win. He couldn't let Sister Eloni harm Lilae.

He finally understood why the Elders had tried to take Sona. They knew of her betrayal before he did, and they were helping him. He wished that they would succeed in capturing her.

Liam knew what would happen if he touched Lilae. He also knew that he had to leave and make it back to the real world as quickly as possible. So he reached for her, to touch her. She pulled away. They both knew what would happen. Her eyes told him that she didn't want to leave. Not yet. Instead, she lay down on the plush grass. She motioned for him to lie beside her. Liam smiled. He knew there wasn't much time, but he would not deny her this wish. He wanted to stay, just as much as she did.

Liam settled onto the grass beside her, his head only inches away from hers. He rested his hands beside him, his fingers right beside hers. Together, they looked up at the sky. It was a beautiful blue, unlike any he'd seen in their world. Knowing where they were made it even more outstanding. He finally noticed the horizon. He could see the tops of the palaces in which the Ancients lived.

Liam rolled onto his side. He leaned over Lilae, and she looked up at him. He'd never wanted to touch someone so much in his life. He held his hand over her face, just above her skin, and closed his eyes. He ran his hand down her cheek, imagining that he was touching her. He could almost feel her soft skin. When his eyes opened, he saw tears trail down her face. Pools flooded her eyes, and he felt his heart break.

She was in pain. He understood. Someone was hurting her. They came here, to heal. He realized how being in the Overworld always healed him both physically and emotionally. He hated to think of what was happening to Lilae right then, as they lay there.

Liam's jaw tensed. He could linger no more. He had to get to her. Her eyes begged him to stay with her. Instead, Liam leaned over her. He lowered his face above hers. Her lips screamed for his. When their lips touched Liam felt a mighty jolt that sent his entire body into frenzy. His eyes opened, and she was still there. She wrapped her arms around his head, and he immediately went to hold her to him.

He kissed her. It was real. Just as he expected, they were torn apart by a bright light. At least, this time, he finally got to touch her, even if it was for but a minute…

Liam opened his eyes and found himself gasping for breath. He fought the water until he realized where he was. After choking the water from his lungs, he calmed himself and made the water support him. He was too weak to do more with his power. He wondered how long he had been underwater.

His eyes widened when he realized that he was being watched.

Mermaids taunted him from below its surface, urging him to come deeper with them. He gasped and looked away. He wouldn't look at them. Their beauty was like a spell. They even sang to him, voices so alluring that he nearly slowed down. Those crystalline blue eyes were enchanting.

He had gazed into a mermaid's eyes before when he were just a child, and he had almost been taken away by them. Mermaids were one of the few creatures that existed in all of the realms.

There was a pack of them, and they were all perplexed.

No one could resist a mermaid.

Liam had one thing on his mind. He had to find get to Lilae. He took a breath and soared beneath the water's surface, stunning the mermaids as they observed this. This particular clan had never come in contact with a Tryan.

His body shot through the water at a speed of the fastest fish. They followed him as closely as they could, right at his heels.

"Are you an elf?" one asked him softly, swimming on her back beneath him.

"Nonsense, I've seen one of those once. They don't like water," said another.

"I didn't ask you!" she shot back, her voice so childlike and innocent.

Liam was amused by this sudden exchange, stealing a quick glance at them.

They were like a dream. Shrouded in a glittering silver light, there were five of them; the others had grown bored with him and already returned to their watery home. Each had a different pattern on its tail and colorful hair. The green-haired one who had asked what he was seemed to be the youngest.

She stared at him, swimming beside him now.

"Where are you going? There's nothing this way."

"Honestly, Kiko, he can't talk underwater. Do you know nothing at all?"

Kiko blew bubbles back at the red-haired one.

"Don't spoil my fun! He is mine, by the way!"

He grinned silently. He found it amusing how they bickered like children. Liam glanced down at them. They looked to be young women. He didn't know much about mermaids. Perhaps they aged like fairies. There was no telling exactly how old they were.

Once again, he shot through the water and then returned to the surface for air.

"*Ahh*, he does need air."

"He can answer me now," Kiko said. "Creature, tell me, what are you?"

He chuckled at being called creature. Surprisingly, they were amusing him.

"I am a Tryan."

"A what?" Kiko asked.

"*Hmm*, I've not heard of such a thing," the purple-haired one said, joining in the conversation.

"I have," said the redhead.

"You lie," Kiko taunted. "You just want to pretend that you're smarter than I, Loilo.

"But I am!"

"You just look older, doesn't mean you know more."

Loilo blew bubbles at Kiko and swam away in a fuss, disappearing into the darkness below.

It was quiet for a while. Kiko still followed; the others gave up and went home.

He found that he was oddly comforted by her company. He looked to the stars to make sure he was still going in the right direction.

"Tell me where you need to go, stranger. Those stars can play tricks on you sometimes," Kiko told him, her voice soft. "Such tricky little menaces those are."

"And what are you?"

She laughed at him. "A mermaid, of course!"

"Right, a tricky little menace is more like it."

"We only want friends."

"And what happens when your 'friends' drown after being lured by you?"

Kiko paused. "Only the bad ones drown."

He glanced at her. She seemed sincere.

"And what about the good ones? The children? The innocent?"

"They learn to breathe water and live happily with us."

Liam was silent, imagining such a thing. He admitted, when he was a child he would have loved to see a mermaid kingdom. He looked below, hoping that he could catch a glimpse of their kingdom but knew he couldn't see such a thing.

The mermaid kingdom was settled upon the very bottom level of the ocean on the deepest rocky terrain. It was way too deep for him to see or venture to. He admitted, he was too afraid to go that deep; who knew what monsters dwelled there?

"Would you like to visit?" she asked him. "I think you are one of the good ones, I do!"

He shook his head, treading through the waves with strong arms. "Not today, Kiko. I must find someone." He wanted to make sure Nani and Rowe were safe, but above all, he mustn't forget why he had set out in the first place. He had to get to Lilae.

"No fair! You know my name, tell me yours now!"

"Liam."

"Strange name I must say. Lee-ammmm. Quite odd."

She swam beneath him then to his other side, almost touching him.

"Who are you looking for, Lee-ammmm?"

"A girl."

"Oh, I see! You like her, yes?" Kiko inquired, her large eyes wide. It was amazing how human they looked from the waist up, yet those eyes were too large and glossy.

"I do," he answered.

Kiko snickered. "Does she like you?"

"No. Well," he took his answer back. "I don't know yet. I think she does. I'm not sure."

"*Humph*! Then why find her? Let her stay lost!" she exclaimed, her tiny voice getting closer and closer as she swam around him.

He laughed at Kiko's surprising childlike innocence.

"She will love me one day." Then he took another breath and went below the water once more.

"*Arrogant* Tryan named Lee-ammmm," she teased softly.

He was deep within his own thoughts again and ignored her taunts. "Why are you following me?"

Kiko smiled. "I like you."

Liam could see the shore far in the distance. "That's nice," Liam answered absentmindedly.

"And why not follow you? I did pull you from the sea floor. So, you are mine!"

Liam quickly turned to her. "*You* saved me?"

Kiko nodded giddily. Her smile widened. "I did."

"Thank you," Liam said, feeling an instant respect for her. Ironic to him, that he had always wanted to talk to a real mermaid but had never expected to meet one like this. "Can you lead me to land? I was heading to the Eura barrier. It can't be too far."

"Of course, but you must promise that you'll come and visit my kingdom someday." She grinned.

Liam couldn't help returning her grin and gave a nod. "I will. Again, thank you for saving me."

Kiko laughed. "I knew there was something special about you. I knew it! I can't wait to tell Loilo!" She swam ahead of him, leading the way.

CHAPTER 52

THE STORM WAS RELENTLESS. Lightning lit up the sky with frightening patterns. The thunder shortly followed, clapping loudly above.

Large droplets of rain beat down onto Dragnor's cloaked head as he flew atop his wyvern, Tari. Its shiny black wings cut through the clouds as it soared through the darkness.

Dragnor had traveled all night to this remote fortress. Eura was the human realm, but the forgotten races still dwelt there. They were secretive folk, keeping to their small hidden cities.

Goblins stood guard, but Dragnor passed through their patrols unseen. Their keen eyes had missed him as he darted above them, as fast as the wind. The tall tower stretched toward the moon and sat in the center of this town made of labyrinths and circular streets.

The goblin folk slept in tiny snug holes dug into the labyrinth walls. Dragnor sighed in relief that he had made it to the tower doors undetected. He pulled the reins of the wyvern and led it down to the ground. He whispered to the creature, and it blended in with the tower walls like a chameleon.

His leather boots sank into a puddle of mud as he stood before the large, thin tower doors. The wood was ancient, a dark oak with dulling gray paint that chipped and crumbled. He turned the rusty knob and paused before pushing them open.

The inside of the tower was dimly lit by tall sconces and torches. The entryway was narrow, leading directly to a set of twin stairs. One set led down. The other was separated by a thin, stone wall and led up.

"Don't linger in the doorway!" someone yelled at him from the bottom of the staircase that led below in a harsh echoing voice. "Are you deaf? Shut the damn door!"

Dragnor did so, shutting the night wind out. He didn't waste time in heading down the stairs. The staircase went deep beneath the ground level, so deep that most would grow fearful. But back in Nostfar, his realm, everyone lived underground. He wasn't afraid; he felt more at home there than he did in the imperial palace. He slept in the dungeons just to remind himself of what it used to be like.

Dragnor crept down the long narrow staircase, following the small trace of light at the bottom. At the landing there was a large cluttered room.

"What brings you down here?" the old man crooned. He was bent over a podium, thin spectacles sitting on the bridge of his narrow, bent nose. He looked down at a dilapidated book. "The hour is quite late to be lurking in these woods, *swartelf*."

Dragnor paused. The man hadn't even glanced at him and had known his race. He straightened his shoulders and looked around the cramped room lit by tall candelabras, their flames flickering and swaying although there was no breeze inside. Not a trace. Shelves of books covered the walls almost completely, and scrolls littered old dilapidated tables. The old floorboards seemed damp, and the air smelled of mildew and mold.

"I need a potion."

"They always do." The old man raised a bushy eyebrow and removed the spectacles. His deep-set blue eyes were clouded with mucous. "What for?"

Dragnor folded his hands. He didn't want to touch anything in that foul room. "An Eternal Sleep Potion."

There was a low chuckle as the man lowered his head and went back to peering at his book. "A fake death potion you mean? You want to put someone into such a deep sleep that those around them think they are dead? What a coward. Why don't you just kill them?" There was a long pause. "Close the door on your way out. Don't let the draft in again."

Dragnor stood his ground. "Make the potion, Vaugner, or my master will surely punish you."

"Oh, yes." Vaugner nodded. "The truth comes out, I see. And with threats, no less."

He didn't bother to lift his gaze, but all humor had left his voice. "I know who your master is." Vaugner closed the book, dust entering the air, and slowly walked around to a nearby chair. He held his lower back as if it pained him greatly. "You think I can be tricked as easily as the mortals of this world?"

Dragnor watched him curiously. Mortals?

"I've been around since the beginning of time. You're nothing but a Shadow Elf cub to me!" He slumped against the chair's back.

Dragnor's eyes narrowed. The old man had a sharper tongue than he had expected. "You'll regret saying that."

Vaugner shrugged. "Will I?"

"I was around in the beginning as well, old man."

"Were you?" Vaugner gave Dragnor a bored yawn.

Dragnor pursed his lips.

Vaugner traced a finger along the chair's arm. "I grow weary these days. Once the Storm and the Flame destroy The Barriers, I cringe to think what horrors they will release." He pointed to himself. "*I* remember why The Barriers were created! Some people choose to forget. Some hide the truth. You cannot hide the truth from someone who was actually there."

"You won't have to worry about it, old man. The Flame will be dead by morning."

Vaugner smirked. "Not likely. You aren't strong enough to even contend with her."

Now, Dragnor smiled. He raised his hands. Flames ignited and ran up and down his arms. He waved the flame before Vaugner.

Still, Vaugner smirked. "What was that, little elf cub?

"I have stolen the Flame's power. I command the power of the Ancients now."

"Was that supposed to impress me?" Vaugner lifted a bushy brow. "You have only tasted her power. No one can take it from her."

Dragnor restrained himself. He could feel Lilae's power, yet he knew Vaugner was telling the truth. He could not completely take the Flame's power. He wanted to rip the old man to shreds. Still, there was work to be done, and he needed Vaugner's help. Instead, he overturned one of the cluttered tables in a fury.

"Do as I say. Make the potion."

"I see what's going on here." Vaugner nodded knowingly. "You're afraid of the gatekeeper!" He laughed. "I see right through you. Not all of the Elders were on the same side. Some still uphold their vows to protect the people of the remaining realms, while… There are those who wish to see them fall. Some who wish to aid in the destruction of life."

Dragnor remained still, as though frozen by Vaugner's words. "Who are you?"

Vaugner shrugged. "No one. A potion maker… right?" He cracked a mischievous smile.

"The Elders are dead, old man."

"Are they?"

"Of course they are." Dragnor paused, remembering what he saw. There was fire and chaos, and every black shadow was covered by the flames. "I was there. I saw Wexcyn turn them to dust. I watched him reshape the entire Underworld. I thought you were supposed to be a wise man."

Vaugner nodded. He rubbed his chin in thought. "You watched him kill the Elders, did you? *All* of them? Interesting."

"Shut up your babbling! I will ask you one last time," Dragnor began, through clenched teeth.

"Don't bother." Vaugner cut him off. "I refuse."

Dragnor raised a hand, the light brighter than any that had ever penetrated that room. He pointed the rays at Vaugner's face and waited for the screams to ensue. When there was nothing but silence then a low snicker, Dragnor quickly lowered his hand in confusion. He saw Vaugner sitting there, shivering with restrained laughter.

Vaugner chuckled, that smug, self-satisfied look on his face that further infuriated Dragnor. Dragnor drew his lips into a snarl.

"Who told you to come here, swartelf?" Vaugner asked between laughs. "Didn't they tell you that I was blind?" More loud laughs.

Dragnor lowered his fists.

"Your cheap tricks won't work on me," Vaugner explained as he began to calm his fits of laughter. "Age," he continued, "has made me immune to your methods of persuasion. Among other things, might I add?"

There was a thick, tension-filled silence between them.

"What do you want with the potion, anyway? It's never been tested on your race."

"It's not for me."

Vaugner raised an eyebrow. "Who is it for?"

"That's none of your concern."

Vaugner shook his head. He sighed deeply and stood. "Has anyone ever told you that you're quite vague?" He smirked, shaking his head as he walked toward the back of the room. "I remember the day Cyden the Prophet spoke the words of the prophecy of the Storm and the Flame. The Ancients gave the people hope."

Dragnor looked up in surprise.

"The day when humans can actually make a stand against the likes of you. I can't believe it's finally come." Vaugner stepped into the shadows, Dragnor's eyes never leaving him. Vaugner turned around with a small box in his hand. It was black, with a single large red ruby set on its lid.

"You've got one more chance," Dragnor said.

"I don't need your chances, you fool!" Vaugner held the box before him. "I've been waiting for you, *Dragnor*, Son of Malikar." he looked at Dragnor pointedly, his eerie eyeballs blind, yet meeting those of the Shadow Elf. "I am not so sure whoever sent you here wants you to survive this night."

Dragnor raised an eyebrow, taken aback at hearing the old man say his name. He had never introduced himself. Moreover, he felt a twinge of panic at the thought that Kavien had betrayed him. He had sent him there. Now, Dragnor wasn't so sure why. Was this errand a trick?

"Truth is I've had a visitor," Vaugner explained, taking out a small silver key from his pocket. Dragnor watched as he placed the key into the lock. "One who wanted a similar potion."

Dragnor started to feel worried. He glanced at the only exit and back at the box. There was something about the box that made him shiver.

Vaugner smiled, his back straightening, making him incredibly tall. "And *she* was much more convincing than you." He turned the key, and the room was flooded with light. It was so bright that Dragnor shielded his eyes and ducked.

"But making potions is not my specialty." Suddenly realization filled Dragnor like a pot of hot water had been thrown on his face. "There was a time when collecting souls was my only occupation," he hissed. "And your soul is ripe for the picking."

Dragnor gasped and turned to run toward the stairs.

"You better run, Swartelf! The Elders don't take kindly to those who escape without permission. And I am much stronger than my brothers and sisters once were. You better run fast!"

Dragnor used his cat-like agility and sped up the stairs, his body disappearing into the darkness. The light of the box chased him, the voices of shadows and spirits calling to him, shouting in muffled tones. The Underworld reached out to him, and he could barely breathe from the fear.

He trembled at the realization that some of the Elders had escaped. He should have guessed it sooner. Vaugner was the only one who could rip Dragnor's soul from his body. If the Underworld was ruled by Wexcyn, where would Vaugner send his soul if he captured it? Dragnor sweated with terror and ran faster than he ever had.

Dragnor felt his heart race, the fear smothering him like a thick blanket. He was too afraid to look back at the whispers that chased him and called out to him. Dread flooded his body as he mounted his wyvern and barely escaped with his soul still intact within his body.

CHAPTER 53

"LILAE," KAVIEN CALLED.

He opened the lid of the chest and saw her lying there. He touched her, and she felt cold. In a panic, he unhooked the collar around her neck and began to lift her from the chest. He gasped when her eyes opened and like wild animal she scratched him across the face.

Kavien wasn't surprised by her actions. He had said some vicious things to her. He had hurt her. She struggled against him.

Kavien tried to hold her down. She elbowed him and used all of her strength to wrench herself free from his arms. With a shriek, she raised a hand to hit him in the throat. Kavien caught her wrist, and she twirled right out of his hands.

"Lilae, *stop*!" He shouted at her. He didn't want to hurt her, but, as she freed herself, she tried to run.

In a flash, he caught up to her and slammed her to the ground. Lilae stared at him in shock at how quickly he had gotten to her. He held her down on the cold marble floor, and she bucked and growled.

"Get off! Let me go!" she wailed at the top of her lungs, and he realized that he was crushing her. He sat up but kept a firm grip on her arms.

He'd never seen her so wild and enraged. It tugged at his heart to see her in that way.

"Calm down, Lilae," Kavien urged, and she shook her head.

"No! Get off of me!" Lilae watched his eyes change color and saw another level of his domination over her. She had failed once again. She began to whimper, seeing how defenseless she was against his strength. She looked at him the way everyone did once they learned what Kavien could do. She'd only seen a glimpse of his power, and it was enough to stifle her attempts of escape.

Kavien felt ashamed. Lilae feared him more than ever, and that was the last thing he wanted. He softened his grip on her and lifted her up.

She was frozen as she watched his face curiously. He never failed at baffling her. He sat her on top of the chest and sat on his knees before her. He held her small hands within his own and looked into her eyes.

"Listen to me, Lilae," Kavien began, and she turned away from him. She tried to rip her hands from his, only to have him hold on tighter.

She bit her lip, and her jaw tensed, but she remained silent. Lilae refused to face him.

His head hun,g and his shoulders slumped. "Why do you always insist on fighting me?"

Lilae shook her head in disgust, thinking in her head that he should know.

"Aren't I good to you?" Kavien asked, and she faced him with a look of incredulity.

"Look at me!" Her face turned red. "You keep me locked in a godforsaken box! You put a collar on me like I am your pet. You let that elf carve spells into my flesh. You let him beat me nearly to death--"

He cut her off with just a glare.

"I did not let him," he told her with a slam of his fist on the chest. "I sent him away. There is no way he can survive what I have sent him to. I sent him to his death, Lilae."

"I don't believe you. I only know what I see, and it is you who has me trapped here. Why do you keep me here? You don't need me. Just let me go!"

Kavien shook her. "What's wrong with you?" he shouted. "Why can't you see that I am protecting you? Do I have to spell it out for you to get it through your skull?"

Lilae tensed. She stared at him. "What?"

Kavien tried to calm himself. He let go of her hands and covered his face. Wexcyn yelled at him. He shuddered.

"FOOL!"

"KILL HER!"

"KILL HER NOW!"

"SHE WILL KILL YOU! YOU'RE SUCH A FOOL!"

"DO IT NOW!"

Lilae leaned forward as she watched him rock back and forth. Her brows scrunched up, and she reached out for him. He caught her hand so quickly that she gasped, and she watched his eyes flicker with light. The whites of his eyes were gone. Shadows ran and lights flashed, and she couldn't help but try and scurry away.

His grip on her wrist tightened and tightened, until the blood began to be cut off. She screamed for him to stop, and, suddenly, he let go.

Kavien jumped to his feet and stumbled away from her. He covered his face in shame. He tried to compose himself. He refused to let them take over.

Lilae began to crawl away, and he slid down to her. He held her close. "Please believe me, Lilae," he begged. He held her in a tender embrace and spoke into her hair. "I never wanted to hurt you. I love you. I wanted to keep you safe."

She listened intently. She was too afraid to move as he held her. Lilae would never forget the horrors she saw in his eyes. She was still too terrified to look him in the eyes, even though they were back to his usual soft gray.

He spoke calmly now, and still she was unsure if he would change on her again. She eyed the exit, wondering if there was the slightest chance of making it.

"I keep you in the chest to make sure that no one can hurt you. I kept you there to keep you from Dragnor's reach. By my side, so I could watch over you. Can't you see that? Can you find it in yourself to believe me?"

Lilae opened her mouth to answer but found herself speechless. He held her at arm's length; seeing the tears in her eyes tugged at his heart.

"I am cursed," Kavien revealed to her bitterly. "It is not just my name. It is everything that I am. My will is not my own. Not until I met you did I have the courage to fight back. Now, I fight Wexcyn every day."

She still watched him with caution.

Kavien waited. The silence was deafening, and he began to wonder if he should have told her so much. He wanted her to know. But, what would she do with such information? Would she be empathetic, or would she hate him even more?

Lilae began to speak, and Kavien felt his stomach twist in anticipation. "You were protecting me?"

He nodded quickly. "Yes, Lilae. I never wanted anything to happen to you. From the day I first saw you. But Wexcyn is always with me. Watching, giving orders. Soon, he will invade the Overworld, and I am to invade Auroria."

She nodded slowly. "And Dragnor?"

He swallowed and looked at her uncomfortably. "You know how the Elder took you from your parents when you were born?

Lilae nodded.

"She protected you, trained you, and maybe even loved you, right?"

"Yes."

Kavien's eyes darkened. "Well, Dragnor killed my family. He took me from my home. He trained me, yes, but with pain. You think you've suffered, Lilae?" He took off his shirt and turned his back on her.

Lilae gasped. Every inch of his back had long, ghastly scars from years of lashings from Dragnor's whip.

"Some say I am lucky to be put on the throne of the Empire. But I think you are the lucky one. I don't even remember what it is like to feel love. My mother and father loved me, and now they are gone. The harem girls love me. But they love my power." Kavien turned back to Lilae.

"I'm sorry," Lilae whispered.

Kavien shrugged. "Don't apologize. It wasn't until you came here that I even remembered what love felt like."

Her eyes met his.

"Somehow, I am stronger than Wexcyn when you are near. Somehow, you keep him at bay."

Lilae raised an eyebrow. "What?"

He shook his head. "It's not important." He changed the subject. "What would you say if I told you I wanted to be free of all of this and run away?" He watched her inquisitive green eyes. "With you."

Lilae pulled back in surprise. He started to smile, waiting anxiously for her reply. She began to open her mouth to answer when there came a knock on the door to his bedroom. They both looked at the door, and Kavien sighed in annoyance.

"Who is it?" There was no answer.

They both looked at the door suspiciously.

Lilae gasped when Dragnor entered the room and threw something at Kavien. Kavien shot to his feet only to be catapulted back into the wall. Lilae screamed when she saw flashing chains holding Kavien's arms against his body. She scurried to the back of the room when a group of high-ranked Sisters followed behind Dragnor.

Lilae looked back at Kavien desperately as they came for her. She fought. Lilae grabbed Kavien's sword from beneath his bed. She knew it was there, it was where he always kept it. It was heavier than any sword she'd ever lifted, and she waited for them to approach.

Kavien was furious. He wanted to kill them all. He struggled to free himself from the chains.

Dragnor grinned. "I thought we were past that now, Flame." He twisted his arm, and she fell to her knees in pain. Her eyes burned with tears, and her stomach knotted. She reached for Kavien, who fought against his chains. They held him in the air, and Lilae remembered the sensation she felt when she was ripped from the sky the day of her capture. Dragnor controlled those chains. They both looked at him in confusion.

Dragnor only grinned. "Thank you, Kavien, for that impressive speech. I always knew you would betray us." He approached Kavien and looked him in the eyes. His grin faded into a look of hatred.

"I'm done pretending to follow your orders, Kavien. It's time Avia'Torena had an emperor worthy of its glory. Wexcyn will understand. He will agree that, although I am not Mithrani, I can lead your people better than you ever could. The Seer is coming."

Lilae fought the pain, but the Sisters used their wands to immobilize her. She was lifted into the air and pulled along, as if by a string, and out of the room.

Lilae screamed for Kavien. She reached for him.

Kavien felt his face turn red with rage as he watched them take her away. The window opened, and his attention was diverted. In flew Sister Eloni. She quietly landed beside Dragnor.

Kavien stiffened. "Where are you taking her?"

Sister Eloni smiled. "To the temple, of course."

Kavien called his power. He would destroy everything in that room. It pulsed out and fizzled.

Dragnor grinned. Sister Eloni giggled.

"My boy, please. Don't embarrass yourself. Don't you know what those are?"

Kavien's face flushed with dread. He looked down. The sparkling chains were tightly snug against his body.

"Those are Cancelling Chains. They cancel any act of power."

Kavien closed his eyes and let out a breath. He had to remain calm, no matter how much he wanted to cry out in anguish. "What do you really plan to do?"

"You really shouldn't have threatened me, Kavien," Sister Eloni said. Her voice was soft yet serious. "I was truly on your side.

After all, Wexcyn chose you. You were supposed to be his champion, and I believed in you. How could you disappoint me so? I don't know what we're going to do with you. So, I have no choice but to invoke a spell on you."

Kavien's eyes popped open.

"No, no. Don't worry. It won't kill you. It'll just put you in a deep sleep. Sure, you'll look dead to anyone who sees you. Your heart will stop, your breathing will slow, but the power will sustain you."

Dragnor nodded. "You have no idea the trouble I had to go through to get the spell."

Sister Eloni rolled her eyes. "You couldn't handle one, old man. I had to kill five of my own girls to make this spell," she hissed.

Kavien watched them. He could only hope they would divert their attention from him, while he tried to think of a way to escape. His muscles bulged as he tried to break through. His hopes were crushed when Sister Eloni turned her attention back to him.

She waved her wand, and his body was moved over his bed. Slowly, she lowered him to the bed and hovered over him. "I will feast on your beloved Lilae tonight. Her youth will sustain me for at least another hundred years." Her eyes narrowed.

"*You* will spend your days reflecting on your betrayal." With a flick of her wrist, she pressed the tip of her wand to his forehead.

He felt the life being sucked out of him and something else seeping into him. He couldn't breathe. He couldn't think. The darkness smothered him, and voices screamed in his head.

CHAPTER 54

TEARS STREAMED DOWN LILAE'S face as the Sisters took her down the corridor. She was still frozen and hovered in the air. Vasira came around the corner. She looked at each woman and then up at Lilae.

"Sister Jedra?" Vasira looked to the woman on the right with a raised brow. "What is the meaning of this? It is my understanding that Sisters are no longer allowed in the palace without permission."

The Sisters, nearly as old Vasira, had hair that reached their waists. Lilae now knew that it meant they had great power. In unison, they looked to Vasira.

"Our business is none of your concern, Vasira. Now, move out of our way," Sister Jedra said.

Lilae nodded her head for her to leave.

Vasira nodded as well, taking her time as she smoothed her dress. "I am afraid I am responsible for the girl's safety. Put her down, and let me lead her to the temple civilly. Or I will have the emperor deal with you."

Jedra smirked. "The emperor no longer has a say in what happens to the girl. This is your last chance to do as I say. Now move." She spoke the word move with such power that Vasira's hair fluttered behind her. Still, Vasira never flinched.

"Just leave, Vasira," Lilae pleaded. She was overcome with worry for Kavien. She had grown to respect and perhaps like Vasira; she didn't want the woman killed.

Vasira met Lilae's eyes. "I'm afraid I can't do that, dear."

Jedra sighed in annoyance. "Have it your way," she said apathetically and lifted her wand out toward Vasira.

A light poured out of it, but, with a sweep of her hand, Vasira did something that made Lilae's blood turn cold. Vasira's eyes went black, and from her hand came a searing light that obliterated the two Sisters before her. They howled and burst into hundreds of black shards.

With a thud, Lilae fell from the air and onto the floor. She shrieked and shielded her face as dozens of screaming girls were released from the Sisters' bodies. Lilae trembled as she watched their translucent souls fly into the air. Vasira frowned and lifted her hand to take the souls.

Lilae watched in stunned silence as Vasira calmed the girls. Lilae was sure she heard their whispers thanking her as they passed through her body and disappeared. As soon as Vasira had killed the Sisters and freed the souls of all of the girls whose youth they had stolen, the hallway quickly fell silent.

Lilae backed into the wall and stared at Vasira in horror. Vasira sighed and looked down at Lilae. Was that a Mithrani skill? Lilae'd never seen anything like it.

"Lilae," she said, holding her hand out to her. "Get up. Quickly."

Lilae looked at her hand suspiciously. She looked into Vasira's eyes. "Who are you?"

Vasira shook her head. "No time. Get up!" She grabbed Lilae's hand and pulled her up. "Dragnor and Sister Eloni will be coming for you. Come!"

Lilae nodded. She was right. Besides, Vasira had just saved her life. She was surprised by the older woman's speed. The woman led her quickly through the halls, her hand grasping Lilae's wrist. Lilae looked at her, perplexed, when they stopped at the kitchen.

"I thought we had more time," Vasira said under her breath. Vasira sat Lilae down in a chair and went over to a pot. She ladled a spoonful of a solution into a clay mug and drank a large sip. She handed the rest to Lilae.

"Drink," she ordered, shoving the mug into her hands. Lilae hesitated, eying the mug with suspicion. She was weak, she was thirsty, but something didn't seem right about the contents of that cup.

Lilae sniffed the contents of the mug and nearly choked at the strong aroma. She looked down at the dark purple liquid that had a consistency of porridge. She frowned up at Vasira.

"What is it?"

"Drink it now!" Vasira forced the cup to Lilae's mouth.

Lilae took a deep breath and allowed the thick mixture to fill her mouth. Vasira tipped the mug until every drop was gone, and Lilae swallowed in one large gulp. Vasira stared expectantly at her face.

Lilae shuddered. She felt her tongue tingle. Then, her throat began to burn. Lilae dropped the mug onto the floor when her hands began to lose their feeling. She shivered and looked at Vasira with wide, fearful eyes.

"What was that?" Lilae stood and felt dizzy. "Did you poison me?" Her voice came out like a whisper, and she felt the room spin. She felt as though she were not really there, as though she was outside of her own body.

Vasira grabbed Lilae by her shoulders and examined her face. She looked deep into Lilae's eyes. "How do you feel Lilae?" she asked. Her eyes were wild with both worry and hope.

Lilae stared at her in confusion. Her hands began to shake, her blood simmered into a boil. She felt something oddly familiar and nearly forgotten begin to return to her. It surged through her veins, making her sweat and breathe faster. There was a rumble in the ground, causing them to lose their balance.

Lilae clutched at Vasira, a sharp pain slicing through her stomach.

"What's happening to me?"

The dishes on the wooden shelves started to rumble and bounce onto the floor with a loud crash. Sacks of food fell over, spilling rice and potatoes onto the floor. The tables and chairs slid across the room as though a strong wind swept through the kitchen.

Lilae held tight to Vasira; she felt as though she were falling into a darkness that wouldn't let her go. Vasira shushed her, looking at the calamity all around them.

"It's working, Lilae." She smiled through tears. "Just hold on, dear. It will be fine." Her smile faded when soldiers burst through the door and stared in awe at the chaos they found.

"What's going on in here?" one of the soldiers shouted, ducking as a skillet flew past his face. They both drew their swords, unsure of what else they could do.

"Bring the girl," the other ordered of Vasira.

Vasira pulled Lilae close to her bosom. "You'd be wise to turn around and leave right now."

"What did you say, old woman?"

Through the haze that Lilae was trapped within, she heard Vasira's words and was shocked, as well, by her power and sudden change in attitude. *Vasira was standing up for her*.

Before either could move away, the soldier roughly shoved Vasira to the floor.

"Know your place, old woman!" he yelled and thrust his sword toward her face to frighten her.

Lilae backed away as they approached her, her skin crawling with energy and her mind clouded by some strange force. She only had the strength to hold her arms up to shield herself. She shrieked when both men were catapulted backwards into the stone wall with such force that they both lost consciousness.

Lilae felt her face drain of color when she saw Vasira stand. Vasira's face faded to reveal one that she knew and missed dearly.

"Delia!"

Delia smiled weakly, her knees wobbling from the use of power.

"Lilae, my dear," she said softly. "Do you feel your power yet?"

Lilae was still bewildered, but she shook free from her awe and grinned.

"Yes!" She came to her feet with a newfound vigor. "I do, Delia, I feel my power again!" Lilae focused on the energy within her and tried to tap into its core. "It's coming back, but I can't *control* it yet!"

"Well, it's not coming back fast enough. Many more soldiers are coming. I can hear them. That blasted Bellen will be coming, too."

Lilae searched the room. When she looked back at Delia, her eyes stung with tears. "Delia." She buried her face in Delia's shoulder. She sucked in long, painful breaths as she thought of all that had happened. "They're going to kill him. He isn't evil after all."

When Lilae pulled back, her face was red and stained with tears. Her heart was still broken.

Delia's eyes darkened. "I know. You saved him, Lilae. You saved him from Wexcyn. He needed to be reminded of what love was. He needed to see that you are not his enemy."

Lilae stared back, overwhelmed.

"You can save him. And then, we can destroy every Bellen in the city. Are you ready?"

Lilae balled up her fist. "I am." She clenched her jaw. "I am *so* ready."

Delia nodded. She reached into her robes, and that old, mysterious bone started to glow. Her eyes widened, and Delia motioned for her to step back.

"What is that?"

Delia ignored her. She closed her eyes and focused. She pulled the bone free from its wire chain around her belt then held it by the joint in the palm of her hand.

She whispered, and Lilae got a glimpse of Delia's true form. Her face flickered. It was suddenly immersed in shadows.

"From crypts of darkness,
I summon thee,
Garion of Urdu,
Come to me!"

Lilae shuddered as a strong wind swept into the room. Delia turned her palm downward and the bone hovered beneath it, as though by invisible string. Lilae slowly backed away as the bone began to spin. The air formed closely around it, sending shards of light into the room. The ground trembled.

The glowing bone took on more bone. Before their eyes the bones connected. Slowly… it formed a body. Without muscle or skin, a human skeleton stood tall above the both of them. A black pool of darkness filled his eye sockets.

Lilae gasped when he stretched out his long arms. Sparks sped along his body, and metal fused to his bones. She looked from Delia to the metal skeleton in disbelief. He hovered like a puppet for a moment, his back curved like an old man with his long arms swaying slowly.

"Garion," Delia called softly.

Garion looked back at her. "Master?" His hollow voice echoed in the room, making Lilae clutch her mouth to suppress a scream.

Delia smiled and looked at Lilae. "Ready?"

Lilae was speechless. She gulped and looked at Garion.

"Master?" Garion called again.

Delia looked him in the eyes, her voice growing serious. She sipped a blue liquid from a crystal vial. "Kill *everyone* who gets in our way! You must not let them harm the girl."

His dark pools of eyes glowed green as he looked at Lilae. He nodded and straightened his back. Lilae jumped when he turned and burst from the room, shards of wood falling to the floor.

"Hurry, Lilae," Delia shouted as she grabbed Lilae's arm to pull her along. "Stay behind Garion, and grab the first weapon that falls within your reach." Her eyes bore into Lilae's. "I want you to make those men and women wish they were never even conceived."

Lilae braced herself for what was about to happen. She heard the footsteps of soldiers thundering down the corridor. She became oddly exhilarated to finally be free to run down those halls that had been her prison for months. She felt her power returning. The fire burning within her was rekindled, and she couldn't wait to make them all rue the day they had kidnapped her.

Garion was charging down the hall with Lilae and Delia running behind him when a group of uniformed palace guards came around the corner. They were running at full speed and stopped abruptly when they saw the skeleton before them. Without pause, Garion knocked the guards down as if they were merely children. His arms were indestructible, and the men toppled over as he slammed them down. He grabbed one by the neck and tossed him into another group with a roar.

"How do you feel, Lilae?" Delia asked.

Lilae smiled as she watched Garion massacre the men. "It is strong, Delia."

"Well," Delia replied, "what are you waiting for?"

Lilae flexed her hands and grabbed a sword from a fallen guard. It felt foreign in her hands after so long. She gave it a good whip to the left and right, the metal swishing through the air. Then, she took off after Garion. Delia was cautious as she regained her strength.

"Stop the girl!" someone shouted, as they tried to get around Garion.

Lilae was fearless again. She dashed through the corridor, slicing everyone in her path. The sword swung and met bone and flesh, and she grinned with bloodlust. All of her pain boiled over into each mighty blow. There were so many. They had flooded the corridor, an entire horde of soldiers.

They tried to smother Garion, but the skeleton would have none of it. Those who trickled through met Lilae's sword. She leapt into the air and crashed down onto two men. They tried to bring her down, but with Evasion, she sidestepped and tricked them into thinking she was in one place, when in fact she was in another. After those were dead, she rested the sword along her shoulder and dashed into the massacre once more.

Blood splattered onto Lilae's face as she laid their bodies to eternal rest. Delia kept up with them until she disappeared into a room. She returned with her willow staff and looked like her old self again.

"Lilae," Delia called. "This way!"

Garion busied himself with smashing heads into the walls and crunching bones with his feet. The sounds nearly made Lilae cringe.

Lilae followed Delia. "What about Garion?" she asked and gasped when, out of thin air, he materialized right beside her. Sparks filled the air when he appeared. One of the sparks snapped at her skin like a bug bite.

Delia paid no notice. "Don't worry about him! Hurry!"

"The emperor! We can't let them hurt him. He was going to escape with me. He can help us."

Delia smiled. "Good girl. I knew if anyone could get through to him, it would be you."

Lilae returned the smile and led the way. Garion continued guarding them from any soldiers brave enough to come down that hallway. Lilae and Delia ran along the hall to Kavien's room.

Lilae felt her pulse racing. She already feared the worst. Kavien was strong. Kavien was powerful. There was no way Dragnor and Sister Eloni could best him. She had seen Kavien in action. She had seen him toss Sister Eloni as if she was nothing.

Lilae burst into the room. Frantically, she ran through the outer sitting room and toward the open door to Kavien's bedroom. It was dim inside. Delia paused in the sitting room, looking around. Lilae ran directly to his bed. She cried out. There he was. Kavien lay on the bed with a petrified look on his ashen face. Lilae shook her head and covered her mouth.

"No. No. No. No!" She rushed over to him and grabbed his face. Her tears fell onto his face. His eyes were closed. His skin was pale and cold. Lilae pressed her ear to his chest and heard nothing. She held his face to her chest. He was dead. He had died because of her. She would never forgive herself. Why did everyone she cared about have to die? Was there any hope for her?

Delia put her hand on Lilae's shoulder. She spoke softly. "Come, dear. We need to leave. I can smell a Bellen."

Lilae looked up and scrubbed her eyes. She held onto Kavien tightly. Even in death, he was a handsome man. His young life had been stolen from him as a child and wasted before he could even live a life of his own. She felt such sorrow for him. Delia pulled her up.

"Let's go."

"I don't think so," Sister Eloni purred. She stepped in from a side door. Delia regarded her coolly.

The small woman floated over. She had her robes pulled off, and, for the first time, Lilae saw her for what she was. She was thin, almost frail. Her white hair floated around behind her.

Lilae glared up at her through a screen of tears.

"I have a claim on this girl. I have been waiting for her."

Delia held out her staff, pressing it to Sister Eloni's chest, blocking her from moving closer to Lilae. "You have no such thing, Eloni."

Sister Eloni looked down at Delia. "And who are you?"

Delia lifted her chin. Something happened to her. A flicker of her true form. Even Lilae froze in terror at the glint of an Underworld form.

"*Gatekeeper*!" Sister Eloni lowered herself to the ground. She fell onto her knees and bowed her head. "Have you come for me?"

Delia looked down at the woman. "Your crimes are great, Eloni. I would have to lead you to the deepest depths of the Underworld before I could find a place for you."

"Gatekeeper. You should understand. I did what anyone would have done, given the chance."

"You escaped once. You will not escape where I send you this time. You cannot cheat death, Eloni. I am death, and I will always find you."

"I did what I had to for my people. We are lost. Like orphans. I had to do what I could to survive."

Lilae watched Sister Eloni's face pale. She was afraid of Delia. She was afraid of death. She had consumed the youth of countless girls to avoid meeting an Elder, and now, one stood before her. Still, Lilae would not let Delia steal her glory. She would not let the opportunity to put one of her demons to rest. She would not let that Bellen talk her way out of her much deserved punishment.

"How could you fault me for being who I am? This is the life of a Bellen. We draw our power from your home. You should understand. It is not fair that you get to use the power of the Underworld to live eternally, when we cannot."

Delia shook her head. "Eloni. You don't understand. I do not live. I do not have life. I am born of death. The same rules do not apply to me."

Sister Eloni held out her wand. "Then you won't mind returning to the Underworld." She raised the wand out and, with a wild look, began a spell. Delia raised a hand and, before she could call her power forth, Lilae slid her sword through Eloni's small back until it pierced through the front of her white sheath dress. Lilae only wished she could have seen the look of shock and pain on Sister Eloni's face.

Delia finished the job by making Sister Eloni's body burst into the same black embers as Sister Jedra and the other Sister had just moments earlier.

"We saw what we needed to see. Kavien is dead. We stopped the leader of the Sisters. Now we must escape from here."

Lilae nodded. She slowly walked over to Kavien's body. She leaned over him and kissed his forehead. "I'm sorry," she said to him, wishing he could hear her. She turned to Delia, gathering her wits and energy to make it out of the palace. Dragnor was still out there.

They raced from Kavien's room to the servant's secret hallways. They went down staircases that seemed to never end. Lilae shuddered, remembering being trapped down in the dungeons only days ago.

Delia spoke hurriedly. "Lilae, do you remember what I tried to teach you that night, back in Lowen's Edge?"

Lilae knew exactly what she was talking about. "Yes." She had to push the vision of Kavien's dead body out of her head.

"Well, now is the time to make it happen. It's our only way out of Avia'Torena! It is the only way to stop the Sisters!"

Lilae could feel the dread rising. She had seen what that Bellen could do. She hadn't time to prepare. The one skill she needed most she had failed at once before. She wasn't sure exactly how that would get them out of Avia'Torena, but she already started to focus on harnessing her power. She refused to disappoint Delia again.

"I have faith in you, Lilae," Delia said. "But you must be ready when we reach the courtyard."

Lilae was silent. She was focused. Determined. She saw the doors that led to the courtyard and took a deep breath. She clutched the hilt of the sword tighter and called out to The Winds. She hoped they would finally respond once more.

"Lilae," they softly called, and she felt her entire body warm with joy.

She beamed as she and Delia finally made their way from the musky, damp, lower wing and out into the fresh air. Lilae's smile quickly fell when she saw Dragnor standing there, waiting for them. Nearly half of the kingdom's soldiers were assembled there, as well, their weapons ready.

Delia held her willow staff toward Dragnor and stepped toward him. When his eyes met hers, his smug smile fell, and he looked as though he had seen a ghost. He stumbled backwards, completely terrorized.

Delia tilted her head as she looked him over. "What's it been, Dragnor, son of the tyrant Malikar?"

Dragnor stood as though frozen, speechless for the first time since Lilae had known him.

"One, two hundred years?" Delia continued, her voice so low and menacing that even Lilae shivered. "And what progress you have made. Who let you out?"

"Gatekeeper!" he said breathlessly.

Lilae's eyes went back and forth between the two of them, confused that they knew each other.

"Yes, yes." Delia stood before him, looking up into his dark eyes, and Lilae saw him shudder before her tutor. "Did Wexcyn warn you that there is a contract on your head? The Elders will hunt you down to bring you back to the Underworld."

Dragnor straightened up. His jaw clenched, and he tried to regain his composure. He glanced at Lilae and the soldiers, who looked on expectantly. They waited for an order.

"I have Inora's protection now, Gatekeeper. My Ancient will protect me," Dragnor said, more to convince himself than anyone else. "You can send me back, but I will just be set free once more."

"It doesn't matter," Delia added. "Whatever it is he has planned will fail. The Flame and the Storm will set things right once more."

"Oh, I assure you," Dragnor grinned, "the Storm will never make it to you."

Delia raised an eyebrow. "Oh, he will. There's nothing you can do to stop him."

Dragnor balled up his fist. "You do know I have all that I need from the girl. Inora has given me the power to absorb that of others. I," he said pointing to himself, "hold the power of the Flame now! It is you who has failed."

Delia laughed softly then and motioned for Lilae to come closer. "Are you sure about that, Dragnor?"

"Your power is no good here, Gatekeeper! Go back to the Underworld where you belong," he shouted. "Go back and let Wexcyn destroy you like he did all of the other Elders."

Delia took Lilae's free hand. "My power may not be as strong in this world," she admitted. "But the Flame's power is!" She squeezed Lilae's hand. "Lilae! Now!"

Lilae held the sword out and took a deep breath. She looked around nervously, and it felt as though time slowed for her. She heard nothing. There was utter silence, but she saw Dragnor give the order to seize her. She watched as the soldiers tried to run toward them as though fighting a strong wind.

She started to sweat, afraid of failure, when suddenly she saw the faces of her family. Tears fell from her eyes as she watched their faces fade and saw what the future would hold if she didn't survive that night. She suddenly glared at Dragnor, and he saw the fire in her eyes.

"Lilae," Delia shouted again, breaking her from her trance. Garion attacked those who were close.

Then, Lilae closed her eyes and let out a long slow breath. She raised the sword in the sky. The fire within her soared up from her toes to her fingertips, and the sword's blade began to glow red with flames. The sadness deep within her made the sky turn red, and, when her eyes opened, she felt Delia's pride. Lilae's eyes were pools of light so bright that the soldiers started to lower their weapons and back away in terror.

Her hair flew as The Winds lifted her from the ground. The wild tresses grew bright red; the soliders feared they were looking at a demon from their darkest nightmares.

"What is this?" Dragnor shouted, shielding his eyes. He looked angrily at Delia. "What is it?"

Lilae shot a look at him that made him take a step back. Those dark eyes of his met hers, and he could read what she wanted to do to him. She growled and pointed her sword at him. His eyes widened, and he raised a hand against her. Dragnor covered his head in his hood and vanished into the shadows. Lilae shouted angrily. She wanted him dead! She wanted to go after him, to make him face her.

Delia looked at her, breathless. “Lilae,” she whispered, giving her hand a squeeze and reaching for Garion’s. “Take us out of here now.”

Lilae stretched higher and suddenly knew what to do. In an instant there was a loud popping sound, and the three of them vanished into the light.

CHAPTER 55

LIAM LOOKED AHEAD AS HE climbed free from the ocean waters. He was exhausted. He pulled himself up onto the sand of the beach. He wanted to rest. He needed sleep, but he had arrived, finally.

Liam could see The Barrier in the distance. The sky above it was visibly darker. Swirls of purple and black topped the hazy aura of The Barrier. His eyes narrowed as he saw something flying toward him. Liam couldn't contain his joy when Nani flew into his arms.

"Liam!" she cried gleefully. She wrapped her arms around him. She kissed him all over his face and smiled at him. "I knew it! I could feel that you were alive!"

Liam hugged Nani tight as he came to his feet. "Oh, I missed you Nani!"

She giggled and planted a dozen kisses on his cheek. "You have no idea how much we missed you, Liam! I am so glad that you are okay!"

"Where's Rowe?"

She flew from his embrace and threw her hand out to point toward the jungle. "He's right there! I knew you were coming. I knew it. We waited for you!"

His gaze followed where Nani pointed, and he saw Rowe running over to them. Liam grinned and hugged Rowe. Rowe rustled his hair with tear-filled laughter. They were both at a loss for words.

"*Aww*, you guys should see yourselves," Nani remarked. "You look just like brothers." She grinned. Her heart felt whole again. "Except, Rowe is the much bigger brother, of course."

"*No time to waste*!" The Winds urged and Liam was brought to attention. The reunion was cut short. There were still important things to accomplish.

"And where have *you* been?" he shouted at them.

Nani and Rowe searched for who Liam spoke to.

"Go!" they yelled. *"The girl! Go! This way!"*

Liam stopped asking questions and grew serious. "All right, guys, we must leave now. The Flame is near. Come on."

They nodded and followed Liam as The Winds led the way. The path to The Barrier was an uninhabitable jungle thick with large slippery tree roots exposed above ground and thatching across the jungle floor. On the horizon, they could see the volcanoes that The Barrier was composed of. Ash littered the sky, and Liam could see lava trailing down canals that the volcano had made; he wondered how the Shadow Elves survived in such conditions.

This piece of land that connected Kyril and Eura was what the whole of Nostfar was like. Dark caverns and odd landforms were the terrain that the Shadow Elves were used to. The ground became smooth with dried and cooled lava.

No amount of sun could penetrate the jungle's canopy. The leaves were big and dark--three times the size of those that Liam knew. They were lush as well, but dark and not as lively; many were brownish red and some were even black. The leaves grew more oddly colored the closer they got to The Barrier.

Liam was careful to avoid the sting flies that surrounded them, swatteing at them with his large hands and splattering blood on his palms.

He wished he had his sword. He felt naked without it. They were so close. It was finally time to see her in real life. Liam couldn't stand the anticipation. It was unbearable.

He could see the broken pillars, and the guardians stood before him. She was there, beyond The Barriers. *Lilae*. The girl from his dreams.

He was anxious, his heart beating out of his chest. The trees fought him, the roots tried to trip him. Liam hacked away at the overgrown vegetation of the jungle with his bare hands, breathing laboriously as plants tried to overwhelm him.

And then, like a dream, he stood before The Barrier, its hazy aura beckoning him. He looked at Nani and Rowe, who were both captivated by the sight, and he grinned.

"Well, are you ready?" Liam asked. They both nodded as they continued to stare.

"As ready as we'll ever be." Rowe prepared himself for what they were about to do.

Nani swallowed hard and managed a small hesitant smile. "We're with you, Liam. To the end."

Liam nodded proudly and took a deep breath. Into the aura he stepped, and, like a blanket, darkness smothered them all.

CHAPTER 56

LILAE, DELIA, AND GARION were sucked into what the the light. Their bodies shot through the sky into a roadway of millions of lights and colors that encircled them like thick water. The air was tight and squeezed their limbs together, pulling them along. They flew for what felt like hours, holding hands and waiting breathlessly for the ride to end.

"Delia!" Lilae screamed when her body started to feel as though it was being ripped apart.

Delia had her eyes closed, and Lilae could tell she felt the same pain. "*Shush,* Lilae. We will be fine," she whispered, her voice wavering. "It's almost over."

Lilae squeezed her eyes shut and was praying for it to end when they were all spit onto a surface that stopped their flight. They crashed onto the ground, and it took a moment for even Delia to find her footing. Garion stood silently, wavering like a mindless puppet.

Lilae opened her eyes and groaned. She lifted her cheek from a smooth black surface and searched for Delia and Garion. She slowly crawled to her feet and nearly fell back down onto the slippery surface, realizing how dizzy the ride had made her. She took in a deep breath and discovered that they were standing at the edge of a rocky cliff.

Lilae looked before them. They were high above a valley of dark water. She felt that she might vomit when she realized just how high they were. Delia looked down, as well, and then at the sky which was a haze of purple. They noticed that the moon was strange, too. It was somehow different, with a more golden tint than the one that Lilae was used to seeing.

The trees were tall and black, and there was ash floating in the air. Lilae jumped backwards when she realized that thin trails of lava slowly slid down the mountain and off the cliff.

"Delia," Lilae called breathlessly, her voice trembling with fear. She felt a sense of dread fill her body, her pulse racing again. She normally sensed when danger was near, and now, she felt it everywhere. It clung to the ash-filled air they breathed.

Delia looked up at her. "Yes, dear?"

"Where are we?"

"The Barrier."

Lilae looked behind her and screamed. She hadn't noticed the two giants that stood guard behind her. They were large, with black cloaks and glowing spears that crossed to show that passing was not allowed.

"The guardians?" The men stared off past them, paying them no attention. Their eyes were full of light, and their faces were serious. Lilae thought that they looked like humans but triple in height and eyes set wider apart.

Delia nodded.

"Which barrier is this?" She had to know. She prayed that it wasn't the Nostfar barrier, where the Shadow Elves and horrifying beasts dwelled. Lilae wasn't ready to battle another basilisk. Any of the four realms but that one!

"It's Nostfar, but calm down, Lilae. It doesn't matter which barrier this is. They will all be destroyed in a moment."

Lilae felt such dread that she had to wrap her arms across her body. Cold goose bumps spread across her exposed shoulders.

"How do we get down?" Lilae wanted to get as far away from The Barrier as possible.

"We don't, dear," Delia said softly and gently took her hand. She smoothed the back of Lilae's hand consolingly. "We must wait."

"Wait!"

"*Shh,*" Delia soothed. "*Shh*! Just a moment. He is coming."

Lilae shot a look of terror at her. "Who?" She folded her hands before her mouth.

Delia nodded toward The Barrier, and they saw the shadow of a figure approaching from the other side. The fog was thick, and they could see nothing but his silhouette. "He who will help you get your child back. He who will help you awaken the Unknown and destroy the evil that will soon walk this world."

"Who is it?" Lilae whispered, as the shadowy figure grew taller as it came closer to the guardians.

"The Storm is coming."

THE END

Thanks for reading! If you enjoyed this book, please consider leaving a review.

Night of the Storm is now available on Amazon.

* * *

Don't Forget to Subscribe to K.N. Lee's Newsletter to Receive Freebies, Exclusive Content, Cover Reveals, Giveaways, Sales, and More!

www.knlee.com

NIGHT *of the* STORM

K.N. LEE

THE HAIRS ON LIAM'S neck stood on end at the ghastly sight that stood before him and The Barrier.

The head of a Tryan man was set on a pike in the middle of the jungle.

"Stay back a female voice boomed from the trees as Liam, Nani and Rowe approached The Barrier. "You are not welcome in Nostfar."

Liam's bright blue eyes glowed in the dark as they shot from pike to the Guardian's that awaited. The open doorway that stretched hundreds of feet into the black sky. The glow from The Barrier's ancient power illuminated the giants before him, swords ready in their massive hands.

They were silent.

Whoever spoke was unseen.

His blue eyes narrowed as he looked up to the tops of the trees. The dark leaves rustled with the wind, yet revealed not even a trace of who spoke.

Shadow Elves. They could blend in anywhere.

"Who speaks?"

"Turn around and leave."

Liam's brows furrowed. "This, coming from an elf in the *Tryan* realm."

"Last warning."

His sword. If only he had it on his hip at that moment.

Pain seared into Liam's leg as a thorny black vine wrapped itself around his thigh and yanked him to the slick black ground of the volcano.

Liam hit his head on the hard packed dirt.

No.

He was so close to The Barrier and finally meeting The Flame. Her face came to him as darkness threatened to take over.

Liam cradled his head with a hand. For a moment, he was disoriented. In a haze, he watched Rowe grab a skinny male Shadow Elf by the neck and slam it into the ground with such strength that the sound of crunching bones filled the dark jungle that surrounded them.

"Kill them. They must not enter Nostfar," the same female voice yelled from the trees as several Shadow Elves jumped to the ground with such agility that they were barely seen.

Liam's eyes widened as they set to attack his greatest friends in the world. He sat up and reached for the vine wrapped around his thigh. The instant his fingertips touched it, the vine lifted him from the ground.

Cool air whipped past Liam's face as he was slung through the air at such a speed that he saw nothing but blackness. His mind raced as he searched for a way to free himself. Before he could react, more vines flew to Liam and snapped themselves around him body, pinning his arms to his side. Like a cocoon, they ensnared him and slammed his wrapped body into the base of a tree that appeared to be dead, yet rumbled like a hungry stomach.

A quick glance at the ground revealed the source of the vines.

The trees were cursed.

Their branches shot through the clearing, attacking his friends and forcing them into a tight space before The Barrier.

"Liam," Nani shouted, as she tried to fly to him. With a broken wing, he could tell that she struggled. The branches blocked her path, ascending as she fought to fly over their blockade.

"I can't get free," Liam said.

Liam looked at the sky. He could summon a storm.

How would that help? He needed the use of his hands to direct the lightning without harming Nani and Rowe. He used all of his strength to try to break through the vines, and yet they only held on tighter, so tight that he found breathing laborious.

A lithe female Shadow Elf jumped down from her spot in the tree top and landed beside Liam. She looked strong, and tall, with leather over chainmail covering her chest and stomach. Her arms were bare, revealing white tattoos and scars. The points of her ears stuck through her auburn hair that looked to be slicked back by mud.

Ferocity filled her brown eyes as she straddled his chest and held her dagger to his throat.

Not now. Not like this.

Not after Liam had already escaped death once. The Ancients may not give him another chance.

He met the eyes of the Shadow Elf. Lilae awaited him. He had to see her in person at least one time before he died.

Almost as if the Shadow Elf woman read his thoughts, she paused, her brow raising as she searched his eyes with her own dark purple gaze.

Nani shot to the ground, faster than Liam had ever seen her fly. She landed in the center of it all. The mayhem that ensued as Rowe fought dozens of Shadow Elves armed with glowing daggers.

She held her hands out before her and closed her eyes.

Liam raised a brow. He'd never seen Nani so calm in the face of danger.

Before his eyes, she started to change.

Smoke began to rise from the ground and up her body as if she'd recently been engulfed in flames. Liam's eyes widened as the trees began to die all around them. Nani's hair went from purple to white. When she opened her eyes, gold light filled them as she held out her small hands.

White power shot from her fingertips. Screams of terror and pain filled the air as her power shot into every Shadow Elf within the clearing and hiding in the trees.

Rowe held up his hands and froze, and yet Nani's power seemed to be selective, leaving Rowe and Liam free from its terror.

The Shadow Elves were reduced to nothing more than bone and guts.

Liam held his breath as even that turned to ash and floated away with the breeze, leaving the three in silence as the intensity in Nani's eyes faded.

He hadn't even realized that the vines had let him free. Glancing back at the tree revealed that whatever Nani had done had killed it, leaving its vines lifeless and shriveled on the ground.

"Liam," Nani called in a small, timid voice.

Liam stood and turned to her. Her white hair gave her an eerie beauty as it was lifted by the breeze. Whatever power Nani had hidden from them all, made her hover off the ground despite her broken wings.

"Nani," Liam whispered.

She smiled and slowly returned to her normal appearance.

She walked to him, Rowe close behind. "Are you okay?"

"I'm fine," Liam said, running his hands through his thick black hair. "But what was that?"

Rowe cleared his throat. "We didn't get a chance to tell you."

"Tell me what?"

Nani ran to him and wrapped her arms around his waist. He looked down at her small face.

"I didn't know until today, Liam," she said.

"Know what? Tell me. I'll understand."

She bit her bottom lip and let go of him. Twirling the ends of her purple hair, she flickered a sheepish look at him.

"I am the Inquisitor," Nani whispered. "Please, don't be cross with me, Liam." She lowered her eyes to the ground as she wrung her small hands. "This is all still very new to me."

Liam took a deep breath.

Inquisitor?

Could his dear fairy friend be one of the keys to saving all of Ellowen?

He picked Nani up and hugged her. "I could never be cross with you, Nani. You are Rowe are my best friends and together we will rid this world of evil."

Liam nodded to The Barrier as the giants started to move from their frozen positions.

"Are you ready for this?"

She smiled at him. "I am."

About the Author

K.N. Lee is an award-winning author who resides in Charlotte, North Carolina. When she is not writing twisted tales, fantasy novels, and dark poetry, she does a great deal of traveling and promotes other authors. Wannabe rockstar, foreign language enthusiast, and anime geek, K.N. Lee also enjoys helping others reach their writing and publishing goals. She is a winner of the Elevate Lifestyle Top 30 Under 30 "Future Leaders of Charlotte" award for her success as a writer, business owner, and for community service.

Author, K.N. Lee loves hearing from fans and readers. Connect with her!

knlee.com

Street team: facebook.com/groups/1439982526289524/
Newsletter: eepurl.com/3L1gn
Blog: WriteLikeAWizard.com
Fan page: Facebook.com/knycolelee
Twitter: twitter.com/knycole_lee
The Chronicles of Koa Series Page: facebook.com/thechroniclesofkoa

Titles by K.N. Lee

The Chronicles of Koa Series:
Netherworld
Dark Prophet
Lyrinian Blade

The Eura Chronicles:
Rise of the Flame
Night of the Storm
Dawn of the Forgotten (Coming Soon)
The Darkest Day (Coming Soon)

THE GRAND ELITE CASTER TRILOGY:
Silenced
Summoned (Coming Soon)
Awakened (Coming Soon)

THE FALLEN GODS TRILOGY:
Goddess of War
God of Peace (Coming Soon)
Love & Law (Coming Soon)

STANDALONE NOVELLAS:
The Scarlett Legacy
Liquid Lust
Spell Slinger

MORE GREAT READS FROM K.N. LEE

Netherworld (Urban Paranormal Fantasy) ***Demons, ghouls, vampires, and Syths?*** The Netherworld Division are an organization of angels and humans who are there to keep the escaped creatures from The Netherworld in check in this action-packed paranormal thriller.

Introducing Koa Ryeo-won, a half-blood vampire with an enchanted sword, a membership to the most elite vampire castle in Europe, and the gift of flight. If only she could manage to reclaim the lost memories of her years in The Netherworld, she might finally be able to move forward.

The Scarlett Legacy (Young Adult Fantasy) ***Wizards. Shifters. Sexy mobsters with magic.***

Evie Scarlett is a young wizard who yearns from an escape from her family's bitter rivalry with another crime family. But this time she may be the only one who can save them.

Goddess of War (Young Adult Fantasy) ***Unsuspecting humans. Fallen gods in disguise. A battle for the entire universe.***

After escaping the Vault, a prison for gods, twin siblings Preeti and Vineet make a desperate journey to the human world where they must impersonate the race they are meant to rule and protect.

Silenced (New Adult – Paranormal Romance) **Silence kept her alive. Magic will set her free.**

Willa Avery created the serum that changed the world as humans, witches, and vampires knew it.

Liquid Lust (New Adult Romance) **Sohana needed a fresh start.**
Arthur--a British billionaire has an enticing offer.
Neither expected their arrangement to spark something more.

Discover more books and learn more about K.N. Lee on knlee.com.